Civilization was in flames.

Paul van Osten of the Reich's Abwehr and Max Schroeder of U.S. Army Intelligence separately decided that there had to be peace—at any price. The only way to achieve that peace was to sign a frightening contract.

It was code-named Operation Double Eagle . . .

AN EXCHANGE OF EAGLES
The Spectacular New Novel
by Owen Sela

"Crackling good suspense in the mold of *The Odessa File* . . . Combines real-life historical figures (Hitler, Roosevelt, Göring, Harry Hopkins, J. Edgar Hoover) with fictional . . . Superbly exciting . . . It is a hair-raising plot in which each detail is worked out with audacity and care."

—Barbara Bannon
Publishers Weekly

AN EXCHANGE
OF
EAGLES

Owen Sela

BANTAM BOOKS · TORONTO · NEW YORK · LONDON

*This low-priced Bantam Book
has been completely reset in a type face
designed for easy reading, and was printed
from new plates. It contains the complete
text of the original hard-cover edition.*
NOT ONE WORD HAS BEEN OMITTED.

AN EXCHANGE OF EAGLES

*A Bantam Book / published by arrangement with
Pantheon Books, Inc.*

PRINTING HISTORY

*Originally published in Great Britain by Hodder & Stoughton
Pantheon edition published May 1977
Book-of-the-Month Club edition published June 1977
Detective Book Club edition published November/December
1977
Bantam edition / June 1978*

ISBN 0-553-11469-7

Published simultaneously in the United States and Canada

PRINTED IN THE UNITED STATES OF AMERICA

To Helen

An Exchange
of
Eagles

Prologue

Sunday, August 27, 1939. Zossen.

All that week the leaders of the West had been concerned with preserving peace. The Pope had taken to the radio and beseeched the strong, by the blood of Christ, to hear him and not turn their power into a destruction. Leopold III, King of the Belgians, had called upon the men responsible for the course of events to submit their disputes to open negotiation. Franklin Roosevelt had sent urgent messages to Adolf Hitler and President Moscicki of Poland urging them to settle their differences without recourse to arms. Premier Daladier had sent Hitler a moving and eloquent letter and His Britannic Majesty's Ambassador to Germany, Sir Nevile Henderson, seemed to be in a state of perpetual motion between Whitehall and the Wilhelmstrasse.

Standing on the hot and dusty barracks square at Zossen Army Headquarters for the Polish Campaign, Paul van Osten knew these well intentioned efforts were doomed to failure. All the previous day the air over Berlin had been filled with the drone of German bombers flying to the east. An SD unit was preparing to stage a fake attack on a German radio station on the Polish border, thereby giving Hitler the pretext he

needed for the invasion of Poland. That sultry August
Sunday, standing in the barracks square at Zossen,
with the sweat dampening the high collar of his tunic,
Paul van Osten knew that world peace now depended
on a phial of acid slowly eating through a strand of
copper wire.

"But I am wrongly judged if my love of peace
and my patience are mistaken for weakness or even
cowardice."

The words reverberated across the square, even
the echo effect of the loud speakers unable to still the
inspiration of that golden voice. The Führer had come
to Zossen to address these the last of his troops to be
moved to the east. Along one side of the square grocery trucks and furniture vans were drawn up in a
ragged line. Because the attack on Poland had originally been planned for the previous Friday, all available army vehicles were already in use on the Polish
frontier.

"I speak to Poland in the same language that Poland has for months past used towards us."

Paul van Osten had been fourteen when the
Great War had ended. He still remembered the bitterness of his father, a Colonel in the 14th Calvary, at the
politicians' betrayal of the army. Years later, while a
military cadet at Lichterfelde, van Osten had experienced the consequences of that betrayal. The huge
burden of reparations had brought about crippling in-
flation. Workers took their pay home in wheelbarrows.
Cigarettes became more valuable than money. The
German Army and the German people had been
emasculated. And it need not have happened. If the
army had acted then, as Dieter Mehl and Baron
Ewald von Kirkdorf and Paul von Osten were acting
now.

At thirty-four, Lieutenant-Colonel Paul van Osten
was a Deputy Director of German Military Intelligence, the Abwehr. He was a slightly built man, with

a high balding forehead. He'd served eight years with the Abwehr, fought with the armored divisions of the Condor Legion in Spain, run an espionage ring in the United States, and was now head of Ast X (West) which had special responsibility for America.

Seven years ago, van Osten had viewed Hitler's accession to power as a good thing. Germany had needed Hitler to give it hope and renew its courage, and despite the brutality of the storm troopers and the low caliber of men Hitler surrounded himself with, van Osten had been prepared to judge the man by the results of his actions. History had taught him that leadership and the practicalities of power often brought moderation.

Over the years van Osten's judgment had been made. The suppression of the press and the churches, the disbanding of trade unions, the persecution of Jews, the growth of concentration camps, the increasing power of the Secret Police, all this had changed van Osten's attitude. But it was only now, when Hitler was committed to a foolish war, that van Osten was prepared to act.

Sixty yards away, from behind a raised and ornate lectern, draped with red and black swastikas, Hitler spoke. A pale-faced man with a narrow tie, wearing a simple field grey uniform. A nondescript man, of medium height, with thinning brown hair parted from the side, now aged fifty. If one met him on the street, without his entourage, without his uniform, one could take him for a commercial traveler. Until he spoke. When he spoke, it was magic.

"There will be no hardship for any German to which I myself will not submit. Henceforth, my whole life belongs more than ever to my people. From now on I am just the first soldier of the German Reich."

Fitted into the lectern stand from which Hitler spoke, was a bomb of British design, shaped like a bottle of Cointreau. It was completely silent, operated by an acid-controlled time fuse corroding a length of wire. The thickness of the wire determined the time between initial contact and the release of the striking pin held by the wire on to the detonator. Three thicknesses of wire had been provided to ensure delays of ten minutes, thirty minutes and two hours between activation and detonation. They were using the thickest wire, because they'd heard that Hitler's appearance at Zossen that day would be delayed by a meeting of the Reichstag.

Unobtrusively van Osten glanced at his watch. 12:22. Eight minutes to go. Beside him, Dieter Mehl stood at ease, his sensitive face expressionless, the dark, languid eyes half closed, his collar-length dark hair tucked well underneath his cap. Beyond Mehl, Ewald von Kirkdorf stood very erect, very military, the dueling scar puckering his left cheek. Paul van Osten did not look for Lieutenant von Epp.

"We shall fight and there will never be another November 1918 in German history!"

12:24. Van Osten stared straight ahead at the platform. Hitler had come without any of the Nazi hierarchy. He stood alone behind the raised lectern, members of his black uniformed SS bodyguard drawn up in a semicircle below him, staring at the assembled soldiers, machine pistols at the ready.

12:26. Dieter Mehl swayed, his body touching van Osten's. There was a peculiar whiteness around his nostrils and his mouth, and the half smile of apology he gave van Osten was tight.

12:28. Van Osten still staring straight ahead braced himself for the shock.

"If England wants to fight for a year, I shall fight for a year. If England wants to fight two years, I shall fight two years. If England wants to fight for three years, I shall fight for three years!"

The second hand completed its relentless arc. Half a minute to go.

"Und wenn es erforderlich ist, will ich zehn Jahre kempfen!" Hitler brandished his fist and raised it high over his head.

There was a rumbling explosion as the soldiers burst into spontaneous cries of *"Sieg heil! Sieg heil! Sieg heil!"* For a whole minute Hitler stood there, clenched fist upraised.

When the cheering had died down he spoke again, quietly, persuasively. "Today you have the Germany of Frederick the Great before you, a Germany that does not capitulate. We know too well what would be in store for us—a second Versailles, only worse."

12:32. The acid was corroding the wire more slowly than expected. The sweat on van Osten's collar was cold. Hitler's ringing phrases beat at his ears, no longer comprehensible, echoing from the loud speakers, a richly golden paean of triumph.

12:35. Hitler still lived. Dieter Mehl had assured van Osten that there could not be an error of more than sixty seconds.

"I have once more put on that coat that was the most sacred and dear to me."

The bomb would not go off. Hitler was finishing his speech.

"I will not take it off again until victory is secured, or I will not survive the outcome."

Abruptly Hitler turned away from the lectern and stepped down. He stopped and turned to face the assembled soldiers. Explode now, van Osten prayed. Explode now. Hitler raised his arm in salute and three hundred soldiers did likewise. Hitler smiled quietly and dabbing at his face with a large white handkerchief, walked away.

"Mein Führer!" Lieutenant von Epp had broken ranks and was racing across the square, his arms outstretched as if he wished to embrace his leader. "Mein Führer!" Von Epp's young face was alive with passion.

Van Osten stared impassively as von Epp dodged the first cordon of SS guards, raced towards the knot of men surrounding Hitler.

"Mein Führer!" Ten yards to go. Eight. Van Osten thought he saw the lumpiness in von Epp's greatcoat pocket where he carried a fused three-pound bomb. Six yards. Von Epp was not going to make it. The SS men were facing him now, machine pistols set at fire.

Abruptly von Epp's hands darted into his pockets. He slowed. Stopped. An expression of amazement crossed his face. There was a sharp clatter of automatic fire and his body cartwheeled backwards to the earth.

* * *

At 5:45 A.M. on Friday September 1, one and a half million German troops moved against thirty-five Polish divisions. Accompanying von Kluge's Fourth Army pushing eastwards from Pomerania was Dieter Mehl. Ewald von Kirkdorf was attached to von Kuechler's Third Army driving south from East Prussia, and racing across the Corridor with Guderian's XIX Corps was Paul van Osten, hoping that the separation of the conspirators would disguise their complicity and that the investigations of the Gestapo and Reynhard Heydrich's SD would be nullified by the exigencies of war.

* * *

Sunday September 3 was bright with sunshine, balmy with the last breezes of a perfect summer. It was a day for fishing or boating or walking in the Grunewald. But for Sir Nevile Henderson and M. Robert Coulondre, Ambassadors for Britain and France, it was a day for war.

At nine o'clock that morning Sir Nevile had attended the Wilhelmstrasse and was welcomed as usual with the SS guard of honor and the subdued roll of drums. Diplomatic niceties were being preserved to the end. At the Foreign Ministry, the Ambassador handed in a note informing the German government that unless their troops were instantly withdrawn from Polish soil, a state of war would exist between Great Britain and Germany.

The contents of the note were read to Reichsmarschall Göring waiting in an anteroom outside Hitler's office in the Chancellery. A similar ultimatum from France was expected within the hour. Göring shook his head in disbelief. He had waited in the Chancellery all morning for his emissary, Birger Dahlerus, to arrange a meeting with the British Foreign Office. Now it was too late. "If we lost this war," he said hoarsely, "God have mercy on all of us."

1

Friday, October 11, 1940.
East Hampton, N.Y.

David Grover Stannard was twenty-six years old,
tall and broad shouldered, with the kind of blond hair
and blue eyes that an aspirant to the SS would have
envied. He'd spent ten of his twenty-six years in Germany, fought the Fascists in Spain and on the streets
of Vienna. Now, he looked over the foot-high stack of
briefs at the grizzled man in the coffee-colored suit
with tailor-made creases and said, "Holland, Belgium,
France. I'll tell you something for free, soldier. The
Wehrmacht are going to piss all over you."

Colonel Alan Berkeley tilted his moustached head
backwards to stare levelly at Stannard. "You just may
be right. That's why we need people like you."

Stannard laughed harshly. "Didn't you know I
fought on the wrong side in Spain? I haven't even got
a passport anymore, and if my father wasn't a partner
in Myers, Hope and Stannard, I wouldn't have a job
either."

Berkeley nodded slowly. "I know all that. I also
know you're half German and used to be a Communist. But I still want you."

"What the hell do you mean, used to be a Communist?"

"I've read everything the FBI and G2 have on you, and a few other things besides. You gave up the Party in 1938."

Stannard looked from the book-lined wall to the scatter rugs on the polished wood floor, looked through the salt-stained glass door at the sea. He'd joined the Party when he was eighteen, because he'd felt like thousands of others, that Communism had all the answers, that Communists cared. "What's so special about me?"

"You've had combat experience. You've fought in Europe, and Europe is where we're going."

"Four years too late," Stannard said bitterly. "Anyway, Spain isn't Europe."

Spain had been different from everything else. Stannard remembered that Good Friday in 1938. They'd been moving since early morning, in a steady, dust-swamped column, peasants with creaking carts loaded high with bedding, sewing machines and cooking utensils, with goats and sheep tethered to the tailboards, mules saddled with sacks of grain and pitiful furniture. Ahead of them the Heinkels had floated in tireless circles over Tortosa, darting silver arrows in a cloudless blue sky. Every three minutes one would peel off and swoop over the town. Then there would be the faint stutter of machine guns followed by the dull thunder of bombs and eruptions of brick colored smoke.

Because the Republicans had been squabbling about ideological differences, and each section had been frightened of a guerrilla force that could be used against them, Stannard's group had been absorbed into the Brigades, and it hadn't worked. For two days they had tried to hold the high ground of La Tarcada

and had been remorselessly beaten back to Vinaroz
and the sea. There were rumors that Aranda's columns
were marching on Tortosa, and as soon as the big
guns could be brought up, the coast road would be
cut. Whether the Republicans knew it or not they
were finished.

Wars were won by guns and armor and bombers
and men, not by ideology. In two years in Spain he'd
learned that and that no one gave a damn about the
peasants. Not even when you came down to it, David
Stannard.

At first he'd told himself it was because of Marx
and the peasants, but now he realized it had been for
himself. He'd wanted the Fascists to be beaten, just as
he had been beaten all that afternoon of January 17,
1934, when he'd protested the arrest of a friend and
been himself taken into custody by the Gestapo. A
nose like a squashed turnip was the only obvious souvenir of that episode. That, and a deep, burning
hatred of the men who had transformed what had
once been his other home into a concentration camp.

"I wouldn't make a good soldier," Stannard said.
"I don't like being bullied and I question orders."

"In my outfit, there will be more explanations
than orders. We want men, not robots. I have been
asked by the President to form a unit for special operations. We are training teams of men who can go anywhere and do anything, operate inside Germany if
necessary."

Stannard lowered the stack of briefs to observe
Berkeley better. He'd always wanted to be involved in
this war, not as a soldier, but as an irregular, a guerrilla fighting on his own, without a chain of command, or cockamamie orders from armchair generals
who couldn't tell their asses from third base. If he
went with Berkeley, it would be like Spain, again.

Berkeley said, "Tell me about Mendenez."

Stannard grimaced. Everyone wanted to know

about Mendenez. He'd been new in Spain then, and Stannard remembered that it had been hot, even in September, even in the mountains. He remembered the narrow track ahead of him, shooting arrow straight down the hill, widening as it crossed the small, scrub-covered plateau before meandering into the fishing village. If he'd had skis, if there was snow, he could have made it to the village in a straight down *schuss*. But there was no snow. There was only heat and flies, sweat and thirst and a special patrol unit of the Condor Legion bivouacking across the track on the plateau below.

They'd arrived an hour previously, maneuvering four battle-weary, grey trucks into a wide circle, just as Stannard and his small group had cleared the tree line. There were about fifty men and Stannard knew they would camp on the plateau that night. The next day they would send out patrols into the mountains, looking for Republicans. When they had scoured the area thoroughly, the patrols would return and they would pack up and go.

It had been rumored that General Mendenez was supervising the operation, but Stannard had not been concerned with that. He was more concerned with the huddle of fishermen's huts pressed together on the beach beyond the plateau. An arms drop was being made in the fishing village in the hour after sunset. Stannard had to get his group there by then.

They had been in the mountains two months. They were tired and thirsty, short of food and more important, short of ammunition. If a German patrol found them they had little with which to fight.

Stannard had eased himself back into the undergrowth, giving surveillance over to Jose Miguel, the picture of the loosely grouped trucks stamped firmly in his mind. The Germans were lighting cooking fires, grey uniformed men spreading over the scrub-land gathering fuel. Stannard knew they would eat and bed down before sunset, so that the light from the fires would not be a warning to the guerrillas they were hunting.

The rest of his group were in the clearing, four men, two women, the burros and Pablo lying in the cart they had commandeered, his face grey with pain from the bullet shattered leg. There was a faint odor of gasoline from the drums one of the burros carried. Gasoline was precious. It had been left behind by the engineers of the bridge they had blown up eight days ago. Stannard had hoped to leave the gasoline in the village for use by a motorized group. He waved quietly as the others greeted him, their concern being replaced by something like hope. "Will it be well, David?" one of the women had asked. Her name was Maria and she was the wife of Pablo who now lay helpless in the cart.

"Sí, sí. It will be well."

Stannard knew exactly what supplies they had. Thirty-eight rounds of ammunition, three hand grenades, a supply of detonators, fuses, plastic high explosive and thermite. They were essentially a sabotage unit, destroying bridges and roads, operating behind the enemy lines and disrupting their means of communication. But there was no question of attacking the German patrol. They were isolated in the middle of scrub-land and there wasn't enough fire power. Unless . . . unless . . . unless Stannard gave them something special. A combination of incendiary and high explosive.

Patiently Stannard kneaded the thermite into the plastic, lubricated the whole with rifle oil. When he had two wet and sticky lumps, each about the size of a tennis ball, he inserted short fuses into them. Then very carefully he laid the masses into the top of the gasoline drums.

By the time he had finished, the sun was nearly

down. He had the men lift Pablo out of the cart and then move it quietly through the trees to the edge of the track. On the plateau below, the Germans were already settling down for the night. Their fires were gentle embers and Stannard could make out the night watch standing beyond the circle of trucks, looking into the fading day.

The sun had almost dropped beneath the sea when the German sentries heard the noise. It was not a startling noise, just the quiet clip clop of hooves and the creak of an axle borne on the evening stillness. A small cart came over the top of the hill, drawn by a single burro carrying a dozing peasant with his white hat drooping over his face and chest.

As the guards watched, there was a shout and a violent clattering. The cart had come to where the track plunged straight and steep down the hillside. The burro had panicked and was running down the hill wildly out of control. The peasant kept shouting, trying to crawl into the back of the cart as it slithered and bounced along the narrow track. The sentries laughed.

And then to their surprise, the peasant jumped off the cart, falling and rolling over and over in a manner reminiscent of the way parachutists fell when they were training. It was only then that they saw the glow in the back of the cart. But it was too late.

The cart leveled out, the burro charged past white-eyed in a shower of stones and loosened earth. Automatically the sentries wheeled round to face the camp, as the cart reached the center of the camp and exploded in a huge, angry orange gush.

It was only two days afterwards that Stannard had learned that General Mendenez, a high-ranking Nationalist officer, had been killed in the explosion.

Berkeley said, "I want you at Springfield. You'll come in as a Lieutenant."

"What alternatives do I have?"

"Only these. You can wait to be called up and sent somewhere in Texas where you'll learn to march in quickstep and practice shooting with wooden rifles. Or you can come with me."

Stannard grinned. "You mean I can volunteer?"

Berkeley laughed. "That's exactly what I mean."

2

Friday, October 11, 1940. Berlin.

Hermann Göring acknowledged the raised arm salute of the guards with an angry flourish of his diamond-studded baton. Followed by a Luftwaffe aide carrying his briefcase, he pushed violently through the doors of the Air Ministry and waddled quickly down a red carpeted corridor.

His head was thrust onto his chest, the long nose seeming to hook over the end of his flabby chin. As he walked, the pale blue eyes stared in cold anger at the carpet ahead of his booted feet. That morning at the Reichschancellery he had been over-ruled. For the first time in seven years, he had been publicly humiliated.

He'd spent all morning at a meeting of the German High Command. The Führer had been there, together with Field Marshal Gerd von Rundstedt, Admiral Raeder and their staffs. They had met to discuss the Führer's Directive of July 17, code named Operation Sea Lion, which detailed the administration of the death blow to England, a *todestoss* that had been delayed for three months and in which the only active participant had been the Luftwaffe.

That morning Raeder had continued to bleat

15

about the weather and the impossibility of landing
three armies on a front stretching from Bristol to Bex-
hill. He did not have the ships and the RAF still controlled the skies above the Channel. With more than a
hint of sarcasm he had reminded the Reichsmarschall
of his July promise to take the RAF out of the skies in
four weeks. Eight weeks after that promise had been
made, Raeder reminded him, the Channel ports had
been bombed, and over a hundred craft assembled for
the invasion had been sunk or damaged, to say nothing of the destruction of munition dumps and provi-
sion stores and casualties to personnel. Now, Raeder
could not guarantee even the landing of a first army,
let alone their supplies or a second or third army. With
the weather deteriorating there was no alternative.
Sea Lion had to be postponed. Indefinitely.

Von Rundstedt had agreed. He was not going to
risk leaving an army of ninety thousand men stranded on English beaches with neither supplies nor
hope of rescue. His men had been waiting in the
Channel ports for nearly three months. The inactivity
and the continuous RAF bombing had inflicted needless casualties and lowered their morale. Besides they
were needed elsewhere. Operation Sea Lion had to be
postponed. Indefinitely.

Göring had protested in vain. Pleaded even. Every night his bombers were over London, pounding
that city into a heap of rubble. In a few days the British will to fight would collapse. In a few days there
would be a surrender without an invasion.

For once the Führer had been openly sceptical.
On the night of September 15 he said the British
claimed to have shot down one hundred and eighty-
five Luftwaffe planes. Losses of that size were unacceptable. Worse. They were irreplaceable.

Even though the true figures for that night had
been fifty-six planes, Göring had not argued too
strongly against the Führer's conclusion. Over the past

three months his losses had been so severe that he knew they could never be made up in time. Besides, not only were the RAF losing fewer planes, but the British were building planes faster than the Germans. And that was something he could not admit in public. To admit that would be to admit that the Luftwaffe had been defeated.

Yet as he strode through the corridors of the Air Ministry, Reichsmarshall Hermann Göring, Commander in Chief of the Luftwaffe, Deputy Führer, Commissioner of the Four Year Plan had to privately admit defeat. True the bombing raids would continue. But the RAF were still in the skies. And Operation Sea Lion had been postponed. And the Luftwaffe had been blamed for it. Worse, Göring had been blamed for it. A year ago, no one would have dared to do that.

As he sat in his office surrounded by models of aircraft in gold and silver, Göring concluded that the Führer had made a serious mistake. Sea Lion would now not become operational till the spring. In those six months, Britain would have recovered from the rout at Dunkirk and the heavy bomber raids. With American help she would have restored her fighter and bomber strength to what it had been before the battle for Britain. After Dunkirk, Erhard Milch, his State Secretary, had said, "If we leave the British in peace for four weeks it will be too late." Now the Führer intended leaving the British in peace for nearly a year! Britain would never be invaded, and the war would be lost.

Göring knew it would be too late afterwards to blame the pusillanimity of admirals and generals, too late to blame those people who had wrongly advised the Führer. "If we lose this war, God have mercy on us." That was what he had always thought and if Germany could not win, then they should strive for an honorable peace.

Göring picked up a good Messerschmitt from his

desk. *He* could achieve such a peace. He moved the
fighter in a low swooping dive. *He* could save Germany. While everyone surrounding the Führer lusted
for a war, he, Hermann Göring, could save the Third
Reich for a thousand years.

He put the plane down and stabbed at his intercom. He instructed his secretary to invite Lieutenant-Colonel Paul van Osten to dinner at Carinhall the following Sunday, and canceled all his appointments
for the rest of that afternoon. Then, locking the door
of his office, he began to write.

*   *   *

Paper, van Osten thought, the life blood of
Intelligence, the rustling bird bones of bureaucracy.
All Germany from the Öder to the Rhine was smothered in paper that spawned like amoebae. Fornicating
paper!

He put down the directive from the Economics
and Armaments Division as Heinz Guertner came in
without knocking. "How many times do I have to tell
you, Heinz, that our families might be neighbors but
this is my private office."

"I'm sorry. I didn't know you were here." Guertner snapped his heels together and threw up his arm.
"Heil Hitler."

"And that doesn't make your intrusion anymore
welcome."

Guertner was a handsome, clear-eyed youth of
barely twenty, with thick blond hair and sun-browned
skin. He was a lieutenant in the Panzergrenadier, and
the army downhill ski champion. Van Osten had
known him all his life, and had Guertner seconded to
him after France, in order to ease the anxieties of
Guertner's father.

Guertner came in and perched on the edge of van
Osten's desk. "Top Secret message for you from Viereck."

Van Osten took the yellow envelope and tore it open.

"What's Viereck doing for us in Washington?"

"Helping to keep America neutral." Van Osten decoded the message quickly. Viereck had entrusted to the captain of the ss *Mattun* three copies of an important War Department file. Indeed the contents of the file were so important that Viereck had informed both Reynhard Heydrich and SS Reichsführer Heinrich Himmler of its impending arrival.

Van Osten clicked his tongue in annoyance. The cooperation of Heydrich and Himmler was something he could well do without.

"What's wrong?" Guertner asked.

"Nothing you can help with." Then seeing the hurt on Guertner's face, "Here take a look at this." Van Osten gave Guertner the directive from the Economics and Armaments Division. "What do you make of that?"

Guertner frowned handsomely over the document. "So German manufacturers are to make no commitments for the supply of goods to Russia after the spring of 1941."

"And what do you deduce from that?"

Guertner frowned in puzzlement. "It says what it says."

"Well, what is the importance of cutting off supplies to Russia? It isn't because Schicklgruber wants to preserve the neutrality of penguins in the Antarctic?"

"No," Guertner replied studying the document again. "We're going to war with Russia. Isn't that what you think this means, Paul?"

"It's an indication," van Osten replied. "No more than that." He lit a cigarette and drew at it thoughtfully. "You realize that if we invade Russia, that would be the end of Germany. If we ever discover that is going to happen, the Führer must be stopped."

"Well, you can ask Göring about Russia."

"What's Göring got to do with this?"

Guertner handed van Osten an engraved invitation.

Dinner at Carinhall on Sunday night, and he hadn't even spoken with Göring in months. On his return from America with the much-prized Norden bombsight, Göring had given van Osten the task of re-organizing the Luftwaffe Intelligence Service. Later, when Göring had been made Economics Commissar of the Reich, he had made van Osten a personal aide charged with the task of overcoming the bureaucracy that clogged the economic life of the Third Reich. Six months before the outbreak of war, van Osten had transferred back to the Abwehr. He had not seen Göring since.

"What can Göring want?" he asked aloud.

Guertner tapped the invitation on the desk. "There's only one way to find out," he said.

3

Sunday, October 13, 1940. Schorfheide.

Carinhall lay deep in the forest of Schorfheide some eighty kilometers from Berlin, an enormous palace built on the site of an old shooting box. A broad avenue nearly six kilometers long led to a grandiosely wide structure of stone, plaster and timber, which housed a swimming pool, a private cinema, a picture gallery, a bowling alley and a taproom. The palace was flanked by the kitchens and servants' quarters, and beside it, reached by sunken steps, stood the tomb of the Swedish countess, Carin von Kantzow, Göring's first wife whose memory Göring revered with an adolescent fervor.

Van Osten had not been to Carinhall for three years. The last time he'd just returned from America and had been something of a hero. Paula had been with him then. It had been someone's birthday, Emmy Göring's or the child, Edda's. There had been a gathering of politicians and pilots, actors and singers from the State Opera. It had been a warm afternoon, with tea and cakes and white wine, music from *Götterdämmerung* and *Fra Diavolo* streaming over the landscaped gardens. Paula had decided that Goebbels who had come with a Czech actress was very much in love.

"Your family is no longer in Berlin." The reproach in Göring's voice jolted van Osten back to the present.

"They are on their grandfather's estate near Königsberg." Unlike other Nazi leaders the Görings entertained lavishly, and usually there was company at Carinhall. Tonight however van Osten and Göring were alone in the vast dining hall, dominated by the Rembrandt which had been a present from Sir Henry Deterding, the founder of Royal Dutch Shell. Having served plates of cold meat and salad, and checked the temperature of the Moselle, even the servants had gone.

"Did you send your family away because of the bombing?"

Göring had once said that if bombs fell on Berlin he would change his name to Meyer. "It wasn't the bombing," van Osten replied, remembering how Paula had snuggled up to him on the way back from Carinhall, smelling of wine and La Roca, saying she hadn't been able to distinguish the actors from the politicians, asking him to drive faster, saying she hoped he would always look like a man in love. Three years ago he and Paula had still been in love. "There were other reasons."

With surprising sensitivity Göring said, "I am sorry I asked. I am sorry for both of you. If there is anything . . ."

Van Osten waved his hand in negation. He did not want to discuss Paula with anyone.

"Did you know the Führer is taking Ribbentrop's advice on the conduct of the war?"

There was bitterness in Göring's voice.

Van Osten said, "Ribbentrop used to sell champagne. He should know a lot about France."

"But fuck all about war! Hess, Heydrich,

Himmler, Goebbels—none of them knows a damn thing about war!"

Van Osten picked up his glass and drank. Alliances between members of the Nazi hierarchy were infinitely changeable, and it was important not to take sides. "Hess was in the Air Force," he said quietly.

"Conscript! Never got a medal!"

Unlike Hermann Göring, van Osten thought. Göring had won an Iron Cross First Class before joining the Air Force. He had flown with Richthofen, commanded the Geswader after Richthofen's death, made twenty-one confirmed kills, and been awarded Imperial Germany's highest medal for valor, the Order pour le Merite—the Blue Max. Oh yes Göring knew about war all right. And proper medals.

"What experience have they got?" Göring demanded. "A chicken farmer, a cashiered naval officer, a champagne salesman, a journalist. Are these the men to conduct a war?"

"There's also von Rundstedt and Raeder and Jodl and a few other military people."

"But does the Führer listen to them?" Göring asked. "You tell me, does the Führer listen?"

Van Osten sipped at his wine, noncommittally.

Göring lowered his voice. "Last Friday, on the advice of these men, Sea Lion was canceled. There will be no invasion of Britain. You understand the significance of that?"

Van Osten nodded. "The war will be prolonged."

"And now the Führer plans to invade Russia."

So the directive from the Economics and Armaments Division was confirmed. "How do you know that?"

"The Air Ministry has ordered two million sets of winter underwear, five million pairs of stockings, one million pairs of fur-lined boots, and one million sheepskins."

"But Molotov is coming to Berlin next month for talks?"

"So did Schuschnigs of Austria, and Chvalkovsky of Czechoslovakia. It is going to be a long hard, bloody winter."

Van Osten pushed his plate away and lit a cigarette. "Given time the Russians can field 150 divisions. There will be no blitzkreig on the way to Moscow."

"My thoughts exactly." Göring took his time lighting a cigar. "There will be war on two fronts and Germany will be defeated. I cannot allow that. I want to see Charles Rieber at eleven o'clock tomorrow."

"Charles Rieber!"

Rieber was an American oil broker, who had been one of the first prospectors into Mexico. When the Mexican oilfields were nationalized Rieber had not joined with the other oil companies in pressuring the American government to impose an embargo on Mexican oil. Instead Rieber had negotiated compensation with the Mexicans. One of the terms of that agreement was that he would arrange to sell Mexican oil to Germany.

Two years ago van Osten had found Rieber, wandering desperately round the Reichsbank, looking for someone to approve his scheme for the sale of Mexican oil. Van Osten had achieved that with an introduction to Göring. But there was nothing Rieber could do to prevent the invasion of Russia.

Göring smiled round his cigar. "What kind of political influence does Rieber have?"

"Enough. A business like Crusader Gulf cannot survive without political muscle. Rieber told me he was once considered for an ambassadorial post."

"Can he get to Roosevelt?"

"I believe so."

"Excellent. Then tomorrow I will give him my terms for a peace that will take America out of this war. With America properly neutral, England will not have the means to fight on. They will have to negotiate a peace, or have peace thrust down their throats."

"Rieber won't do it. He's making a lot of money out of this war. He won't do anything to change that."

"True," Göring laughed. "Very true. But I promise you that this time, he will."

Van Osten walked across and looked at a portrait of Göring's pet lion cubs. He wished he could believe that Göring wanted to achieve such a peace. But having worked with him he knew that Göring was indecisive, emotional, a frightening amalgam of opposites. He played the buffoon but had steel enough to create the Gestapo. He covered the walls of his dining room with bad impressionists and indifferent moderns, but had an expert knowledge of medieval painting, and the picture gallery contained three Cranachs, a van der Weyden and a collection of Boucher nudes. He pillaged the art galleries of Europe, but no sequestered property hung at Carinhall.

"It won't work," van Osten said. "Even if Rieber agrees to do it, neither Churchill nor the Führer would consent to such a peace. In fact, Reichsmarshall, I should remind you that the Führer has specifically forbidden any attempt at peace."

"That is why I only speak of it to those I trust."

Van Osten turned slowly. He was being involved in a conspiracy. But if there was a conspiracy to oust Hitler, Göring was not the man to lead it. Three years ago it might have been possible. But Göring had given up the Gestapo to Himmler, screwed up the battle for Britain, and made a mess of the Economics Ministry. Now he was only a fringe person, tolerated for what he once had been.

From the head of the table Göring flicked ash from his cigar. "Knowing what you know, the question you have to ask yourself is, are you for Hitler? Or are you for Germany?"

Van Osten walked quickly back to the table and sat down. "Hitler and Germany are indivisible."

"Yet once they were not."

"At the beginning, in 1929—"

"At Zossen," Göring said harshly. "In 1939."

*   *   *

Göring pushed a glass of cognac along the table to van Osten. "The father of the late Lieutenant von Epp flew with me in the Richthofen Geswader. You know how we old fliers are. Always the last to surrender, and deeply concerned with honor. The night before he died Lieutenant von Epp wrote to his father, explaining what he was doing and why. His father had to tell me so that I at least would understand that his son was not a traitor."

Bitterly van Osten remembered that Göring's rise to power had been based on the information contained in the files of the Berlin Political Police, that Göring's penchant for blackmail died hard.

"Two names were mentioned," Göring went on. "Dieter Mehl and Baron Ewald von Kirkdorf."

"You should place such information before the proper authorities."

"I like patriots. Now more than ever Germany needs people like von Epp, von Kirkdorf, Dieter Mehl and Paul van Osten." Göring paused and looked directly at van Osten. "If there is opposition from the Führer I look to you to overcome it."

"How?"

"On the weekend of the 13th December Eva Braun and the Führer will be staying at Lech, a ski resort in the Arlberg. Details are in this folder. It will be easier than Zossen."

A second chance, van Osten thought. Not for Göring, for Germany. But Göring's support was not enough. "An assassination at Lech will not resolve your problem," van Osten said.

"Why not?"

"Because there will be a struggle for power within the Reich."

"Would not the Deputy Führer automatically succeed Hitler?"

Van Osten shook his head.

"Himmler?" Göring asked. "Goebbels?"

"It will be the SS against the Army."

"Right now the Army will support me. Victory will go to him who moves first."

"And to the one who controls Berlin."

"With my Luftwaffe I could take Berlin."

"You could bomb Berlin," van Osten said. "Destroy Berlin. But to take it you need troops. One division of parachutists would be more use than the entire Luftwaffe. What kind of support can you guarantee?"

"Tropp, Deputy Director of the Berlin police is my man. Also Brauer of the Fasschirmjäger Göring training at Hildesheim. I can guarantee you three battalions of paratroops."

With that and the police they could take Berlin, hold it for long enough to bring out the Army and Luftwaffe in support of Göring. "There are conditions," he said. "If I agree to do this thing, I want to use my own people. Mehl and Kirkdorf must be brought back from Paris and Amsterdam. I also want a cover, a winter operations directive from OKW. And I want unfettered access to Luftwaffe resources."

Göring smiled tiredly. "Consider it done."

4

Monday, October 14, 1940. Berlin.

Göring met with Rieber punctually at eleven o'clock. Rieber was a gangling, wide-shouldered man of about fifty, craggy-faced, with hard blue eyes under bushy white brows. He wore a generously cut turquoise blue suit illuminated by a hideously garish tie.

Göring gave Rieber a glass of Sekt and forgetting that Rieber didn't smoke offered him a Dutch cigar.

Rieber's narrow mouth tightened. He'd been forced to spend the weekend in Berlin because Herr Scholl had refused to conclude the business of exchange credits. "I am here without State Department approval," he said brusquely. "I should be in Lisbon today."

"Transport to Lisbon can easily be arranged." Göring sipped the bubbly Sekt and eyed Rieber casually over the rim of his glass.

Rieber said, "I have not been able to conclude my business with Herr Scholl."

"I know," Göring said. "That is because I wanted to talk to you about exchange credits myself."

Rieber's shaggy eyebrows met in a frown. Exchange credits were the bane of the Mexican oil deal. In the past the problem had been dealt with by Herr

Scholl who was one of fourteen Finance Assistants at the Ministry of Economic Affairs. Göring's sudden interest was ominous. "The position is most unsatisfactory," Rieber said. "My clients have supplied over eighty million dollars of oil and have received goods and services of only nine million."

Göring's expression was one of injured innocence. "But the remainder is held in accounts in their name!"

"In blocked accounts, in Germany, in their name."

Göring said, "I can make an order now for the release of twenty-five per cent of the blocked funds."

Rieber frowned. Herr Scholl had never gone above ten per cent, and now Göring had more than doubled that, without any obvious reason. "Because of the delays they have suffered and the amounts involved, my clients wish to have thirty per cent of the funds released."

"Consider it done," Göring signed a release order and handed it to Rieber.

Rieber was still puzzled. No one did anything for nothing, least of all Hermann Göring. He said, "Of course my clients will make a contribution to the economy of their largest customer. It is their wish that this contribution be handled through your Ministry."

"That will not be necessary." With men like Rieber, everything inevitably came to money. In this case, cheap money. Göring sipped at his Sekt and said, "I.G. Farben scientists have discovered a method of producing oil from coal."

Rieber leaned forward, placing his palms on his knees. He'd heard rumors about the synthetic oil process. This was the first confirmation that the I.G. Farben scientists had succeeded. If the oil they produced was cheap enough and refined enough, current oil technology would soon be obsolete. Europe would become the center of oil production. German Europe.

"At present they do not produce sufficient oil even for our needs. But in two years—" Göring flung out his arms expansively. "In two years they will supply the world!"

Rieber said, "If there is anything I can do to—"

"I have recommended that I.G. Farben appoint your company, Crusader Gulf, as exclusive distributors of synthetic oil throughout the Americas."

Rieber's breath caught in his throat. An exclusive license for the United States alone would turn Crusader Gulf into a major oil company and increase the value of his holdings by over a thousand per cent. He coughed, clearing the tightness in his throat. "What do I have to do?"

"Simply ensure there is peace between Germany and the United States. Without that the development of the oil process will be delayed, our exports will be embargoed, and we will not be able to trade with American companies."

"I am a businessman, not a politician. How can I ensure that there is peace between our two countries?"

"Paul van Osten tells me you have political influence in Washington, that you know President Roosevelt."

Rieber knew Roosevelt, had supported him in '32 and again in '36. But the man was a failure, senile and over impressed with his own image. Rieber didn't like him, and did not trust him either. "I know Roosevelt," he said.

Göring leaned over the desk, thrusting a bulky envelope at Rieber. "In this envelope is a letter I want personally delivered to the President. It contains my terms for an end to this terrible war. My terms for a just and lasting peace."

Rieber had not met Roosevelt since the summer of '38, not since the great man had reneged on his half-hearted promise to endorse Rieber's ambassadorial aspirations. "I may not be able to the President," Rieber said. "I might have to deal with Harry Hopkins or Cordell Hull."

"I don't know Hopkins, but if you can't see Roosevelt, Hull will do." Göring picked up a silver-plated Stuka. "Now, Mr Rieber, your interests are the same as Germany's."

Rieber stood up. "How shall I convey Roosevelt's reply to you?"

"You will convey it to Paul van Osten. Go and see him at the Tirpitzufer and make the necessary arrangements. You will find that he is arranging for a Luftwaffe plane to fly you to Lisbon, and that he has a contract with I.G. Farben for you to sign." Göring stood up. "Go in peace."

Thursday, October 17, 1940. Arlberg.

When the bulb over the hatch winked green, van Osten signaled to von Kirkdorf and crawled to the rear of the Heinkel taking the chunky Zeiss photoreconnaissance camera with him. They'd driven down to Munich that morning with Dieter Mehl, armed with a requisition for the plane, hoping for one of the latest Junkers fitted with three motorized cameras that scanned the ground simultaneously. They were told that Luftwaffe Transport Command had no such planes, not in Munich anyway. So they'd been given a hand-held camera and this tired Heinkel bomber with a veteran pilot who liked missing mountains by a mile.

Van Osten lay flat on the floor beside the camera and punched a large hole in the perspex. The roar of the twin Jumos became deafening. The wind rushed in, in an arctic blast. Below him stretched the jagged range of the Arlberg, rugged mountains rising to over two thousand meters, their peaks packed with snow. Von Kirkdorf grabbed his ankles and van Osten thrust his upper body and camera through the opening he had made.

The slipstream wrenched at him, threatening to tear him from the fragile grip round his ankles. The camera bobbed and dragged him outwards, its unsupported weight tearing at his wrists. Even behind his goggles, his eyes began to stream and the landscape blurred. Within seconds his fingers were transformed into separate stalks of pain, his face and exposed upper body, covered with a jelly-like numbness. At two thousand five hundred meters, the temperature was just above freezing, even in October.

His lips were torn from his teeth in a pain filled grin. Below the peaks of the mountains was pasture land, dotted with grazing cattle. He could make out the ordered boundaries of farms clinging precariously to the hillside, cottages, dark green clusters of pointed pine thrusting upwards at the sky. The twin ribbons of the chair lift running up the foot of a mountain enabled. him to identify Lech. It was Austria's first mechanized lift, which was perhaps why Eva Braun wished to ski there. At the foot of the lift, there was a small village, houses with pointed roofs, a single narrow church spire, a road.

Van Osten took his first photograph, turned the spindle for the next shot and found his fingers rigid with cold. Desperately he wrenched it, feeling the skin split, his blood freeze. The spindle moved and he took another photograph. And another. Another. He kept photographing frantically until the plane pulled away and the village was a tiny speck before his watering eyes.

"Enough to freeze the balls off a brass monkey," he stuttered, as von Kirkdorf dragged him inside.

"Brass monkeys don't have balls." Von Kirkdorf pulled him away from the opening, pressed him to the floor, threw his greatcoat, life belts and oiled paper over him.

Van Osten's teeth chattered uncontrollably.

"Next time you go."

But on the way back, van Osten went, knowing that as he was prepared for the shock of the cold and the wrench of the slipstream, he would be able to observe more. A third of the way, about a thousand meters up the mountain overlooking Lech, well away from the clusters of farm buildings, was a wooden chalet, built into the side of the mountain, two storeys high, its upper storey surrounded by a large balcony. A small track led away from it, upwards and to the right, to an old farmhouse and outbuildings. Below and to the left, the track crossed a tiny ledge, then broadened out still moving down the mountain, crossing the ski lift and ending in a large field. In the winter, one could follow the track and ski through the field to Lech. Van Osten loosed off twenty more shots before the chalet where Eva Braun and the Führer would stay, and the village became indistinguishable.

There was no possibility of repairing the shattered perspex and all the way back to Munich, the near arctic wind rushed through the hole, pulling the temperature, even in the pilot's cockpit, down to near zero. Van Osten sat in the co-pilot's seat, face blue with cold. He had to say something to the pilot. The flight out of Munich would have been logged and even Luftwaffe movements were checked by the Gestapo. He had originally thought of asking the pilot to fly over other parts of the Arlberg and pretend to take photographs. But in those temperatures, and at that height, he hadn't dared risk the camera falling from his frozen fingers.

Van Osten gestured downwards with his thumb. "What's it like in the winter?"

The pilot concentrated on flying. He was an elderly man, with an expressionless, wizened face peering out of a large flying helmet. "Snow," the pilot said. "Just snow."

"It would be a good place to train Alpine troops?"

"Anywhere in the Arlberg would be a good place to train Alpine troops," the pilot said.

"It's not only the training, it's the billeting, making sure they have places to sleep and food and beer. That place Lech, looks as if it might do."

"You'll have difficulty getting there in the winter," the pilot said. "From next month we begin transporting the Waffen SS into Lech for winter training."

* * *

Afterwards they picked up Dieter Mehl in Munich, where he had gone to collect architect's plans of the chalet.

"A thousand pounder from the air," Dieter said. "That'll do it."

Huddled in the passenger seat, still feeling the cold despite a covering of two greatcoats, van Osten repressed a smile. "No big bangs," he said. "The chalet is tucked into the hillside. It will have to be an attack on skis, with thirty or forty men."

"Too many," von Kirkdorf said, from behind the steering wheel.

"The chalet will be protected by Hitler's bodyguard and the Waffen SS will be in Lech."

"So what? Even the SS can't ski up mountains."

"There is still the bodyguard," van Osten said. "We need forty men."

"A typical infantry solution," von Kirkdorf said. "Using those methods we'd never have taken Rotterdam." Von Kirkdorf had gone in with the 16th Airborne which had taken the bridges across the Nieuw Mass River. "More than five or six men, and your security is shot to hell."

Dieter, sprawling across the rear seat cried, "Impossible! We need at least twenty men. We screwed up in Zossen because we did things on too small a scale."

"Our problem in Zossen," von Kirkdorf said drily, "was detonators that went kaput."

Van Osten stared into the dark beyond the shaded headlamps remembering Spain and the cart exploding in the center of the camp, the day Mendenez had died. "A small group could do it," he said. "If they were the right men, and we had explosive incendiaries."

Dieter said, "We have no such things in Germany."

"We can get them," van Osten said.

"But what about the men?" von Kirkdorf asked.

Van Osten said, "We can each pick one trustworthy person. I'll take Heinz Guertner. He's an excellent skier, and I've known him all my life."

Von Kirkdorf picked Josef Lipski, a Pole whom they all knew. Lipski had once been an ardent Nazi, fought with the Freikorps on the Polish border. A Stuka machine-gunning refugees on the road out of Warsaw had changed all that. His parents, sister and younger brother had all been killed, and soon afterwards, von Kirkdorf had taken him into the Abwehr.

Dieter said, "Manfred Lessing."

Van Osten frowned. Lessing was a burly Swabian, a former policeman who had joined the Abwehr eighteen months previously. "Lessing's sister is married to a Gestapo officer."

"Well, he should read some of Lessing's reports."

"I've read some of Lessing's reports," van Osten said sharply. "If anything, they protest too much."

"Manfred's alright," Dieter said. "Anyway, he's my choice."

If they were too careful, van Osten thought, they would never have enough men to mount the operation, and second choices were likely to prove second best. "Fine," he said, "we'll arrange a briefing when the photographs are ready. Tomorrow, Ewald, you have to sort out the security arrangements."

"Mel"

"Yes. You're the best actor amongst the three of us."

*　　*　　*

Franz Becker felt the chill of his flight deep in the marrow of his bones, as still clutching his flying helmet he made his way to the bar in the pilots' mess at Munich Airport. Looking about him furtively, he ordered a schnapps with a beer chaser. His hand shook as he raised the glass to his lips. Becker knew he'd been flying too long. He'd started back in 1922, flying Junkers F13s on the South American route and later, Ju-24s for Deutsche Lufthansa. He'd been on the reserve list when war broke out, too old to fly those fast new Messerschmitts, or take Heinkels or Junkers on bombing runs. So they had assigned him to Transport Command and given him this Heinkel 111, which like him, had seen better days.

Today, with the chill wind from the shattered perspex whistling through his cabin, swooping in broken cloud around the peaks of the Arlberg, he had been sure he was going to die. That mad van Osten from the Abwehr had forced him five hundred meters below the Hoher and the Paracier-Spitzel He shuddered at the memory and ordered another schnapps.

He was on his fourth schnapps when he became aware of a young, fresh-faced man beside him. A civilian, wearing a brown suit, a snap brim hat and a brown leather motoring coat. As a civilian, the man had no business in the pilots' mess, but in this new Germany, there were all kinds of civilians, with strange and frightening powers. The young man slid a glass of schnapps along the bar towards Becker.

"Had a good day, Franz?"

"Same as usual," Becker grunted. He always tried to avoid men like this. They were overbearingly smart, and insatiably curious. They wanted to know where he had been, what he had done, and he hated telling them. But he told them, because if he did not, there would be a black mark somewhere against the name of Franz Becker, and Franz Becker could not afford black marks.

"Not the same as usual," the young man said. "What happened to the perspex?"

"It shattered."

"From the wind or from the equipment that was loaded onto your plane?"

"From the equipment." Becker finished the schnapps in one fiery gulp. "A camera was being used and they had to break the perspex."

"Where did you fly?"

"Over the Arlberg." Hoping to dissuade the man, Becker said, "It was for the Abwehr."

"You wouldn't know who the Abwehr officer was?"

Becker did and Becker told him.

Friday, October 18, 1940.
Washington, D.C.

You could tell when the President was angry. Normally he read, holding the paper in front of him, head thrown back slightly, tilting the sheet from side to side. Now as he read the report brought by the representative of the English SIS, he tilted the paper furiously.

The English wanted his Ambassador recalled. He was hindering the British war effort and obstructing Anglo-American liaison. The secret agent produced evidence of an article the Ambassador would publish five days before the presidential election indicting the Roosevelt administration, proof of the Ambassador's claim that he could put twenty-five million Catholic votes behind Wendell Wilkie.

Deliberately the President tore up the report and

drafted a cable. 'THE LIQUOR TRADE IN BOS-
TON IS NOW CHALLENGING AND THE GIRLS
OF HOLLYWOOD MORE FASCINATING. I EX-
PECT YOU BACK HERE SATURDAY.'

Twenty-five minutes later, when Rieber called
for the sixteenth time, the President was thinking of
those twenty-five million votes. Rieber, who was a
friend of the Ambassador's, had been calling to discuss a German offer of peace. The President could
not discuss such an offer with a man like Rieber. At
the same time he could not be shown to have refused
to discuss such an offer. That refusal would be con-
veyed to the Ambassador and was politically dangerous.

The President spoke to his Appointments Secretary. "Call Charles Rieber and have him see me here
tomorrow at noon. You'd also better get someone from
the State Department—Morton Stevens, I think. And
oh! Grace, better have someone from G2 (C) here as
well. No, not that man Schroeder, ask General Clark
Winters if he will be so kind as to attend."

Friday, October 18, 1940. Berlin.

Colonel Erich Hoerlin had a small office in the
Reichschancellery, from which, in the absence of General 'Sepp' Dietrich, he commanded the one hundred
and twenty SS men who comprised the Leibstandarte
Adolf Hitler. Hoerlin was a big man, blond, ruggedly
handsome, with thoughtful blue eyes which many
women thought romantic.

The responsibility of protecting Germany's Mes-
siah lay heavily upon Hoerlin, and his task was not
made easier by the Führer's abrupt and wilful change
of plans, the Führer's contempt for security men and
his firm belief that the providence which had chosen
him to lead his people would always protect him. Before Dietrich had gone on leave, he had entrusted

Hoerlin with the security arrangements for the Führer's meeting with the Japanese at Innsbruck and afterwards at Lech. Lech was enough to give anyone a nightmare.

A wooden chalet halfway up a desolate mountain, inaccessible by road, and at that time of the year, surrounded by snow. His picked team of thirty-six men would be exhausted after the meeting at Innsbruck and could not be expected to maintain the best vigilance for a whole weekend afterwards, in freezing temperatures, with food and shelter a good two hours away down the mountainside.

As if that was not enough, now there was this foppish civil servant from the Air Ministry saying that his relief team would have to be transported by road all the way to Lech. With snow-covered roads and the probability of blocked passes, Hoerlin knew it would take them at least two days to get there, if they managed to get there at all.

"This is impossible," he cried. "I cannot conceive that our august Luftwaffe does not have one Junkers to spare."

Von Kirkdorf had spent all morning at the Air Ministry, using the signed authority van Osten had given him to extract information. Now, immaculately clad in a formal black suit and wearing a high, winged collar that had been fashionable at the beginning of the previous decade, he ruffled his papers. "Two Junkers," he said softly. "The capacity of a Ju-52 is eighteen persons. You require two, and you want them on standby for the entire weekend. I am afraid it is not possible. Another weekend perhaps, but not the weekend of December 13th. It would be better if the Führer would postpone his visit."

Clot of a bureaucrat, Hoerlin thought. They expected everyone, even the Führer, to arrange their lives according to their pedantry. Dietrich had told him that the meeting at Innsbruck had been set up after long negotiations. No variation was possible and the Japanese were already on their way. The Führer would rather change his bodyguard than cancel the meeting. "The transport must be provided."

Von Kirkdorf leaned forward, thrusting the files at Hoerlin. "See for yourself. A third of the available aircraft are scheduled for overhaul. Requisitions for theaters of war have exceeded estimates by sixty per cent. It is contrary to the Führer's directives to divert aircraft from the war."

"But we need only two aircraft."

"As I said, any other weekend but the 13th. We are falling behind with replacements, our losses over Britain were much higher than anyone knows. Our manufacturers have let us down. We have aircraft without engines, and engines without aircraft to fit them. Each time we have to replace the undercarriages on the JU-52s we have to buy a complete set of spares costing one hundred and twenty thousand marks. And those undercarriages break up so easily."

"We all have problems," Hoerlin said. "I want those aircraft."

"If we could let you have them," von Kirkdorf said, "we would. The last thing Reichsmarshall Göring wants is to expose the Führer to unnecessary risk. Will the nonavailability of your second group expose the Führer to such a risk?"

"We will protect the Führer, somehow."

Von Kirkdorf said, "Yours is a great responsibility. A divine responsibility. I want you to know, I did my best to procure the aircraft for you."

Hoerlin gave von Kirkdorf a resigned smile.

"Reichsmarshall Göring said to me, that if this nonavailability of aircraft endangered the Führer in any way, he would persuade the Führer to alter his plans."

Hoerlin did not want that. In the middle of fighting a global war, the Führer did not want to be disturbed about the traveling arrangements of his bodyguard. If Göring spoke to the Führer about that, Hoerlin would never hear the end of it. "You can tell the Reichsmarshall that the absence of those eighteen men will make no difference."

Von Kirkdorf shook his head slowly. "I cannot tell him that. He will want to know why you wanted thirty-six men in the first place, especially when we have all been ordered to ensure that resources are not wasted."

"So, you've saved yourself two aircraft."

"I must confirm to Reichsmarshall Göring that the arrangements for the Führer's protection are adequate. Reichsmarshall Göring is very devoted to the Führer."

Hoerlin said, "I can't discuss the Führer's security arrangements with you."

"I understand," von Kirkdorf said. "I will make arrangements for you to talk directly to Reichsmarshall Göring."

Hoerlin did not want that. Göring was overbearing and demanding. Defeated in his attempt to hold on to the Gestapo, he was looking for another unit, loyal to him and close to the Führer. What better way to form such a unit than send a small body of his paratroopers to give the Führer additional protection, to work with the SS bodyguard, and finally replace them.

"We have other ways of dealing with the problem," Hoerlin said. "If we can't use men, we will use money and fire power, to make each man more effective. The Führer's chalet will be surrounded with fencing, and the perimeter will be protected with machine gun nests. We will build roads up the mountain from Lech so that the Führer can complete the entire journey by car. We will commandeer existing farmhouses and billet our men within easy reach of the chalet. You can tell Reichsmarshall Göring that so he need have no concern for the Führer's safety."

"I will," von Kirkdorf said, "and I promise you he will be most relieved."

5

Friday, October 18, 1940. Washington, D.C.

Berlin W8, den
Leipzigerstr. 3.

16.10.40

Der Reichsminister der Luftfahrt
und Oberbefehlshaber der Luftwaffe
Ministeramt

The President of the United States,
1600 Pennsylvania Avenue,
Washington, DC,
United States of America.

CONFIDENTIAL
AND MOST
SECRET

Dear Mr. President,

The Third Reich now constitutes a United
States of Europe. The former territories
of Austria, Poland, Czechoslovakia,
Holland, Belgium, Luxembourg and France

are part of and submissive to Germany.
The armed strength of Germany is such
that it is only a question of time
before the British Empire is brought
under the hegemony of the Reich.

Nevertheless it is recognized that such
further victories as Germany will
achieve can only be at the cost of a
prolonged war. Germany is gravely
concerned about the great political and
economic upheaval which would result
from such a war, and for these reasons
wishes to make certain proposals to the
United States of America.

There is no doubt that a protracted,
modern war will result in the extinction
of both neutrals and belligerents. This
is not to the advantage of the United
States who because of the consequent
lowering of living standards will lose
its best markets.

A prolonged war will also end European
civilization as we know it. The British
Empire will inevitably be destroyed, and
this must lead to the end of the white
man's control of the world. A protracted
war will weaken Germany as well as the
other belligerents, leaving Russia and
Communism to grow stronger, allowing
Japan to extend its influence in the
Pacific. There is no doubt that these
reasons are of vital importance to the
United States.

Consequently it is proposed that Germany
and the United States should accept and

promulgate an agreement on the following
basis:—
(a) Germany will keep Danzig, the Polish
     Corridor and all its former terri-
     tories ceded to Poland by the Treaty
     of Versailles.
(b) All overseas Colonies which Germany
     had before 1914 and which are
     currently administered by other
     countries either under mandate or
     other forms of control, will be re-
     turned to Germany forthwith.
(c) Germany's military conquests since
     March 1940 are to be recognized and
     the countries so brought within the
     administration of the Reich will
     continue to be administered under a
     German mandate.
(d) Germany will receive substantial
     financial aid to enable her to
     obtain necessary raw materials and
     goods to adjust her level of economy
     to an appropriate basis.
(e) The Unted States will bring its
     admittedly powerful influence to
     bear upon England in order to
     persuade that country to accept the
     terms of the settlement herein
     outlined. In any case, the United
     States will cease supplying goods
     and other war materials to England
     on a cash and carry or any other
     basis and will support Germany in
     its efforts to gain a just,
     equitable and lasting peace. As a
     last resort, the United States
     would supply goods and war materials
     to Germany, which would be shipped

under the protection of the armed
might of the United States.
(f) The question of Czechoslovakia will
be decided at a conference between
representatives of the Governments
of the United States and the Reich.

Acceptance of these terms would achieve
a just and lasting peace. In addition,
any efforts made by you to secure such a
peace would not only enhance your
reputation as a world statesman, but
enable you, if such is your intention,
to leave office in a blaze of glory.

Yours faithfully,

GÖRING

The President laid Göring's letter on his desk. Acceptance of Göring's terms meant leaving Europe in slavery for a generation. But he could not reject those terms too obviously. He looked over the top of his half-framed glasses at Rieber. "We are most grateful to you, Charles." He moved his head to indicate Morton Stevens and General Clark Winters. "All of us here."

Rieber eyed Stevens and Winters cautiously. They were meeting not in the President's Oval Office, but in the Executive Study, beyond the Lincoln Sitting Room which the President used as a living room, library and informal office. It was sometimes referred to as the Yellow Oval Room because Dolly Madison had done it up in yellow damask and some of the Louis XVI chairs were bright yellow. The President sat behind a green inlaid desk in a wheelchair that had no supports for his arms.

"What on earth were you doing in Germany, Charles?"

Rieber was prepared for that. "I was in Lisbon on

business, when I received Reichsmarshall Göring's invitation. It seemed the right thing to do, so I went."

"And you did not choose to discuss the subject of this invitation with our people in Lisbon?" That was Morton Stevens, serious-eyed, crew cut, in his late thirties, one of Roosevelt's brightest Under Secretaries of State.

Rieber looked at Stevens. A tidy, conservative man, he surmised, a man devoted to his career. "With respect," Rieber said, "I felt it would be easier all round if I went without official sanction. I may have been wrong, but that was my decision at the time."

Stevens' pale eyes behind the square, rimless glasses were devoid of expression. "Your passport was valid for Portugal, Spain and Switzerland. You had no business going to Germany."

"On the contrary, I had a duty to go to Germany, with or without State Department approval. Over there, young man, the world is exploding into little pieces. I think I have done something to stop that."

"Visa regulations are made for everyone's benefit," Stevens said. "There are penalties—"

"I think under the circumstances," the President interrupted, "we can overlook Mr. Rieber's small transgression. Tell me about Göring, Charles. Why do you think he has made this offer of peace?"

"I think he genuinely wants peace. I do not pretend to know what his motives are, but I am certain of his sincerity."

"If so, why did he not use normal diplomatic channels for his offer?" Morton Stevens asked.

"I don't know. If I were asked to guess, I'd say he felt that I could ensure that his offer was read by the right person at the right time."

"And does Herr Hitler share Reichsmarshall Göring's views on peace?"

"I am not aware of Hitler's views."

The President asked, "What were your impressions of Germany?"

Rieber hesitated, intimidated more by the presence of Winters than Stevens. Winters he knew was the Head of Army Intelligence Branch, G2 (C). "I wasn't in Germany long enough to get any valid impressions."

The President inserted a cigarette into a long holder. "Did the people seem happy, well fed, and confident? I hear talk of rationing and food shortages."

"They believe their hardships are temporary and that the war will not last long. They have been told that Britain will be defeated soon."

"So they don't know the battle for Britain has been lost?" A quick pull at the cigarette. "How did you find Germany, Charles? Was it very different from America?"

"As I said, I wasn't there long enough. But it isn't like America."

"I know. You just went in and out. Well, you must leave this to us. We're going to work on it right now, and please believe me, we will stop at nothing to achieve a just and enduring peace. Thank you for everything you have done."

Rieber said, "I am pleased to have been of service, Mr. President."

"One more thing." The President held the cigarette away from his face. His jaw jutted. "We take over from here. You will find the oil business is safer and more rewarding, even if you occasionally have to breach the Neutrality Act. Remember, diplomacy is best left to the experts." He placed the cigarette holder between his lips at a jaunty angle. His smile broadened and his eyes twinkled. "Now," the President said, "I must run."

Which Rieber thought was a strange thing to say, when the man had long ago lost the use of his legs.

* * *

Afterwards, the President turned to Stevens and Winters. "Well gentlemen, your views."

Stevens was the first to speak. "It's a German ploy. If the Germans were really serious they would have made a formal offer."

"I don't agree," Winters said. He was a stocky man with close cropped white hair, a stolid ruddy face. At the time, the whole of G2 consisted of hardly more than a hundred people. An Army of less than a quarter of a million men, with arms and equipment for less than one third of those, and which had not fought for twenty years had little use for Intelligence. G2 (C) was concerned with counter-espionage. However the President had given the responsibility for counter-espionage within the United States, to the FBI. So G2 (C) confined itself to estimating the strength and disposition of foreign armies from open sources of information. "It may be that Göring is perfectly sincere in his offer of peace," Winters went on. "The defeat of his Air Force may have taught him something."

Stevens said, "Göring's sincerity or lack of it is unimportant. He cannot make those proposals effective unless they are sanctioned by Hitler."

"Perhaps Hitler is using Göring as a front?" Winters suggested.

"That's ridiculous. Göring is acting without Hitler's authority. Hitler dominates Europe. He wants to dominate the world. He will not stop now. I would have thought that was obvious even to the simplest military mind."

Clark Winters colored. Colonel Max Schroeder should have been at this meeting. Schroeder actually dealt with Counter Intelligence and knew about these things. But Schroeder and the President disliked each other and had recently fallen out over the President's proposal that G2 (C) should co-operate with the British Secret Service. "You can't discount the possibility," he protested.

"A possibility that has no relationship to reality as we know it."

"What is your opinion of the proposals themselves?" the President asked.

"They are unacceptable," Stevens said. "We can get better terms, especially if the German government is headed by Göring."

"We cannot fight this war," Winters said. "We have neither the troops nor the equipment. It will take a year at least before we are anywhere near ready. We should talk peace."

The President eyed Winters keenly. "Talk peace with Hitler? Or talk peace with Göring?"

Stevens said, "Hitler's word is worth nothing, Mr. President. That has been shown to us time and time again."

"And Göring cannot talk peace as long as Hitler is around. I wonder . . ." The President looked up at the smoke drifting from the end of his cigarette holder. "I wonder if our fat friend Göring has plans to get rid of Hitler. That's something your people should know about, General. That's the kind of intelligence we need."

"We haven't the—"

"The British would know," the President interrupted. "You should have agreed to co-operate with them."

"We can find out, if we have to, Mr. President."

"Good. Find out then if Mr. Göring has plans to deal with Mr. Hitler. Find out also if he needs any help."

Stevens looked at the President with horror.

"After all," the President continued, "it's time we gave the Germans some kind of aid."

"What the President means—" Stevens said.

Roosevelt smiled directly at General Winters. "The President," he said, "was only thinking aloud."

      ✽   ✽   ✽

"Thinking aloud!" Colonel Max Schroeder exclaimed. "You must be out of your mind, General. Who thinks aloud when he can think silently? The President was giving you an order."

"Morton Stevens didn't seem to think so. He tried to stop the President."

Schroeder looked at Winters pityingly. "What did you expect him to say? Come round to my office and let me give you written orders in triplicate?"

"We should not interfere in the internal affairs of other countries," Winters said.

"And we mustn't forget Hitler is the legally elected representative of the German people. Let's send him flowers."

Winters was regular army and had been given command of G2 (C) only because of Roosevelt's dislike of Schroeder. Schroeder didn't resent Winters for that. He got on well with Winters. Each left the other alone, Winters concerning himself with administering G2 (C) and Schroeder dealing with practical intelligence matters and the avoidance of J. Edgar Hoover's pudgy toes. Schroeder saved all his resentment for Roosevelt.

"Can't we get clarification from the President?" Winters asked.

Patiently Schroeder explained to him that the President had to be able to make a plausible denial. If they succeeded in discovering Göring's intentions and they helped him eliminate Hitler, and they weren't found out, and there was peace, Roosevelt would run for a fourth term. If they failed they'd be disowned and might even be shot. "The Chinese say that he who loses is a bandit, and he who wins is a king."

"And what if we do nothing?" Winters asked morosely.

"Then we have our budget slashed and we get disbanded, and if we're lucky, we get jobs in a new intelligence outfit run by Roosevelt's friends."

"If we do we're doomed, if we don't we're damned."

"Exactly," Schroeder said.

6

Saturday, October 19, 1940.
Washington, D.C.

Colonel Max Schroeder pulled gently at his cigar as he stood by the cloakroom of the Washington Hotel, watching the elegantly dressed diners collecting their overcoats. It had been a splendid dinner. Excellent food, plenty of conversation, speeches short and to the point.

One hundred and fifty of Washington's most influential people had been there. Schroeder would never have been able to get in, if not for his high-ranking Intelligence status and the personal intervention of Senator Nye himself.

The dinner had been organized by the Committee to Defend America First. Two weeks before the election the Committee had gathered together the people who mattered most and given them their message. Keep America out of the war. Keep Roosevelt out of the White House.

Charles Lindbergh had been there, modest, unassuming, intense with a desire for peace. "This war," he had said, "is the climax of all political failure."

Schroeder agreed with that. There was a joke

53

going around Washington. Snow White now only had six dwarfs because Dopey was in the White House.

"We are in danger of war today not because European people have attempted to interfere in America, but because we American people have attempted to interfere with the internal affairs of Europe. Our danger in America is an internal danger. We need not fear a foreign invasion unless American people bring it on through their own quarreling and meddling with affairs abroad."

Lindbergh had been to Germany before the war, was a friend of Reichsmarshall Göring. The diners had given Lindbergh a standing ovation, and they had cheered long and loud when Senator Burton Wheeler said that Roosevelt's new Triple-A plan would plough under every fourth American boy. Decent, well meaning, influential people had cheered. Schroeder looked at them, crowding in the doorway for taxis, elegant in their evening clothes. These people were America. This was the way of life they wanted to preserve. At that moment, Schroeder had no doubt America wanted peace.

Charles Rieber came into the lobby, stepped round the little knot created by Henry Ford and Joseph Kennedy huddled in conversation. Rieber was talking to John Foster Dulles as he came level with Schroeder.

"Good evening Charles," Schroeder said.

Rieber looked at him with surprise. "I didn't expect to find the army at a pacifist gathering."

"Peace is war by other means," Schroeder said. "Do you have time for a drink?"

Rieber hesitated momentarily and looked at Dulles. Dulles nodded acquiescence. "Come round to the house," Rieber said.

*   *   *

Rieber lived in Georgetown, an area of steep, cobbled streets, with picturesque views of the Potomac. His home on Prospect Street was old and large, solidly built, with a lounge that occupied the whole of the first floor. It was elegantly furnished with Georgian chairs and sofas and tall chintz drapes.

"State's furious about your making contact with Göring," Schroeder said as they entered the lounge.

Rieber unfastened his bow tie. "Tough on 'em. Bourbon okay?"

"Bourbon's fine. Ice and water."

"State's furious because I did in two days what they haven't been able to do in ten years. Those boys at State spend too much time sitting on their brains. Do you know how long I've been waiting to get compensation from the Mexican Government? Two whole years!"

"My heart bleeds for you Charles," Schroeder said. "But over at G2 (C) we've heard some funny stories about Mexican compensation."

"Malicious lies," Rieber snorted. "State's furious because I've done their job for them and achieved peace."

"They don't see it that way."

"What other way is there to see it?"

"They think you are being used by Göring. They don't believe Göring can deliver. They are going to reject his offer."

"They're mad," Rieber said walking to the bar. Very steadily he poured bourbon into glasses, added ice. "War," he said softly, "I have seen war on land and sea. I have seen blood run from the wounded. I have seen men coughing out their gassed lungs. I have seen the dead in the mud. I have seen cities destroyed. I *hate* war. Do you know who said those words, Max? Franklin D. Roosevelt." Rieber brought Schroeder his drink. "Franklin D. Roosevelt who has never been near a battlefield in his life!"

"All that proves is Roosevelt is a liar. What's new about that?" Schroeder had not come to talk about Roosevelt.

"We should have been warned by that speech, Max. Roosevelt is sick in mind as well as in body. He has dreams of great and secret power. Dangerous dreams for all of us."

"I can't buy that." If Roosevelt was going to war, Schroeder wanted facts.

"Why not?"

"No American President wants to involve America in a European war. The people wouldn't stand for it. Congress wouldn't approve of it."

"Bullshit," Rieber said. "Roosevelt hasn't got any choice. Remember that catch phrase his Brain Trust people thought up? Spend your way out of a depression. Well, after a time you need to spend money on more than good works and charity. Those new armament factories are it, Max. Roosevelt needs those factories as much as the British. Take them away and unemployment goes zooming up, right back to where it was at the height of the depression. Ten million, fifteen million and every one of them a vote against Roosevelt. The man could never stand that! He'll keep on churning out armaments long after the British stop paying for them. He'll turn America into the biggest arsenal in the world, because that's the only way you can spend your way out of a depression."

Schroeder knew nothing about economics. All he knew was that Rieber's argument fitted his concept of Roosevelt and the New Deal.

"Oh come on, Max. You intelligence buffs know how it will be done. One day there will be an incident. An American ship will be sunk by a U-boat. The American people will be outraged. They will not know that the whole incident was stage-managed. They will ask for and get war."

Like the *Panay*, Schroeder thought. The *Panay*

had been a US Navy gunboat which had been strafed and sunk on the Yangtze river by Japanese aircraft. There had been tremendous public outrage, shrill demands for war. But the Administration had accepted the Japanese apologies, agreed that it was a mistake, buried the matter as swiftly and surely as the bodies of the American seamen had been swallowed up by the murky brown waters of the Yangtze river.

It hadn't been an operation run by G2 or Naval Intelligence. Schroeder was sure of that. He knew the authority had come from higher up.

Schroeder had special reason to remember the *Panay*. His nineteen-year-old boy, his only child, had died that day, his body ripped apart by the machine guns of the dive bombers, incarcerated in the blaze of an oil fire, lost forever in a place he had no business to be.

If Roosevelt wanted war he must be stopped. Schroeder had no doubt of that. But Roosevelt didn't want war. He wanted Hitler eliminated so there could be peace.

Schroeder dragged his attention away from the *Panay*, forced himself to concentrate on what had brought him to see Rieber. "Can Göring overrule Hitler and implement such a peace?"

Rieber considered the question carefully. "All I can say with authority," Rieber paused to emphasize the word, hoping it would color the rest of his statement, "is that Göring would not have made such an offer unless he felt certain he could keep his part of the deal. I've known Göring a long time. He is a brave, determined and dedicated man. I've never known him to make a promise he couldn't keep."

Schroeder asked, "Does Hitler know of Göring's offer?"

"I think not."

"Did Göring tell you how he would deal with Hitler?"

"He would have been mad if he did."

"Okay, so how does Göring plan to implement this peace? Don't you see, Charles, if we know that, we have a deal."

"I wish I knew," Rieber said. "I really wish I knew. There are a lot of us who want to see peace in Europe. But I don't know what Göring plans to do about Hitler."

"Can you find out?"

"No. The arrangement with Göring is that I do not see or speak or write to him again. Roosevelt's reply is to be communicated to one of his associates, Paul van Osten."

So Göring was trying to isolate himself. Which meant that the whole plan was a fake, or that Göring too was looking for a means of plausible denial. "Do you feel you are being used, Charles? That Göring is carrying out some devious scheme and sent the proposals through you, because you could be so easily denied?"

Rieber shook his head. "No. I'm totally convinced of Göring's sincerity."

"Who's van Osten?"

"He is young, thirtyish, used to be one of Göring's assistants at the Ministry of Economics. He is now with the Abwehr."

"What rank?"

"Lieutenant Colonel."

"Then he's been with the Abwehr some time. Would he be the kind of man to kill Hitler?"

Rieber shook his head. "No, not Paul. He is too nice. He's one of those very correct Germans, honest, dignified, honorable, an aristocrat with principles."

Which was just the kind of person who would want to get rid of Hitler. "I'd like to meet him," Schroeder said. "Can you arrange that?"

"I could try. Where will you meet?"

"In Switzerland," Schroeder said. "Geneva or Zürich."

"Geneva," Rieber said. "The food is better."

"Anywhere in Switzerland," Schroeder said. "As long as it's next week."

Sunday, October 20, 1940. Berlin.

In his small Schoneburg flat, van Osten woke late. It was an *eintopf* day, when all one could get in a Berlin restaurant was a cheap stew for the price of a huge meal. The difference was supposed to go to Winter Relief, but van Osten knew that it only went to swell the war contribution, so he fried himself some bread, ate it with two slivers of bacon and drank ersatz coffee made from roasted barley. Then he read Hesse, and punctuated by the clatter of the S-bahn, tried to think about selflessness.

To care and not to care, to act and to sit still, to achieve and yet preserve detachment. Whether the assassination plot succeeded or failed wasn't important. What was important was the part van Osten played in it, his own fulfilment. Rubbish! If Hitler were allowed to live, if there was no peace, hundreds of thousands would suffer and die, and not only Germans. Lech had to succeed.

Early in the afternoon they told him there were two radio messages at the Tirpitzufer. By then, he was reading Thomas Wolfe whose extravagant prose translated so well into German. Van Osten decided to abandon *Look Homeward, Angel,* and drive over to the office. It would pass the time till he went over to the von Ritters' for tea and a game of chess with Karl.

It would have been different if Paula and the children were with him. A Sunday lunch, the best that rationing would allow, and afterwards a ramble in the woods playing boisterous games with the children, or a visit to the zoo. He missed the children. He missed

Paula. There were, he thought, too many empty
spaces between the days.

The first radio message was from Rieber. He took
his time decoding it, filling out the empty spaces. The
State Department had rejected Göring's offer of peace
because they did not believe he could implement it.
But Rieber had persuaded US Army Intelligence
Branch G2 that such implementation was a possibility. They were sending a Colonel Max Schroeder to
discuss it and he would be in Geneva on the 26th,
staying at the Hotel Cornavin. If van Osten could
make the meeting, he should cable Rieber at once.

Viereck's message said he was returning to Berlin
immediately, to report on the progress of the anti-
Roosevelt campaign. Viereck also wanted to take back
with him to America, one hundred thousand dollars,
in order to settle bills which would be outstanding by
election day.

That one hundred thousand dollars was a serious
problem. All the money the Abwehr had for the anti-
Roosevelt campaign was exhausted. The only thing
left was *Judengeld*.

Van Osten sent Viereck a message instructing him
to come to Geneva instead of Berlin, sent Rieber a
message confirming that he would be at the Hotel
Cornavin on the 26th, and decided to see Canaris
about exit permits as soon as possible.

7

Monday, October 21, 1940. Berlin,

Paul van Osten sat with Heinrich Himmler and Reynhard Heydrich round a small table in a somberly furnished room at 8 Prinz Albrecht Strasse, the headquarters of the Gestapo. It was a fine room, built when things were done in a big, solid way, with generous windows and curtains of dark velvet. In front of each of them was a copy of the file which had been brought by the captain of the ss *Mattun* and rushed by motorcycle despatch from Hamburg.

The file was thick, cleared for three star Generals and above. A legend on the cover proclaimed, 'IF YOU HAVE NOT BEEN CLEARED FOR THIS INFORMATION RETURN TO RECORDS SECTION IMMEDIATELY.' The file contained detailed plans for the intrusion and continued involvement of the United States in a total war against Germany. The target date was the spring of 1943, by which time the Americans expected to have an army of five million men.

Van Osten looked up from the file. Even a totally controlled German Europe could not produce that manpower or that wealth of arms. If America entered the war on that scale, Germany was finished. Peace now, was therefore imperative.

Himmler was reading methodically, taking careful notes in pencil. He was a pale, mild-looking man with spiky brown hair, steel-rimmed pince-nez and a neatly trimmed moustache. Like Hitler, he had been born a Catholic, and van Osten recalled that he had used Jesuit discipline to build up the organization of his SS. Forty years old, Himmler was chief of all German police and Reichsführer of the SS.

The SS or Black Order as Himmler called it, was the elite organization of the Nazi party. Its members were supremely fit, intelligent, totally loyal and racially pure since at least 1750. They had murdered Roehm and his SA stormtroopers in 1934, and since then had become the most powerful organization inside Germany.

Reynhard Heydrich was Himmler's deputy. Himmler called him his *triebfeder*. Quick and intuitive he was indispensable to Himmler. Heydrich was thirty-six years old, an expert fencer, skier and violinist. He was very tall, and very lean, with a long handsome face, blond hair and eyes that were blue, hard and intelligent. He headed the Directorate of Reich Security, the RSHA, which controlled all sections of the police, security and intelligence, with the exception of the Abwehr. Heydrich also controlled the intelligence service of the Nazi party, the *Sicherheitsdienst-Inland*, the SD, and through the RSHA, controlled the Gestapo. Now as he finished reading he looked thoughtfully out of the window and waited for Himmler.

Neither Himmler nor Heydrich should have seen this file. They were supposed to confine their interests to the internal security of the Reich, and Viereck should never have forwarded copies to them. Not that it made any difference now. If Roosevelt wanted war, there was no opposing it.

Himmler indicated that he had finished reading by clearing his throat and looking at the others mildly, like a schoolmaster with two of his favorite pupils. "This is a military matter. These documents must be handed over to OKW."

Heydrich swiveled in his chair to look at his chief. "Before we do that we should ascertain two things. Can the military resolve this problem? Are the files genuine?" He eyed van Osten.

Van Osten said, "These files have been provided by one of our agents in the United States, George Viereck. Viereck got the original from a clerk in the War Department, who is loyal enough to our cause to be a member of the German American Bund."

"How did this clerk get the file?" Heydrich asked. "It is marked for very restricted circulation only."

"It was given to him for return to Records, by an officer in a hurry to visit his pregnant wife at Bethseda Naval Hospital. Viereck has no doubt that it is genuine."

Heydrich said softly. "Our congratulations to Herr Viereck."

"You are Military Intelligence," Himmler said to van Osten. "Does the army have any plans to repel an invasion of this type?"

"We have always understood that the Führer wishes to avoid war with the United States."

"And now it seems, we have no choice." Heydrich tapped the file in front of him. "These are not contingency plans. These plans show a determination to have war at any cost. We have no hope of peace."

Heydrich's intuition, van Osten thought, had gone directly to the heart of the matter. Roosevelt wanted war, and Göring's peace mission was already a failure, unless the Führer was killed and Göring given control of Germany. Now above all, Lech had to succeed.

Himmler asked, "If we prepared now, could we repel such an invasion?"

Van Osten selected his words carefully. He had to show faith in the super Wehrmacht. "It is a question of numbers. We can never mobilize more than two and a half, three million men. Our troops will be facing an overwhelming superiority of men and equipment."

"And God is on the side of the big battalions," Heydrich smiled.

Van Osten smiled back gratefully.

"How do the American people feel about such a war?" Heydrich asked. "A few months ago I received a copy of a Roper poll which showed that sixty-four per cent of the American people were opposed to involvement in a European war."

"That figure is reducing," van Osten said. "The bombing of Britain has made more people support American involvement."

"What are the precise figures?" Himmler asked.

"It's now about fifty-fifty, and falling."

"So Roosevelt does not have all his people behind him. How can he go to war?"

"He can create an incident," van Osten said, "and by 1943, public opinion might have changed."

Heydrich dropped his pen on the table and leaned back against his chair, arms draped around the back rest. "There is only one solution. Roosevelt must be disposed of. If the American people are not one hundred per cent committed to war, then a new President in his first term will not drag them into it." He smiled again. "America as we all know is a democracy."

Van Osten reached for a cigarette and stopped. Himmler did not approve of smoking. Van Osten drummed his fingers on the table. Murdering an American President was unthinkable. If the murder were carried out with the customary crudeness of the

SD it would start a war, not stop it. But without such a murder, war was inevitable. So if such a deed had to be done, then it better be done by the Abwehr. If such a deed had to be done, van Osten knew, it was his responsibility to do it. Meanwhile, he had to stop Heydrich turning this particular thought into action. The Abwehr and the SD were rivals, and though by agreement, foreign espionage was deemed to be the province of the Abwehr, Amt VI of the RSHA was SD Ausland, which had foreign agents and carried out missions abroad.

"Roosevelt may not be President much longer," van Osten said.

Himmler and Heydrich looked at him inquiringly.

"The Presidential elections are in two weeks. There is considerable opposition to Roosevelt. He is running for a third term and that is not considered to be in accord with the spirit of the American Constitution. They call it the Führer–Prinzip."

The two men looked back at him unsmiling. The Führer–Prinzip was taken seriously by the Secret Police of the Third Reich.

"How will the Abwehr ensure that Roosevelt is not elected?" Heydrich was leaning back in his chair, the pale blue eyes looking intently down the long face.

Van Osten said, "We're running an anti-Roosevelt campaign in the United States."

"And how does one do that?"

Van Osten bit back a remark that none of those present had experience in fighting free elections. "We are trying to convince the American people that Roosevelt is not for them. We take advertisements in the press and on the radio, we hold meetings and subsidise cover organizations. We provide information about Roosevelt's duplicity."

"All this must cost money," Heydrich said.

"Where does the Abwehr find foreign currency for this esteemed purpose?"

"We are using funds surplus to the requirements and talents of the Italian Secret Service."

Heydrich's smile implied that was well phrased. "What is the probability of your success?"

"High. We are most optimistic. It will be foolish to move against Roosevelt until after the elections."

"But after the elections, what?" Himmler asked.

Heydrich said, "If Roosevelt wins, he is to be killed. There is no alternative to that."

Himmler remained silent, his fingertips pressed to his temples, thinking. Finally he said, "Your logic Reynhard, always your damned logic . . ."

Heydrich's damned logic was impeccable. Van Osten asked, "The question Reichsführer is who is to do it?"

"Those who are most fitted." Himmler knew that SD Ausland had nothing comparable to the Abwehr network in America. He smiled weakly at Heydrich. "Our friend here must look after it."

"It will not be easy," van Osten said.

"It is only by overcoming difficulty that you become worthy of the Reich." Himmler's pale grey eyes raked van Osten. "You must have the inner compulsion for this task. You must will yourself to do it."

"Yes, Reichsführer."

"I wish to be kept informed of your progress," Heydrich said.

"As far as that is consistent with the operation."

Heydrich smiled. "Let us talk again after the elections. Meanwhile we wish you every success."

*　　*　　*

Van Osten placed Viereck's message on Canaris' desk. "We haven't got a hundred thousand dollars," he said. "We'll have to use the Jew."

"Is there no other way?"

Van Osten shook his head. "Can you arrange exit permits for Friday?"

"For which destination?"

"Basle," van Osten said. "I don't want the Gestapo to know we're going to Geneva."

Canaris looked thoughtful. "The Jew must come back, you know."

"We're taking everything else from him," van Osten said.

"It's the law."

Van Osten shrugged.

"The law may be wrong, but we have to keep within it. We have to be practical."

Van Osten wondered what the Jew would think about that. "We do what has to be done," he said and left.

* * *

When van Osten returned to his office, Heinz Guertner was arranging the latest batch of directives on his desk. He looked up at van Osten. "Good grief, Paul, you look as if Hermann Göring fell on you."

"I haven't been with Göring. I've been with *der Alte Mann*." Van Osten flung himself into his chair and gestured at the desk. "Anything interesting?"

"No, just the usual. Jews can only breathe through one nostril, and then only if they are facing Mecca."

"I wish a few other people were ordered to do that," van Osten said darkly and lit a cigarette.

Heinz took the pack from the desk and toyed with it. "French?" he asked. "Black market?"

"No. A present from our agent in Paris." He looked at his watch. "Sit down, Heinz. Your fiddling about irritates me."

Heinz replaced the pack of cigarettes, straightened the photograph of Paula and the children and sat.

"Ever thought how this war is going to end?"

"Well . . ." Heinz frowned handsomely. "We'll invade England and that will be it."

"No," van Osten said. "We're not going to invade England for a long time. Sea Lion has been canceled and the Luftwaffe have lost the battle for Britain."

"What is going to happen?"

"It seems we are going to invade Russia."

Guerther gazed blankly back at him.

"History tells us that the time for invading Russia is not yet. The first thing you were taught was never to get involved in a war on diametrically opposed fronts."

"Yes," Guertner said. "I remember that."

"We're going to have to stop the Führer."

"We? How?"

Van Osten eyed Guertner levelly till he saw comprehension dawn.

"Oh my God! Not really, Paul! Not you!"

"Yes," van Osten said. "I'd like you to join us. You will have a splendid opportunity to ski."

*   *   *

Over at the Schutz Weinstuben, Mehl and Lessing having long finished their *eisbein* were on their third bottle of chilled Beaujolais. They agreed that horrible things were being done in the Third Reich, things that made one ashamed to be a German. Harmless lunatics were being murdered together with Jews, Gypsies and Poles. There was forced labor, forced starvation and forced prostitution. Civilians were arrested and tortured without cause. Lessing and Mehl had once compiled interminable lists of these incidents, compiled references and cross references. Germany was rotten with barbarism.

And it had to be stopped. Yes, sir. It was going to be stopped. Now.

Lessing blinked at Dieter, his low set eyebrows,

swarthy features and shaven head giving him an expression of brutal cunning. "How?" he asked.

Dieter ran a finger round his throat. "Lop off the
head and the body withers."

Lessing's cheek twitched involuntarily. "I think
that is a good idea," he said.

*   *   *

Von Kirkdorf told Lipski about the place and the
people involved in the attempt on the Führer's life.
"Well Josef, do you want to join?"

Behind the heavy moustache Lipski's teeth
gleamed in a smile, the flesh around the grey eyes
crinkled. "If I say no now, you will have to cut my
throat."

"Right," von Kirkdorf said.

"I join," Lipski said. He reached across the table
and gripped von Kirkdorf's hand. His smile was replaced by an expression of the utmost sincerity. "I
want to join," he said. "I am proud you invited me."

8

Tuesday, October 22, 1940. Berlin.

The basis of the Third Reich's system of internal security was its files. At Gestapo Headquarters in the Prinz Albrecht Strasse, Amt IV C, Records and Preventive Detention controlled files on nearly three quarters of a million people. Each file was alphabetically indexed by name and by nature of the suspected offense and cross indexed to suspect groups and known associates, marked by tabs which ranged in color from red to pale grey to denote the potential danger of the suspect.

At 103, Wilhelmstrasse, SD-Inland had its own comprehensive filing system. Here, even rumors were catalogued together with the results of the SD's frequent public opinion polls, the records of its investigations into cultural and scientific matters and details of over a quarter of a million suspects.

At Heydrich's direction there was little exchange of information between the SD and the Gestapo. All requests for exchange had to be authorized by Heydrich himself or by a small committee of SD intimates who were the only people who had unfettered access to both sets of records. Heydrich maintained that this was because the SD was only a party organization, while the Gestapo was a government agency. The truth was that in Nazi Germany, knowledge was power and that total knowledge was best restricted to those least likely to abuse it.

Knowledge being power, Heydrich also had a private filing system stored in a room in the Wilhelmstrasse, three doors down from Heydrich's own small office there. The room was guarded, combination locked, and only Heydrich had the combination. Here was stored information on the characters, weaknesses, habits, and scandals of the industrialists, high ranking military officers and political leaders of the Third Reich, information on Goebbels' passionate love affair with a Czech actress, details of Göring's art deals and copies of his accounts at the Deutsche and Thyssen banks, records of Himmler's involvement with hypnotists and a psychiatric analysis of his stomach cramps. In those bulky, fireproof filing cabinets there was even documentation concerning the uncertain genealogy of Adolf Hitler.

Reynhard Eugen Tristan Heydrich had come a long way since that meeting on Himmler's chicken farm at Walterudering, nine years ago. Then, Heydrich had been unemployed, expelled from the Navy because of an affair with an industrialist's daughter. Himmler had been head of the SS, a force of less than ten thousand men, nothing compared to the hundreds of thousands of Roehm's brown shirted SA stormtroopers. When they met, Himmler had been nervous, and fearing that Heydrich was a member of Naval Intelligence, had given Heydrich twenty minutes to outline the organization of an SS Intelligence Service. Drawing on half remembered ideas from thrillers and his own sparse experience, Heydrich had sketched out what such an Intelligence Service should be. Now, he controlled such a service, but that was not enough.

One day, Heydrich knew, the posts of Führer and Reichschancellor would be separated. The Führer would become the Head of the Reich but the Reichschancellor would be the man with the real power. That was the job Heydrich wanted, and the essential first step was to control *all* the police and intelligence services of the Reich, including the Abwehr.

Which was why he had brought the information concerning Paul van Osten to this room where he had a special filing cabinet devoted to the activities and personnel of the Abwehr. He took out Paul van Osten's file. Van Osten was a year younger than he, came from an old army family, which in peace time farmed estates in East Prussia. Van Osten had served in Spain, had brought back the Norden bombsight from America. Göring had rewarded him by having him reorganize I/Luft, the Luftwaffe Intelligence Service, transferred him afterwards to the Economics Ministry, when Göring had replaced Dr Schaat as Economic Commissar for the Reich. None of which explained why van Osten had flown over the Arlberg with an aerial camera, nor why his friends, Dieter Mehl and Baron Ewald von Kirkdorf should have returned so suddenly from Paris and Amsterdam.

Heydrich replaced the file regretfully. There was nothing there and he would have to move carefully. Van Osten was a favorite of Göring's, and Canaris had often said that van Osten was the best officer he had. So Heydrich would have to wait. But he was used to waiting. For years he had lived in Himmler's shadow and he knew that when facing superior odds, cunning was of more use than brutality.

Tuesday, October 22, 1940. New York.

The roar of the twin Wright Cyclones deepened as the TWA DC 3 skidded down the air waves to Floyd Bennett Field. The last time Schroeder had flown it had been in one of those Ford Tri-Motors, with wicker seats for the passengers and cabin decoration that was intended to make one feel one had never left home. The interior of the DC 3 was more functional. It looked like an aircraft, even from the inside.

Schroeder was on his way to New York to connect with the Pan Am Clipper which left Port Washington for Lisbon on Wednesdays. The US Army did not encourage its officers to fly everywhere, and normally Schroeder would have traveled to New York by train. But there was a man Schroeder had to see in New York. He had spent all of Monday trying to get to this man, the one person who could resolve the problem of assassinating Hitler.

As the DC 3 swooped towards the runway, Schroeder tightened his seatbelt. The assassination of a political leader was a simple thing. Eight years previously, he had worked with the Secret Service detail guarding President Hoover. At that time, he'd made a close and careful study of political assassination. Archduke Ferdinand of Austria, Prime Minister Spencer Perceval of England, Edward Drummond, Secretary to Sir Robert Peel, Senator Huey Pierce Long Jr., and three American Presidents.

Shooting was the usual method of political assassination. Usual because it made the most sense. You were at a safe distance from your victim, the weapon was neither too bulky nor too heavy, and called for a skill which could be easily learned. Provided you could aim straight, there was little left to chance.

To date the Americans had the worst record of all. They had shot at one in five of the men they had elected President. Shot and *killed* one of every ten Presidents. Lincoln, Garfield and McKinley, all murdered, all shot, and that in a country whose politics were not attuned to coups or mass murder.

So what was the difficulty in killing Hitler? All it would take was one man.

Schroeder checked into the Victoria on 7th and 51st, then took a cab down 7th Avenue to the address he had been given on Broadway. There were queues for a matinee, outside the Palace Vaudeville Theater and the Metropole Café advertised a Dixieland band. Times Square was garish even at that time of the afternoon and the New Amsterdam Theater was advertising the forthcoming Ziegfeld Follies.

1450 Broadway was an office building, housing wholesale clothing suppliers, typewriter manufacturers, theatrical agents and the Manhattan Simplex Distribution Co., World's Largest Distributors of Wurlitzer Automatic Phonographs.

Schroeder was asked to wait in a small lobby with a furiously typing secretary. A few minutes later, he was ushered past two burly men, into a large room overlooking Broadway. A small man sat behind a desk with his back to the window. He was no more than one hundred and forty pounds, and wore a neat blue suit and bow tie. His face was pinched, dominated by a large nose and a full lower lip. Schroeder knew this man was thirty-eight, but he looked a good five years older. His hands were the strongest part of him, large and with scarred fingernails. He looked like an artisan who had gone into business on his own account. Schroeder could not believe that he was in the presence of Meyer Lansky, who since Lepke Buchalter had been arrested, ran the National Crime Syndicate.

"Johnny Toriano said you wanted to see me about Lucky."

Schroeder nodded. Now that the moment had come, the enormity of what he wanted seemed ridiculous.

Lansky looked down at a piece of paper on his desk, on which was written, Schroeder's name, rank and his title at G2 (C). "But you're not from the FBI?"

"I work for Counter Intelligence."

"And Counter Intelligence can help Luciano? Counter Intelligence can secure his release?"

Schroeder hesitated. Lansky was a man who expected promises to be kept. "I cannot guarantee that," he said.

"I thought so. And what you want to see me about, is it official?"

Schroeder hesitated. Lansky was a cautious man. Before he did anything for Schroeder, he would check him out in depth. "It is unofficially, official."

Lansky remained impassive, waiting with controlled patience.

"We think there would be an end to war in Europe, if Hitler were disposed of."

"I'm a businessman," Lansky said. "I have no concern with politics."

"But you know someone who could help us?"

Lansky thought about that for a moment. Then he said, "No."

Schroeder said, "If Hitler were killed, the persecution of the Jews would be stopped. Don't you want to do something to help your own people?"

"I cannot help them in this way." The brown eyes gazed steadily at Schroeder. "There is no one I know who can. You might find someone else who would say he could do it. The price will be very high. Two to three million dollars. But he would lie to you. The fact is that it cannot be done."

"All it takes is one man."

"One man who is an actor, who has lived in Germany, is very brave and is able to shoot. A man who will do it, knowing he will not survive the attempt. I do not know anyone like that."

"Your friend Luciano? Can he not help? He must have contacts in Europe?"

"Luciano is in jail. How can he help?"

"If he were released?"

"But you cannot guarantee that. Even if you could, it would be difficult." Lansky paused, staring at his desk. "Every action has its consequences, you understand. The people who do this thing will have too much power. Power frightens other people and makes enemies. It will not be good for business."

Lansky stood up. "If it has to be done, use one of your people, without other connections. That is the only way."

The interview was over.

9

Wednesday, October 23, 1940. Berlin.

The six of them sat round a large table in the briefing room of Abwehr II. Spread on the table were the aerial photographs of Lech and the plans of the chalet which Dieter had brought. On another table stood bottles of Moselle, Sekt, and Tattinger champagne. The room smelt of wine, tobacco and burning wood.

"For a start," van Osten said, "let's forget why we are doing this. Let's simply concentrate on blowing up the chalet." He reached out and pointed to the village of Lech. "There will be two SS divisions here. So we have to come in from above. On X day minus one we land by parachute here." He pointed to a flat field about three hundred meters above the chalet, well above the tree line. "We remain hidden all of X day, and in the late evening we ski down and attack the chalet. Hopefully we will have a supply of high explosive incendiaries. We demolish the chalet with those." Van Osten pointed to a narrow trail leading from the chalet to the right of the photograph. "This trail leads to Warth. As you can see the slope is gentle and you needn't keep to the trail. This is our escape route. At the end of the trail you will find transport waiting to take you away from the scene." He looked at Dieter. "Do you want to tell us about the chalet?"

Dieter got to his feet and tapped the photograph with a pen. "As you can see the chalet is built into the side of a hill. It's structure is timber on a stone foundation. It is reached by going down these steps here, and going through this glass fronted porch. Beyond the porch is a heavy wooden door opening onto a broad corridor. To the left of the corridor are stairs going up to the first floor. To the right, a kitchen and dining room. At the end of the corridor is a large lounge which runs the entire length of the house. The lounge looks down the mountain, and is more than adequately provided with French windows.

"Upstairs there are five rooms, two small rooms at each end of the house and three large rooms in between. The entire upper storey is surrounded by a balcony, and more important, is entirely constructed of wood. You will also note that it stands clear of the hillside and that the distance from the balcony to the edge of the hill is only fifteen meters.

"On the night in question, the central of the three large rooms will be the Führer's study. That to the right of it will be his bedroom and the room to the left, the bedroom of Fraulein Braun."

"How very chaste," von Kirkdorf murmured.

"How will the place be guarded?" That was Guertner.

Von Kirkdorf said, "There will be guards above the chalet and on the slope below it. We will have to defeat those guards by force of arms or stealth. There is no alternative to that. But, there are three points in our favor. One, the attack will be after dark, so we will not be seen. Two, the attack will be made on skis, so we will be silent. Three, it is only necessary for one of us to get through."

"Four," van Osten said, thinking of the camp in Spain and the runaway cart charging down the hill, "we don't have to get into the chalet, or right up close to it. If we get the high explosive incendiaries and we fasten them to a sled, then all we need to do is launch the sled at the chalet with enough force to leap the fifteen meter gap."

"After that," Lipski said, "kavoom!"

"What about equipment?" Lessing asked.

"Let's go into that now," van Osten said.

And for a whole hour they did. They would need skis, sleds, snow smocks, parkas, machine pistols, a machine gun, emergency rations for two days, a four-wheel drive Horch to remove them from the scene. By the time they finished, van Osten had a list three pages long.

"One more thing," von Kirkdorf said. "Training. All of us are less than one hundred per cent fit."

"Also," Lipski interrupted, "I have never jumped with a parachute."

"Some weeks before the operation," van Osten said, "adequate training will be provided. Our cover is an order from OKW to form a group of Alpenkommando." He smiled. "I have told OKW that you gentlemen are it."

Thursday, October 24, 1940. Berlin.

Zossen. The word stuck in Heydrich's throat. A plot to assassinate the Führer. He had been in charge of the inquiry for over a year and so far had not found the traitors.

Heydrich was in the basement of 103 Wilhelmstrasse poring over the Zossen file. The room was not sound proofed and from the interrogation room next door, Heydrich could hear occasional shouts interspersed with the sound of the old man sobbing. The late Lieutenant Karl von Epp had been a member of 12 Panzer. He came from an old military family. His father had been one of those First World War fighter

aces who in 1918 had refused to surrender. A warrior!
A man of honor!

Lieutenant von Epp's friends, soldiers and men of
honor, had been arrested, interrogated and tortured.
But none of them had been able to explain why their
colleague had suddenly gone mad and tried to kill the
Führer.

Heydrich had interviewed von Epp's father, a remote, arrogant man who had reminded Heydrich of
the repulsive Grand-Admiral Erich Raeder, the officer who had terminated Heydrich's brief naval career.
All Lieutenant von Epp's father had said was that on
his last leave the boy appeared to have been strongly
influenced by an older man. Not an army man. Someone outside, but still concerned with soldiers. The boy
seemed to resent, and here Heydrich had detected a
vindictiveness in his father's demeanor, that the Commander in Chief of the German Army had been dis-
missed on trumped up charges of homosexuality, and
that the evidence had been provided by the SD.

That accounted for motive. Heydrich thought. But
what about the means. The only lead he'd had so far
were the detonators taken from the bombs found in
von Epp's pocket. They had been scrapped as useless
by the Third Army Ordnance Depot, sold to an ammunition manufacturer in Essen. The ammunition
manufacturer had stated that the detonators were useless and had been scrapped, and produced his store
ledgers to prove it.

Heydrich thrust the file into a drawer, slammed
it shut, and went across to the interrogation room. His
finely shaped nostrils quivered at the stench of sweat
and urine. The old man had fouled himself. He was
strapped to a chair in the center of the room, straggly
grey head collapsed on a scrawny chest. The lower
part of his face was covered with blood and there
were ugly bruises on his ribs, forehead and cheeks.

Heydrich lit a cigarette to kill the stink. "How far have you got?"

Ernst Jahnke, sweating even in rolled up shirt-sleeves, took off the knuckledusters as he approached Heydrich. He was a dark, compact man, with a pugilist's face, the heavy shoulders and powerful gait of a wrestler. Heydrich had recruited him from the Berlin Police, which Jahnke had joined after having been expelled from Berlin University for street fighting. Jahnke said hoarsely, "He still says he doesn't know the man. They only met twice. Once when the man asked him about the detonators and the second time, when he bought them."

"How was he paid?"

"Cash. Reichsmarks."

Heydrich picked his way carefully across the floor spotted with blood, vomit and urine, and stood in front of the old man. Jahnke, with less circumspection, raced across and pulled the old man's head upright.

"This man you sold the detonators to, what did he look like?" Heydrich spoke quietly, reassuringly, with even a touch of warmth.

"I told . . . I told . . . the others . . ."

The man could hardly move his tongue inside his battered mouth. The eyes that looked up at Heydrich were glazed with pain and exhaustion.

"Tell me, old man, and all this will cease." He gestured to an assistant to give the man water, waited patiently while it was drunk.

"He was a tall man . . . nearly two meters."

"Fat or thin? Dark or fair?"

"Thin . . . dark, with hair down to his collar."

"How old?"

"Like you . . . young."

"Why did you sell the detonators, old man? Was it because you needed the money?"

"No . . . not money. That man . . . was Gestapo."

"How do you know that? Did he show you a card?"

"No . . . no card. He said . . . Gestapo."

Heydrich knew there was no way the Gestapo would have been involved in Zossen. Which meant someone outside but still concerned with soldiers. Someone outside and still concerned with intelligence.

Abruptly Heydrich turned on his heel and stalked to the door, beckoning Jahnke to follow him. In the corridor outside he ordered Jahnke to have the man cleaned up, and taken back to his cell. The old man was to be made as comfortable as possible, given proper food and allowed to sleep. As soon as he was fit Jahnke was to have him look at the photographs in the SD's confidential file of Abwehr agents.

Friday, October 25, 1940. Geneva.

Geneva was covered by a blanket of low cloud. The lake was grey, seeming to mould with the mist that covered the hills surrounding it. In the offices of the Swiss Bank Corporation, Paul van Osten stared at the mist and tried not to look at the face of the man seated beside him.

The man's name was Solomon Tauber. He was a Jew who once had jewelery stores in Stuttgart, Tabinger and Baden Baden. He'd also had an illegal account at the Swiss Bank Corporation in Geneva. The jewelery stores had been appropriated by the Reich. The proceeds of the illegal bank account would soon be appropriated by the Abwehr.

Van Osten tried to dissociate himself from the morality of the situation. The money had been illegally held and was therefore lawfully, the property of the State. The Abwehr was an arm of the State, had discovered the existence of the funds, *needed* them. It was the need that made it morally justifiable. Hitler and Roosevelt both had to be stopped. And what was a Jew's life savings if that was achieved. Yet, van Osten could not bring himself to look at the man in the ill-fitting suit who sat beside him and spoke in a despairing voice.

"And you wish to withdraw all your funds, Herr Tauber?"

The Jew nodded.

"You wish them transferred to Germany?"

"No," the Jew said, pausing to look at van Osten, "I want to take it out now. In cash. In American dollars."

"You are no doubt considering an investment," the bank manager said. "The bank has an excellent—"

"It is not something with which the bank can help," van Osten snapped.

The bank manager smiled ingratiatingly. "We have known Herr Tauber for a long time. Naturally we wish to continue the relationship."

Perhaps you'd like starving with him in a concentration camp, van Osten thought, savagely. Perhaps you'd like wandering around in threadbare clothes with a yellow star on your chest. "There's nothing you can do to help," he said.

The bank manager looked away from his blazing eyes. "You'll have the money in a few minutes," he said and remained silent until the money was brought.

*   *   *

Twelve kilometers after the border with Vichy France, van Osten turned the BMW into the woods. It was dark, and he could barely see Tauber, seated in the passenger seat. He drove the car gently down a forest track, listening to the leaves squelch beneath the tires. When he thought he'd gone far enough, he stopped. He could not explain to himself the reason for what he was about to do.

"You," he said turning to Tauber. "Get out of the car."

Tauber looked at him in surprise, then fear. "I can't," he said in a low voice. "I have to return to Germany."

"Don't tell me what you have to do, pig," van Osten snapped. "Do as I tell you. Get out of the car."

Tauber hesitated, then gingerly opened the door. "What are you going to do with me?"

"Nothing. Just go."

Tauber still hesitated. "But where will I go? I have no friends, no money."

Van Osten took a thousand dollars from the roll that had been Tauber's and gave it to him. "Go," he said. "Go, now."

Tauber was still uncertain. "But—but what—"

"You have your life," van Osten said. "For God's sake go!"

Slowly Tauber backed away from the car, then turned round and shambled into the forest. Van Osten waited until the Jew could no longer be seen, then turned the car round and drove back towards Geneva.

Saturday, October 26, 1940. Berlin.

After the blue lit dimness of the night club, the alley was pitch black. Strains of Lale Andersen's 'Lili Marlene' drifted through the baize curtain, hung in the air momentarily, moaned, died. A soldier's song followed. '*Wir Fahren Gegen England*.' Dieter Mehl grinned in the darkness. No one was sailing to England. Not that year.

The girl clutching his arm stumbled and fell against him, deftly cursing the blackout. Ever since September, when the RAF had bombed Berlin, its lights went out at sundown. Dieter grabbed the girl's arm and kissed her roughly on the side of her face. "Don't worry, *liebchen*. We'll soon be home."

Dieter Mehl was pleasantly drunk. There was nothing else to do in Berlin on a Saturday night in wartime, except get pleasantly drunk and find someone to screw. That was the way poets and soldiers lived. This one, she had a head as well as a body. She read women's magazines, found out Du Pont had brought out new stockings, made of a synthetic material which was just as smooth as silk and lasted four times as long. Found out too that Dieter had connections with America, and had the brashness to ask him to get her a few pairs.

Dieter was interested in the stockings too, but not as presents for lady friends. The Abwehr would be interested in the new material. If it was smooth as silk and stronger, there were other uses for it. He had sent away for a dozen pairs.

The faint greyness ahead of them was the Kudamm. Dieter steered the girl round to the left, to where his car was parked. One more bottle of Niersteiner, a few records on the gramophone, Karin adored something called 'All or Nothing At All' with Harry James and someone called Frank Sinatra, then bed. For Dieter Mehl that was the pattern of Saturday night.

There was a black Mercedes parked arrogantly across the curb. Only the Gestapo dared park like that. Dieter moved to guide the girl around the car. A door opened and two men climbed out onto the pavement. They wore heavy leather coats and had hats pulled well down over their foreheads. They kept their hands in their pockets when they spoke.

"Hauptmann Mehl."

Dieter froze. Karin had seen him often enough in civilian clothes, slept in his apartment often enough to know he had no uniform. Suddenly hearing his military title, she must realize that he was a secret policeman.

"I do not answer to that title outside office

hours," Mehl said tightly, aware of Karin's fingers clawing into his arm, whether from fear or surprise that he was so well known to the Gestapo, he was not sure.

"There is urgent work for you. Please come with us."

Mehl repressed a drunken giggle. The Gestapo were trying to act like gentlemen. "I am busy," he said. "Can't you see that?"

"We will arrange for the young lady to be taken home."

"What is it? Who wants me?"

"General Heydrich himself. A matter of the utmost urgency."

"I will find my own way home," Karin said, her tone non-committal, releasing his arm as she spoke.

Impulsively Dieter threw his car keys to one of the men. "It's an Opel coupé a few meters along on the left. Take my friend home, and bring the car to me at the Wilhelmstrasse." He bent and kissed Karin quickly and stepped into the Mercedes, beside the submachine gun clipped between the seats.

An urgent summons from Heydrich at two o'clock in the morning could not be good news. If there was work that was urgent or important, Heydrich would not be rounding up members of the Abwehr. It had to be something else. He tried to relax and think about other things as the car crept under the Brandenberg Gate, the pinpoints of its shaded headlamps barely illuminating the roadway ahead.

At SD headquarters he was taken straight to Heydrich's office. Heydrich was sprawled behind his desk, cleaning his service Luger. A civilian stood at ease before the desk, an elderly man with hugely bruised lips, no teeth and a monumental swelling on his cheek.

Dieter felt his breath catch, the blood leave his face, his veins grow cold. The old man with no teeth turned and stared at him for a moment and then

turned back to Heydrich and nodded. Heydrich remained very still, lolling in his chair. A small smile
played at the corners of his mouth; he seemed quite
affable. Only his eyes were blue and pale and filled
with a coldness that burned. Heydrich waved the old
man out of the room.

When the man had gone, Heydrich swung his feet
off the desk and put away the Luger. Then slowly,
deliberately, looking all the while at Dieter he
reached forward across the desk and closed the file
that had lain open on it. Dieter could see the name on
the file. Zossen.

"Sit down Hauptmann," Heydrich said. He kept
his hand on the file, his eyes still on Dieter.

Dieter knew that he had only days to live. Long,
pain filled days. Heydrich would want to know who
else had been involved. In a sudden panic, Dieter
wondered how he would stand up to torture.

"As a loyal soldier of the Reich," Heydrich said,
"you will be glad to learn that we now know who was
involved in the plot to kill the Führer, at Zossen, fourteen months ago." His eyes never left Dieter's face.
"You do not say anything Hauptmann. Are you not
pleased?"

"I am pleased," Dieter said.

"Good, good. In a while they will all be dead, except one." Heydrich paused and lit a cigarette, pushed
the pack over to Dieter. "You may smoke."

It was an old trick. You offered a man a cigarette, watched him extract it from the pack, light it,
noted if his fingers trembled. "I have been in a night
club," Dieter said softly. "I think I have maybe drunk
a little too much. My hands shake."

"Don't worry. It's Saturday night." Heydrich drew
ruminatively at his cigarette. "I hear you have been
brought back from Paris to join a special unit of Abwehr Alpenkommando." He drew a sheet of paper towards him, embossed with the insignia of the OKW.

"You, Paul van Osten, Baron von Kirkdorf, Heinz Guertner, Manfred Lessing, Josef Lipski. Is that correct?"

"I believe so," Dieter said. Then added despondently. "They're always forming special units."

"Do you have any idea of what you are supposed to do?"

"No. I was only notified of my impending transfer and asked to be in readiness to move into the training area at a week's notice."

"And where is the training area?" Heydrich asked.

Dieter swallowed. "I don't know."

"Van Osten has been taking pictures over the Arlberg. Did you know that?"

Dieter shook his head.

"It is in his report," Heydrich said. "He was looking for a suitable place for training Alpenkommando." Heydrich smiled pleasantly. "I am sure he must have told you that. You are good friends, aren't you."

"Yes," Dieter said. "We're friends." Heydrich probably knew the names of everyone who'd been involved in Zossen, Dieter thought miserably.

"Then he would have told you?" Heydrich's high pitched voice was cajoling.

"I have not seen Oberstleutant van Osten for a few days."

"Ah," Heydrich said, noticing the sudden switch to formality. "You work together don't you?"

"I'm at Abwehr Central in the Potsdamerplatz. Van Osten is at the Tirpitzufer. Besides," Dieter added, "he is not in Berlin now."

"Where is he?"

"In Geneva," Dieter said.

"Ah yes, Geneva. Something I believe to do with a Jew." Canaris could authorize van Osten's exit permit, but a Jew had to be cleared through the Gestapo. "I personally approved the exit permit."

"So he has not been able to give me details of this new unit."

"Even though he brought you back specially from Paris," Heydrich said. He remembered quite clearly that the copy of the exit permit provided to him by the Gestapo, had shown that van Osten wanted to take the Jew to Basle. The activities of Paul van Osten were becoming quite intriguing.

"I am making you an offer, Hauptmann Mehl," Heydrich said. "I would like you to transfer to the SD."

"But—but—"

Heydrich raised a hand. "Oh, I don't mean officially. What I do mean is from now on, I want you to work for me. Do you understand that? For me. I want to know everything that happens with van Osten and his Alpenkommando. I want to know what happens in the Arlberg."

"It's highly unusual," Dieter protested.

"So," Heydrich said, "was Zossen."

10

Saturday, October 26, 1940. Geneva.

Paul van Osten was enjoying Geneva. There were
lights in the streets and real food instead of cardboard
cutouts in the shop windows. There were cars driving
about with unshaded headlamps and his first impulse
had been to warn someone in authority about the possibility of a British bombing raid.

Peace was good! He'd eaten at the Au Fin Bec,
pâté and steak and cheese, a liter of wine, cognac and
coffee, enjoying the food, enjoying even more just
looking at the huge dishes of butter on the table and
not having to surrender coupons. Today, while waiting for Schroeder, he had gone and looked at the
enormous white building of the League which had
once held so much hope for mankind, strolled afterwards in the Rue du Marche thinking how pleasant it
was that there were no military vehicles scurrying
around, no blank faced, shuffling queues, no anti-
aircraft guns disfiguring the parks and the tops of
buildings, and most of all, no fear of bombing or the
Gestapo. In only a year he'd forgotten what peace was
like.

He asked the desk clerk to inform him discreetly
of Schroeder's arrival and spent time afterwards in his

room, studying a photograph of Schroeder which he had brought from the Ast X (West) archives. The photograph was five years old, part of a group picture. Schroeder was in evening dress, and the enlargement had blurred the detail. Schroeder was looking sideways at the camera, a square jawed man of medium build, in his early forties. He had a finely shaped nose, a good, sensitive mouth, crew-cut hair, and a strangely unmarked face. The suddenness of the flash light had given the eyes a fanatical gleam. It was a strong face, determined, but there was something about it that van Osten couldn't quite place. He couldn't tell how that face would react to his plans for peace.

* * *

Schroeder had been in Geneva before, when he'd been a Military Attaché in Paris. Van Osten had left a note saying that he would see him in the bar at seven, and an hour after he arrived, having bathed and changed into a double-breasted plaid suit, Schroeder set off on a walk.

It was a mellow evening, the small trees in the Place de Montbrillant brown and sparse with autumn. Schroeder felt better as he walked, less helpless than he had done during that diurnal train journey. The air in Geneva was crisp and clear with a freshness he had not found in any other part of the world.

As he walked, he thought about Paul van Osten. The FBI had pictures of him taken some years ago. Van Osten had been in America then, working as a salesman for a German engineering company, and the FBI had suspected that he was in fact, a spy. But there had been no information to support that, and all the FBI had apart from his photograph, was the address of a rooming house on New York's East Side.

Rieber had told Schroeder how he had met van Osten at the Economics Ministry and how van Osten

helped him through the bureaucratic maze of the
Reich. Van Osten obviously had some influence inside
Germany. Equally obviously, Göring trusted him. The
question was whether van Osten would in turn, trust
Schroeder.

*   *   *

Van Osten had finished the schnapps and was
nursing the beer chaser when Schroeder came into the
bar, walking with the quick, direct gait that van Osten
found so very American. Schroeder's plaid double
breaster made him look shorter and wider than he
really was, and his spiky crew-cut bristled over a
moist forehead. He looked much older than the photograph. It was not the face, which was still unwrinkled,
nor the fact that the crew-cut was much sparser. It
was, van Osten realized, the man's expression of controlled resentment.

Van Osten swiveled on the bar stool and waved.
"Greetings! What do you drink? Our countries are not
at war, so we can be friends."

Schroeder eased himself onto a stool, and shook
hands with a hard, pawing grip. "You are van Osten,"
he said. In the flesh, van Osten's face was more mo-
bile, the premature baldness more emphasized.
Schroeder noted the sensitive mouth, the way the
deep-set blue eyes looked straight back at you. Van
Osten was obviously keenly intelligent and, in his pale
grey suit, looked more like a prosperous business executive than a member of the Secret Service. Schroeder
said, "Now about this Göring business—"

"Afterwards," van Osten said clutching his arm.
"What will you drink?"

"I don't suppose they have bourbon, do they?"

Van Osten shook his head.

"I'll have a gin and tonic then."

"You'd better make it a large one," van Osten said
and ordered.

When their drinks had been served, van Osten asked, "How goes it in America?"

"There are only two things that concern America now," Schroeder growled. "This war and the Presidential elections." He swallowed his drink.

Schroeder's voice carried. Instinctively van Osten looked around. Even in neutral Switzerland walls had ears. "Who is it going to be?" he asked. "Roosevelt or Willkie?"

Schroeder took a long pull at his drink. "Roosevelt," he said. "I'm a Republican, but I'm sure that on November 5, Roosevelt's going to be back in the White House."

Van Osten thought fleetingly of Viereck and his isolationst campaign. "Why not Willkie?"

"Because Willkie is an Iowa farmboy playing at politics. He had no program. Deep down he supports Roosevelt's New Deal and social security and all that pinko crap. He's just standing there saying, 'Me too!' He's even taken to calling Roosevelt the champ. People *like* champions, for Chrissake!"

"You think Roosevelt is a champion?"

"I've never known what to think of Roosevelt. Never been able to make the man out. He's too much of a—" Schroeder licked his finger and held it up as if trying to discover from which direction the wind was blowing. "But he's going to win."

And it was too late to stop Viereck or save any of the money that had already been committed. And if Roosevelt was going to win, it was too late for peace.

Schroeder said again, "Now about this Göring business—"

Van Osten silenced him with a gesture. "Later," he said, quietly. "There are spies everywhere."

"This is a neutr—" Schroeder started to say, but van Osten's steely glance stopped him.

*   *   *

Van Osten selected a table near the kitchens where the clatter of utensils and the constant passage of waiters would keep other diners away and hopefully neutralize any hidden microphones.

They ordered fresh trout from the lake, Chateaubriand, a bottle of Brouilly and a carafe of iced water for Schroeder. Van Osten ate with great appetite. Eating in Geneva was very different from the dreary life sustaining ritual it was in Berlin.

"We're interested in the Göring proposals," Schroeder said.

"Not so loud."

"Okay. Sorry." Schroeder looked round. There were less than a dozen other diners in the room, all of them Swiss, or possibly German. Schroeder wasn't sure he could tell the difference at a cursory glance. "Your paranoia is infectious, did you know that?"

"Paranoia is a delusion of persecution," van Osten said. "In Germany persecution is no delusion."

"Is that why Göring wants peace?"

"Not Göring, Germany," van Osten pushed away his plate of trout, its bones picked clean and gleaming whitely. "While we are spending money on arms and soldiers our economies stagnate. We build nothing. We sell nothing. We only destroy. If the war continues for much longer, all Europe will be like that." He pointed to his plate. "And America will have no trading partners."

"Okay. How will you bring about this peace?"

"Why do *you* want peace?"

That was a question Schroeder hadn't expected. "It's obvious, isn't it. Peace is better than war."

"And how fully are you committed to peace?"

"All the way. War does not solve problems. The last war gave us Versailles and a rampaging Germany."

"We have achieved our *lebensraum*," van Osten said.

"I do not want to see the blood of American boys being shed in a useless war."

"You may not have any choice," van Osten said, "and I'm not only talking about American soldiers. I'm talking about American civilians."

"What do you mean?"

"You know what I'm talking about. What do you know about the Columbia Project?"

Schroeder knew very little about the Columbia Project. All he knew was that G2 had to provide security for a bunch of scientists working under conditions of great secrecy to develop a new weapon. There were rumors that it was a new kind of bomb, but Schroeder did not know anymore than that.

"Do you know how devastating this new weapon will be?" van Osten asked.

Schroeder shook his head.

"It's to do with an atom of uranium," van Osten said. "I don't suppose you read *Naturwissenschaften?* Never mind. I have copies for you in my room. When an atom of pure uranium is bombarded by neutrons, it splits. When it splits, it releases more neutrons which cause more atoms to split. A chain reaction, do you follow? The atoms keep splitting and releasing energy till in the end there is an explosion of the most terrible violence."

Van Osten paused and started on the Chateaubriand. "The theory has been proved. Lise Meitner and Frisch confirmed it by experiments in Copenhagen. They repeated it at the Pupin Physics Laboratory in New York. The results were identical. The atoms they split released two hundred million volts of electricity. Do you know what that means? A uranium bomb will be twenty million times as powerful as TNT!"

Twenty million times as powerful, Schroeder thought. Good God! One of those bombs in the lake could blow up the whole of Geneva. "And America has this weapon?"

"Not yet. Maybe in two years. In two years, Germany will have an atom bomb, also. You have your Columbia Project, we have our Uranium Verein. Unlike your Columbia Project, the Uranium Verein is part of the Heereswaffenamt, the Army Weapons Department. We get our uranium from the Jachymov area of Czechoslovakia. I give you these details, so that you can check them, if you want to."

"The question is," Schroeder said, "will anyone use this bomb?"

"The thing you foreigners forget," van Osten said, "is that the worst thing that can happen to Germany is to revert to the nothing it was before 1939. Unlike America, Germany has nothing to lose. By 1942, we shall have the new Messerschmitt 242, a bomber powered by jet engines. It will be capable of carrying a plane load of bombs all the way across the Atlantic."

"Oh my God!" Schroeder said.

"I can show you copies of the specifications," van Osten said. "So you see why there is no point in prolonging this war, why prolonging it can only destroy all the participants. Britain is finished. They may carry on fighting, they may even win battles, but their empire is lost and they will never again be the most powerful nation in the world." Van Osten paused and sipped at his wine. "With its resources, America could rule the world. Maybe, Germany too. A different Germany."

"I promise you now," Schroeder said, "that I will do anything to stop the prolongation of this war, and help you build a different Germany."

Van Osten moved his hand palm down over the table-cloth in a silent, beating movement. "That's one hand applauding your sentiments. You say you want peace, yet when we offer peace, you reject it."

Schroeder said, "The State Department rejected your offer because they don't believe Göring can implement such a peace. That is why I have come, Paul, so that you can convince me that Göring can do what he has promised." Schroeder finished eating and took out a cheroot. "Give it to me straight. Hitler doesn't know and wouldn't approve of Göring's proposals, isn't that right?"

"That's right."

"And in order to implement the Göring proposals, you will have to get rid of Hitler."

Van Osten smiled sarcastically. "And you have come to help me dispose of Hitler?"

"If you need such help and if it will bring peace."

"But what if Hitler is not the only obstacle to peace?"

"I want you to know that we are going to work together to remove all obstacles to peace."

Van Osten went silent, tracing a pattern on the tablecloth with the unlit end of his cigarette. "There can be no peace," he said softly, "as long as one person or one country wants war."

"Of course."

"There can be no peace as long as Hitler or Roosevelt wants war."

Schroeder jerked the unlit cheroot from his mouth. "Don't be ridiculous, Paul! The only reason Roosevelt rejected those proposals was that he didn't believe they could be honored. Without Hitler it would have been different. Roosevelt does not want war!"

Van Osten leaned across and placed his fingers on Schroeder's lips. "Not so loud, my friend. Come up to my room. I have something to show you that will make you change your mind."

* * *

Over coffee and cognac in van Osten's room, Colonel Max Schroeder read the file that had been taken from the War Department. As he read he muttered, "Bastard!" Then by way of embroidery, "Lousy

double-crossing bastard." Through sheer vindictiveness Roosevelt had excluded G2 (C) from the war.
"Lousy double-crossing bastard," Schroeder muttered
again and spat out the sodden end of his cheroot.

He had no doubt the document was genuine. The
type face, the idiom, the terminology were all clearly
War Department. Besides, van Osten would not have
risked blowing whatever game he was playing by producing a forgery. And it made sense!

The reasons for American involvement were those
so often stated by Roosevelt. Democracy had to be
saved. America needed a friendly Europe. The spread
of Fascism had to be contained. If the British fleet
were surrendered the Atlantic would be dominated by
an unfriendly power and America would be forced to
defend itself on two oceans.

The time for America to get involved in a European war was now, while Germany's resources were
stretched and the British were keeping them at bay.
But Ordnance reported that it was impossible to both
supply Britain and equip the forces needed for an invasion of Europe. Besides America did not have an
army capable of invading Europe.

The American regular army consisted of 227,000
troops, smaller, Schroeder thought, than the Czecho-
slovak Army which had been so casually surrendered
to the Nazis. Equipment was only available for 75,000
of those 227,000 regulars, and the draftees under the
Selective Service Acts were having to make do with
improvisations. The Army Air Force consisted in the
main of P-40s, most of them still carrying World War I
equipment. The only properly armed and manned
force was the Navy, but they were needed for the defense of the Pacific against the Japanese.

By 1943 America would have a force of five million well-trained, well-equipped men. That army
would be more than a match for the Axis.

It was also likely that by 1943 the American people would regard Nazi Europe as an accomplished fact, especially if by then Britain had fallen. That was one reason, therefore, why Britain should be given all moral and material support to continue the conflict.

But whether Britain fell or not, America would be involved by 1943! If the American people would not recognize the danger of fascism, then such awareness would be thrust upon them.

The *Panay* over again, thought Schroeder, except this time the lives would be those of non-combatants. He skimmed through the detailed estimates of the men and equipment needed for the invasion of Europe, the form such an invasion would take. If Britain survived, the invasion would be through Northern France. If it didn't, through Italy and the Balkans and the soft underbelly of Europe.

Damn Roosevelt!

"So you see," van Osten said softly, "if you want peace you need to do more than merely get rid of Hitler."

Schroeder gazed at him blankly. A war in which both sides were equipped with atom bombs! Destruction on a scale much more terrible than that caused by the hurricane which had ravaged New England and blown whole houses over Long Island Sound! A war of the worlds! And this time there would be no soothing CBS announcers saying it was only a play produced by Orson Wells. This time it would be for real.

Van Osten said, "There will be only scorched earth."

Schroeder shook his head doggedly. "There must be an alternative to that."

"Only one. Peace now." Van Osten took a long time lighting his cigarette. "This is our responsibility. We cannot walk away from your countrymen and mine. We have to go in and clear up the mess the politicians have made."

"By doing what?"

Van Osten said, "With the loan of a few high explosive incendiaries from you, I propose to kill Adolf Hitler."

Schroeder stared at him in amazement. The unsayable had been said. One German had decided that Hitler was expendable.

"But that isn't enough," van Osten added. "If he is elected, I want Roosevelt dead."

* * *

The idea was crazy. A life for a life, two lives for world peace and no new devastating bomb. Two lives for a million. An exchange of . . . eagles. It was crazy, but worth it.

It was also treason. As long as Roosevelt was President, he was Commander in Chief of the Armed Forces, Schroeder's ultimate superior. It was not only treason, it was mutiny.

"Doppel Adler," van Osten said. "That's what we will call it, Double Eagle."

Schroeder stared at him unseeingly. He wasn't thinking of names, he was thinking of consequences. If Roosevelt went, he would be succeeded by Henry Wallace. Wallace was unpopular with the Democrats, had been accepted as a Vice-Presidential candidate only at Roosevelt's continued insistence. He was not a man who could take the American people to war. He couldn't carry Congress or the Senate and as one not elected to Presidential office, would not dare to create a situation that made war unavoidable. No, if Wallace succeeded Roosevelt, he would have no alternative but to seek peace.

Schroeder and van Osten talked through half a bottle of cognac, late into the night. The exchange was limited by van Osten's accessibility to the Führer, and the need for the exchange to be completed swiftly. Hitler was perpetually surrounded by an extensive bodyguard, and his quarters in Berlin, Rastenburg and Berchtesgaden were veritable fortresses. There was little advance notice of his movements. He came and went so suddenly, he seemed to be acting on impulse.

And now there was Lech . . . both murders would have to take place within forty-eight hours of the 14th December.

"We will not have a problem with Roosevelt," Schroeder said. His face was flushed, his eyes puffy. He drew at his cheroot, squinting against the smoke. He told van Osten that Roosevelt would have to be killed by an American, whose motive would not be connected with the war. One man, one bullet, Schroeder said, thinking of Lincoln, McKinley and Garfield. The traditional way.

"Within forty-eight hours of the 14th December," Schroeder mused. "What happens if we double-cross each other?"

"We are allied in the cause of peace. If you ever think of betraying Double Eagle, think of twenty million tons of TNT on New York."

"But if the betrayal on either side was accidental, or unavoidable?"

"That must not be allowed to happen."

"The best laid plans . . ."

"Then it is necessary that each of us has a representative on the other's side who will check, report and approve on the progress of the operation. Someone who will confirm that any failure was an act of God."

"And confirm any success," Schroeder added. "I wouldn't put it past Goebbels to broadcast Hitler's death just to have Roosevelt killed."

"My representative will be George Viereck," van Osten said. "He will contact you immediately after the election. You will give him a biography, career details, personal statistics and a photograph of your representative. Your man will have to be young, fit, able to ski, shoot, use a radio, handle explosives, take care of himself in unarmed combat, be able to live rough if necessary, and, most important, be able to pass as a German."

"But he cannot take part directly in the mission," Schroeder said. "His job is to monitor it and provide confirmation to me."

"The confirmation must be instantaneous," van Osten pointed out.

"It will be. He will use a radio and a code known only to him and me. I will make the arrangements to ensure that the message will get through."

Van Osten said, "If you get Roosevelt first, I shall make similar arrangements." He splashed cognac into their glasses. "To the success of Double Eagle," he said.

Schroeder raised his glass. "To a happy and peaceful exchange."

11

Sunday, October 27, 1940. Geneva.

George Viereck reached the Hotel Cornavin
shortly before noon, barely two hours after Schroeder
had left Geneva. He was an insignificant looking man
of about sixty, with a narrow face and pale eyelashes,
thinning and much receded grey hair parted from the
side. There was a curious immobility about his face,
and if he betrayed any emotions at all, it was with his
eyes which shifted and danced continuously behind
silver framed spectacles. He dressed conservatively in
single breasted dark suits, had a polite demeanor and
an air of having known better things.

Over lunch in a nearby restaurant, Viereck told
van Osten he was glad to be back in Europe, eating
food different from Washington hamburgers which
the Americans had taken to calling liberty steaks.

The mood in America was changing, Viereck
said. The people were being won over by Britain's
continued resistance to the Luftwaffe. There were
even V for victory brooches on sale in the shops, V for
Britain's victory. The brooches were quite fashionable.

"Will Roosevelt find support for joining the war?"
van Osten asked.

"It's possible," Viereck admitted. "If he is re-elected," and gave van Osten a knowing smile.

Van Osten found it difficult to like Viereck. Viereck had spied for Germany in the First World War, worked in America then, lived outside Germany since. Canaris had brought him back into the Abwehr because of his knowledge of foreign countries and his experience of America, had forced him on Amt X (West) when the Abwehr decided to oppose Roosevelt's re-election.

But there was no doubt that whatever the result of the election, Viereck had done a good job on the anti-Roosevelt campaign. He had spent Abwehr dollars as if they were his own, produced reports that were models of conciseness and accuracy, given independent and farsighted counsel on American affairs, created effective propaganda for the isolationist cause.

Yet van Osten didn't quite trust him. It was partly his manner of shifty reserve, the feeling he gave of having more knowledge than he was prepared to divulge, the slightly superior way in which he accepted instructions. Van Osten suspected that Viereck had been thrust upon Canaris by Heydrich, that the master spy of the last war was serving two masters, but he had no way of proving that.

Still as far as the exchange of eagles was concerned, van Osten had to use Viereck. There was no one in America with the skill or experience to run such an operation, except van Osten, himself. But van Osten had to be at Lech on the 14th December.

"How do you think the elections will go?" van Osten asked.

"Close," Viereck replied, "very close. Willkie has only just started to make the American people frightened of involvement in this war. The press is solidly for Willkie. Not only Hearst, but papers like the *Daily News* and *The New York Times* which used to support

Roosevelt. Willkie is still behind in the opinion polls, though he is making up ground fast."

Viereck took out a list of the costs of the operation against Roosevelt. A cool one and a half million dollars. Van Osten whistled. If Roosevelt was elected Canaris would use his head for a croquet ball and Heydrich would take over the Abwehr for Christmas.

Viereck began explaining the expenditures. The bulk of the money had gone on radio and press advertising, radio spots based on the Republican Party's campaign—"When your boy is dying on some battlefield in Europe and crying out, Mother! Mother!— don't blame Franklin D. Roosevelt because he sent your boy to war—blame yourself because you sent Franklin D. Roosevelt back to the White House."

Full page advertisements had been taken out in almost every leading American newspaper. Viereck showed him two. The first was from *The New York Times* of June 25th.

DELEGATES OF THE REPUBLICAN NATIONAL CONVENTION, AMERICAN MOTHERS, WAGE EARNERS, FARMERS AND VETERANS! STOP THE WAR MACHINE! STOP THE INTERVENTIONISTS AND THE WARMONGERS! STOP THE DEMOCRATIC PARTY WHICH WE BELIEVE IS THE WAR PARTY IN THE UNITED STATES AND IS LEADING US TO WAR AGAINST THE WILL OF THE AMERICAN PEOPLE!

Another advertisement from the *Chicago Tribune,* at the time of the Democratic Convention read:

DON'T LET THE DEMOCRATIC PARTY, HISTORICALLY THE PARTY OF NON

INTERVENTION, BECOME THE PARTY OF INTERVENTION AND WAR, AGAINST THE WILL OF NINETY-THREE PER CENT OF THE AMERICAN PEOPLE!

The cost of inviting fifty Republican Congressmen on a three-day visit to the Party Convention in Philadelphia was put down at three thousand dollars and that of sending reliable isolationists to Chicago for the Democratic Convention at two thousand. As a consequence, both parties were now firmly committed to avoid involvement in foreign wars.

Nearly one hundred thousand dollars had been paid to one George Hill, secretary to Representative Hamilton Fish, for arranging isolationist speeches and pamphlets to be distributed under the 'frank' of his employer. More money had been spent on obtaining similar help from other sources, and nearly one million two hundred thousand pieces of mail had been distributed free, under Congressional frank.

All that effort and money, van Osten thought, and yet no certainty. He gave Viereck the hundred thousand dollars. "Can't anything more be done?" he asked.

"No," Viereck said. "Now, fate will decide."

Van Osten lit a caporal and smoked it thoughtfully. "If Roosevelt is elected there is something more that will have to be done. Roosevelt will have to be assassinated."

Viereck looked at him expressionlessly. "The Abwehr will do that?"

"No. American counter-intelligence will." Swiftly he told Viereck of the American side of his arrangement, and what he wanted him to do.

"Why are American counter-intelligence doing this?"

"They are opposed to the war. They feel if Roosevelt is elected America will come into it."

"And what do they want the Abwehr to do for them?"

"Nothing," van Osten said. "Nothing at all."

Viereck's face remained expressionless. Even the eyes went still. Van Osten could not tell whether Viereck believed him or not. Then, without warning Viereck smiled and reached into his pocket. "I have a souvenir for you," he said and handed van Osten a campaign button, across which was written in large letters, "We don't want Eleanor either!"

Tuesday, October 29, 1940.
Springfield, Va.

Stannard and Oldfield jogged through the woods with a staggered pounding of booted feet, their calves heavy and sore from the continuous movement, their shoulders raw from the persistent tugging of the sixty-pound packs each of them carried. Their breath was harsh and dry in their throats, their bodies coated in sweat.

They'd been commanded that day by an idiot. He'd force marched them till late afternoon, right into the trap set by Raiding Group B. Their force, Attacking Group A, had scattered under the onslaught. Deliberately Stannard and Oldfield had left them, were now trying to make their way back to base along this little known path through the woods and across the rope bridge across the ravine.

They came out of the woods together, stood for a moment in the fading sunlight, panting harshly. To their right was a narrow trail, sandwiched between the end of the woods and the ravine edge, moving slowly uphill and curving round the promontory where the woods ended, where the thin yellow bridge dangled across space.

They moved along the trail wearily, Stannard by the ravine's edge, Oldfield skirting the woods. Sud-

denly ahead of them a machine gun chattered, spewing bullets into the soft earth around their feet.

Quickly, instinctively, Stannard hurled himself to
the ground, slipped off the trail, slid down below it,
body pressed to the earth. Bastards! They'd expected
someone to try to get back this way. But a machine
gun nest! Bastards!

Slowly Stannard raised his head to the level of
the trail and looked. Oldfield was down, crawling into
the wood. The machine gun chattered again, a tenta-
tive exploratory burst. The gun was in the woods,
right on the promontory covering the bridge and the
trail with a right-angled sweep. Bastards, Stannard
thought again, and then he saw Oldfield gesture that
he was going to try to make it through the woods.

The machine gun chattered again, not so exploratory this time, throwing stinging earth into Stannard's
face. He slipped down the trail edge, settled down behind his Thompson 1928 submachine gun.

The Thompsons were new issue, and the Weapons
and Tactical Co-ordination Unit had been given special priority, unlike those poor slobs of conscripts who
were still being trained with wooden weapons. Fat
lot of good they'd be if the American army ever went
into Europe.

Stannard edged the Thompson on to the trail and
fired a short burst. The gun was awkwardly long and
heavy and with its .45 bullets tended to fire high.
Stannard much preferred the captured German Ber-
mann MP35 he'd used in Spain. The machine gun
started up again, bullets whipping noisily through the
undergrowth, scouring the trail and the woods in a
long vicious hail of fire.

Berkeley, the commanding officer of W & T C U,
had warned them that at Springfield they played
games for real. They used live bullets and expected
only the toughest and the best to survive. Stannard
whipped the Thompson up, stuck it onto full auto-

matic and fired a long burst at the machine gun nest. He knew where it was now, could see the glow of the tracers they used. As the machine gun started its reply, Stannard rolled himself forward along the edge of the trail. The closer he got to the bridge the better. The closer he got to the machine gunner the better. He stopped and fired a short burst, then ducked down again and slammed in a fresh magazine.

He had no thought for fatigue now, no sensation of sweat covering his body or the dryness of his mouth. There was room in his head for one thought only. Get that bastard gunner, then get across that bridge.

At that moment he heard the dull thump of two grenades exploding close together, saw the flash through the trees, where the machine gun nest had been. Instinctively he raised the Thompson and poured a stream of automatic fire towards the flash.

Afterwards there was silence. Stannard watched, waited. Nothing. He counted to twenty, still waiting, then saw a figure move through the trees. Oldfield. He waited till Oldfield reached the track, stood in full view of the machine gun nest. When nothing happened, he got to his feet and raced for the bridge.

"Good work, Mike," he panted as his boots hit the rope, feeling the whole contraption bounce above space. Still holding the warm Thompson in his right hand, he dragged himself across with his left. Mechanically he estimated the distance. Twenty yards to go, felt the bridge bounce and sway as it took Oldfield's weight, bounce and sway, move slowly down and up and down and down and down and—JEESUS!

The bloody bridge was going. Stannard felt his body thrown down and forward, his left arm tense with the shock of his weight, his booted feet flail uselessly through air.

"David!"

Oldfield was below him, hanging desperately

onto the rope, sweat-rimmed fingers slipping help-lessly, Stannard let the Thompson go, dropped his right hand, gripped a sleeve, a wrist, locked on, felt as if a metal rod had been smashed across his shoulders as they took the weight.

The breath whooshed out of his lungs as they swooped across the ravine like weights on the end of a pendulum. The rope tore at his clenched palm. A whip-like pain cracked across his shoulders. Below him were the tops of the trees, a sluggish brown stream meandering through rock, rocks and trees and the sheer face of the ravine's edge. David swung his feet to meet it, felt his boots scrape on rock, felt the slamming jar that threatened to fold his legs into his stomach, felt the pressure ease as they swung away. Now there was time for a tortured gasp of air, before they slammed again into the rock face.

And stayed still.

Stannard felt the rope take the weight of Old-field's body, heard Oldfield say, "Okay David," brought his right hand up to grasp the rope and hung there listening to the blood pounding in his head.

Tuesday, October 29, 1940. Berlin.

Van Osten huddled deep in the passenger seat of the Opel as Dieter told him about the meeting with Heydrich. "He knows about Zossen, Paul. He's got the information from the storekeeper from whom I bought the detonators."

"What else does Heydrich know about Zossen?"

"Nothing else, so far. But I don't know for how long. I don't know what I will do or say if he has me tortured."

"Heydrich cannot have you arrested," van Osten said. All actions of the Gestapo were above the law, but they could not arrest Army officers. Where Army officers were concerned, they had to be content with making reports to the man's superior officer.

"That's fine," Dieter said. "That takes care of the Gestapo. But what about the SD? Will they decide to keep within the law?" Dieter and van Osten both knew that the SD frequently acted extra-legally. The SD had participated in the assassination of the Austrian Chancellor Dolfuss, and before Holland had become part of the Reich, they had created a diplomatic incident by kidnapping two British Intelligence officers from Venlo, just inside the Dutch border with Germany.

"We have powerful friends," van Osten said.

"But does Heydrich know we have powerful friends?"

"If he arrested you, he'd find out damned soon."

"I'm no hero, Paul. Take me out of the operation. Send me back to Paris."

"You won't get away from Heydrich in Paris."

Dieter played with the wheel, jerking the car from side to side, the tires yelping as they bounced over the joins in the roadway. "What if I had an accident?"

"That's no solution. Heydrich can always interrogate you in the hospital. Whatever you do, Dieter, you cannot get away from the man."

Rushing along the Avus Autobahn in frosty darkness, van Osten considered alternatives. Cancel Lech? Impossible. The whole future of Germany was at stake. Besides, the deal with Schroeder was done, and Göring was committed.

Van Osten said, "I cannot cancel Lech. Lech must go ahead at any cost."

"I don't think I can go through with it."

"If I take you out of the operation, Heydrich will know you've talked to me. He will immediately interrogate you over Zossen. No one in the Abwehr can stop him doing that. I am going to keep you in the operation, but from now on, you will only know what I tell you. If Heydrich thinks he has penetrated our operation through you, then he isn't going to waste time infiltrating anyone else. And we will tell Heydrich just what he needs to know."

"Alright. So what do I tell Heydrich the next time I see him?"

"Tell him that we're training to go into Russia. Tell him we're being sent on a survey expedition. That's the story I've already fed back to Heydrich. Because your information checks with what Heydrich already knows, he will believe you."

"I hope so," Dieter muttered. "For all our sakes, I hope so."

Wednesday, October 30, 1940. New England.

The Presidential retinue had been traveling all that day, stopping for speeches at New Haven, at Meridan, at Hartford and at Worcester. Ten minutes before each stop, the President would cease whatever work he was doing and have his valet sent into him. His trousers would then be taken off and the metal braces clamped to his legs. The President would personally lock and test them before putting on his trousers again. When the train stopped, he would walk down to the end of it, squeezing sideways along the aisle on the arm of General 'Pa' Watson or Sam Rosenman or Prettyman, the valet. He would then ease himself onto the platform at the rear, holding himself erect all the while and make his speech. When it was over, he would be slowly turned round and helped back to his private compartment. There he would take off his trousers and remove the braces with great glee, before dressing again and settling down to work.

The President had been crippled for nineteen years. The train carried special ramps so that he could be wheeled in and out, and when he disembarked, his

coach had to be 'spotted' so that if there was an incline, it was not so steep that the ramps could not be
used.

Normally the President loved train journeys. He
enjoyed watching the passing countryside and informing whoever was seated with him of the history and
political sympathies of the towns they passed through.
Today however, there had been little time to look out
of the window. Five speeches had to be made, one of
them a major speech in the Boston Arena. The Presidential Pullman was crowded with people working on
that speech.

The President sat in a low-backed armchair, studying the original draft Missy LeHand and Grace
Tully waited patiently before portable typewriters,
ready to make amendments in quintuplicate. Sam Rosenman and Robert Sherwood sat together before car-
bon copies of the speech, pens at the ready, and
Harry Hopkins was by the window, his copy of the
speech on the seat beside him, frowning thoughtfully
at the roof of the car.

The President's advisers were worried men. A
fortnight previously, Wendell Willkie, under pressure
from the professionals within the Republican party
had altered his tactics. Gone were the personal attacks
on Roosevelt's arrogance in breaking the tradition of
Washington and Jefferson by running for a third term,
on the nepotism that had made Elliott Roosevelt a
Captain in the Army Air Force. More important, finished also was the bipartisan approach to foreign policy. Willkie now called Roosevelt a warmonger,
charged that if Roosevelt were elected, America
would be involved in a foreign war within five
months, cried that votes for Roosevelt meant wooden
crosses for America's sons, brothers and sweethearts.

Contemptible though Roosevelt's advisers
thought Willkie's tactics were, there was no doubt that
they were effective. A bank had advertised in the

Chicago Tribune that all its officers were voting for Willkie. An insurance company informed its policy holders that Roosevelt's election would render their policies worthless. Gallup showed Willkie closing rapidly on Roosevelt, and friendly newspapermen had warned there was now a danger that Willkie could be swept to the Presidency on a tidal wave of hysteria.

That day, at each stop, the Presidential train had been inundated with telegrams. They all said the same thing. The President must guarantee the mothers of America that their sons would not have to fight. If he could not make that solemn promise, he may as well pack up and go.

At the last stop, Harry Hopkins had collected a telegram from Ed Flynn, Chairman of the Democratic National Committee. If the President could not assure America there would be no involvement in a foreign war, then the election was lost. Like it or not, the Strategy of Terror was working.

"But how often do they expect me to say that?" the President demanded. "It's in the Democratic platform and I've repeated it a hundred times."

"They don't seem to have heard you the first time," said Robert Sherwood, the playwright and currently the President's speech writer. "Evidently, you've got to say it again and again and again."

The President looked down through his pince-nez at the passage they had been working on before Hopkins had given him the Flynn message. That passage assured the parents of the draftees that their boys would be well fed, comfortably housed and properly looked after.

"How about this?" the President asked, scribbling in an amendment. He coughed and cleared his throat. "And while I am talking to you mothers and fathers, I give you one more assurance. I have said this before and I shall say it again and again and again. Your boys are not going to be sent into any foreign wars."

"That'll do it," Hopkins said.

Sam Rosenman however, looked dubious. "The Democratic platform uses the words 'Except in case of foreign attack.' I think that phrase should go in."

"You can't put that phrase in, Sam. Everyone knows we will fight if we are attacked. If somebody attacks us, that isn't a foreign war, is it? Or do they want me to guarantee that our troops will be sent to battle only in the event of another Civil War?"

Wednesday, October 30, 1940.
Washington, D.C.

Berndt von Schramm was a minor diplomat, persuaded to assist Viereck in his hate-Roosevelt Campaign by the Abwehr allowance of 600 marks a month. He also dealt with queries from the Ministry of Propaganda, which recently seemed to be collecting every bit of gossip and scandal they could find on Roosevelt and his family. Eleanor Roosevelt slept with Negroes, the President had gonorrhea, and his mother was a drug addict. Now as von Schramm drafted a reply to the latest inane query, he kept the Silvertone radio on softly, half listening to the latest episode of the Lone Ranger.

He wrote: "The Roosevelt family was founded by Claes van Rosenvelt, who sailed from Holland to New Amsterdam in 1640. There is no doubt that van Rosenvelt was Dutch. The name Rosenvelt derives from the locality where the family lived, that is to say, the Field of Roses, or Rosen Velt. The Rosen Velt is located on the island of Tholen, near Zeeland. It was not, so far as I can ascertain, a Jewish island. Having traced President Roosevelt's genealogy, I cannot confirm that he has Jewish blood.

"In response to your second question, President Roosevelt appears healthy in body and in mind. The reports about him having seizures, writhing on the ground, chewing carpets and frothing at the mouth are quite obviously fabrications. He is no more insane than any other national leader, today."

Berndt signed the message and thought that would teach Goebbels to keep bothering him with idiotic queries, walked over to the icebox and took out a beer. American beer was as good as German he thought walking over to the radio and turning it up.

12

Heydrich had always believed that the object of a police apparatus was not to make arrests but to monitor and influence thought, not to liquidate the opposition, but to anticipate and control it. Which was why Paul van Osten intrigued him. Intuitively he knew van Osten was up to something, and before he could manipulate it, Heydrich had to discover what it was.

He reviewed the facts. Van Osten had flown a photo-reconnaissance plane over Austria. Doing what? Not looking for a billet for six Alpenkommando surely, which was what he'd reported he'd done, and if he wanted to estimate the height of a mountain he would have done better to have looked up from the bottom than fly over the top. And why had Dieter Mehl and von Kirkdorf been summoned to Berlin?

And what was the connection between that and Geneva? A week ago van Osten had left Germany, crossed the frontier into Switzerland accompanied by a Jew, Solomon Tauber. On Monday, van Osten had returned *without* the Jew. Also, van Osten had gone to Geneva instead of Basle. Why? What was he trying to hide? What was he doing?

117

Judengeld? Heydrich thought that was disappointing. He wanted van Osten for more than extorting money from Jews and giving them their freedom. Hoarding money abroad? That was better. It was a capital offense but there was no drama to it, no convoluted process of interrogation and evasion, no watching and prying, none of the fascination of the hunt. With currency offenses, you had the information and confronted the man. It was boringly simple.

But van Osten was not a boringly simple person. His traditions were those of the Army officer, not the *nouveau riche* businessman, grown fat already from one year of the war. With van Osten, Heydrich knew it wouldn't simply be a question of money.

Dieter Mehl would give him the answers, or give him the answers van Osten wanted him to give. But in time he would get the truth out of Mehl and in order to check Mehl's story, he had to find out what van Osten had really done in Geneva. Heydrich sent for Ernst Jahnke and told him to do precisely that.

Thursday, October 31, 1940. Schorfheide.

After the other visitors left, Tropp, van Osten and Major Lothar Brauer went up to the attic where amidst the low pitched whirring of model trains they discussed how they would take Berlin.

Göring stayed in the dining hall. The discussion would take at least an hour and detail bored him. Besides, now that he was committed, he was frightened and full of a sense of betrayal. Conspiring to murder Hitler was somehow different. Even the mass murders of Roehm and the SA had not caused him such anguish.

He had been with Hitler for nineteen years. He thought back to that meeting in Munich's Königsplatz. Then Göring had been an out of work war hero and Hitler, just another politician in a shabby trench coat, with a lock of lank brown hair plastered over his fore-head and a ridiculous moustache. That November day, Hitler hadn't even spoken, but Göring had felt a bond spring between them, and that night he had told Carin, "I am for that man, body and soul." For nine-teen years he had been Hitler's man, body and soul. So what had changed now?

It was not he, Göring, who had changed. It was Hitler. Hitler had moved away, favoring those who told him what he wanted to hear. These days Göring only saw Hitler by appointment, no longer addressed him by the familiar Du. And surrounded by these men who knew nothing of military matters, Hitler was leading Germany to destruction.

Göring had to act. He was right to act, right to accept help from outside the Party. The bullet wound in his thigh pulsed painfully. It was significant that of all the Nazi leaders who had participated in the beer hall putsch, *he* was the only one to have been shot. Was it because he'd always had more courage? More vision?

Was that why they all treated him as a buffoon now? Why Hitler surrounded himself with others, Speer, Ribbentrop, Bormann, Goebbels, even that termite, Himmler.

Göring finished his brandy at a gulp. Damn them all! He would do it!

*   *   *

In the attic which extended the width of Carin-hall, van Osten stood under exposed rafters and eaves, pointing at a wall map of Berlin. Göring was fright-ened. Tonight, he'd invited five other people to din-ner, so that if Heydrich ever investigated there would be an innocent explanation. He had sent the three of them to this vast room filled with an elaborate con-struction of railway tracks so that the cricket-like buzzing of the speeding trains would confuse any hidden microphones. Van Osten knew Göring was capable of panic. If Göring panicked he would abandon the conspiracy. Worse, in order to protect himself, he would expose it.

"The radio stations," van Osten said, touching each of them on the map, "they all must be seized. The opposition must not have the means of publicizing resistance," thinking of the eleven bars of the Chopin polonaise, which repeated every thirty seconds, a year ago, had proclaimed that Poland still fought.

Lothar Brauer said, "We're going to be fully stretched. Our first wave is only three battalions." Brauer was thirty-three, good-looking, well built, with crew-cut silvery blond hair and steady blue eyes, a veteran of Eban-Emael and holder of the Knight's Cross.

"Then we will have to do it." At fifty-four Tropp was older than van Osten and Brauer, a tall man with a bony face and a semicircle of cropped brown hair on an otherwise bald head.

Tropp was the Assistant Director of the Berlin Police and van Osten did not want the police to be in action too early. He worried about Tropp. Tropp was obstinate, involved, van Osten suspected, because of a vendetta against Himmler and an ambition to be the strong man of the new regime.

Brauer said, "There is no other way, Paul. Not unless the Abwehr have units to spare."

"The Abwehr is fully extended." Van Osten smiled. "I suppose we'll have to rely on the police."

When Göring joined them an hour later, the plans were complete. Three battalions of Brauer's FJR 1 would land at Tegel and Templehof. From there they would be transported to various points in Berlin in vehicles provided by the police and Luftwaffe Transport Command. Their objectives would be the Reichschancellery, SD headquarters in the Wilhelmstrasse, the War Ministry in the Bendlerstrasse and the homes of Heydrich and Himmler.

Tropp's men would move on the Gestapo headquarters in the Prinz Albrecht Strasse, on four key police stations and all the radio stations. Then, if Brauer had been able to persuade their Commanders, the remaining six battalions of the 7th Air Division would fly in from Hildesheim and reinforce Göring's hold on Berlin.

"The only problem," Brauer said, "is the SS barracks at Lichterfelde."

They all turned to Göring, massive and outrageous in his Master Hunter's uniform with its full sleeved silk shirt, leather tunic and massive hunting knife. Göring stared thoughtfully at the panel that controlled the trains. Göring had been a cadet at Lichterfelde, and his special police, the *Landespolizeigruppe Göring* was stationed there. If Göring were to commit them to the attack, then his support was assured and there would be no possibility of betrayal.

Van Osten looked at the railway tracks twisting past farms and forests, towns and villages, past railway stations and castles, through tunnels bored under papier-mâché hills. At one end of the room was a six-foot-high mountain, and at the other, a model of the celebrated French Blue Train rushed past scenery like that of the Riviera.

Göring tripped a switch. A goods train shunted across the marshaling yard, an engine took on fuel, a speeding express swerved quickly over points. Everyone looked at the trains.

Göring said softly, "My police will take Lichterfelde."

Van Osten breathed out audibly.

Then Göring smiled. "Now let me show you how I would take Berlin." He laughed as he pressed the button on the panel. Van Osten gasped as a squadron of Stukas emerged from the rafters, each gliding half-way across the room on taut wires, to drop their bombs with unerring accuracy on the Blue Train.

Friday, November 1, 1940. Washington, D.C.

Schroeder stared past Alan Berkeley's trim figure at the rectangle of grey sky beyond the office window. "We need one man," he said, "who can ski, shoot, handle explosives, use a radio, take care of himself in a scrap and be able to pass as a German."

Berkeley crossed elegantly trousered legs. "I can think of a dozen trainees at Springfield who'll fit that specification, but none of them will be ready till the end of December."

"We need him in two weeks," Schroeder said. "And we want the best."

Berkeley shook his head. "We'd love to co-operate, Max, but it can't be done. Not in two weeks."

"We can't wait till the end of December."

Berkeley said, "Believe me, I'd like these people operational as soon as possible. I don't know what to do with them after December. I can't have them sitting around waiting for a war to start."

"Who is the best trainee at Springfield?"

"They're all equally good."

"Cut the crap, Alan. Someone's got to be better than the rest."

"Well," Berkeley said, "if you're twisting my arm, the two Americans are slightly ahead."

"Americans!" Schroeder said. "I thought you were training foreign agents."

"No, just agents."

"The names of these Americans?"

"David Stannard and Michael Oldfield."

There it was, one or the other. It was a pity they had to be Americans. Schroeder would have to cover that. When whoever was selected reached Germany, all trace of his American origin would have to be obliterated.

"This mission is classified AI," Schroeder said. "No records are to be kept. I want the man delivered with his service record. No copies are to be kept. There must be no trace of him having been at Springfield. In other words Alan, I want him to disappear from the face of the earth."

"My best man? You must be joking. I won't agree to his release."

"I have the orders of the President himself," Schroeder said. "It could end the war."

"May I see the orders?"

"Come on, you know better than that. When did Presidents give written orders for missions of this nature?"

"I'm going to need something in writing," Berkeley insisted.

"*I'll* give you orders in writing," Schroeder said, "and you can show him as transferred to G2 (C)."

"Does his mission have a name?" Berkeley asked.

"Call it Double Eagle."

Schroeder watched Berkeley leave, slim and erect, grizzled silver head virtuously upright. It was a pity Berkeley had been so insistent about written orders. The man who killed Hitler would never leave Germany alive, but he would be a hero. There was no way Roosevelt's killer would be that. And the man who organized that killing would have too much power and have to be eliminated. Berkeley would know who that man was, so Berkeley would have to die.

Friday, November 1, 1940. Berlin.

Heydrich sat talking to Dieter Mehl in a bar near the Ku damm. "Surveying in Russia," he said in his high pitched voice, "how interesting. Do you think Hauptmann, that the Führer will invade Russia?"

"I only carry out orders," Dieter said.

"Come, come my friend. You are more than a *unteroffizier*. You are a clever man, otherwise you would not be in the Abwehr. Now tell me, what is your conclusion?"

Dieter realized he had made a mistake. Despite the swallow of beer he'd had hardly a minute earlier, his mouth felt like a dry sponge. "I—I believe we will invade Russia."

"Oh good, you're starting to think. Now tell me, is this invasion of Russia a good thing or a bad thing for Germany?"

"If the Führer decides to invade Russia, it must be the right thing to do. Only he knows all the facts."

"That's better," Heydrich said. "You see how easy it is to think. Why was van Osten flying over the Arlberg?"

"He was looking for a place to train us."

"Has he found such a place?"

"I don't know."

Heydrich's eyes were diamond bright, diamond hard. "That is not very enterprising," Heydrich said. "I expect those who work for me to have enquiring minds. Where do you start training and when?"

"We start training on the first of December," Dieter said. "In the Arlberg."

"Where in the Arlberg?"

"I don't know yet. Van Osten hasn't told us. I cannot ask him anything for fear of making him suspicious."

"Or for fear of knowing the answer," Heydrich said. "Have you told van Osten of our arrangement?"

"No," Dieter said.

"What are you doing between now and the first of December?"

"Map reading courses. Physical training."

"Why do you think van Osten used an airplane to find billets for six men?"

"It—it was the quickest way, I think."

"And he took aerial photographs, for what?"

"I think he was testing a camera. He might want to use it for an aerial survey."

"The camera was an old Zeiss," Heydrich said. "It did not need testing. What pictures did he take?"

"Oh—just the Arlberg. Mountains and valleys, farms."

"You will find out exactly where, Hauptmann. Do you know why he went to Geneva?"

Dieter shook his head.

"Or who he went with?"

"No," Dieter said.

Heydrich threw some money on the table for the beers. "I will see you again shortly," he said. "The next time, please, do not attempt to lie."

Dieter watched the tall, arrogant figure stalk out of the bar. As he raised the glass of beer to his lips, his hand was shaking. He hated Heydrich, he thought, he hated van Osten, he hated everything about this new and terrible Germany.

Monday, November 4, 1940. Geneva.

Hugo Sperle, Chief Inspector of the Touristpolizei in Geneva, was a large bellied, big boned, placid man, trying to enjoy what was left of his work. That summer of the war had been a poor one for tourism and he'd had very little to do, so the visit of a detective from the Berlin Kriminalpolizei was something of an event.

Sperle liked the dark-haired German, a steady looking, polite young man without the disdain detectives usually had for the tourist police. The detective was investigating a business fraud, and suspected that the people concerned might have crossed into Switzer-

land. Even in war time, Sperle reflected, crime went
on. Quite cheerfully he offered the German the police
copies of hotel registration cards for the week ended
27th October. It was no trouble and Sperle was proud
to demonstrate that the Swiss could be efficient too.

Ernst Jahnke was pleased at Sperle's efficiency.
He started with the first class hotels. After all a high-
ranking officer in the Abwehr would hardly have
stayed in anything less. The Beau Rivage, the
Bergues, the Richmond and the Rhone. Not much
luck there, and not that many visitors, either. The
Russie, the Angleterre, the Phenicia, the Cornavin.
Ah, success at last. Van Osten had stayed three nights
at the Cornavin, from the 25th to the 27th. Another
German had stayed two nights. George Viereck, with
an address in Massachusetts Avenue, Washington.
More intriguing yet, a Colonel Max Schroeder of the
American army had also stayed at the hotel. In fact,
thought Jahnke, the only person who had not stayed
at the Cornavin was the Jew.

He thanked Sperle profusely and promised to let
him know the result of his investigations. Then he
went over to a café in the Rue de Lausanne and made
a telephone call to Berlin.

13

Tuesday, November 5, 1940.
Hyde Park, N.Y.

The speeches were over. The campaigns had ended. Millions of dollars had been spent, countless billions of words spoken. 49,815,312 people had gone to the polls, most of them, in all probability, having committed themselves to one candidate or the other, before a word had been spoken. There was nothing more the candidates or their party organizers could do. Now, the people of America would decide.

In the Big House, one and a half miles to the south of the village of Hyde Park, forty people had lunch and waited. The first results would not be known till later that evening.

The Big House was not particularly elaborate. Various owners had added wings to the original frame and clapboard structure, given it a front of Georgian stucco, shallow steps and a broad porch under a colonnaded portico leading into the front hall. It stood on a green rise, about half a mile from the Hudson River; the old families almost always built some distance away from the river in order to avoid the New York Central railway track. It had a splendid view of the river and the old trees, and smooth grounds sloping down to the Hudson gave the house an impressive quality.

After lunch, which had been presided over by the President's mother, the President, Harry Hopkins, General Watson and Doc McIntire settled down to a game of poker. As usual, the President secreted his chips in various pockets, so that he would always have a reserve.

Mrs. Eleanor Roosevelt set off with a friend for a walk through the autumn woods, to her cottage, Val-Kill. She was not looking forward to another four years in the White House. There was a lack of privacy there and many of the things she had to do meant little to her. Still she hoped that if victory came, it would be large, a decisive mandate for liberal government. She hoped that her husband would do all the things he had wanted to do, and knew had to be done, but had been restrained from doing, because of political considerations. Four years more in the White House would be a considerable job of work, and she hoped that whatever happened for the country today, it would be for the best.

Everyone, except the President and his mother, came to Val-Kill for supper that night. It was a stand up affair, cream chicken and rice, cake, ice cream and coffee. While they were eating, the first returns from Connecticut came through. They were good, but it was too early to judge yet.

Around nine o'clock everyone returned to the Big House. In the front hall, amidst the display of birds collected and stuffed by the President as a boy, the portraits of Sarah and James Roosevelt, the statue of the President, which even though it had been sculpted in 1911, almost prophetically showed him without legs, were Mrs. Sarah Roosevelt with several lady friends, sewing, knitting and chatting. They paid little attention to the radio in the room.

In the dining room were the President in shirt

sleeves, his two sons, his uncle Fred and Missy. During the evening, this group would be added to by various members of his staff, friends and campaign workers. The room was littered with charts and tally sheets, and the President sat before telephones which linked him with the White House and Ed Flynn at the Biltmore. In a little cubicle off the dining room, teletype machines chattered away.

The guests spread themselves out, in the library, in the little study off the foyer; and upstairs in Harry Hopkins' bedroom, listening to a fifteen dollar radio were Robert Sherwood and his wife, Madeline.

The results were coming in steadily, and they weren't good. Iowa had predictably gone for Willkie, but so had Indiana, Kansas and Vermont. Five states with 37 votes and all the President had so far was Connecticut with its 8 committed votes. If the trend continued Willkie would undoubtedly win. North Dakota, South Dakota, Nebraska, three more states and 15 more votes for Willkie.

"He's winning just where we expected him to win," the President said equably, but Harry Hopkins downstairs now in the dining room looked worried. No one could gauge the public reaction to Willkie's last minute terror tactics, and in the last two days of the campaign at least three polls had shown Willkie marginally ahead.

Just after ten o'clock the result from New Jersey came through. New Jersey for Roosevelt with 16 votes. Then New York with a massive 47. Then Virginia with 11, Illinois 29. The country was going for Roosevelt. Maryland 8, New Hampshire 4, Pennsylvania 36, the Roosevelt states were coming into their own from Rhode Island through Wisconsin to Wyoming.

By eleven o'clock Ed Flynn claimed victory and at midnight there was a parade of Hyde Park townspeople, a band playing "The Old Grey Mare" and a hastily improvised placard bearing the legend, "Safe on Third."

Safe, but for how long?

Tuesday, November 5, 1940. Washington, D.C.

That afternoon, while the country chose its Chief Executive for the next four years, Schroeder visited the Secret Service Records Office in the Treasury Annex. Al Hine, the officer on duty, remembered Schroeder from the time Schroeder had been attached to the President's detail. Schroeder greeted him warmly. He asked after Al's wife and kids, invited his opinion on Disney's *Fantasia*. Schroeder had worked long enough in Washington to realize that you got as much done by knowing the right office boy as the right senator.

"We've got a problem, Al," Schroeder said. "With all this war hysteria, we've got a hunch that some kraut is going to take a shot at the President."

"Someone's always threatening to do that." Each year the White House received some five thousand letters which directly or indirectly threatened the life of the President. The Secret Service together with the FBI checked out each and every one of the writers. Some of them were harmless cranks venting their spleen on the most obvious symbol of government and bureaucracy. Others simply hated all Presidents. Still others only wanted to be noticed. Very few had the motivation and the opportunity to carry out their threats. Nevertheless every single person was checked, put on file, and if the President ever visited a locality where the threatener lived, nut case or not, he was placed under special surveillance.

"I'd like a look at the files," Schroeder said.

"Isn't this a Secret Service matter?"

"We're concerned," Schroeder said. "The State

Department, too. Some of these people could and should be deported."

"You want the German files then?"

The German files were the last thing Schroeder wanted. "I'd like to cover the field," he said. "We don't want these people in the army, if we can possibly help it. We don't want to train them to kill properly." Schroeder knew he'd fluffed it. It would have been better to have made a routine check on a specific matter. Now Al Hine might not be suspicious, but he would remember.

Al Hine thought it was unusual for a Colonel to come looking for that kind of information, when it could so easily be obtained by a routine interdepartmental request. He could of course refuse Schroeder. But Schroeder was a full Colonel and G2 worked in ways as idiosyncratic as those of the Service. If it was legitimate, he'd get an almighty barracking.

"Okay," Al said, "let's start with January 1940." He'd already decided to send a report of the incident upstairs. Then if anything went wrong, it wouldn't be his responsibility.

Wednesday, November 6, 1940.
Washington, D.C.

"The future of our country is inextricably involved in events beyond our shores . . . Let no American think that he can expect freedom or generosity or even good business from a dictator's peace."

Supporting himself on the rail of the viewing platform at the rear of the Presidential train, his great shoulders hunched forward, and speaking without notes, Franklin Roosevelt spoke to the crowd that had come to Union Station to welcome him back to Washington.

Roosevelt seemed all head and shoulders, Schroeder thought, head, shoulders and voice. He looked tired, the shadow under the deep set blue eyes seeming permanent, the long wrinkles that framed his mouth deeper and more set than Schroeder had seen them before. Roosevelt was a tired old man, obsessed with war.

"We too can be attacked and not necessarily by standing armies. We can be attacked as Norway was attacked, by treachery and surprise built up over a number of years. Their spies and the secret agents are already here and in Latin America."

Schroeder felt a twinge of guilt. He was one of those spies. A spy, but not a traitor. The traitor was Roosevelt, and it was good for America that spies like Schroeder were closer to the heart of the administration than even the President knew.

Schroeder had not wanted to come to the station, not wanted to see the man he had promised to kill. But such a sighting was necessary. Details observed now, could prove significant later. Besides, Evelyn had wanted to come.

For the first time since that terrible evening of the 12th December, Evelyn had asked to attend an official ceremony, allowed herself to be exposed to the sight of men in uniform. That evening Schroeder had been potting the tree he had bought for Christmas. Evelyn had been ironing his dress shirt for a dinner party at the Pattons'. The radio had been on, tuned to the Lucky Strike Hit Parade. Schroeder remembered the tune they had been playing, something called 'Harbor Lights', remembered the sudden interruption, the short brutal newsflash.

The SS *Panay* had been sunk!

His first thought had been for Evelyn. He had moved to turn the volume low, when he'd seen her standing white-faced by the living room door.

"Bobby," she'd whispered, "please God, not Bobby. Please God, don't let it be!"

Afterwards they had waited for more newscasts, for more information, for telephone calls, waited till they heard the measured footsteps come up the drive, saw the serious faced Navy officers, unbelieving still because it had happened so far away, heard the terrible confirmation, numbly accepted the brief condolences.

It had all been so bloody pointless. And it would happen again, to thousands of other parents. Schroeder took his gaze away from the group of figures on the viewing platform of the train, looked past them to the massed band of the US Marines, and the crowd of officials sprinkled with the uniform of blue and khaki, looked to the policemen grimly holding back the crowd at the end of the platform. Those people there hadn't voted for war! Those people there hadn't even been asked to make the choice! All they had done was select personalities, differentiate between one sales campaign and another. And for that they were condemned to die!

Evelyn's fingers were biting into his uniformed sleeve. She was staring straight ahead of her, tense, frightened, as if she realized that that man with the enormous shoulders and huge, freckled head had sent her son to a needless death.

"And one thing I make clear, and over this there has been no disagreement with our friends of the other party. Our primary aim is to overcome this foreign threat, by whatever means. Our primary aim is to restore to those countries which have been victims of the dictators' lust for aggression, their rights, their freedom, and their dignity. And again I say, by whatever means. It is our unswerving determination that the democratic way of life shall not be ended and not only in this hemisphere."

The applause thundered out, echoing and resounding under the cavernous roof of the station. James Roosevelt moved imperceptibly nearer his father, supporting him with his body, so that the President could take his hands from the guard rail and acknowledge the cheers. He waved and then smiling, receded slowly into the train. The band began to play "Happy Days Are Here Again," while the crowd cheered and cheered and cheered.

Schroeder unloosed Evelyn's arm, took out the camera from her handbag. Everywhere flashbulbs popped, everywhere there were sharp reports and blinding flashes. If he had a gun, Schroeder thought, if he had a gun concealed in a camera, he could take Roosevelt now.

The cheering people did not know, could not know the full horror of the war this man they applauded so wildly would lead them into. If Roosevelt had his way this wildly cheering crowd would in two years time be dead, slaughtered by a holocaust that had been foretold in Chapter 24 of Matthew. The sun would be darkened, the moon would not give light, the stars would fall from heaven. Armageddon! That was the only end to the war that Roosevelt wanted.

And Schroeder remembered yet another quotation from Chapter 24 of Matthew. "For wherever the carcass is, there will the eagles be gathered together."

The eagles were gathered together.

So be it.

Wednesday, November 6, 1940. Berlin.

Paul van Osten was not entirely unprepared for the summons from Heydrich. What he had not expected was its directness or its urgency. Heydrich had telephoned him without the assistance of a secretary or aide, had insisted that they meet right away. Their difference in rank dictated that the meeting take place at the Wilhelmstrasse, Heydrich's territory.

Van Osten felt his heart sink as he entered that sparsely furnished room, looked into Heydrich's sharp-featured, triangular face. Heydrich was in uniform, the black tunic of the SS setting off the silver oak leaves on his collar and the single silver chevron on his sleeve. The hard blue eyes raked van Osten's blue suited figure, the black clad arm shot upright in acknowledgment of van Osten's conventional salute.

He'd lost points for that, van Osten thought, sitting down at Heydrich's command. No Hitler salute, no uniform. But he hoped he'd gained a psychological advantage, let Heydrich know he was not to be intimidated.

"Did you have a good journey to Switzerland?" Heydrich asked.

Surely not a polite ice breaker. "It was a comfortable journey," van Osten replied. He needed a cigarette desperately, but Heydrich wasn't smoking, and hadn't given him permission to do so.

"You are aware, that it is illegal for any person or organization other than the Reich Security Service to collect or utilize the so called *Judengeld?*"

"I am aware of that," van Osten replied, feeling surprisingly calm. "The wealth which the Jews had, we have taken from them. We ourselves have taken none of it. Individuals who have offended against this principle will be punished according to an order which I issued at the beginning and which threatens: He who takes so much as a mark shall die."

Heydrich smiled. "Reichsführer Himmler will be flattered that you remember his precise words."

"Neither the words nor the deeds of Reichsführer Himmler can ever be forgotten," van Osten said. He knew that Heydrich paid only lip service to Himmler's elaborate SS rituals and absorption with Teutonic folklore. "Is there anything specific relating to *Judengeld* that you wish me to investigate?"

Heydrich laughed. He liked that. Any specific matter. He would have liked to have told van Osten there was a specific matter. The case of a missing Solomon Tauber. "We have had reports that there are some intelligence officers who believe they have a right to extract these funds and use them for their own benefit or that of their units. I am glad you agree that such an act is illegal. I am sure you know it carries severe penalties."

Pointedly van Osten looked out of the window. Heydrich was on another fishing expedition, he thought. Well let him fish. The longer he took to find out the truth, the better the chance of success at Lech.

"I will circulate a reminder to all Abwehr personnel," van Osten said, regretting the impulse that had made him release the Jew. There had been no agreement about that. That would have contravened Himmler's directive. It had been an impulse, a dangerously generous impulse.

"Contrary to your expectations," Heydrich said, "Roosevelt was elected President."

"I've heard the news," van Osten said. "We are very disappointed."

"Is that all you can say?" Heydrich exclaimed. "How much did that campaign of yours cost? A million dollars? Two million?"

"One and a half million dollars," van Osten said. "Approximately."

"Squandered!" Heydrich clasped his forehead in a wildly theatrical gesture of despair.

That came from having parents who were opera singers, van Osten thought. Pity Heydrich couldn't sing. A successful operatic career might have spared Germany the ravages of the blond beast of the Reich. "We had to try it," van Osten said. "He who dares, wins."

"You lost!" Heydrich's lips curled contemptuously. "You wasted valuable foreign currency!" He leaned back in his chair. "It would have been cheaper to kill Roosevelt. What are your plans for that?"

"They're made," van Osten said, and stared directly at Heydrich.

A silence filled the room, a silence that grew increasingly hostile, as each man waited for the other to speak.

Finally Heydrich said, "It is an order from Reichsführer SS Himler himself that the operation be carried out under the supervision of the SD."

"That is an order I cannot carry out, without written instructions from my own superior, Admiral Canaris. My apologies, but the agreement of 21st December 1936 between SS Oberführer Best and Admiral Canaris specifically provided for espionage and counter espionage outside Germany to be carried out by the Abwehr, without supervision from any other organization. The activities of the SD under that agreement were confined to breaches of paragraph 163 of the Penal Code covering—"

Heydrich waved his hand irritatedly. "I know the details of that agreement," he snapped. "I will speak to Canaris about giving you the appropriate orders." And that, Heydrich knew, would take months. Canaris was his neighbor and they rode together on Sunday mornings, but on a matter like this Canaris would never give way. He was an impossible man!

"Until then," Heydrich said, "the SD is only too pleased to co-operate. Is there any help you need, Oberstleutnant?"

"We have all the help we need," van Osten said quickly, then realized that was a mistake.

"And too much help can be confusing," Heydrich said softly. Then quickly before van Osten could pick up the point, "When will this mission be completed?"

"By the middle of December."

"Good," Heydrich said. "Good. I hope you will have better fortune than in the election campaign."

A warning about *Judengeld*, questions about the elimination of Roosevelt, hardly matters for such an urgent meeting. Puzzled van Osten asked, "Is that all, sir?"

Heydrich's lips parted in a humorless smile. "Should there be anything else?"

Heydrich watched van Osten leave, thinking the outcome of that meeting could fairly be called a draw. He picked up a paper knife thoughtfully and ran it lightly over his nails. The assassination of Roosevelt. Van Osten would not lie to him about that. Roosevelt would have to be killed or van Osten explain why. And he had volunteered a deadline. The middle of December. Van Osten would not have done that if he didn't have a plan that was certain.

What plan?

Schroeder? The meeting with Schroeder. Could van Osten have arranged with Schroeder for the murder of Roosevelt? Incredible! Impossible! There could be no motivation for Schroeder to do such a thing. It didn't even bear thinking about. Typical van Osten though. Subtle and effective. No! That line of reasoning was too far fetched to contemplate. Better stick with facts. Better get at the truth.

Better wait for Dieter Mehl.

Wednesday, November 6, 1940. Washington, D.C.

From his office in the West Wing of the Munitions Building, Schroeder gazed thoughtfully across the parks and gardens to the inspiring façade of the Lincoln Memorial. It was, he reflected, a poignant view for a future Presidential assassin.

The phone on his desk rang, the urgent double ring of his direct line. Schroeder picked it up.

"Colonel Schroeder?" An elderly voice, not one he recognized.

"Yes."

"I am to tell you Double Eagle will fly."

"Who is this?"

"Viereck. You have been expecting me. You have something for me."

"No . . . not yet."

"I was told you would have something for me to-day." The voice was irritable, petulant.

"There have been delays," Schroeder said.

"What delays? Everything should have been ready today." The petulance was turning to suspicion.

Schroeder said, "I can't go into this on the phone. But everything will be alright. I promise you it will be alright."

"When will I have the information?"

"Give me a week."

"I will meet with you on Monday the 11th."

"Where?" Schroeder was answered by the click of a receiver being replaced and the purr of a dialing tone in his ear. Goddamn Viereck's suspicions, he thought, goddamn his arrogance. Schroeder hoped that he would not report adversely to Paul van Osten.

Soon afterwards, Schroeder drove downtown, still in his uniform. Uniforms were unfashionable in peace time and during phoney wars, and most days Schroeder wore civilian attire. Yet today, when for the first time in months he'd worn a uniform, everything he did verged on treason.

Grimly he circled the block twice before finding a 5¢ slot near the Crusader building on 14th Street. As he walked by Garfinkel's he noticed a window full of blonde moppet Shirley Temple dolls, BB air rifles and Buck Rogers Disintegration Guns. He'd once bought Bobby a BB air rifle, which in a most unmilitary manner Bobby had exchanged for a battered Kodak Brownie. If Bobby had stayed with cameras he would have been alive today, Schroeder thought and turned into the Crusader building.

Rieber's office was on the topmost floor, with a view of the Treasury Building and General Thaddeus

Koscinzko's corner of Lafayette Park. Unlike the General, Rieber was grimly effusive.

"Come on in, Max. You look magnificent in uniform. Tell me, are uniforms going to be fashionable this year?"

"Yes," Schroeder said, sitting down heavily. "Unless you help me do something about it."

"Me?" Rieber asked. "Look boy, I've already done my share for peace."

"State will have nothing to do with your proposals," Schroeder said, "until the Germans can show them what they mean to do with Hitler."

Rieber spread his hands palms upwards on the table. "I can't do the impossible. What the Germans do with Hitler is a political and military matter. How did you get on with van Osten?"

"I saw him in Geneva."

"And did he tell you what Göring is going to do about Hitler?"

"That's only the half of it. We're going into this war, Charles. Whatever happens to England, we're going in."

If there was war Rieber's agreements with I.G. Farben were worthless. If America won that war, those agreements would be discovered, Rieber and Crusader destroyed. If America won, those secrets would be taken from Crusader and divided among the majors.

"What makes you so sure?" Rieber asked.

"I'm sure, Charles, sure as God made little apples and pigs can't fly."

"So nothing came of your meeting in Geneva?"

"Enough came of that meeting in Geneva for me to say that it is possible to avoid this war."

"That's very encouraging Max, very encouraging."

"What's your stake in peace? Don't expect me to believe that you went to Berlin and risked the wrath of the State Department because you love humanity. How much is peace worth to you, Charles?"

Rieber stopped considering how he could take Crusader out of the deal with Farben. "Peace is worth to me what it is worth to any businessman. If there was peace, we could start trading with Europe again. It's as simple as that."

"And trading with Europe is worth a great deal to you, yes?"

Rieber shrugged.

"You realize what I am doing is unofficial?"

Rieber nodded. Plotting the murder of a foreign head of state, even someone like Hitler, was diplomatically unjustifiable and downright dangerous.

"So I am unable to use government funds. I need money."

Rieber calculated carefully. If it was not too much money and if he could hand it over cleanly, perhaps it would be worth it.

"How much?"

"Twenty-five thousand dollars. That's a lot less than the Mob would charge you for the job."

"What else?" Rieber asked.

"I need a place not far from Washington, very quiet, very secluded. I'll need to use it for two to three weeks with no questions asked."

"What do you need it for?"

"To train my operative."

"Okay," Rieber said. "I'll send you round the twenty-five thousand in cash tomorrow and you can use Crusader Farm. It's out near Laurel. There's no one there, except the guards."

Schroeder stood up. "Keep the guards. I'll probably need them. And I'll give you back the money I don't use."

Rieber stared at him in amazement. For the first time in his life, he thought, he'd met an honest man.

14

Friday, November 8, 1940. Springfield, Va.

It was the last day of jungle training. For the past two weeks, Weapons and Tactics Co-ordination Unit had crawled through dense foliage, swung Tarzan-like on creepers, paddled boats along narrow streams choking with leeches, waded chest deep through swamps, been on a three-day survival exercize living off the jungle. They were haggard, bearded, had lost some of their vibrant tans; there were dark circles around their eyes and they smelled of old sweat, dried mud and jungle dirt, but now, when they moved through the jungle, they moved like animals, not men.

Lying motionless in a tree looking down at the narrow trail, Stannard wondered whether it would be like this in the Pacific. For one thing it wouldn't be as cold as Springfield. Not in November. They did a magnificent job of simulation here, but they sure as hell couldn't do much about the weather.

Stannard concentrated on the track eight feet below, a narrow ribbon of mud through the foliage. They were on a hunting exercise. He was one of the hunted. In a few minutes the exercise would be over and they could return to base. Stannard had turned the tables on his pursuers. He had doubled back and was now lying in wait for them.

One day he'd be on the run for real, in a tropical jungle, or a rock-strewn mountain slope, a coral atoll or across bare scrubland. No matter. He'd been trained on all kinds of terrain at Springfield. A survivor of the Weapons and Tactical Co-ordination course could, and probably would be dropped anywhere, at any time, and have to survive.

Stannard heard a cautious rustle and went very still, breath floating softly between his parted teeth. The crunch was followed by the squelch of a footstep in the mud. Then silence. Whoever it was must have crawled to the edge of the track. A few seconds, then another squelch. The man must be at the place where the marsh crossed the track. And soon the man would have to break cover.

Seconds later, Stannard saw the top of a khaki hat low against the shrubs, the khaki clad body almost indistinguishable from the undergrowth. Let him come, Stannard thought, looking behind the man into the forest to check if there were any others. No. Only one man. Which made it just right.

The man edged out of the undergrowth, straightened up slightly, looked down the track, and seeing it empty, straightened up still further. Let him come, Stannard thought, five yards, four, three. He let himself fall from the tree, swinging his body loose in an arc, landing lightly on his feet in front of the man.

Startled by the whirring of the air, the man looked up, stepped back. It was Mike Oldfield. As Stannard landed, he swung his hand back, for a jab at the windpipe. For a split second his eyes brightened as he recognized Stannard, his hand hesitated. In that split second, David Stannard kicked him in the testicles.

With an agonized rush of breath, and a tortured scream, Oldfield folded forward, his body curving

round the boot, lifting off, falling face down in the
mud. Stannard took him by the shoulders, turned him
round. Oldfield was pale, making deep, sobbing
noises.

"You hesitated," Stannard said. "Never do that.
Not for me. Not for anyone. If you make up your
mind to kill. Kill!"

Oldfield writhed from side to side, his hands between his thighs. Stannard picked him up, put him
across his shoulders, began to lope gently along the
track, back to base. As he ran, his eyes roamed the
undergrowth, in case someone jumped him.

Never let up, never relax, that was the lesson of
Springfield. React, react, react. Except when you
were attacking and then do it hard, hard, hard and
fast. Two of the instructors were British Commandos.
They didn't play games either and kicked the shit out
of anyone who did.

*   *   *

In the tower, high above Springfield, Max
Schroeder watched the exercise through glasses.
Berkeley was with him, and when he saw Stannard
lope out of the jungle area, carrying Mike Oldfield, he
said, "Looks as if Stannard's your man."

Schroeder grunted and eyed the rangy figure
through the glasses. There was muscle there alright,
and litheness. The boy was an easy mover, cat-like,
using only the muscles he needed and no more. A bit
on the skinny side perhaps, but he carried the other
man as if he were cotton.

Schroeder focused the glasses on Stannard's face.
Flat cheek bones, a three-day growth of beard, surprisingly sensitive mouth, matted blond hair bleached
by the sun running down to his collar. He must be
about six foot two, Schroeder thought, would look
splendid in dress uniform. He looked at Stannard's

eyes. They were blue and tired, but there was spirit in them and an indomitable hardness.

"How good is he, mentally?"

"Quick and thorough," Berkeley replied. "An excellent improvisor."

"What happens if he has to kill?"

"We hope that everyone who has been through here will be able to kill when the time comes. That's what we train these men for. To kill. To kill whenever necessary, without question. But it's difficult to tell how any of them will react the first time. No matter how many men you've trained, or how hard you've worked them, you simply cannot say this one will do it, that one will flunk it."

"What about Stannard?" Schroeder asked, thickly.

"He should be alright," Berkeley said. "He's killed before," and moved to indicate they should go down to lunch.

Friday, November 8, 1940. Berlin.

Two days previously, van Osten had sent Dieter Mehl to Bremen. His business was to deliver two Afus, small spy radios especially developed for the Abwehr by Telefunken, to a steward traveling on the North German Lloyd freighter *Schwaben*. Dieter had prolonged the journey as long as he could, but today he'd had to return to Berlin and the imminent threat of Heydrich.

Van Osten had briefed him thoroughly on his cover story, but that did little to assuage his fears. The blackout in Berlin seemed unnaturally sinister, the movements of people along the shaded pavements full of secret menace. Dieter told himself that he should not be alone, and drove slowly from bar to bar, trying to find Karin. He drank schnapps and beer and Riesling and burgundy, a little gin and some kirsch, remembered he hadn't eaten since lunch and by the time the last bar closed, discovered that he was quite drunk.

He stood swaying in the street, heedless of the few people brushing against him in the darkness. If not for the war, he would have been a writer, Dieter thought. He still wrote poetry. He even looked like a poet. The girls often told him he looked like Byron. If not for the war he would have published one or two slim volumes of poetry, some bad novels and a lot of journalese. But there was no place for writers in the Reich, or poets or journalists. The only safe form of writing was stenography, and then only if you took down Goebbels' words accurately.

Dieter belched and lurched up the street, trying to remember where he'd left his car. It was no use. He'd lost his car. Heydrich had lost him. Dieter giggled and lit a cigarette, lifting his coat to shield the flame from the wind. A man in an old pilot's leather windcheater lumbered towards him, moving with the measured gait of a practiced drunk.

"Haben sie streichholz, bitte?"

Dieter held out his lighter, glimpsed a youngish, round face, a pair of slanted eyes looking quizzically at him over the wavering flame. The next moment a fist, large, solid and practiced exploded into his middle, and as he gasped and bent double, a mighty hand crashed against the back of his neck. Dieter felt himself thrown forward, miraculously caught by his jacket, suspended with his face inches from the pavement. Then he was thrown face downwards across the rear seat of a car which drove furiously away, while he retched helplessly and panted for air.

Friday, November 8, 1940. Washington, D.C.

At forty-five, J. Edgar Hoover had been head of the FBI for sixteen years. He was a powerful looking man nearly six feet tall, with a sturdy body that was starting to run to fat. His face was round and clean shaven, with a thick mouth and penetrating black eyes. In transforming the FBI from a political pigsty into a much envied, professional, respectable and incorruptible law enforcement agency, Hoover had become a legend. Dillinger, Pretty Boy Floyd, Baby Face Nelson, Ma Barker, Machine Gun Kelly, Lepke Buchalter, the Bureau's successes were already part of American folklore and all over the country, little boys wore tin G-Man badges, carried G-Man guns, read G-Man comic strips and saw G-Man films.

J. Edgar Hoover's hobby was collecting finely blown glass. He was unmarried and lived with his mother. He had two close friends, both of whom were in the Service. Hoover's work was his life. He usually worked late and always paid attention to detail.

The detail he was paying attention to, late that particular night, was the report he had received from one of the agents assigned to watch the offices of Meyer Lansky at 1450 Broadway. Seventeen days previously, Colonel Max Schroeder, Deputy Head of G2 (C), US Army had visited the Chief of the National Crime Syndicate and successor to Lepke Buchalter's Murder Inc. Not that the agent's report had referred to these organizations. Hoover always maintained that there was no such thing as organized crime in the United States, and that the National Crime Syndicate and Murder Inc. were inventions of feverish and under-employed imaginations of reporters for the sensational press. Nevertheless, a US Army officer and a Deputy Head of Counter-Intelligence had no business consorting with gangsters, not even if he was leaving for Europe the next day.

If not for the report which had reached Hoover that day, the matter would have simply gone into the file that Hoover had been building on Max Schroeder since the mid 1930's, when Schroeder had been involved with the right wing Townsendites and the Union Party. The report emanated from the office of the President's Secret Service detail. Three days previously, Schroeder had visited Secret Services Records, inspected certain potential assassins' files, and because manuscript copying of any kind was forbidden, requested photocopies of the personal summaries from five files. The names were attached, and the Secret Service now requested that the FBI check the matter out.

Five names. Horace Bush, Patrick McNeady, Abe Brodie, Carmel Panatour, James Emmanuel, spread from Louisiana to Kansas. G2 (C) could well be hiring assassins, Hoover thought, or more likely radicals. It was not something he could question Schroeder about. So he instituted checks on the five men, and decided to wait and see what developed. Then he considered how he could get to Lansky, to find out what Schroeder had seen him about.

Friday, November 8, 1940. Berlin.

"Zossen," the man asked, "who else took part in Zossen?" They were in a basement room with colorless walls, the only illumination a desk lamp shining directly into Dieter's face. The man in the old pilot's windcheater had said he was Wolff Brandt of the Berlin Gestapo. The stocky man with him was Ernst Jahnke of SDD-Inland. Dieter had been arrested on the orders of General Heydrich. In due course he would be charged with the highest form of treason, conspiracy to murder the Führer. Unless he talked. In which case, Brandt was authorized to make a deal. And that had ended the polite part of the interrogation.

"There were over a hundred of us at Zossen," Dieter said and relaxed, waiting for Jahnke to hit him. The blow caught him on the side of the face and he pitched out of the chair, scraping his palms on the ce-

ment as he fell. Slowly he picked himself up and arranged himself on the chair.

After the brutal, amazing shock of the first
blows, Dieter found he could stand the pain and the
humiliation. Maybe it was the alcohol, or perhaps he
had more physical courage than he'd thought. But the
pain of the blows was only temporary and was as
nothing to the hard core of defiance that each blow
stimulated. The more he was beaten, the less he
would talk, Dieter vowed. That was the only way he
could win.

"Tell us what you did with the detonators."

"I never had any detonators."

"The storekeeper identified you."

"He was mistaken."

"Be reasonable, Mehl. We know there were others
involved. Give us their names and all this will stop."

"There were no others," Dieter muttered thickly.

The blows rained on his body and on his face,
short, solid punches that slammed the breath from his
body and made his broken teeth grate. The more they
hit him, the less it hurt, Dieter thought. The more
they hit him, the less he would talk.

"Why do you think we dared arrest you? Don't
you think we know? We know all about Zossen. Your
friend van Osten wasn't as brave as you. You've held
out long enough, Mehl. Tell us who else was involved."

"Himmler," Dieter said, "and Ribbentrop."

A blow lifted him off the chair, flung him awkwardly, sideways. He saw the anger on Jahnke's face
as his head cracked against the cement. Dieter managed to laugh, before everything went black.

❈   ❈   ❈

They weren't taking any chances. He was
strapped naked to the chair. His body was lathered
with sweat and between his feet was a pool of vomit

that smelled sourly of stale wine. His shoulders and ribs were covered with ugly bruises, blue and purple and black. Blood trickled slowly from his smashed nose, dripping warmly onto his thigh. An eye was puffed shut and there were large weals on his cheeks and a sore gap where his front teeth had been. The inside of his mouth was caked with dried blood. Dieter knew he'd never look like Byron again. But he still wouldn't talk.

There were more men in the room now. He could see the hands reaching into the pool of light from the desk lamp. Jahnke's hands covered with black hair, Brandt's, square and stubby, the long, pale slender hands of Reynhard Heydrich. A violinist's hands. Every Sunday Heydrich played the violin with Frau Canaris. He was said to like chamber music, Mozart and Haydn and in Nazi Germany, the music of Mendelssohn was banned.

Brandt was asking him about the Arlberg, again. Dieter repeated that it had to do with the invasion of Russia, focusing with his good eye on the shadows behind the light. The pain in his fingers increased.

His hands were strapped behind him, the fingers held in metal gloves, with sharp spikes that pierced the flesh.

Why had van Osten used an airplane? To see if an aerial survey of Russia was possible. The pain increased. Dieter screamed. Paul had briefed him well. Paul had given him all the answers. As long as he kept to the answers, they'd never break him. Never. Never.

The questions stopped, the pain momentarily ceased. There was a row of angry burn marks across his chest, already blistering. He couldn't remember when they had done it. Had he talked? From behind the light a voice asked, "What was van Osten doing with the Jew in Geneva?"

"Identification," Dieter muttered. "Verify . . . if he had . . . assets."

"Why Geneva if the exit permit was for Basle?"

"We'd heard . . . an account . . . of a bank . . . Geneva." Dieter's head slumped on his chest.

"Did he?"

"No."

"Where is the Jew?"

"In his shop." Dieter could feel the blood running down his fingers, hear the spikes grate against bone. The pain grew more intense, filling his hands, filling his body. He struggled feebly. The pain was filling the room, his long, wailing scream was filling the room. He heard footsteps scrape the cement.

Then there was peace.

* * *

The chill of water mingled with the chill of sweat, the acrid stench of ammonia stung his nostrils, his throat choked with vomit, damp strands of hair stuck to his forehead, his feet were spattered with blood and urine and vomit. Dieter came round. The metal gloves had been removed; his fingers were bloody, sore and stiff. One of the burn blisters on his chest had burst. And the light on the desk had been turned away from him. Over his own stertorous breathing was the murmur of voices. They had given up, Dieter thought. He had won. He had outlasted them. Paul would be proud. The whole Abwehr would be proud.

Brisk footsteps. After all this, the sound of brisk footsteps, a hand holding two copper clamps and a length of wire. Dieter watched impassively, uncomprehendingly, as the clamps were fastened onto his nipples, watched numbly as a larger clamp was fixed to the head of his penis. They were going to castrate him, Dieter thought, at first without emotion, then with a savage, primeval fear that made his body tremble, his breath grow harsh through broken teeth.

Just within the circle of light thrown by the desk

lamp, was a square box. On one side of it was an on/ off switch and facing Dieter was a rubber knob, protruding from the box, capable of being moved around a scale marked one to five.

Dieter felt the room move, as if he was caught by a giant wave. The voices faded into a comfortable drone. Suddenly, there was Brandt's voice, from a great distance away, its tone unbalanced as if Dieter could only hear on one side of his head.

"Tell us about Viereck?"

"Viereck . . . who is Viereck . . ."

"Why did Viereck meet with van Osten in Geneva?"

"Abwehr . . . business." Dieter could hardly get the words out. "Roosevelt . . . election . . . must be . . . stopped." He couldn't concentrate anymore. The pain in his body had dulled. His mind had dulled too. He saw Jahnke's hand move the black rubber knob to four, the fingers rest insect-like on the on/off switch.

"What has Viereck to do with Roosevelt?"

"Election . . . detonators . . . man mistaken . . . not me . . . no one at Zossen."

Jahnke's voice. "What was van Osten doing with Colonel Max Schroeder of US Army Intelligence, in Geneva?"

"Paul . . . Schroeder . . . I don't know." He rolled his head from side to side. "Water."

"Here is the proof."

White cards before his face. Didn't want cards, wanted water. Hotel registration cards. Schroeder. Van Osten. They had met in Geneva. Paul hadn't told him. Hadn't briefed him. He had been betrayed. After all the pain, he had been betrayed.

"Why did they meet?" Jahnke snapped.

"I—I . . . don't know."

Jahnke's finger tripped the on/off switch. Dieter's body snapped outwards, curving against the

straps. His head arched backwards, his eyes defied
the bruises and opened very wide. He screamed. One
word. "Lech." As his body flopped back he gurgled,
and his tongue protruded. His head jerked straight
and sagged sideways while the eyes continued to stare
at his interrogators.

❉   ❉   ❉

Heydrich switched off the tape recorder at the
sound of Mehl's scream. Whether Mehl had been
drinking a lot before his arrest, or had been beaten
too severely before the administration of the shock,
whether the filth on his body had proved too effective a conductor of electricity or Jahnke had made a
mistake, all was now irrelevant. What was important
to Heydrich was to dispose of Mehl's body and find
an alternative means of discovering what Mehl had
known.

Heydrich had had no right to incarcerate Mehl.
No right to torture and kill him. If Canaris or van Osten ever learned the truth, there would be revenge
taken, and open war between the agencies. Open war-
fare between the agencies was not what Heydrich
wanted. That way, Germany would suffer, the Führer
would be displeased, and Heydrich would bear the
consequences. So Mehl had to be disposed of. Tidily.

"We have carried away a thousand corpses and
remained decent. That is what has made us hard."
Heydrich reflected on Himmler's words as he sent for
four men from the SD Technical Department in Dell-
bruchstrasse. When the men arrived, he told them
what he wanted done.

For hours afterwards, the sound of Mehl's scream
stayed with Heydrich, his acute musician's ear repro-
ducing that single piercing note with overpowering accuracy.

Licht! That was what Mehl had screamed. He
played the recording again. Light! A confusion with

electricity? A prayer? A protest at the encroachment of perpetual darkness? Heydrich had to know, had to tie it in with van Osten's overflight of the Arlberg, the disappearing Jew and the meetings in Geneva.

He wished he could arrest van Osten. But van Osten was untouchable. Touch van Osten without proof and the wrath of Göring and the cold blooded hatred of Canaris would explode around him. He could not arrest van Osten but he could talk to him. He was perfectly entitled to ask him about the Jew.

Which left Geneva. Viereck had been in Geneva. Viereck would know about the meeting with Schroeder. Heydrich sent an urgent message to the SD agent in Washington, ordering him to find out what Viereck was doing in the United States, and to remind Viereck that he owed his employment by the Abwehr to General Heydrich.

Saturday, November 9, 1940. Berlin.

The car lay on its side, its metal fused by the impact and the heat, the smell of burnt rubber and leather still hanging over it, heavy and acrid. The Opel had come straight off the road, smashed a gap through the fence, bounced off a tree, rolled over and exploded. The marks of its passage scarred the wintry earth and the flames had seared leaves and left a brown patch of burnt grass about the wreck. A seat lay twenty yards away, intact and vividly blue against the greeny brown of the earth.

A few yards away also, surrounded by a hastily erected screen of bedsheets, lay charred flesh and bones in the vague shape of a human body. From the shape of the wreck, an indentification disc, and a number plate that had survived the impact, van Osten and von Kirkdorf had agreed the remains were those of Dieter Mehl. But they'd had to look at the body with its charred skin flaking away, the exposed tissues burnt black in places, the obscenely protruding tongue. If Dieter had been immolated in a blazing car, that was what he would have looked like.

Van Osten walked away through the cold, grey morning to the gap in the hedge, away from the smell of charred flesh and charred rubber. The field was dotted with policemen, and there was an ambulance with a blue flashing light. And Dieter was dead.

"No brake marks," van Osten said, pointing to the road.

"If Dieter had been drinking he wouldn't have known he was going off the road."

"Heydrich was after Dieter," van Osten said. "For Zossen."

Von Kirkdorf looked back at the wrecked car. "Even Heydrich could not have organized all this." He scuffed the earth with the side of his shoe. "Does Heydrich know about Lech?"

"He wanted Dieter to tell him."

Von Kirkdorf looked down at his shoe, looked down at the torn earth by the roadside. "Did Dieter tell him, do you think?"

"I don't know."

They walked together up the road to where van Osten had parked his BMW. "Do we abandon Lech?"

"Not yet," van Osten said. "Not till we're certain that Heydrich knows."

*   *   *

"It happened like I said. The car skidded. Dieter was probably driving too fast." Dieter's father repeated, "Yes. Dieter always drove too fast," as if the memory was some consolation.

"It was all over very quickly," van Osten said, sorry for the sturdy, Thuringian farmer trying to force comprehension by the repetition of detail. "We are arranging a military funeral."

"No," Dieter's father said. "We would like to bury Dieter here. That is, if it can be arranged."

"It will be arranged," van Osten said.

"Thank you. Thank you . . . I don't think Dieter would have liked a military funeral. He wasn't really a soldier, you see."

Van Osten put the phone down, slumped into a chair, pressed his palms against his eyes, his mind still rankling with details of post mortems, coroner's certificates and transport. I'm no hero, Dieter had said only a week ago. Poor, frightened, soldier-poet Dieter, killed for a better Germany.

There was an imperious pounding on the door, someone using a fist like a gun-butt. Van Osten froze. Only the Gestapo knocked like that. Heydrich was rounding up the Zossen conspirators.

Without quite knowing what use it would be, he dropped his Walther into his pocket and went to the door.

The moment he opened it two uniformed SS guards sprang into the apartment, ugly and arrogant, powerful in their black uniforms with the forked lightning symbols streaking across their caps and collar tabs. The guards swept the apartment with their Erma MP 38's. Van Osten kept his hand on the Walther.

Standing in the corridor, his trim figure clothed in an elegant brown suit, his blond hair glinting in the sunlight was Reynhard Heydrich. Van Osten's first impulse was to shoot him, to freeze the supercilious smile on those haughty features forever. The guards in the apartment, the two guards flanking Heydrich in the corridor wouldn't stop him. But he remembered Lech, told himself the target was Hitler not Heydrich, told himself that if he was about to be arrested, Heydrich would not have come to do it.

Slowly he loosed his hand from the Walther. Just

as slowly he backed into the apartment, allowing Heydrich to enter.

"I am sorry to come unannounced," Heydrich said, waving the guards out of the room, noticing the cautious way van Osten took his hand from his pocket, noticing also the jaw covered with dark stubble, the red rimmed eyes, the tousled hair above the high forehead, the strain in van Osten's usual manner.

"There was something I wanted to talk to you about," Heydrich went on. "An inquiry we received last night. As I was in the neighborhood. . . .."

"You're welcome," van Osten said through a dry mouth.

"But not if it is inconvenient." Heydrich had expected van Osten to have a bigger apartment than this. It was not suited to a senior officer of the Abwehr. Only one bedroom, and sparsely furnished, the clatter of the S-Bahn outside, an atmosphere like a monk's cell. A telephone, a Blaupunkt radio, a gramophone, a collection of classical records and books, Heine and radio telegraphy and *romans policiers* in French and in English. Wryly Heydrich thought there were no *romans policiers* in German these days. Goebbels had banned all writing which made the police look incompetent.

"You look tired," Heydrich said. "I hope *der Alte Mann* is not working you too hard."

Van Osten noted the use of Canaris' nickname. Heydrich was trying to be friendly. So that he could replace Dieter Mehl with Paul van Osten?

"A friend of mine was killed in a car accident last night. I have had to help with the funeral arrangements."

"My sympathies," Heydrich said seriously. "Would it be anyone I know?"

"Yes," van Osten said. "Dieter Mehl."

Heydrich looked blank. "So many names. So

many faces. You know how it is. Please convey my sympathies and those of the RSHA to his family."

"What was it you wanted to see me about?"

"It isn't very important," Heydrich said. "If I had known about your friend, I wouldn't have troubled you. This matter can wait."

"You're here. Let's get it over with."

"It's about the Jew, Solomon Tauber. You obtained an exit permit for him, two weeks ago."

"So I did."

"He hasn't been seen since."

"I can hardly be expected to keep tabs on every wandering Jew. After we came back from Basle, I left him outside his shop."

"What business did you have with him in Basle?"

"Abwehr business." That was something Heydrich didn't dare push. Yet.

Heydrich smiled thinly; only his mouth moved. "I see. Returning from Basle, you must have crossed the border at . . . Rheinfelden?"

"There isn't anywhere else," van Osten said.

"That's right. If you were returning from Basle. We have not been able to find the re-entry permit for Solomon Tauber."

"I suggest you have your people check again. I suggest you also check that he hasn't been removed to a place of safety. That is what you people call concentration camps, isn't it?"

Heydrich was still smiling, his eyes still glacial. "The Jew is missing," he said. "His re-entry permit is missing. Isn't it logical to deduce that he didn't return?"

Through his tiredness and his grief, van Osten realized that Heydrich was still investigating, that Dieter had not talked.

"Dieter Mehl too was investigating the case of a disappearing Jew," van Osten said.

Heydrich cocked an inquiring eyebrow. "And is that relevant, Oberleutnant?"

"Bruno Heydrich Suss," van Osten said slowly, "founder of the First Halle Conservatory for Music, and known to his colleagues as Isidor Suss. In fact Mehl provided us with a copy of Riemann's Musical Encyclopaedia for 1916, which has an entry for Bruno Heydrich, real name Suss."

Heydrich's face flushed with anger. He drew himself up to his full height. "I warn you Oberstleutant van Osten that I have repeatedly fought and won court actions for that kind of racial slander."

"But in those cases," van Osten said, "the defendants did not have the benefit of Mehl's researches into the Registry Office for Civil Marriage in Halle."

"What researches?" Heydrich demanded. "There have been no researches. Mehl was in Paris."

Van Osten did not say anything. He had played Canaris's trump card. From now on, Heydrich would either be a friend, or ten times as vicious an enemy.

Heydrich turned on his heel and walked out of the room.

A Jew in an elite Aryan order, van Osten thought. No wonder there was no limit to his need for power.

15

From where he sat near the Chain Bridge in Pali-
sades Park, Schroeder had a view of the railroad, the
chimneys of the Dalecarlia Filter Plant and the Potomac. A huge blimp hung high over Arlington, carrying sightseers at a dollar fifty for twenty minutes. It
was bitterly cold and Schroeder's fingers and toes felt
like icicles. Viereck was twenty minutes late and soon
they would be closing the park.

These Europeans filled their spying with mys-
tery, made great play of assignations at sunset, and
strange passwords. Schroeder wished he'd had the
sense to force Viereck to meet him in a cafeteria in
downtown Washington. The park was emptying, the
light was translucent and without shadow. Schroeder
felt foolish mopping his face with a handkerchief each
time someone passed. The sprightly old man whom he
had first observed ten minutes earlier hurried by.
Stopped. Took out his handkerchief, mopped his face,
came over and sat down.

"It's a cold night, tonight."

"Are you George Viereck?" Schroeder asked,
thinking to hell with passwords.

Viereck looked at him, thinking that even in civilian attire, Schroeder looked Army, deciding it had to do with the straightness of the shoulders, the crowsfeet round the eyes, the direct way of looking at you. "You must be Colonel Schroeder. You have something for me?"

Viereck spoke in a low voice, as if surrounded by the darkening emptiness of the park, there was still a chance that he might be overheard. He was a shifty looking man with the air of an impoverished aristocrat, and he sat alertly upright on the bench, his eyes glinting knowingly.

Schroeder reached underneath his overcoat and gave Viereck the envelope. With a deft movement, Viereck thrust the envelope underneath his own coat.

"You'll find everything you want in there," Schroeder said.

"The man will be required in Zürich by the end of the month. Has that been arranged?"

"That will not be a problem."

Viereck said, "The envelope is sealed. I will have to open it."

"I thought you were sending it by diplomatic pouch."

"No," Viereck said. "I may have to communicate by other means." The previous day, Sunday, Viereck had been carpeted by the Chargé d'Affaires. Not only was the Dies Committee on Un-American Activities investigating the Embassy's involvement in the election campaign, but a scurrilous message implying that Hitler was a lunatic, had been sent to Germany by Viereck's assistant. Viereck was now prohibited from using the Embassy's radio, telephones and diplomatic pouch, and he was dubious about using the Abwehr radio network which van Osten had warned him had been probably infiltrated by the SD and more dangerously, by the FBI.

"What other means?" Schroeder asked.

"That's my problem," Viereck said curtly. "When and where will you do it?"

"It will have to be on or about the 16th of December. Our target leaves Washington in nine days on a fishing trip. There is no time between now and then."

"You haven't told me where," Viereck said.

"Because I don't know where, yet. It depends on his schedule. For the moment, I think Union Station may be a good venue. I'll tell you more, next time we meet."

"Who will do it?" Viereck asked, "and how will it be done?"

"In the time honored way. One man with a gun."

"Have you found such a man?"

"Not yet. The man will have to be someone who is slightly unbalanced. Presidential assassins have always been mentally unstable. I have the means of contacting such a person. Then I have to provide him with the opportunity and the motivation. After that it is as simple as pulling a trigger."

"You cannot use a lunatic," Viereck snapped.

"The man I have in mind, is not a lunatic. He is simply a man who is obsessed. Our task is to provide him with the means of satisfying his obsession."

"There must be someone else who can do it? Someone more stable?"

"No," Schroeder said. "This is not a job for which you can contract an assassin. The man has to want to do it . . . I'm sure this will work."

Viereck wasn't that sure. A lunatic doing it could result in failure, and arrest, and perhaps a world war. Roosevelt only needed an excuse like that to attack Germany. "I must be able to choose the man."

"Impossible."

"And if I don't approve of your choice?"

Schroeder hesitated. "Then we will discuss alternatives." He was sure Viereck wouldn't have been picked unless he was good, but there was too much at stake for Schroeder to concede him interference rights. "I want to make it clear, that this is my operation."

Viereck stood up, small and frail in the fading light. "Subject to my overall approval, Colonel. That is what was agreed. Pick your man and let me see him."

"You'd better let me know where I can contact you," Schroeder said. "I'm not going to spend the rest of my life freezing to death in parks."

Viereck muttered a telephone number. "There will always be someone there to take a message," he said, and walked briskly towards the Canal Road exit.

Tuesday, November 12, 1940. Washington, D.C.

Watching the enthusiastic crowds, the battered brown fedora being repeatedly doffed, the flash of that famous smile move across the screen in grainy black and white, Schroeder was pleased to see that security procedures had not changed much since he'd been at the White House. They still used cars in front of and behind the Presidential Cadillac, still used flank and shoulder men. It was a well tried system, been proved effective over forty years. It was the proud boast of the Secret Service that since the Congressional Bill of 1901 had given them the responsibility of guarding the President, they had not lost a single one.

Yet.

Over the past few days, Schroeder had considered alternative means of completing his assignment. Poison. Not possible. All food parcels were automatically sent to the Department of Agriculture for testing. If the contents were incapable of being analysed, or contained food that went off quickly, the parcels were destroyed, a fact which Roosevelt, who liked

oysters and shell fish, had been known to complain
about. Further, no White House food was ever ordered by phone, and never left to be delivered. It was
always bought on the spot and taken away immediately.

A parcel bomb was too chancy. Most of the President's mail was opened by someone else, and besides
every parcel was X-rayed at a special laboratory on
the grounds.

The Presidential train was always preceded by
pilot coaches containing Secret Service men. The distance between the trains varied from occasion to occasion, and in any case, probably due to the fact that he
could not brace himself against the movement of the
train like a normal person, the President hated speed.
So the Presidential train rarely traveled at more than
thirty-five miles an hour.

An attempt inside the White House was impossible. Getting in was difficult. Getting out afterwards,
impossible. And since McKinley was shot with a gun
concealed in a bandage, no visitor was allowed to approach the President unless his hands were exposed.
Of course, the White House was Washington's best
known fire trap, but that was too melodramatic a solution, and Schroeder could not rely on chance.

The newsreels confirmed his original decision.
The best place was in the street. There the President
only had the local police and the Secret Service detail
to protect him. Not even his car was bullet proof. The
President of the United States was only allowed seven
hundred and fifty dollars for his car. In that respect,
Schroeder thought ironically, Al Capone was better
off.

He was watching a motorcade in New York. Suddenly a man darted towards the President's car, waving a bottle. Drunk perhaps, innocently joyous, but
the Service Service were if anything, over zealous. In
a flash the forward right Secret Service man had de-

tached himself from the phalanx running beside the President's car and attacked the intruder. The man with the bottle was hurled to the ground and within seconds, the forward right position had been taken up by a man from the following car. It was smooth, controlled, effortless. Schroeder knew the routine. Deal with intruders as fast as possible, leave the police to make the arrests. Close the gap quickly and for the man by the President's shoulder, never under any circumstances leave your position, unless you are relieved.

The President was most vulnerable in a slow motorcade, or because of his infirmity, getting in or out of a car. Because of his infirmity the Secret Service always knew where he was. But if attacked, the President could neither duck or weave or dive or run. He was literally a sitting target.

And the newsreel he had just seen had given Schroeder an idea. He now knew exactly when and where he would make the attempt. He'd spotted the one thing the Secret Service had overlooked.

*   *   *

Viereck spotted the man while he was parking the Dodge outside his Eye Street apartment, a lumbering sort of fellow who looked like a middleweight wrestler turned beer salesman. Viereck had seen him lurking about the embassy, deduced from his arrogance and his brutal looks that he worked for the SD or the Gestapo.

"You waiting for me?" he asked in German.

"Nein—ja." The man hesitated in confusion. Then he said, "Yes."

"Let's go inside and talk."

The man's name was Helmut Schirach, and he was the SD agent in Washington. Why someone so doltish as Schirach had been assigned to Washington,

Viereck couldn't understand, unless the SD thought it a city of little importance.

"I have some questions for you from General Heydrich," Schirach said without preliminaries. "What were you doing in Geneva on the 27th of October? What are you doing in America now that the election is over?"

Viereck was irritated. He did not want to be involved in an internal war between intelligence agencies. Whether Canaris or Heydrich won that battle was a matter of indifference to him, as long as he could sell his talents to the victor. Also, Heydrich had no business sending an oaf like Schirach to question him. Schirach would have a hard time being a messenger boy for Western Union, let alone interrogating someone with the experience of George Viereck.

"My compliments to the General," Viereck said loftily, "but what I did in Geneva and what I am doing in America is none of his business."

Schirach lumbered to his feet, and spat his cigarette onto the floor. "You will tell me," he said. "That is an order."

"The General is well aware of the regulations governing activities of the Abwehr abroad," Viereck said. "If he has forgotten, no doubt you will remind him."

Schirach moved towards him. "You will tell me," he repeated ominously.

As he approached, Viereck eased out the silver plated Derringer he always carried. "Wait right there, Schirach, or you won't even be able to say hello to your General anymore."

Schirach stopped, staring wonderingly at the gun.

"You have a lot to learn in this business, young man," Viereck said. "The first lesson is, never telegraph your intentions. The second is, don't try to teach your grandfather to suck eggs."

"But General Heydrich—"

"You think you can walk in here and say General

Heydrich this and General Heydrich that, and I jump about and tell you everything? What are you, man? An imbecile? What did they send you to Washington for? To see if grass grows on your brain?"

"But I have orders—"

"Then show me the damn orders, fool. Prove to me that you are an officer of the SD."

The man took out his party card and put it on the table together with his SD membership card. The oaf walked round Washington with that, Viereck thought disgustedly. What were German agents coming to. The man gave Viereck a radio message from Heydrich.

Heydrich felt he was owed a favor. He wanted Viereck to take sides. Heydrich wanted van Osten.

Since his meeting with Schroeder, Viereck had worried about why he had to send details of a US Army Lieutenant who had been trained as a commando, to van Osten. Worried too about the unnecessary participation of US Intelligence in a plot to assassinate Roosevelt. Van Osten had told him less than he needed to know. It was the kind of situation for which Viereck required insurance.

He looked up at Schirach. "Tell Heydrich that what I have to say is much too important to be entrusted to an oaf like you. The General should contact me direct, by phone. Tell him I am forbidden the communication facilities of the Embassy."

"But the General is not in Berlin," Schirach protested.

"I shall wait until he returns," Viereck said.

16

Thursday, November 14, 1940. Bermuda.

Norah Bradley, Examiner at the British Imperial Censorship Office did not quite know what to make of the material in the brown envelope on her desk. It was addressed to a Paul van Osten at Auster Neuheit AG, in the Schoneburg area of Berlin and contained a photograph and typewritten letter which seemed like a normal item of business correspondence. She read the letter again.

Dear Paul,
          I thank you for the introduction
to the Sonndheim Novelty Manufacturing
Company. I met with their chief director
now, and he is very anxious to fulfil
our order. There are problems but of
small size. They say they cannot deliver
until 16th December and delivery will be
made at Union Station. I trust this will
not upset your customers. I am also
thinking they will have production
problems especially with the means of
delivery.
          However...

The letter meandered on for two more paragraphs, reporting on sales, the state of the writer's health and transmitting warmest wishes. At the end of the letter was a reference to the photograph.

I am enclosing a photograph of Fritz's boy. You will see how much he has grown.

Norah Bradley felt something was wrong. "Graham," she said to young Sommerville who shared the office with her and had been rejected by the Army because of flat feet. "Do we have anything on a Paul van Osten?"

Young Sommerville not only had flat feet. He had a horror of direct questions. "Just a second, Miss Bradley, just a second and I'll check." He picked up a black ledger and turned over the pages, murmuring, "Pee, pee, pee for Paul . . . should I look under P or O, Miss Bradley?"

"Don't shirk, Graham," Norah Bradley said icily. "Look under P and O and V."

Sommerville looked under P and O and V, muttering "Vee-ay, vee-ay, vee-o. No, Miss Bradley. Nothing on Paul van Osten," before snapping the ledger firmly shut.

Norah Bradley then asked young Sommerville to take the photograph and the letter to the lab. Half an hour later, the letter, the photograph and young Sommerville came back. The lab said the letter was clean.

"Oh dear," said Miss Bradley, "how boring." She wondered what to do next. Miss Bradley knew something was wrong. She felt something was wrong. Miss Bradley believed in intuition. She also believed in spirits. When she was in London, she talked to her deceased brother once a week. Here in Bermuda however, it was more difficult. There were no mediums, only witch doctors, and the spirits did not like the sunshine. Despite that, she *knew* there was something wrong with this letter.

She looked at it again. The Germans were using new secret inks these days, called 'Apis' and 'Betty', which required to be developed by complicated solutions of ferrous—chloride and salt, or calcium—ferro—cyanide and other things. Things had been much simpler in the Great War. She remembered then the Germans had used 'Pyramidon', a pain killer freely available at any chemist, and easily developed with iodine.

"Graham," she said, "take this back to the lab and ask them to try it with an iodine reagent."

"No one uses that kind of ink, these days," Sommerville said. The walk to the lab was hurting his feet, and besides he knew that the Germans were using a new technique called *Mikropunkt*.

"Do it," Miss Bradley ordered.

When Sommerville returned, he was running. He thrust the letter at Miss Bradley. On the reverse were the words, '*Doppel Adler*', followed by a short biography of someone called David Stannard.

Doppel Adler. Double Eagle. That was a coin worth twenty dollars. Not a young man with close cropped blond hair and a charmingly aggressive expression, wearing an open necked military shirt.

David Grover Stannard was twenty-five years old, going on twenty-six. His height was six foot two inches and he weighed one hundred and seventy pounds. His father was a lawyer, and his mother who had been a German actress, had died in 1933. There were dates set next to German cities, presumably the time the young man had spent in Germany as a child. He'd been in Europe every year since 1932, visiting Germany during the even years, and Switzerland and Austria in the odd. A very *bohemian* life.

It seemed that he'd skied on the American Olympic Team in 1936 and then fought in Spain for two years. He was a temporary Lieutenant in the United

States Army, was familiar with explosives, a good marksman, an expert skier, and expert also in unarmed combat. Quite a violent young man, Norah Bradley thought, and what was he doing anyway, getting mixed up with the Germans?

The young man reminded her of her cousin Mary's second son, except Mary's boy was only five feet eight.

This young man must be a spy. But then the Americans were not at war. And they didn't have spies. Perhaps he was a German spy. Oh dear, that would be disappointing. She decided to take the letter to Mr. Pennyworthy Upstairs.

Mr. Pennyworthy had also worked in Intelligence during the Great War, and at one time had shared an office with Sir Compton Mackenzie. After the war Sir Compton Mackenzie had returned to writing and Mr. Pennyworthy to his job in the Post Office. Now he was a Senior Examiner at the British Imperial Censorship Office and was generally referred to as Mr. Pennyworthy Upstairs.

Mr. Pennyworthy pursed his lips and blew through them as he looked at the photograph and the typewritten sheet. "You're quite right, Bradley. It looks pretty fishy."

"I knew it," Miss Bradley cried. "I knew it as soon as I felt the envelope. I had vibrations."

"You were quite right," Mr. Pennyworthy said. He paused and looked out of the window at the golden afternoon outside. Pity there was a war on. He'd quite like a paddle in the sea. He cleared his throat and said, "What I want you to do is this. Take copies."

"Yes, Mr. Pennyworthy," Miss Bradley said.

"Take one set of copies for us here and send a second set to the British Security Office in New York. They'll know what to do with this.

"And the letter?" Miss Bradley asked.

"Oh, when the ink has faded, send it on to Mr.

van Osten. I'm sure he wouldn't like to be kept waiting for his mail."

Thursday, November 14, 1940. Berlin.

Even though Heydrich had had to wait three hours to speak to Viereck it had been worth it. Even though they had spoken on an open line, Viereck had said more than enough.

Geneva was of no consequence. Viereck had gone there to collect funds for the Abwehr campaign against Roosevelt. Which solved the riddle of the disappearing Jew. *Judengeld!* But that was insignificant compared to the rest of Viereck's news.

Van Osten was conspiring with American intelligence to assassinate Roosevelt. Incredible! Totally, wildly unbelievable! But true.

The operation was called Double Eagle, and Viereck was monitoring Schroeder's plans for murder. And why Viereck, Heydrich thought. Why should a miserable old has-been like Viereck control the assassination of the century? What had van Osten to do that was more important than that? And why Double Eagle? Double Eagle was an American coin. It was also the two-headed eagle on the old Austrian flag.

A two-headed eagle? That wasn't Roosevelt. Roosevelt had nothing to do with Austria. Hitler? Was that why American intelligence were co-operating with van Osten? Was that why van Osten was going to the Arlberg?

He picked up the phone and called Heinrich Himmler. What, if anything, was happening in the Arlberg during the middle of December?

Himmler was surprised that Heydrich didn't know. Training exercises for winter operations had been scheduled for the Waffen SS.

Heydrich said he knew that. Was there anything else?

Himmler gave a disgusted snort. Yes, *die blode kuh* intended skiing in Lech at the same time.

Reynhard Heydrich smiled. *Die blode kuh* was Himmler's epithet for Eva Braun. And Mehl's last word had been Lech not Licht. Lech was where it would all happen!

"Is anything wrong?" Himmler asked.

"No, no," Heydrich said. "Quite the contrary, Herr Reichsführer. Everything is good. Very good."

So now he knew. Double Eagle, an exchange of assassinations. Roosevelt for Hitler. *Se non e vero, e molto ben trovator.* If it was not true, it certainly was a happy invention. God preserve that *wunderkind,* van Osten.

With Roosevelt dead America would not enter the war. The only people who would benefit from the Führer's death were the Army, the Abwehr and Göring. Göring! Göring had always wanted peace, also Canaris, the Abwehr, perhaps even van Osten. But neither Germany nor Heydrich needed peace. Not for two years. In two years, Reynhard Heydrich would be ready to succeed Adolf Hitler.

Still, Van Osten would not dare such an exercise without powerful support. Göring. Replacing Hitler with Himmler was no advantage for Germany and van Osten would see that. It had to be Göring. Göring must know and approve of van Osten's plan. If he could trap Göring now . . .

That was the brilliance of van Osten's plan. Van Osten was untouchable. Arrest him and Roosevelt lived, war with America became inevitable, and the man behind van Osten went free.

For now Heydrich had to support Double Eagle, had to monitor the operation, penetrate it. He looked at the list of van Osten's Alpenkommando. Cunning, not brutality, he thought.

Monday, November 18, 1940. Springfield, Va.

Stannard had just finished breakfast when he was summoned to Colonel Alan Berkeley's office.

"At ease," Berkeley said and leaning back in his chair, began to fill his pipe. "Sit down."

Stannard sat.

Berkeley concentrated on filling his pipe, stubby fingers kneading tobacco in the bowl. "I want you to know that you are the best Communist we've had through Springfield," Berkeley said. "And the best trainee."

"Yes?"

"I am telling you this because I don't want you to feel that anything has gone wrong with you, here at Springfield. I have orders to release you from Springfield immediately."

"But—"

Berkeley lighting his pipe, raised one finger from the bowl to silence Stannard's protest. "I know," he said, the phrase distorted by the clenching of his teeth around the mouthpiece. "I know," smoke trickling out of his mouth. "You haven't completed the course yet."

"I don't like leaving things unfinished."

"Well," Berkeley had his pipe drawing smoothly now. "You will finish it. But not in the way you think. You've been selected for a mission."

"In Spain?" That was the only place where he had operated. That was the only *logical* place to send him on a mission.

"I'm sorry, I have no details. All I know is that it is an important mission and they want the very best. That's you." Berkeley paused to look thoughtfully at Stannard. "I want you to return to your quarters immediately, pack up your belongings and report to Colonel Max Schroeder of G2 Army Intelligence at eleven o'clock today. You should confine your farewells to as few people as necessary. You don't owe any-one explanations."

A sudden thought struck Stannard. At Springfield they were very much cut off from the outside world. "We aren't at war yet, are we?"

Berkeley shook his head slowly. "You are, sol-dier," he said.

After Stannard left, Berkeley carried out the next part of his orders. Orders he didn't understand but which had come from Schroeder himself, in writing. He collected together Stannard's service record, the record of his courses at Springfield, his leave passes and mess bills, every official recognition of Stannard's existence and set them aside for transmission by mes-senger to Schroeder at G2. Then he called for the course registers and had Stannard's name obliterated. For the sake of proper records, he filed a copy of Schroeder's order in Stannard's empty file, scribbled across it that Stannard had been transferred to Dou-ble Eagle.

Monday, November 18, 1940. New York.

In the British Security Office on 86th Street, Laurence Cullen was the only person who'd heard of David Stannard. Stannard was an American skier, a downhill racer who had crashed badly at Garmisch–Partenkirchen. Cullen had been at the 1936 Winter Olympics. In 1936 he'd been one of M16's best men in Germany. Too good in fact. By 1937, the SD had a price on his head. Which was why HMG with a great show of compassion had returned him to England, and now, sent him away from the war zone to help create and run the British network in America.

Unlike Norah Bradley, Cullen did not get any vi-brations from the Stannard documents. Cullen was a man who dealt with facts. Fact one. There was no rea-son why a photograph and career history of a temporary Lieutenant in the United States Army should be sent to Germany. Fact two. There was even less reason for this information to be sent to Paul van Osten, who if Cullen remembered rightly, was one of those nicer Germans who worked for the Abwehr.

Those two facts led to an inescapable conclusion. Stannard was a spy. A spy for the Germans. The photograph and other details were being sent so that he could be officially recorded in their registers as an agent. As long as they maintained such bureaucracy, Cullen reflected, the Germans would never have an effective Secret Service.

He decided to run a check on David Stannard. A Lieutenant in the United States Army should prove easy to trace.

He was.

Monday, November 18, 1940.
Washington, D.C.

David Stannard marched smartly across the room, stopped two feet from Schroeder's desk, pounded to attention, snapped his arm in a salute.

Schroeder winced. No one had saluted him that close, that precisely and that noisily in two years. Stannard towered over him. Just over six feet, huge of shoulder, deep of chest, filling out the khaki shirt. Lithe too, an impression of taut animal energy. Clear, unrelenting eyes, a determined mouth and despite that, a good looking lad. Hard though, hard as stressed concrete. Schroeder couldn't have picked better.

"Sit down, soldier." Schroeder reached for a cheroot. "We're sending you to Germany. You leave on Wednesday's Clipper to Lisbon. From there you will go to Zürich. Here are your tickets, route and radio codes. Sign this form and a passport will be delivered to your hotel this afternoon." He pushed a fat envelope across the desk.

Stannard signed the form, opened the envelope and glanced casually at the contents.

"The codes are to be memorized and destroyed. Your cover is that of a physical education instructor on a skiing holiday."

Armchair colonel, Stannard thought. A civilian trying to look military and with so much evangelical fire in his eyes, the man must be a saint or a nutter. "Why am I traveling under my own name?"

Schroeder's mouth twisted petulantly. He didn't like being questioned. "We don't have the facilities for forging passports and we can't bring State in on this. Besides, to get out from Germany afterwards, you'll have to be one hundred per cent clean."

Stannard nodded. He had forgotten they sometimes checked passports at Bermuda.

"In Zürich you will be met and given a new identity which will take you into Germany. There you will report to Lieutenant Colonel Paul van Osten. Your cover will be that of a serving officer in the German Army."

"So if I'm found out, I get shot as a spy." He'd bet five to ten Schroeder had never seen real action in his life. All these intelligence freaks were like that. Theorists. Weirdos.

Schroeder didn't want to think of Stannard dying. "You mustn't be found out. So no calling up old friends, no frequenting old dives. You get out of sight and stay out of sight. There'll be plenty of time to visit people once this war is over. At your hotel in Zürich, there will be a crate containing a dozen high explosive incendiary bombs. You are familiar with their construction and use?"

"Yes. How will the bombs be delivered to Zürich?"

"As part of a diplomatic consignment to our attaché there." He saw the challenging look on Stannard's face. "He knows nothing about your operation."

"What do I do with van Osten?"

"Van Osten is going to blow up a chalet in Austria. I want you to monitor the operation, give me your opinion of van Osten's plans. You will not take part in the operation, however. Immediately after the chalet has been destroyed you will inform me of that fact on a fixed frequency radio that you will be given before you leave Washington."

"It doesn't seem much of a job," Stannard said. "Why can't van Osten destroy this chalet by himself and tell you about it afterwards?"

"Because I don't trust van Osten."

"Is it the chalet or the people inside the chalet who are important?"

"The people inside. Van Osten will tell you who they are at the appointed time."

Stannard threw the envelope on the desk and stood up. "Shove it," he said.

"What's that you said, soldier?"

"Shove it. A phrase customarily used to—"

"I know what it means." Schroeder's face colored. He hadn't been spoken to as crudely as that since he'd been a subaltern. "Even been on a charge, soldier?"

Stannard looked at him coolly. "Ever been in a war, Colonel?"

Schroeder realized he couldn't put Stannard on a charge without publicizing the fact that he was recruiting personnel from Springfield, and revealing the purpose of Stannard's mission. "Sit down," he said, quietly.

Stannard remained standing. "Let's get something straight, Colonel. If you want me to risk my life going into Germany, carrying bombs, masquerading as a German, you will forget all this smartass intelligence crap about need to know."

"You have to trust my judgment as to how much it is safe for you to know."

"No," Stannard said. "Where my life is concerned, *I'll* decide what I need to know." If Schroeder was going to put him on a charge he would have done so already. The fact that he had not done so was significant. "So you'd better make your mind up real fast, Colonel. Either you're running a proper intelligence operation or a treasure hunt."

Schroeder looked down at his desk, away from Stannard's implacable gaze. "You're going to Germany," he said, "to kill Adolf Hitler."

"Geronimo!" Stannard sat down fast.

"It's an irregular operation, irregularly authorized by an irregular President. Your control is me. Between us, we're going to stop this war."

For Schroeder and the President the war might stop, Stannard thought, but it was unlikely that he would live to see the peace.

"Will you do it?" Schroeder asked.

"Yes," Stannard said. There was nothing else he could say.

Tuesday, November 19, 1940. New York.

Laurence Cullen put down the phone from Colonel Alan Berkeley. Alan Berkeley was West Point Academy, an officer and a gentleman. Officers and gentlemen didn't lie. Colonel Alan Berkeley had just said, "There is no David Stannard at Springfield."

Worse. He had added, "There is no Lieutenant David Stannard in the entire US Army."

Brilliant officer though he might be, Berkeley could not know the name of every single lieutenant in the US Army. Which meant he was telling Cullen to mind his own damn business.

Cullen's business was finding out why Stannard's photograph had been sent to Paul van Osten. Berkeley had lied which meant the mailing of Stannard's photograph had official sanction.

If Stannard was a Springfield trainee, he was a doer, not a thinker. People like Stannard were only used on active missions. There was no conceivable reason why America should involve itself actively with Germany.

Which meant that it was not America, but certain persons in high places in America who had sent Stannard to Germany. Cullen recalled that Poland, Holland, Belgium, and France had been subdued by the Germany Army, only after they had been weakened from the inside by efficient fifth columnists. Had the High Command of the American Army been penetrated by the Germans? Improbable. America was too far from Europe, it's Army shared neither common tradition nor common training programs. But still Stannard was out of circulation and Berkeley had lied.

Cullen took the next flight to Washington. There was another way he could find out what had happened to David Stannard.

In Charlie's Bar on K Street, Sergeant Bill Kerr of the Fifth Commando Regiment said he'd taught David Stannard at Springfield. "Bloody good he was too, but then the lad had experience."

"Experience?"

"Yes. Two years in Spain. Operated as a guerrilla. Probably had more experience than all of us had at Guernsey. It seems he killed one of their Generals."

"Where's Stannard now?" Cullen asked.

"He's finished."

"Has he completed his course, then?"

"No. He had three weeks more to go. They shouldn't have taken him off. He was a bloody good lad."

"Did he get into any kind of trouble?"

"No. By the time we've done with them, those lads have no energy for trouble. He just didn't turn up yesterday. Or today. I had a word with his mate, a chap called Oldfield. He'd seen Stannard last morning, soon after breakfast. Stannard told him he was being transferred to another unit. All very hush hush. Couldn't tell Oldfield anything more about it."

Kerr looked at his empty glass.

"Want the other half?" Cullen ordered the drinks.

Kerr said, "There's something funny about this Stannard business."

"What especially?"

"This morning, his name wasn't on my roll."

"Because he'd been transferred to another course?"

"No. The name had been removed from the roll. It was as if he'd never been there."

"You're sure it wasn't a mistake?"

"Of course I'm bloody sure. After you called, I sneaked into Records and checked. Springfield has no trace of Stannard having been there. There is no file, no record sheet, no course report, no instructor's detail, nothing."

"But there must be some indication of where he's gone and what he's doing?"

Kerr shook his head. "There's only one thing," he said. "There's a piece of paper where his file should have been. Orders from a guy called Schroeder in G2 obliterating Stannard together with a note that he has been transferred to something called Double Eagle."

In New York, the next day, the Stannard affair, as Cullen was already calling it, grew more mysterious. Bermuda reported a David Stannard on board a Pan American Clipper bound for Lisbon.

Cullen radioed Lisbon, gave them a detailed description of Stannard, and asked them to put a six-man tail on him, all the way through Europe.

Afterwards, Cullen started to clear his desk. He decided that in order to find out what Double Eagle was all about, he'd have to work out of Washington.

17

Wednesday, November 27, 1940. Zurich.

David Stannard reached Zürich at 3:30 that afternoon and checked in at the Savoy Baur en Ville in the Paradeplatz just off the fashionable Banhofstrasse. That he thought was a luxurious mistake. No physical education instructor, even an American one, could afford first-class hotels in Zürich.

Stannard unpacked and showered. Then, he lay down on his bed and wondered how to pass the time in Zürich. In Washington he had been confined to a suite at the Madison. In New York he'd only been allowed to visit his father. Those restrictions did not apply to Zürich, which was just about his kind of luck. Fun in Zürich! Fun and Zürich were mutually incompatible. Some spook with a weird sense of humor must have planned his itinerary.

Stannard hadn't been in German-speaking Europe for four years. The last time it had been the Olympics. He could have beaten Schneider that day. Easily. That day everything had been right, especially the way he'd felt inside. He'd felt like gold. He remembered it clearly, streaking out of the gate, body crouched, wind whipping around his ears, the snow thrusting at him through his flexed knees. He'd been going like hell. At two hundred yards he'd already had half a second on Schneider. Then a binding had snapped and he'd cartwheeled into the trees.

Afterwards, the wise ones had said, more guts than sense, lucky to get away with only a fractured tibia. Stannard grinned ruefully. He'd never been that good before, he'd never be that good again, he'd never make it to an Olympic gold.

This year there were no Olympics. Stannard's grin widened. He wasn't even an amateur anymore.

The phone rang.

Stannard sat upright. It couldn't be for him. He didn't know anyone in Zürich. No one knew he was in Zürich.

The phone rang again.

It must be a mistake. It had to be a mistake. Then he remembered that he was going to be met at the Savoy. Perhaps his contact had arrived sixteen hours too early. He picked up the phone.

"Hello David, is that you?" A woman's voice, young, bright, cheery. Just what he needed, but how did she know who he was and where he was? The articulation was English, with the faintest hint of a continental inflection. Obviously an English girl who'd lived a long time in Europe.

"Who is this?" Stannard asked.

"Susan Witney, darling."

Susan Witney, darling or no darling, who the hell was Susan Witney?

"Oh! I don't suppose you remember I got married, did you? The name was Susan Lenglen. Do I have to remind you? Berlin, 1936."

Berlin 1936. Susan Lenglen. Stannard remembered. It had been after the accident and she'd come instead of her friend, the physiotherapist, who'd caught a bad cold and did not want to infect Stannard while his resistance was low. Susan Lenglen had taken him for a drive through the Grunewald. She had been impressed with the manner and cause of his accident. Olympic downhill skiers were a rarity in any girl's book, even if their resistance was low.

At the time he'd thought she was merely a celebrity hunter, and having notched up her score, would not return. But she had. Two or three times, when Stannard was able to hobble on crutches, and afterwards when he was able to walk, they'd had a brief and proper affair, with visits to the theater, tea at the Kempinski and sex in his apartment afterwards. They had not, he was certain, been in love.

The affair had petered out, when Stannard went to Spain and her father, who was a chemist for a Swiss pharmaceutical concern, was recalled to Basle. It had been one of those casual flings that spring up between likeable strangers in a foreign city. Stannard hadn't thought of Susan Lenglen or Witney as she was now called, for over two years.

Her voice came through the receiver, slightly raised, slightly anxious and slightly annoyed. "It is David Stannard I am speaking to, isn't it?"

"It is."

She laughed. "I'm so relieved. For a horrible moment I thought I'd been making advances to a dreary old Swiss. How long are you staying, David?"

"I don't know," Stannard said, which was the truth. Then he remembered that he should know. "Just tonight," he said.

"How awful! It's been such a long time, darling. I'd love to see you!"

But no one was supposed to know he was in Zürich. No one could have known he was in Zürich. So how the hell did Susan Lenglen/Whitney find him?

"What about the Witney side of the family?" Stannard asked.

"That went *kaput* a year ago. A quickie marriage and a quicker divorce. He got me on the rebound from you, darling. It was damn silly."

But not as silly as her story. Stannard was positive there'd never been any question of love or rebound, but he had to see her. He had to find out how she knew where he was, and he wanted to see her face, when she told him. "I'm going down to the bar for a drink," he said. "Could you meet me there? Perhaps we could have dinner afterwards?"

"I never thought you'd ask," she cried, voice quivering with excitement. "I'm just round the corner from you. I'll be in the bar before you get there." She put the phone down with a happy laugh.

* * *

She was seated at a corner table when Stannard got to the bar, and he felt mildly surprised at how attractive she really was. The intervening years had fined her down and given her poise. The long hands were still beautiful, no cracked nail varnish now, and the long legs were still slender. She dressed better these days with accessories that matched. She was wearing a smartly tailored suit with a little beret fastened into her brown, page boy style hair. For a brief moment she looked impossibly younger. It was only when he went up to her that he saw the tiny lines about the eyes and mouth, the humor and brightness in the brown eyes, the assurance in the way she turned to greet him, that he realized that she was no longer half girl and half woman, and was far more attractive than she had been four years ago.

Stannard ordered a white lady for her and a gin and tonic for himself.

"I don't suppose you've taken up smoking yet," Susan said, selecting a Players from a pack on the table.

Stannard shook his head.

"I thought not." She gave him a book of matches so that he could light the cigarette for her, something she would never have had the confidence to do before.

"Tell me, darling, what brings you to Zürich for only one night?"

Stannard grinned. "What do you think? Skiing. I leave for Davos tomorrow."

"You don't! I've waited years for this moment, and you rush off to Davos. Why didn't you tell me you were coming?"

"I thought you lived in Basle, not Zürich. Which reminds me, how did you know I was here?"

"I saw you, my love, striding through those doors, over there. I couldn't talk to you then, because I was in a tram on the Banhofstrasse. As soon as I could, I called."

Stannard knew she was lying. Not from her expression or the inflection in her voice, but from the fact that Stannard had checked into the Savoy at around four o'clock. If she'd seen him then and was so much in love with him she would have got off that tram and called him immediately afterwards. And if she had seen him walk into the hotel, she must have seen the skis protruding over his shoulder.

"Let's eat," he said. "I'm famished."

* * *

She took his hand when they went in to dinner, released it reluctantly when they sat at the table. She kept looking at him with a strange intensity while they ate, and halfway through the meal, she placed her foot between his, and gripped his knee with her thighs. She spoke animatedly of what had happened to her since Berlin. Her father, whom David now remembered, worked for Hoffman La Roche, had been summoned back to Basle. She'd met Witney there, married him on impulse and gone to live in England. But it hadn't worked. It was him as much as her. He'd been too English and she'd . . . she had been foolish. She should have known that after David there couldn't have been anyone else.

As he told her about his teaching job she kneaded his knee between her thighs. It was disturbing and strangely pleasant. Not once did they talk of politics or war or what each of them were really doing.

Over the brandy she said, "Oh baby it's all over so soon."

"It needn't be," Stannard said. "Let's go upstairs."

She looked down at her glass and colored. "I can't, darling. I'd love to, but I can't," impulsively reaching out and placing his hands between both of hers. "You see, they know me here. My father lives in Zürich now." She laughed shamefacedly. "He's got a reputation to keep."

"I understand," Stannard said, even though he didn't. What the hell kind of game was she playing at? Ferreting him out pretending she loved him madly, thrusting her body at him, then discovering she couldn't go to bed. Any other girl and Stannard would have thought, cock-teaser.

"We can't go upstairs, but we can go to my place," she said still holding his hand. "My father is away in Basle, till Friday."

* * *

All the way in the taxi she chattered brightly, nervously, her hand clenching and unclenching in his.

Once inside the apartment she pulled him to her, covering his face with kisses, rubbing herself against him, crying, "Oh darling, darling, darling. Oh David!" Her hands already underneath his jacket, twisting hopelessly at his shoulders.

Stannard found himself tugging impatiently at her clothes, tugging at a brassiere that would not unhook. He wrenched her naked body to him, his mouth

covering hers, his hands fondling and kneading her
flesh. He'd forgotten how sexy she was, he'd forgotten
how lovely she was. God he'd forgotten . . .

They fell to the floor together, writhing on the
rug before the fireplace. He entered her hard and
fast, thrusting into her with hammer blows, pounding
her flesh. Her fingers twined themselves in his hair,
pulled his face to hers. "Oh David darling, darling,
please," her passion stimulating his, grunting as she
moved with him, at him, fast and furious, hard,
bright, wanting to fill her, till he could stand it no
more, and came in a long, shuddering release.

They made love another time, in her bed, slowly,
with less passion and more tenderness, Stannard working himself inside her and she seeming to rise up,
splay out, draw him down and down everlastingly
down into her. "Love me darling, love me, I loved you
always, David, David, it's been so long!"

Thursday, November 28, 1940. Zurich.

He came to the hotel in the grey morning, full of
a strange energy, his body vibratingly alive. Susan
Lenglen/Witney. Who would have thought it. He remembered her face underneath his, as he walked into
the lobby, the fast shut eyes and honey colored hair
streaming over the pillow. Who would have thought it,
Susan Lenglen/Witney. He didn't want to leave
Zürich. He didn't want to blow up a chalet. Was it
only last night he'd said that Zürich and fun were incompatible?

Stannard collected his key from the concierge and
went up to his room. There was a fresh smell to it, and
an air of abandonment. He stepped out of his clothes
as he crossed the room, opened his suitcase, stopped.
Stared. His clothes were not the way he'd left them.
The straps on his ski bag had been fastened one notch
looser than was his custom. In the bathroom, his razor

had been opened and his shaving cream taken out of its holder.

He slipped into a shirt and slacks, went downstairs to the storeroom. The case with the defused bombs and radio set was untouched. He returned to his room relieved.

As he'd guessed, Susan Lenglen/Witney had lured him away from the hotel so that someone could make a leisurely search of his room. Who? It had to be the Germans. Who else would be interested in what he was doing in Zürich.

So Susan Lenglen/Witney was a German spy. Should he let her know he knew, or should he pretend that nothing had happened and that he was only a physical education instructor on his way to Davos?

He took a taxi back to Susan's home. In daylight, he could see it was set back from the road, surrounded by a wall, protected from the street by a slender iron gate. A uniformed Swiss porter stood before the gate. The gentleman must be mistaken, he said. Doctor Lenglen and his daughter had gone away ten days ago and had not returned yet. No one had been in the house last night. He knew, because it was his duty to insure that no one entered the house in Doctor Lenglen's absence.

* * *

His contact arrived at precisely 10:30, a tall man, elegantly clad in a three-piece suit with a carnation in his button hole, a monocle in his left eye, a flourishing Prussian moustache and a dueling scar to complete the caricature of a German aristocrat. Stannard hoped his name wasn't van Osten. If it was, he was getting out fast.

The man greeted Stannard with a light click of the heels and an outstretched hand holding an engraved visiting card. "Baron Ewald von Kirkdorf," the man said.

Stannard didn't have a visiting card. For a confused moment, he tried a salute, but the Baron caught his hand.

"No, no my dear chap. You don't salute me because I am a Baron. I've done nothing to deserve it, and if you knew what my family had done you wouldn't want to salute anyway."

Von Kirkdorf stepped back and looked David up and down. "I trust you had a pleasant journey."

"It was slow."

"Ah, that's the French for you. We Germans are supremely efficient. Soon we will make the Italian railroads run on time."

If he went on like that, Stannard thought, he'd have to blow up his bloody chalet all by himself. "Perhaps the Italians don't want their trains to run on time."

"What the Italians want or don't want is of little concern. They will do as they are told, because the Führer says so." Von Kirkdorf sighed. "If they still won't run on time, I suppose we'll have to alter the timetables. It will never do if the German nation got a reputation for unpunctuality."

Stannard didn't know whether to laugh, or to be angry.

Von Kirkdorf stretched out a hand and ran finger and thumb thoughtfully along the lapel of Stannard's jacket. He clicked his tongue in disappointment. "American tailoring," he said. "*Mein Gott!* One would have thought they were still cutting bearskins for cavemen."

"There's nothing—"

Von Kirkdorf raised a finger imperiously. "I have some good German suits for you," he said. "Let us go up to your room and try them."

"But I don't want any German suits."

Von Kirkdorf smiled thinly. "Like the Italians, what you want or don't want doesn't matter."

They went up to Stannard's room, von Kirkdorf

ordering a porter to bring up an old, battered case that must have been expensive six years ago. "Napoleon was wrong," he said. "The English are not a nation of shopkeepers. They're a nation of tailors. I wish Hitler would decide to invade the place or make peace. I need another half dozen suits."

"Your country is at war," Stannard snapped, "and all you can think of is clothes."

Von Kirkdorf taking out a suit and laying it on the bed, turned and looked at him, icily. "Your country is not yet in the war," he said. "What, if anything, do you think about?"

"Conquering Germany," Stannard said tightly. "Like we did the last time."

"That would be nice. And afterwards we might even sell you Volkswagens, if the various ministries concerned can ever get together and build the wretched things." He held up a grey flannel suit. "Very German, don't you think? Admirably designed for a champagne salesman or a traveler in ladies lingerie. Put it on."

"I'm not putting it on," Stannard protested. "My own clothes are perfectly adequate."

"That's a matter of opinion," von Kirkdorf said. "They're much too vivid, especially for someone who is trying to cross the frontier masquerading as a German."

"Why the hell didn't you say that in the first place?"

Von Kirkdorf raised an eyebrow. "Should I have?"

While Stannard dressed, von Kirkdorf made him speak German, congratulated him on his command of the language and then, still speaking German, told him what they would do next. Stannard would store all his belongings in the hotel, except for his skis, the bombs and his passport. The passport would be hidden in a secret compartment in the bag von Kirkdorf had brought. Then he gave Stannard a passport in the name of Karl Schmidt, a driver's license, an identity card, a ration card, a book of petrol coupons and two letters from a sweetheart in Bremen. Karl Schmidt, von Kirkdorf explained, was exactly his age and exactly his build. "He is your *döppelganger,* only remember he was born in Bremen and has been working for the Abwehr in Switzerland for the last four months. Your direct superior is myself." Here von Kirkdorf bowed, "and your rank is that of Captain. You will address me as Major at all times when third parties are present."

"*Jawohl,*" Stannard said.

"Now," von Kirkdorf said, "we practice the salute to the almighty Schiklgruber who with some luck will not live a thousand years. You draw yourself up so," von Kirkdorf drew himself erect, pulling in his chest as he did so, "you stamp your heels so, and then you throw your arm upright at an angle of forty-five degrees to your shoulder, with a snapping motion of the elbow that should, if you are any good at saluting or do it often enough, dislocate it. We have more Generals on sick leave through saluting than through any other cause."

After Stannard had learned to salute satisfactorily von Kirkdorf asked him to check the contents of his suitcase.

"What's this?" Stannard held up a bottle of French perfume and two bottles of whisky.

"I should have thought it was obvious," von Kirkdorf said.

"I don't drink whisky," Stannard said, "and never use perfume."

"Good. Then once we have crossed the border, you can give them to me."

"But it's illegal to import these articles into Germany."

"Illegal for Germans, yes. For the Secret Service,

no. Customs will think it very suspicious if an Abwehr man returns to Germany without smuggling something. Is there anything you would like to take in?"

"Have you ever learned to say anything simply and concisely?" David asked.

"No," von Kirkdorf replied, "to do so would be boring, inartistic and rude."

They left soon afterwards in what was probably one of the last Duesenbergs built. It was an SJ with one of those magnificent straight eight, 420 cubic inch displacement engines made by Lycoming. It was installed in a handsome roadster chassis, and as von Kirkdorf showed him later, was capable of traveling at over a hundred and twenty miles an hour. Von Kirkdorf had the top down and though it was a trifle wintry, Stannard thought they left in considerable style.

Thursday, November 28, 1940. Berlin.

Two weeks previously, when Heydrich had decided to live with Double Eagle, he had ordered the Frontier Police to inform him of the movements of any of van Osten's Alpenkommando, across Germany's borders. As the Frontier Police were subordinate to the Passport and Aliens Service of the RSHA (Amt IV F) and the Kriminal-polizei (Amt. V), Heydrich's personal directive was carried out with total diligence and efficiency.

Ten minutes after von Kirkdorf and Stannard had crossed the German border, the information was on Heydrich's desk. At eight o'clock that morning Baron Ewald von Kirkdorf had crossed into Switzerland at Basle. He had returned shortly before noon, crossing at Schaffausen, accompanied by one Hauptmann Karl Schmidt, of the Abwehr. Particulars of von Kirkdorf's car and the perfume and whisky they had smuggled into Germany were annexed, but Heydrich had no interest in that. Heydrich was interested in the uncanny similarity between the physical details shown on

Hauptmann Schmidt's passport and the description of
David Stannard, sent to him by Viereck.

Amazing coincidence, he thought, though not
such an amazing coincidence, if you knew how it was
done. A more rewarding coincidence was the Gestapo
file on Stannard.

In January 1934 he had been involved in a dis-
turbance at a Berlin café, involving the civil rights of
one Hans Burckner. Stannard had been interrogated,
and as the offense was minor and Stannard was
American, released. The cross reference to Burckner's
file showed that Burckner had been arrested in November 1937, charged with "insidious attacks against
the government", tried by the People's Court and
transported to a concentration camp where he had
since died.

The Gestapo had been concerned at Stannard's
inclusion on the American Winter Olympics Team, but
in view of the Führer's directives on Olympic year and
the Olympic ideal, had not protested his entry into
Germany. Throughout his stay he had been kept under close and discreet surveillance but no evidence of
subversion was found, both during the Olympics and
the months afterwards, which Stannard spent in Germany recovering from his accident.

Stannard had subsequently served with the Inter-
national Brigade in Spain and was reputed to have organized the successful attack on General Mendenez. A
cart with bombs, a runaway Trojan burro, what an
ingenious idea, Heydrich thought. Stannard was obviously a resourceful, courageous and dangerous man.
Heydrich admired resourcefulness and courage, and
after reflection decided that Stannard's presence
made the odds on the success of van Osten's operation
a little too favorable.

He sent for Brandt, gave him Stannard's description and alias, told him he wanted Stannard to disappear. It had to be done discreetly. The Abwehr must

never know the truth, and there must be no direct confrontation with the Abwehr. It was important also that Stannard be buried under the name of Karl Schmidt, so the American Embassy would not be involved.

That done, Heydrich telephoned Colonel Erich Hoerlin of the SS Leibstandarte Adolf Hitler and reviewed the security arrangements for the chalet at Lech. Heydrich was satisfied that the perimeter fence around the chalet would prevent a runaway load of bombs from crashing into it.

Then, meticulous to the last, he had the personal details on Stannard's German passport checked with the Registry of Births and Deaths in Bremen. Afterwards he took a note of the passport number and requested the Foreign Ministry to confirm whether it was one of the many blanks they had issued to the Abwehr.

* * *

In Washington, some six hours later, Laurence Cullen received a message from Zürich. As expected, Stannard had arrived the previous day, and stayed at the Savoy Hotel. An opportunity had been created for his personal effects to be examined. Nothing had been found.

That morning he'd had an appointment with someone who looked like a German aristocrat. After talking for about an hour in his room, Stannard and the German had left in a Duesenberg roadster. The agent's taxi had not been able to keep up with the big car, which had been driven at a reckless speed all the way to Schaffausen, where together with Stannard, it crossed the border into Germany.

Blasted nuisance, Cullen thought. His German agents were very thin on the ground and he would have to expose them to the risk of trailing Stannard and finding out what Double Eagle was about.

18

Thursday, November 28, 1940. Berlin.

Berlin was full of men in uniform and military vehicles darted urgently about the city. There were bomb craters in the Tiergarten from the RAF raid two weeks ago, and an atmosphere of weird excitement, as if war and the possibility of unexpected death had given a purpose to people's lives.

Stannard was given an apartment near the Tiergarten, which was guarded at all times by two uniformed men. Here, von Kirkdorf said, Stannard's bombs and radio equipment would be safe from the routine searches the Gestapo made of hotels, and it was less likely that he would be subjected to the casual interrogation with which the Gestapo sometimes welcomed hotel guests.

The apartment was large with a splendid view over the park, comfortably furnished and well provisioned with drink and cigarettes. There was a connection in the wall for a radio aerial, but von Kirkdorf asked him not to send any messages as the radio monitoring system in Berlin was very good. Stannard refused von Kirkdorf's invitation to dinner. He knew that von Kirkdorf had set out from Berlin at five o'clock that morning and that they were to have a busy day tomorrow.

After von Kirkdorf left he checked over the equipment and thought about Susan Lenglen. According to the rules he should report the matter to Schroeder, who would pass the information over to the English. Susan had married an Englishman, was therefore English, had therefore committed, was committing, treason!

Susan would die.

There was a certain balance in that. Last night, she had presumed on an old affair to seduce him. To betray him. Last night, while opening her body to his, while taking and giving pleasure, she had sent him to his death. For that, she deserved to die. For that there was no forgiveness.

There was little food in the apartment so he decided to go out and eat. The apartment was in the Budapesterstrasse, not far from the Kudamm. Stannard decided to find a small place in a back street, where the chance of meeting an old acquaintance was remote. The guard waved him out into the darkened streets.

Blackout was a new experience, cars crawling past throwing tiny rectangles of light from shielded headlamps. No street lamps, curtains drawn in every building, every building black. In Spain, he'd been in the countryside. Bombing attacks on towns had been rare, but that had been another war. There hadn't been this darkness or the virtual absence of people on the streets. It was eerie, and unreal.

With some difficulty, he found a restaurant and ate. Underneath that supercilious exterior, von Kirkdorf had turned out to be extremely pleasant. He was a good officer, concerned about detail, hiding his concern under a mask of superficiality. He hadn't told

Stannard much about himself, and Stannard hadn't told him about Susan.

He finished his meal, surrendered his coupons and went back into the dark and empty streets, standing in the restaurant doorway to allow his eyes to adjust to the darkness. War was a hell of a business. Already he was involved in it, not knowing quite how or what he was supposed to be doing. He set off for the apartment. If not for war, he might even have fallen in love with Susan Lenglen. But war reduced everything to basics. People were what they were and you ceased to have illusions about them. What mattered were how people loved, lived, fought and died. That was all there was to it.

The footsteps interrupted his thoughts. He realized they'd been behind him, synchronized with his since he'd left the restaurant, fitting into a narrow rhythm. Now the footsteps had faltered, breaking the rhythm, making Stannard aware.

He didn't have a gun and wasn't carrying a knife. A knife would have been hard to explain, if he'd been stopped on the street by the Gestapo. In any case he hadn't been expecting trouble on his first night in Berlin.

Stannard increased his pace. The footsteps behind him accelerated. Stannard kept up the increased pace for ninety seconds, then slowed down to something below his normal pace.

The footsteps behind him continued at the faster pace. Perhaps the man had realized what Stannard was doing, and was trying to allay his suspicions. Stannard walked on, feeling his body tense as the footsteps drew nearer. They were the footsteps of a burly man, weighing about 190 pounds. The question, thought Stannard, was not how big, but how fast and allowed the man to draw closer to him.

If the man went by, he would do nothing. He would simply observe what the man did next. Then,

for the first time he felt that something was seriously
wrong. The man behind him was walking directly in
his tracks, not to one side as if he wished to overtake.
Stannard turned his head. The man was five feet behind him, a square, bulky figure in a dark overcoat,
hat pulled down over his face. Then a voice in front
and to the right of him said, "Stannard."

Instinctively Stannard looked in the direction of
the voice. At that moment the man behind him seized
his shoulders and pushed him into a recessed doorway.

There was another man there, also wearing dark
clothes. Stannard glimpsed a faint pallor of skin and
the gleam of eyes under a pulled down hat. Another
gleam too, solid and metallic. The man's gun was hardly
a foot from Stannard's stomach.

"*Was is Doppel Adler?*" the man asked. His German was strangely soft, an accent Stannard hadn't
heard before.

"*Was is Doppel Adler?*" the man repeated, more
urgently.

Stannard concentrated on the gun, and the grip
on his shoulders.

The men were too close, Stannard thought. Recessed doorways were no place for interrogations.
Without warning, he flexed his knees, lowering his
body, and loosening the grip of the man behind him.
At the same moment he swung his left hand outwards,
and slammed away the gun. His right hand shot forward in a straight arm jab, fingers folded over, tearing into the gunman's solar plexus. The man gasped,
folded, only to smash his chin against Stannard's vi-
ciously upraised elbow. The man's head rocked backwards, smashed into the door. The gun clattered to
the floor.

The man behind was trying a stranglehold. For a
moment Stannard leaned back, giving the man his
weight, then raising his foot he brought it savagely

down on the man's instep. The man screamed, loosened his grip. Then Stannard was tearing at the fingers round his throat, going for the little finger, twisting it back as he turned round to face the man holding him away, forcing the man to lean sideways, with the pressure on the trapped finger.

"Who are you?" Stannard asked.

He was answered by a shout. "What is going on there? What is happening?" A curtain was drawn back. Light fell across the street. There would be police and Gestapo, Stannard thought, and releasing the man's fingers, punched him hard to the body before stepping round him and running through the darkness to the apartment.

19

Friday, November 29, 1940. Berlin.

"Welcome to Berlin," Paul van Osten smiled.
"What does it feel like being Hauptmann Karl
Schmidt?" Stannard looked very like his photograph,
except the hair was more blond, the skin more
burned, the expression of relentless determination,
more emphatic. If looks were anything to go by,
Schroeder had sent him a good man.

"I've got a higher rank in this goddamn Army,"
Stannard grinned, "but lower pay. You guys would be
better off in the British Army."

"We haven't seen the British Army for so long,
that we're starting to think they've demobilized."

Van Osten was younger than Stannard had expected. He'd imagined a lieutenant colonel in the Abwehr to be nearly as old as Schroeder. But in war
time, Stannard reckoned, promotions came quickly
and wondered what van Osten had done to have
earned his.

Van Osten led Stannard over to the long table by
the window where the aerial photographs of Lech
were spread out. "It's a perfectly simple operation,"
van Osten said, "and I promised Schroeder that you
would be exposed to only the smallest risk."

Van Osten was something of an ascetic, Stannard thought. It showed in the leanness of the body, the steadfast expression in the light grey eyes. He had a good face, honest, with a sharp nose and firm mouth and a high, balding forehead. Stannard liked van Osten.

Van Osten placed a finger on the photograph, by the chalet nestling into the hillside. "That's our objective. We're going to take it out, with your bombs. On Sunday five of us leave for Hildesheim for training. Von Kirkdorf you have already met. The others are Josef Lipski, Heinz Guertner and Manfred Lessing. You will meet them at lunch."

Stannard approved of that. In clandestine operations it was necessary that people knew each other. Better still that they liked each other. But most important, that they trusted each other.

"At Hildesheim we train as parachutists and commandos."

"What combat experience have you all had?" Stannard asked.

Van Osten told him. He himself had been in action in Spain and also served with Guderian's XIX Corps in Poland.

Von Kirkdorf was an ex-member of the German Flying Sport Association which had once provided the legal basis for training 'amateurs' to fly. After a flying accident he had joined I/Luft and then, on van Osten's recommendation, transferred to the Abwehr. He'd been with von Kuechler's Third Army in Poland, and that summer, had spearheaded the 16th Airborne into Holland.

Dieter, van Osten thought, and remembered that Dieter was dead, and Lech had to go on. Heinz Guertner had joined the Abwehr fresh from Military Academy. He had seen service in France, but not much action.

Lessing was ex-police with experience in controlling street demonstrations and in unarmed combat. He was also an expert with explosives.

Lipski's experience covered street fighting in Warsaw, skirmishes on the German-Polish borders and a few months' service with the regular German Army.

"Why them?" Stannard asked.

"You work with what is available. They can ski and they can fight, and they are prepared to die. We cannot demand anything more."

There was no answer to that. "Tell me about the operation," Stannard said.

"On the night of the 14th December we will be parachuted to this place here." Van Osten pointed to a flat field about three hundred meters above the chalet. "We will remain concealed there until early evening when we will bomb the chalet. You will wait at this point here." Van Osten's finger moved to a narrow road about four hundred meters below and to the right of the chalet. "when you see the chalet explode you will immediately leave the area. You will not stop for anyone or anything." Van Osten's finger traced the small road that led from the point at which Stannard should wait, to what looked like a little village. "This village is called Warth. You will drive through it following the road to Au. Au should be high enough for you to transmit your message. There you will abandon your Alpenkommando uniform, equipment and your radio, change into civilian clothes that will be provided and drive as near as possible to the Swiss border. Then using your American passport you will cross over into Switzerland." Van Osten paused and smiled. "After that, all that remains is for me to wish you a pleasant journey home."

"What about you lot?"

"There will be transport waiting for us. We hope to be able to ski away afterwards."

"How will the chalet be guarded?"

"A perimeter fence, four machine gun nests and

sixteen members of the SS *Adolf Hitler Liebstandarte* patrolling the perimeter in shifts." Van Osten smiled. "And down here in Lech two divisions of the Waffen SS on winter training."

"And you still think you can do it?"

"We do not have the luxury of choice."

Stannard walked away from the table on which the photographs were laid out. "How many people know of this operation?"

"Max Schroeder, the five people involved in the operation and you."

"Wrong," Stannard turned. "Nine people know of this operation, or know enough to want to find out more." He told van Osten about Zürich and Susan Lenglen, about the two men who had attacked him the previous night.

Immediately van Osten thought, Heydrich! But if Heydrich knew about Stannard, he had to know about Double Eagle. But how could Heydrich know about Stannard? "The operation is secure," van Osten said, tightly. Even if Heydrich knew, he couldn't have Schroeder's man panic and call off the operation.

Stannard stared at him, impassively. That didn't explain Susan Lenglen or the two men. "You'll have to do better than that," he said flatly.

Van Osten asked for a description of Susan Lenglen and the men, for Susan Lenglen's address in Zürich and then gave instructions for Stannard's information to be checked.

When he finished, Stannard said, "There are two things I don't like about your plan."

"What, exactly do you not like?"

"With just two weeks training your group is going to do a night drop over mountains onto a snow covered field that looks as if it measures a hundred by forty. Five will get you ten, someone is going to drift off base, you're going to lose half your equipment and someone's going to get hurt."

"That's what von Kirkdorf says," van Osten replied. "It was my decision to use parachutes. As I see it, we go in early morning or late evening, when the parachutes will be relatively invisible against a grey winter sky." Van Osten smiled. "When there is light enough to see but not be seen. I agree we run a risk of losing some of our men and equipment. But if we go in by glider, and it crashes or lands in the wrong place, then the whole mission has to be written off."

"That's the chance you'll have to take," Stannard said. "If you lost half your men or half your equipment the mission is fucked up anyway. Besides, with the parachutes, you're landing much too close to the chalet."

"It's above the tree line," van Osten protested. "The trees will give us cover."

"Not if the Waffen SS run into you on a training exercise. Also, the plane carrying parachutists must get closer in than one towing a glider. It has to be all or nothing, I'm afraid."

Van Osten thought about it. Finally he said, "Two of you and one of me. We still have some democracy in Germany. I agree. Ewald can fly the glider and we will land here, on the Zuger Tabel."

The proposed landing place was on the opposite side of the mountain to the chalet, probably a day's march away. "It looks fine," Stannard said.

He spent the rest of the morning going through van Osten's requisition list. He was amazed at the thought and planning that had gone into it. If he'd had that kind of support in Spain, he'd have smashed the entire Nationalist Army. It was a shame his role in Germany was restricted to that of an observer.

There were skis, snow shoes, sleds, snow smocks, emergency rations, a paraffin stove, whitewashed tin helmets, and instead of tents he had arranged for each man to be issued with ingenious white triangles called

Zeltbahns which could be used as capes, or joined together to make a light and convenient tent.

In addition each man would be issued four egg type grenades, a double-edged knife, a Walther P38 and an MP 38 machine pistol. They would also take with them one MG 34 machine gun, ten belts of ammunition for it and one spare barrel, a mortar, the latest 8 cm Kurzer which van Osten said was only half the weight of the standard Granatwerfer. There would also be a flamethrower, again the latest model, weighing only fifteen kilos and projecting five jets of flame at over eight hundred degrees centigrade.

If anything, Stannard thought, they were over armed. The operation had more than an even chance of success, which was all that could be expected in the circumstances. Subject to his making a survey of Lech, Stannard told van Osten, he would tell Schroeder that.

* * *

For obvious reasons, the Abwehr did not have a staff canteen. They lunched instead in a private room at the Kaiserhof, each man filtering in separately, only Stannard and van Osten going in together. It was all very melodramatic, Stannard thought with amusement, then remembered that the operation had been penetrated.

Guertner was the only one in uniform, the single lieutenant's pip gleaming dully against the field grey with the distinctive apple green shoulder straps of the Panzer-grenadiers. He looked hardly more than twenty, much too young for this operation. He told Stannard he was looking forward to winter training, he would have won the Grand Slalom for Germany if there had been Olympics that year, instead of war.

Lessing was less effusive, a dark and beetle browed man with close set, suspicious eyes. Even if van Osten hadn't already told him, Stannard would have had little difficulty in spotting his police background. He was a watchful, calculating, mistrustful man who didn't say much and listened carefully to everything around him.

Lessing and Guertner should be replaced, Stannard decided. One was too young, the other too redolent of Gestapo. Which left von Kirkdorf and Lipski.

Von Kirkdorf was his usual effete, arrogant self. He sent the wine back twice, pretended he'd never met Stannard before. He was insufferably arrogant, but Stannard liked him. His coolness went deep and Stannard felt sure he would retain it under the most difficult circumstances.

Stannard liked Lipski too, a sturdy Pole with a drooping Mexican moustache and a shy smile that made his eyes sparkle. He spent most of the lunch baiting von Kirkdorf, offering him his monthly ration of petrol, so that there would be thirty-seven gallons more for the Duesenberg.

Afterwards, back in van Osten's office, Stannard asked about Guertner and Lessing.

"They have to stay," van Osten said. "It's too late to get anyone else." Then seeing Stannard's concern, "Don't worry, I've known Heinz Guertner all my life, and we have checked Lessing out thoroughly."

But Stannard still worried.

Saturday, November 30, 1940. Berlin.

"Die Fahne hoch, die Reihen fest geschlossen
SA marschiert in ruhig festen Schritt.
Kameraden die Rotfront and Reaktion erschlossen."

The beerkeller was pleasantly noisy and crowded. Smoke hung heavily about the low rafters. The young men in the far corner of the room sang with gusto, banging their steins and slopping beer over the top of the piano. Most of the men in the beerkeller were young, blond stalwarts wearing black uniforms on which the silver SS runes gleamed. Mingling freely with them were other men, not in uniform, some even dressed in sweaters and slacks. And there were women too, neat, clean, and well-dressed, chatting amiably to the young gods of the Reich.

"MARSCHIEREN MIT UNS IN IHREM GE- ISTE MIT."

The whole room joined in the last line of the Horst Wessel, even the two men playing chess at a table well away from the piano. In one of the booths lining the room, Heydrich banged his stein on the table with a final Geiste mit and smiled at his companion. "More veal? More beer?"

His companion chewing rapidly nodded. He had not eaten like this for months. A slender, dark-haired girl walked unselfconsciously up to the piano amidst a spattering of applause and began to sing.

Heydrich said, "As you see, we look after our own."

His companion knew that the beerkeller was exclusive to members of the SS and SD, a place where food was not only available but cheap. He felt at home here, he felt he belonged.

"You must join us," Heydrich said.

"I'd like to."

"After you have finished your Alpenkommando training in Lech."

The man choked.

Heydrich eyed him coolly. "Don't be upset. We know what is going to happen in Lech. The SD knows everything."

"I was only told to report for training," his companion said, all appetite suddenly gone.

"We know, we know. What is going to happen isn't your fault. You have been misled by your superiors."

A blonde girl went by, wearing tights and carrying a tray. "Zigaren, zigaren."

Heydrich reached out, took two packs of cigarettes and tossed one to his companion. "You must tell me everything that is happening at Lech," he said. "Every little thing."

His companion started to eat again. "I always intended to," he said.

* * *

Even though it was late on Saturday night, Gestapo Inspector Wolff Brandt was in his office. The disposal of David Stannard alias Karl Schmidt was proving to be a more difficult problem than he had anticipated.

His men had spotted Stannard leaving the Abwehr offices in the Tirpitzufer, followed him to an apartment in the Budapesterstrasse. They had shadowed him for two days, and the only time Stannard had left the apartment was to travel to the Abwehr offices. He went back and forth in a staff car and his apartment was guarded by armed soldiers.

Brandt had waited in his office late that night, hoping, that being a Saturday, Stannard would have gone out to dinner, to a nightclub, or find himself a woman. But Brandt's agent had just telephoned. The lights in Stannard's apartment had been turned off and it seemed he had gone to bed.

Despite the lateness of the hour. Brandt felt Heydrich should be informed of the situation. Heydrich liked nightclubs and drinking. Brandt hoped that late on Saturday night he would be in a good mood.

To Brandt's relief, Heydrich was in an excellent mood. "My dear fellow, don't worry about a thing," he said in that high-pitched voice of his. "I will take care of everything for you. Let me call you back in five minutes."

Five minutes later, Heydrich called back. Stannard would be leaving for Munich the next day, to take a flight over the Arlberg. He would be alone, and if Brandt could manage it, he should get as much voluntary information as possible from Stannard, before finally disposing of him.

Saturday, November 30, 1940.
Washington, D.C.

Ever since he had decided to kill the President, Schroeder had become fascinated by the man's activities. He'd taken to buying every Washington newspaper and reading with great avidity the daily reports put out from the pressmen on board the *Tuscaloosa*. The President had caught a fish. The President had spoken to Harry Hopkins. The President was looking well. The President was looking forward to returning to Washington and getting on with the job.

One correspondent, however, revealed that the President would not be coming straight back to Washington. Before he returned, he would be visiting an ex-Harvard friend, who had an estate near Arlettesburg, Va.

Interesting, Schroeder thought all Roosevelt's friends were Establishment. Arlettesburg was interesting too. He would take Evelyn for a drive out there, tomorrow.

20

REPORT OF AGENT CLINTON KERMODE. 9/27/40
Subject, Carmel Panatour who lives at
Breaux Farm, Cayenne, Louis.

When interviewed, subject admitted
sending attached letter dated 9/5/40 to
the President of the United States.
Subject added that if I had come to get
him, then there was going to be
shooting. Subject is 5' 5", weight
approximately 120, receding brown hair,
close set brown eyes, thin scar across
nose, protruding ears, thin face,
pointed chin, narrow mouth.

Subject was born at Breaux Farm on
6/18/01. Breaux Farm is about twelve
acres, mainly poultry and livestock and
is about four miles south of Cayenne.
Subject lives alone. He has no family
and his parents are both dead. (Mother
12/2/16. Father 7/11/30.)

On 6/10/24 subject married Therese
Raquin, daughter of a local bar owner.
The marriage lasted just over one year,
Therese Raquin dying in childbirth on

September 6 1940

Mr President

    You aint goin to be President no more. You is wrong to run three times when Jefferson and Washington didnt. Your toady judges and smartass New Dealers aint goin to get you into the White House this time coo if you look like winning we is goin to stop you dead.

    We are the people you talk about in your fireside chats on the radio. We the farmers and the workers and the poor people of this nation think you is a pig. You work with the FAT PIGS in the oil companies and railroad companies and SCREW THE PEOPLE.

    In eight years you have not helped us. All you do is give work to your boys. You dont care about us farmers in Louisiana cos we are Hueys people and you were durn scared of him. You never earned a nickel in your goddam life so you dont know how us people really feel. We not going to let you be President again, thats for sure.

    When John Lewis was with the workers at General Motors you were cavhayin around with fat pigs like Astor and opening motels where men can go with women who are not their wives and innocent young girls get raped. For this you will BURN in HELL.

Your New Deal is bullshit. Seven million people are still out of work, starving etc. You know that better than us and you still run for President! But you're no good Mr President. Every idea you have you stole from Huey. Huey was a better man than you will ever be. You never thought of sharing wealth before Huey did 'cos Huey was smarter than you when he was in knee britches, than you are at sixty. But you try to be President three times and he not once.

You were right to be scared of Huey. We got news for you Mr Dictator President. You better stop running for President cos you shore never is going to make it. In my dream, Huey he told me so.

Huey talked to me in my dream. You cajuns fool away, he said. Whatever hicks want to do they got to do it for themselfs. You are letting the fellows in stripped pants take everything away from you. You are my friend. You must go in and stop them. You must REVENGE ME! There was blood on the white of his dress shirt when he said again REVENGE ME.

His blood memory is still hot in my eyes, Mr President. You did not shoot him but you paid for the bullets with your mothers money. If you become President a third time, then you will pay the blood price.

That I promise you.

7/18/25. A few months after her death
her family moved from the area. Subject
moved to New Orleans and is understood
to have taken a job as a traveling
salesman. His visits to Cayenne were
infrequent until shortly before the
death of his father.

Subject has lived at Breaux Farm since
his father's death. For a period of two
years after his father's death, he lived
at the farm with one Miss Sadie Stanton.
Miss Stanton left subject apparently due
to his prolonged and continued violence
towards her. Owner of Sho-Nuff Bar,
Cayenne, William MacMurfee confirms that
on at least three occasions he met Miss
Stanton in Cayenne when she had blacked
eyes, or bruises on her face.

After his return subject appears to have
taken interest in farming and local
politics. Worked actively for Huey Long
during his election campaign for United
States Senate. Subject apparently boasts
of close friendship with Long and his
associates. Shortly before Long's death,
subject maintained that on Long's
accession to Presidency he would
receive an important job in connection
with relieving the poverty of the
farmers in Louisiana.

Subject held for questioning on 10/7/33
in connection with a suspected breach of
Sullivan Act.

Subject charged with conspiracy to
murder William Carter, a journalist

opposed to Long. Charges dropped for lack of evidence.

Subject was held for questioning in connection with the murder of Hubert Frey, a lawyer opposed to Long. No charges brought.

1/2/35 subject held for questioning with regard to assault on Joseph Medwick, a politician who urged the reform of the Louisiana legislature. No charges brought.

Subject appears to have been gravely affected by death of Senator Long. The day after Senator Long's death, subject appeared in the Sho-Nuff Bar, brandishing a revolver and trying to collect a posse to avenge the Senator's death. At the time, subject was heard to state that Roosevelt's men were behind the murder of Senator Long and that he would get the bastards.

For the last few years subject has remained on the farm. His unpredictability and his unpremeditated violence appear to have made him less desirable to Long's successors. He has not participated in politics since 1935. He has a local reputation as a recluse and eccentric and on at least two occasions has fired shotguns at passersby in the belief that they wished to steal his land.

The annexed letter is the seventh the subject has written to the President.

It is not recommended that any charges
be made, though the subject should be
placed under special surveillance should
the President visit Louisiana.

*   *   *

The blacktop stretched for miles, reaching for the
low hung autumn sun. Huey's road. Before Huey
there had been thirty miles of paved road in the
whole goddamned state. Thirty miles! Before Huey
there had been no hospitals for the poor to go to, and
precious few schools. In a State crossed by rivers and
swamps there were few bridges, and those there were,
levied a toll. The State itself was run like a large company town, by the sugar, lumber, gas, electrical and
railroad interests, by rich politicians from New Orleans and Standard Oil.

In seven short years Huey changed all that. In
seven short years there were over two thousand five
hundred miles of paved road, there were schools and
free hospitals, there were free text books and toll free
bridges, there were night schools for adults and the
control of the corporations was broken.

There was also a thirty-four storey Capitol building in Baton Rouge in front of which now stood a gi-
gantic bronze statue of Huey Long, wearing a double-
breasted suit, bug-eyed as ever, looking like a
rumbustious traveling salesman. In those seven years
the power of the out of state corporations had passed
to Huey Long. Long personally controlled the legislature, the judges, the policemen, the tax collectors, the
banks and the governor.

Long had been born in Winn Parish, the sixth
child of a hog farmer and his fifteen-year-old bride.
Always precocious, with a voracious appetite for reading, he had completed the three-year law course at
Tulane University in eight months and was a lawyer

by the age of twenty-one. Afterwards, he served an appropriate novitiate for politics, by working as a traveling salesman for such diverse items as kerosine home lamps, Black Draught laxative and lard. In 1928 he had been elected governor. In 1932 he became a United States Senator, leaving Louisiana to be governed by a crony, appropriately called Okay. In 1935 he scared the shit out of Roosevelt and the Democratic Party.

Long was the first Southern politician since the eighteenth century to have a national vision. The dream had come to him at three o'clock one Washington morning, in the form of a political program where no one would have more than five million dollars and no family would earn more than a million, where every family would have a homestead worth five thousand dollars and an annual income of two to three thousand. Working hours were to be limited and holidays guaranteed. By the end of 1935 there were 27,431 chapters of Share the Wealth Societies throughout the nation. There were over four and a half million members, and if Long had run for President in 1936 there was no doubt that he would have drawn three to six million votes away from the Democrats and Roosevelt.

On the 8th September 1935 Long had returned to Louisiana to attend to some minor problem with the legislature. A frail young man was waiting for him. His name was Carl Weiss, a doctor whose father-in-law, a judge, had been thrown out of his job by manipulation of votes. As Huey strutted across the Capitol, Weiss shot him under the ribs with a small pistol.

Immediately Weiss was cut down, his body ribboned with sixty-one bullets. But it was too late. Two days later Long was dead.

Dead, but not forgotten. The poor of Louisiana in the bayous would not forget. The wool hats, the red necks, the cajuns would not forget. The Carmel Panatours would not forget. For now and always they were Huey's people.

* * *

Schroeder had taken four other names from the Secret Service files. One of the men was dead, another was in a mental home, and of the rest Panatour looked the most capable. The man was a loner, delicately unhinged, bitter. He'd never had anything, lost everything he'd loved. Had Therese Raquin borne him a child, his life might have been different. But she hadn't, so he'd become what he was, twisted and violent, obsessively reliving the few short moments in which Huey Long had brought a vestige of glamour into his tawdry life. Panatour had one advantage over all the others. Unlike most would-be murderers of Presidents, Panatour had participated in killing before. Which was why Schroeder had picked him.

Schroeder turned off the blacktop onto gravel, heading along the loop towards Cayenne. He'd been driving two days, southwards, away from the cotton fields, the neat whitewashed shacks and big houses, driving towards the low red hills and clumps of black-jack, towards where the second growth pines clustered together amongst the black stubs of burning for sheep grass.

The pine forests of a long time ago had been cut down by the mills and the railroads. They'd put up the mills and laid the tracks and erected the commissaries and paid a dollar a day to the people swarming out of the broomsage. When there weren't any more pines the lumber mills and the railroad companies had gone. Gone too were the men with the broadcloth suits and gold rings on their chubby fingers. Only the dollar a day men remained watching the red clay earth wash away. There were about three hundred of such men in Cayenne, a dirty town that smelt and felt of hardness and poverty. Heads turned slowly as

Schroeder edged the Packard through the town and northwards again onto the dirt road, clouds of dust billowing behind the undulating suspension. Breaux Farm. He hoped Carmel Panatour was what he expected him to be.

Panatour was a short, slight, scruffy man with a receding forehead and pointed chin, eyes that were red rimmed and burned defensively like a frightened dog's, a lonely, terrified person, in whom the seeds of violence were not deeply buried. He wore filthy overalls, a tattered jersey, and cradled a shotgun aggressively across his chest.

"What you all want?"

The house behind him was a small rectangular box, grey and unpainted, with a tin roof and shuttered windows. Behind it was a row of gable-shaped chicken coops, a barn, a dilapidated stable and a hog trough. The far end of the farm must have been swampy, because against the bare ground it was unnaturally green.

"I want to talk," Schroeder said. "To talk about a dream. To talk about Huey Long."

The ancient flea-ridden dog that had come snarling out at him, wandered away and settled down beside the porch. Panatour swung the gun towards Schroeder. Hate now blazed in those red-rimmed eyes. "You git your ass outa here, do you hear me? You git movin' right away."

Schroeder shrugged and turned on his heel. "Blood on a white shirt," he said softly. "That's the way it was. The blood memory of Huey Long will not be revenged." He turned to face Panatour. "Huey laid down his life for the likes of you. For what? Once, when I was at his pappy's place Huey showed me the pig trough. I bet I dumped ten thousand gallons of swill into that trough, he said. I bet I slopped five hundred head of hogs out of this trough. And, he said, by God, I'm still pouring swill. Poor Huey."

"You git right out of here." But there was ño conviction in the man's voice.

"I'm going," Schroeder said. "I'm going."

"You ain't from these parts. You got no right talking like that. We's Huey's people."

Schroeder said, "That is what Huey said to me. These are my people, for them I will even lay down my life. And he did. Now he speaks to me from beyond the grave and he says the men in striped trousers are stirring again. He says remind my people that no one does anything for hicks and cajuns except hicks and cajuns. Stop the fat pigs in Washington."

"When did Huey say that to you?"

"In my dream. Huey sent me here to find someone who would look after his people. To find someone who would revenge his death."

"You're like the last son of a bitch that came here," Panatour said. "You're from the FBI."

"No," Schroeder said. "I'm not from the FBI. I'm not from these parts. I worked with Huey in Washington, making things easy for him, so he wasn't bothered by corporation lawyers and such. Let me show you something." Very slowly Schroeder reached for the photograph he'd had the lab boys doctor. It was a photograph of an exuberant Huey Long, one hand raised in the air, the other slapping his thigh. And sharing the joke with him was none other than Max Schroeder. An expert could spot the differing gradation of background, but in the fading evening light, it was unlikely that a half crazed farmer would.

"Got any more pictures?" Panatour asked. The gun was now cradled under his arm and his shoulders hung slack.

"I haven't any more pictures on me," Schroeder said. "That is my favorite. That is how I always remember Huey."

Panatour thrust the photograph into his overalls

pocket. "I will keep this. I ain't got no pictures like this of Huey."

"I'll get you some," Schroeder promised.

"Come into the house," Panatour said.

They sat on the front porch and he brought out a jug of corn liquor. "It's good," Panatour said holding it up to his mouth, pouring it straight down the throat. He watched Schroeder acutely as he did the same.

"It's good," Schroeder agreed and tried to keep from spluttering.

"Tell me about Huey," Panatour said. "Tell me what it was like in Washington."

Schroeder told him. For two hours, Schroeder told him, lies, fabrications, magazine stories, half remembered myth. He told him how Long had once pissed through another Senator's legs, how he had once received some high falutin' delegation in green pyjamas, how he'd danced through the Senate mocking Prince Franklin and Lord Corn Wallace.

At each anecdote, Panatour threw his head back and laughed, a high-pitched asthmatic wheeze, that made the tears start from his eyes. "That's our Huey," he would choke. "We is Huey's people!" And then he would pass the jug of corn liquor.

Then Schroeder told him how one month before he'd returned to Louisiana, Huey had told him that enemies were plotting his death. There was going to be one man, one gun, one bullet.

"But that's how it happened," Panatour cried. "One man, one gun, one bullet." He shook his head in amazement. "Goddamn it and Huey knew!"

Schroeder nodded sadly. "Yes, Huey knew. But he did it for you and for me. And now we sit here and drink corn liquor while his ghost walks the State, crying for revenge."

"I wanted to revenge him," Panatour said. "The night he died, I went into Cayenne but no one would come."

"Folks will come now," Schroeder said. "I'll come, I have it all arranged. It is what Huey wants. The only favor he asks."

Panatour looked down at the jug of liquor and said, "I have dreams too."

"I know," Schroeder said softly. "It is a sign that Huey wants you. Huey wants you to pull the trigger."

Suddenly Panatour erupted from his chair. "I'll kill the bastards!" he shouted. "I'll kill the son of a bitching bastards!"

Schroeder pulled him back into the chair. "Not now," he said urgently. "Not now. It has to be done in Washington. You and me together."

"None of the boys from here?"

Schroeder shook his head. "No. It has to be you. You're the one who has been chosen."

Panatour giggled. He liked it. He liked the idea of using the gun, pulling the trigger.

The rest of it was easy. Panatour agreed to come to stay on Rieber's farm. As they set out for Virginia, Schroeder felt the worst of it was over. Only the waiting was going to be difficult.

21

The autobahn was four lanes of dark and deserted carriageway. There was a gas shortage and
much private transport had been commandeered by
the Army. Besides that, long-distance travel at night
was hazardous, because of the danger of British air
raids and the more frightening danger of being
stopped and interrogated by the Gestapo.

Stannard was not worried about the prospect of
British air raids or the Gestapo. The last British raid
had been nearly a month ago, on the anniversary of
the 1923 beerhall putsch, and he'd been told in America, that the British were running short of bombers. So
far as the Gestapo were concerned, van Osten had
given Stannard a special pass, signed by Göring himself which stated that Hauptmann Karl Schmidt was
engaged on urgent Luftwaffe business and was not to
be hindered, delayed or interfered with.

He kept the Citroen at a steady 100 kph across
the flat plain from Nurnberg, heading towards the
Franconian Jura and Bayreuth. Van Osten had provided him with the Citroen, a Light Fifteen model,
barely two years old, with wide curved front wheel

arches separate from the body, and a sloped back radiator with chevrons. Driving to Munich yesterday he had found the car awkward, clumsy, had special difficulty with the gear lever protruding from the dashboard. Familiarity had however transformed that. With its front-wheel drive and ground hugging suspension, Stannard found it was possible to corner the car incredibly quickly, found that the heavy steering grew light and precise at speed, that the engine was unburstable. He felt at one with the car now; and could drive without thinking about it. He thought instead about his flight over Lech, earlier that afternoon.

Lech and the Arlberg had been covered in snow. A square, wire perimeter fence was being erected round the chalet with machine gun emplacements at each of the corners. The track which ran down across the ski lift to the large field above Lech was being broadened and built up into a motorable road.

The chalet itself was rather more than one thousand meters above Lech, built into the hillside so that its upper storey was level with the flattened slope of the hill that rose above it. About two hundred meters above the chalet the hill leveled out, dipped into a deep ridge before rising steeply again above the tree line to the narrow plateau on which van Osten had originally intended to drop his parachutists.

An attack could be made from the ridge, Stannard decided. If they could get there and if the two machine guns above the chalet could be eliminated.

Headlights blossomed in his driving mirror, vibrating over the concrete slabs of the autobahn. A car traveling very fast.

The hill on which the chalet stood was part of an interconnected range of mountains. It could be possible to get to the chalet in a day from the landing spot they had picked for the glider, far to the west and above the chalet, but still necessitating a climb of about four hundred meters and some treacherous travel across snow bound country. That way, they would approach the chalet and the ridge from the top, and if the attack were made in the early part of the shortening evenings, the attackers would be nearly invisible.

The most dangerous phase of the operation would be the attack on the chalet. There van Osten and his men would be outnumbered, but they would have the advantage of surprise. If their training was as thorough as their requisitions, they had more than an even chance of getting away with it. Of course one or more of them could be killed. But that was an acceptable risk. And all it needed was for one man to get through. One man with the bombs. One bullet riddled, dying man. If he got close enough to the chalet, Hitler would be killed. And if Hitler were killed, there would be peace and an end to the German nightmare.

The Citroen slowed as the autobahn climbed up the foothills of the Jura. Stannard gave the car more gas, twisted his rear view mirror over as the car behind him closed right up, filling his driving compartment with light. A big powerful car, traveling very fast. One moment it was behind him, the next it had drawn alongside, to pass. Stannard leaned forward to pick a lower gear for the steepening hill.

Out of the corner of his eye he saw a small orange flash, heard a sharp crack, felt a wild stinging of glass against his cheek. The other car was pulling away as he realized his window had been punctured, and that he had been shot at. The car was a black Mercedes already out of range of the Citroen's headlights. Stannard took his hand from his blood wet cheek, braked violently, heeled the Citroen over in a sweeping U turn. The car bounded over the central reservation, throwing its tail in a rapid, squealing lurch, responded instantaneously to the flick of the steering, the flooring of the throttle, swayed and straightened, accelerated rapidly down the fast lane back towards Munich.

He knew he'd been spotted in Munich, but he hadn't expected this. Waiting in the mess for the pilot of the Focke Wolf Fw 189a to finish warming up the engine, he'd been approached by a lieutenant wearing the black uniform and the death's head emblem of a tank destroyer crew. The man's name was Muller and he seemed to remember Stannard from a skirmish at Lys when Hauptmann Karl Schmidt had led a platoon against a Belgian T-13.

Stannard had known the man was lying. Schmidt's biography had made no reference to Belgium. Schmidt had been in intelligence throughout the war, working first in France and then in Zürich but the man refused to be dissuaded. He had met Hauptmann Karl Schmidt at Lys, had seen Hauptmann Karl Schmidt receive his tank destruction medal.

Stannard had tried to walk away. The man had followed, insisting that they had met afterwards in Bremen. Panzer Lieutenant Muller was probably just as big a fake as Hauptmann Karl Schmidt but Stannard had no way of proving that, or of getting away. Finally he had told Muller that he was with the Abwehr, and reminded him that careless talk cost lives. Before Muller could challenge that, the pilot had come in and announced that the aeroplane was ready.

Stannard kept his right foot pressed to the floor, pushing the Citroen to its maximum. But the maximum was not enough. The Citroen was a rugged, all day cruiser just able to make 160 kph. Unlike the Mercedes whose two and a half or three liters gave it a top speed of nearly 200 kph. It was being driven flat out too, overhauling the Citroen rapidly. An autobahn was no place to match manoeuvrability against power.

Stannard scanned the roadside for an exit. On a narrow, twisting road, perhaps he could keep them away. But he was heading the wrong way for Berlin, and unfamiliar with side roads. If he left the autobahn, he could drive into a dead end or run out of fuel. And that would be that.

The engine note kept up a sustained roar as he sped back to Nurnberg. Could he lose them in the town? No, Nurnberg was thirty kilometers away. They were closing up now, they would catch him easily in thirty kilometers.

Stannard waited. At Springfield they'd prepared him for a motorized war. The approaching headlights grew larger in his mirror. He'd done this once before at Springfield and written off a bulbous Ford sedan. With firmer suspension and front wheel drive he'd have a marginally better chance.

He hoped.

The headlights bored into his back, illuminated his dashboard with pale yellow luminosity. Above the sound of the racing engines, he heard the crack of a pistol shot.

Stannard touched the brake firmly, released it, swung the car quickly to the left, then threw in the clutch and yanked the wheel round to the right. The car flung itself sideways, seemed to teeter on the outer edges of its wheels. Angled headlamps flared across the central reservation and empty carriageway. The sound of squealing tires filled his ears, the stench of burning rubber his nostrils. He was pressed against the door as the car heeled over and for a moment he thought it would roll. Then he let out the clutch and floored the accelerator, twisting the car round upon itself, forcing it to spin with its own forward motion, seeing the world turn round with him, hearing an awful bumping and grinding, feeling the car shudder as if it would shake itself apart. Then he was round staring into the headlights of the onrushing Mercedes, driving towards it at seventy kilometers an hour.

The driver of the Mercedes had barely time to

react. Tires shrieked. The Mercedes nose dived on locked wheels. Its lightened rear end lifted, swung wildly sideways, snaked horribly towards the speeding Citroen. At the last moment the driver released the brakes and swerved. The swinging stubby tail of the Mercedes caught the Citroen a glancing blow. A headlamp shattered. The Mercedes swayed past, rising incongruously on two wheels. Stannard glimpsed an unwinding coil spring, a vibrating exhaust pipe, then the Mercedes was rolling over the central reservation, doors flying open like wings, glass and rubber curling through the night. Stannard gunned the Citroen across the reservation back onto the proper side of the road, stared wildly at the wavering beam of his single headlamp, took the Citroen up to its maximum speed and held it there, all the way to Berlin.

Monday, December 2, 1940. Washington, D.C.

There were far more uniforms about the room than at the beginning of the year, Laurence Cullen thought. It was as if America was consciously committed to war. Cullen was lunching with Alan Berkeley at the Services Club and conversation over the Russian salad and asparagus had been confined to whether America would enter the war and how the British were bearing up. Halfway through the steak and chicken Maryland, Cullen asked, "What's your man Stannard doing in Germany?"

Berkeley paused in his eating. "We have no one called Stannard."

"Then I take it that it's open season on Double Eagle," Cullen said. "I mean Double Eagle is nothing to do with you, is it? It's okay if we interfere?"

Berkeley looked down at his plate. "I can't talk about Double Eagle. It's A1 classified. And if I were you, I'd keep clear of it."

"Sorry," Cullen said. "You aren't at war with Germany. Yet you put a man into Germany. Why? We're interested. We have to know."

"I can't talk to you about it," Berkeley said. "I haven't the authority. I haven't the knowledge. I'll have to get clearance to talk to you about this."

"Do that," Cullen said. He looked down at his plate. "The steak is very good here."

Monday, December 2, 1940. Berlin.

Paul van Osten said, improbably, "Look at your face. You've been going with women again." That was a half joke. Van Osten still worried about Zürich and Susan Lenglen.

"Women with claws like glass splinters," Stannard said, and told van Osten about the shooting the previous night. "And there's nothing in your newspapers about an accident on the E6."

Van Osten had no doubt it was Heydrich. The men in Berlin, Susan Lenglen, the men in the Mercedes, all SD or Gestapo. "It would be better if you left Berlin," he said.

"You mean abandon the operation?"

"No. I mean you come training with us at Hildesheim. No one will be able to get to you there."

"Hell, Paul, I was railroaded into the American Army. What're you trying to do. Conscript me into the Wehrmacht?"

Van Osten laughed. "Yes, and when America enters the war you will end up shooting yourself. Think about it, David. You will be safer at Hildesheim."

"What happens if they find out I'm American?"

"Better than your being found in Berlin. At Hildesheim we will say you are an Abwehr recruit being trained for operations in America." He paused and lit one of his smelly cigarettes. "In our world there is no truth. Only interpretations of truth."

If he went to Hildesheim, Stannard thought, he'd

have a better idea of how the group was making out. He'd be right on top of the operation, know immediately if anything went seriously wrong. And there was no doubt it would be safer than Berlin.

"Also," van Osten said, "if you are going to check the requisitions against deliveries, and satisfy yourself that our equipment is adequate, it would be more convenient if we were together."

"Okay," Stannard said. "You've sold me."

"Meanwhile you'd better keep this." Van Osten gave Stannard his Walther.

Stannard hefted the gun, testing its weight and balance. "What have you found out about the men who attacked me in Berlin?" A pause while he realized he both wanted and didn't want to know about Susan Lenglen. "What have you found out about Zürich?"

"We do not know yet who attacked you in Berlin. One of our agents visited the address you gave us in Zürich. The apartment is occupied by an invalid doctor who has not left the house in two years. Neither he, his wife nor his housekeeper remember anyone like you or Susan Lenglen. Are you sure you got the right address?"

David nodded. "Check out her father. His name is Lenglen too. He is with Hoffman Laroche."

"We've already done that. Dr. Lenglen lives by himself in Basle and has done so since September 1939. His daughter Susan lives in Surrey with her ex-husband's family. He has not seen her since the war began."

And there was no way of quickly checking that. "Who is trying to stop this operation?"

"The Gestapo, Heydrich and the SD."

And they were on the periphery already, Stannard thought. Already he was under suspicion, which meant that someone had talked. "The raid cannot go on," he said. "You've got to abandon it."

"Impossible." Slowly van Osten crushed out his

cigarette. "We've waited sixteen months since the last attempt at Zossen. We will never get Hitler as unprotected as this again. We have to do it now, for all our sakes."

"With the Gestapo already on to you?"

"The Gestapo don't know. They're focusing on you, because they have learned of your arrival from Immigration. Don't worry. If they were only half certain, they'd pick us all up. But they haven't, and now they're going to lose you. Look David, they have only twelve days to find out. Twelve days isn't very long, and that is all the time we need."

Stannard allowed himself to be convinced. He wanted to be convinced. At the outset he'd determined that the elimination of Hitler was a good thing, and nothing would divert him from that. Even if he had to do it himself.

"So every hour is a victory," he murmured.

Van Osten tapped the photographs on his desk. "Let's be positive. Let's check how we're going to do it. Let's go over the plan of actual attack."

Their meeting went on for the rest of the morning and when it finished both men felt confident the attack would succeed.

Stannard was leaving the Abwehr offices when he saw the tourist, a small jockey-like man in an electric blue suit, carrying two cameras. Something about the man attracted Stannard's attention. There were few tourists in Berlin, fewer still parading along the Tirpitzufer. The man was looking directly at him and as Stannard stared inquiringly back, the man looked down into the lens of one of his cameras and took three rapid pictures.

"Wait!" Stannard shouted, launching himself down the steps. "Wait!"

But the man was already running up the street. Stannard raced after him taking one stride to the other's two. The little man was no athlete, was weighted down with cameras. Stannard overhauled him rapidly, was reaching out for his shoulder when his feet were kicked from under him and he sprawled forward on the pavement on knees and flattened forearms. Shoes rushed past his head as he collected himself, got to his feet, but it was too late. The camera-carrying little man and a burlier companion were climbing into a Mercedes parked at the top of the Tirpitzufer.

Monday, December 2, 1940.
Laurel, Maryland.

Panatour stood by the paddock in the hazy afternoon sunshine, a rumpled, brittle-looking figure. The grass around his feet was littered with spent cartridge cases. At the far end of the paddock were a row of targets. Schroeder noticed that the area around the bullseye on each of the targets was nearly shot away.

Panatour turned as he heard their voices, lifted the .303 Lee Enfield threateningly.

"This is a friend of Huey's," Schroeder called. "He has come a long way to meet you."

Panatour looked from one to the other of them, the rifle still held across his body.

"Good afternoon," Viereck said.

"You're no friend of Huey's," Panatour said. "You're not even American."

"Huey knew a lot of people in Washington," Schroeder said, persuasively. "Not all of them were Americans."

Panatour lifted the rifle to his shoulder, squinted along the barrel at Viereck. Schroeder heard the rustle of clothes as Viereck's hand moved towards the inside of his jacket.

"He's only got blanks," Schroeder muttered out of the side of his mouth, hoping Panatour hadn't found a box of live cartridges in the farmhouse.

Beside the wooden stock of the rifle, Panatour's

mouth quivered, his fingers curled round the trigger, appeared to press it twice, his body simulating the movement of recoil, the barrel moving from Viereck to Schroeder. "Bang, bang," Panatour said. "Both of you is dead." Then turning round he loosed off a shot at the target.

Slowly Viereck relaxed.

"You like my shooting, Max?" Panatour asked, still looking at the target.

"It's pretty good." Schroeder walked up to him. "Here, I brought you two more boxes of cartridges."

Panatour took them thoughtfully, then raised the rifle and fired again.

Back at the farmhouse, Viereck said, "He won't do. He's totally insane."

Schroeder said, "We're not concerned with the condition of his mind. All we're concerned about is whether he can shoot accurately."

"And whether he is under our control."

"Panatour is controllable," Schroeder said.

"Half controllable by you," Viereck snapped, "and that is not good enough. This job must be done by someone who knows what he is doing, someone who will be responsible to us."

"It isn't your operation," Schroeder said.

"You'd better get someone else."

"In that case the operation will have to be postponed until long after the weekend of the 14th."

A strange look crossed Viereck's face. "It will not be postponed," he said. "I will personally supervise it. I will accompany this mad man, carrying my own weapon, and see that the job is done properly."

"I don't know if I can make arrangements for two people."

"You must," Viereck insisted.

"But you—" Schroeder said, "you. When did you last fire a gun?"

"I have considerable experience with rifles and

revolvers. I fought in the Imperial Army and I belong to two rifle clubs in Washington. Now, will you tell me the time of the assassination and show me the place?"

Monday, December 2, 1940. Berlin.

Shortly after eight o'clock, walking with slow steps, the Führer came into the ante-room where Reynhard Heydrich waited. The Führer wore a simple field grey uniform with a white shirt and black tie. On his left breast was the Iron Cross First Class which he had won in 1918, together with the Black Ribbon of the wounded.

Heydrich jumped to his feet and saluted.

Hitler returned the salute with the familiar upraised arm. "We have just stopped for dinner, General," the Führer said. "Would you care to join us?"

Heydrich decided not. Dinners at the Reichschancellery were austere affairs. While Hitler was served his vegetarian food and Fachinger mineral water, the guests had soup, meat with vegetables and a sweet, accompanied by bottled beer or cheap wine. Moreover, there was no knowing how long the meal would go on, or who would be there. If some of the party intellectuals from Munich had been invited, Heydrich knew he would die of boredom.

"I am sorry, mein Führer. I have to return to the Wilhelmstrasse."

Hitler said, "You wish to see me on a matter that is urgent and personal."

"Yes. We have discovered the existence of a plot to assassinate yourself and Fraulein Braun when you visit Lech this month."

"And have you arrested the plotters?"

"No, mein Führer. We only know of the plot, not who the perpetrators are."

"They will not kill me," Hitler said. "As you well

know, there have been many attempts and none have succeeded. I am Germany's destiny. They cannot succeed."

"It is possible that either you or Fraulein Braun may be hurt in the attempt. I know that there will be two divisions of Waffen SS in the area, but the best they can do is exact retribution. They are little protection against a single fanatic."

Hitler said, "I have been greatly concerned about Fraulein Braun's skiing. She is very useful to us here, and she might break a leg."

Heydrich nodded sympathetically. He knew the Führer was also concerned about Fraulein Braun's sunbathing, in case she got skin cancer.

"But we will go to Lech," Hitler said. "My meeting cannot be postponed, the Führer cannot alter his arrangements every time some fanatic wants to kill him." Hitler paused, allowed those intense eyes to fix themselves on Heydrich. "Especially when there are so many clever young men in smart black uniforms, who will find these fanatics and eliminate them."

22

Wednesday, December 4, 1940.
Washington, D.C.

Cullen laid the photographs and extracts from David Stannard's service record on General Clark Winters' desk, then walked to the window and looked down at the Reflecting Pool with its images of grey sky, the Washington Monument and the Lincoln Memorial. Beyond the pool, Potomac Park was empty, the river beyond it ominously turgid. Over the far bank, an airplane moved like a silver arrow.

"You aren't in the war, yet you have an operative in Germany," Cullen said. "This is a photograph of your operative, taken outside Abwehr headquarters in Berlin. His name is David Stannard and we want to know what he is doing there."

Winters would have liked to have known too. He tapped the photograph with his finger. "This picture looks kind of blurred."

Cullen crossed over to the desk. "That's because it was sent by radio, through the courtesy of a friendly newspaper. I'll have more and better copies by Saturday."

Winters remembered how the British had exposed a German agent called Westrick with the help of friendly newspapers. Adverse publicity could harm

G2 far more than the President's enmity. "We're perfectly entitled to run an operation inside Germany," Winters said. "It's our war too."

"But we're the ones who are doing the fighting."

"You'd better discuss this with Max Schroeder. Let me get him in."

Schroeder came almost immediately, a well-built figure, fresh complexioned, smooth-faced, very military. He took care of himself, Cullen thought, but felt the man's paleness was disturbing. Those fair eyebrows and pale eyelashes deprived his face of all expression, except resentment.

Schroeder's lips tightened in suppressed annoyance as he studied the photographs. Viereck was an idiot to have sent information like that by ordinary mail. He put the documents back on the desk and looked directly at Cullen. "This information is correct. David Stannard is in Germany."

"The question, Colonel, is what is David Stannard doing in Germany?"

"I can't answer that, I'm afraid. His mission is to do with the Columbia Project." Schroeder turned to Winters. "You know how security-minded they are."

Cullen said, "Give us an outline without specifics."

Schroeder had his story prepared. "We're doing your dirty work for you. We're pulling out a scientist called Jaroslav Mayek who was kidnapped in Switzerland by the Gestapo. We have established lines with the Abwehr on this. So get off our backs and stay off." Schroeder knew Cullen would never be able to confirm that.

"Why are the Abwehr helping you?"

"Because we have certain common aims. Like preserving peace."

"Preserving peace," Cullen said bitterly. "The Germans are preserving peace!"

"And I wouldn't run to Hoover or the President

with this information, if I were you," Schroeder said. "The peace-loving American public might not take too kindly to the liaison between the British Security Office and certain domestic agencies."

When G2 (C) had refused to co-operate with the British, the President had brought about a secret alliance between the FBI and the British Secret Service. Hoover had insisted that no other government department should be aware of his alliance with the British Secret Service, not even State. Cullen was aware that both G2 and Naval Intelligence had refused to co-operate, knew too that if the secret was exposed, the British would have to cease operating inside America. "There is no such alliance," he said.

Schroeder smiled tightly. "And there is no one called David Stannard in Berlin."

Cullen said, "In that case, I'm sorry I've taken your time."

*   *   *

Back in his own office Schroeder decided that Cullen would not stop now. He'd bypassed Berkeley and gone to Winters. Now that he had been blocked he would go back to Berkeley, ask more questions, raise suspicions.

There was only one thing to do. Stannard had to be isolated. The chain that linked him to Schroeder and Springfield had to be broken. He sent a coded radio message to Berlin. "Double Eagle has been infiltrated. In future you will only accept orders signed by me and transmitted in this code. All other orders from whatever source will be ignored. Acknowledge."

*   *   *

Later that afternoon, Schroeder went over to Water Street where among the fish markets and boatyards was a jobbing printer. There he collected and paid for five hundred visiting cards in the name of

Mr. George C. Viereck of Viereck Industries Inc., whose offices were in New Jersey.

Then he called on the helpful young man at Ordnance.

"I have it ready for you, as promised," the young man said. "We pride ourselves on being able to deliver on time." He showed Schroeder an attaché case on the outside of which was fitted a telephone handset. Then he opened the case and showed Schroeder the apparatus inside. "Of course when we've done, the case will be sealed. I have left it like this so I can show you what happens. Your radio signal is transmitted by this," the young man picked up a small metal case, about twice as large as a packet of cigarettes, "and activates this device here." He pointed to a curved piece of metal. "That moves the plunger against the detonator."

The young man moved the plunger with his finger.

Schroeder closed his eyes.

"Relax," the young man said, "it isn't armed yet. If it was, both of us would be playing harps and singing hymns."

Schroeder looked round the room, estimating its size, wishing the young man wasn't so flippant. "I'll collect it on Friday," he said.

"Yeah, right," the young man replied. "And I promise your *kraut* won't know what hit him."

Thursday, December 5, 1940.
Hildesheim.

The fourth day of training and everyone except Stannard moved splay-legged and muscle bound, stiff as boards, peering at their surroundings with glazed, exhausted eyes. Van Osten had picked the toughest division in Germany to train the group for Lech, the 7th Air Division, the conquerors of Eben Emael.

Seven months ago, Eben Emael had been re-
garded as the most impregnable fortress in the whole
of Europe. Situated at the junction of the Meuse and
the Albert Canal, it consisted of a series of underground
galleries lined with steel and concrete, with gun towers
protected by armour plating and manned by 1,200 men.
Eben Emael had fallen to just 80 men from Hildesheim.

With that as an example, Lech should have been
a piece of cake. Except, with Eben Emael the 7th Air
Division had been able to practice for months, re-
hearsing landings on models of the fort, experimenting
with methods of effectively silencing its guns. No
such preparation was possible with Lech. For a start,
no one knew exactly what the situation would be on
the night of the 14th, and to train specifically for an
attack on the chalet would publicize their objective to
the whole division. More important, there was not
enough time.

So van Osten had insisted that the training course
made them as fit and tough as possible in the time
available.

Major Lothar Brauer accepted the challenge with
much *schadenfreude*. Each morning the group was
woken at 6:30 and taken for a run by an extremely fit
Stebsfeldwebel who had enough lung power at the
end of half an hour and three miles to bellow, "Keep
your bottoms moving there!" Then followed half an
hour of brisk calisthenics, breakfast and an hour's
gunnery. The rest of the morning was spent in practic-
ing close combat techniques or knife work, or if a sa-
distic instructor felt inclined, a route march with full
packs and lugging two light machine guns complete
with spare barrels and ammunition belts that weighed
five pounds each. They had an hour and a half to collapse over lunch which was followed by more running, jumping or climbing, all in full uniform, then
more gunnery before a merciful halt was called at
seven o'clock in the evening.

It was a vicious, body-breaking system, similar to the one employed at Springfield, with one fundamental difference. At Springfield they endeavored to build up endurance, self-confidence and initiative. Here they paid more attention to rigid discipline and created endurance by pushing a man beyond his limits. Everything was done by the clock, everything to order, everything was done over and over again until the set target was achieved.

Stannard's own exceptional fitness became a matter of comment. The Stebsfeldwebel wanted to know which regiment he had been attached to before joining the Abwehr and why he wasn't a parachutist. Guertner and Lessing, both of whom Stannard had bested in unarmed combat questioned him closely about his experiences during that belligerent summer of 1940.

Though the group was stiff and weary and sore, neither the routine nor the sheer physical arduousness had broken any of them. They were a good group, and lying in his cot that might, Stannard wished he was going with them to Lech.

Thursday, December 5, 1940.
Washington, D.C.

When Laurence Cullen called in at the Justice Department, all he had to do was insure that he had on a fresh white shirt and a newly pressed blue suit. Hoover insisted that everyone who worked for him or with him was always neat, clean and properly dressed. Cullen also took care to arrive five minutes early. Hoover was as punctual as he was precise.

Cullen had just enough time to pay his respects to the relics of former Public Enemy John Dillinger before he was ushered into the Director's presence.

Cullen placed copies of both sides of Viereck's letter, the photograph that had accompanied it, and the photograph taken outside Abwehr Headquarters, on Hoover's desk.

Hoover studied them intently, then said, "This boy's got no business in the US Army. He's got no business traveling abroad. None of those pinkos who fought in Spain are allowed passports."

Cullen said, "G2 (C) have put that man into Berlin to work with the Abwehr and pull out a very important scientist, who they allege was kidnapped by the Gestapo."

"Stannard's a Communist," Hoover said as if that were the end of the matter.

"There are also," Cullen continued, "three inconsistencies in the G2 story. Firstly, Stannard is not an intelligence operative. Secondly he cannot, however good he is, single-handedly bring out anyone from Germany. Thirdly his service records and details of his training at Springfield have been erased."

Hoover asked, "You're saying the Communists have penetrated G2?"

Cullen said, "I don't know about that. Why do you think Stannard's record has been erased?"

"Because if he is found out, there should be no connection with the United States. There is nothing so very unusual about that."

Cullen pointed to the photocopies of Viereck's letter. "What about the letter? Could you find the writer?"

Hoover studied the letter. "The address is probably a fake, we don't have the envelope or a copy of the postmark and it is nearly three weeks old. We haven't a hope in hell."

"I've instructed the Censor's Office to hold any other letters with similar handwriting."

Hoover sighed. "We'll have to wait till then. Anyway, what's your gripe about this boy Stannard being in Berlin?"

"Why," Cullen said. "I want to know why. Alan

Berkeley tells me his mission is so highly classified that he cannot even talk about it. All he is prepared to admit is that there is an operation called Double Eagle. Then Schroeder feeds me a cover story as full of holes as Gruyère cheese *and* he threatened to expose our relationship with the FBI."

Hoover's mouth tightened. "Backmail," he said. "I don't like blackmail." Cullen could see Hoover was worried about that. "I don't like blackmail," Hoover repeated. "Let's see what we've got on Max Schroeder."

"And David Stannard?"

The FBI's filing system was not as exhaustive as Reynhard Heydrich's, but it had a record of every known member of the Communist Party, past and present. In twenty minutes, both files were brought to Hoover's office.

Stannard's file contained much that Cullen already knew. A record of his family background, his skiing, his service in Spain. The new factors were the name of the general Stannard had killed, and the fact, that at the outbreak of the war, Stannard had attempted to join the British Army and been rejected because at the time they were not taking Americans.

As he read, Cullen theorized. Stannard was a known Communist, but had yet been selected for specialist training at Springfield. Whoever recruited him the second time must have known of his background, *and ignored it*. Which meant that others at Springfield were sympathetic to Communists, which meant that high up in the US Army, there were Communists, and which meant that Stannard's mission to Germany was to do with the Russians.

In August 1939, Communist Russia and Fascist Germany had entered into an alliance. It was an alliance of convenience and Cullen knew that it had proved expensive for Germany. They'd had to cede parts of Poland and Rumania, had to suffer increasing Russian domination of Eastern Europe. The alliance was not expected to last long. So the Russians could reasonably be using an American Communist. For what though? Stannard had killed Mendenez and surely the answer lay there. Stannard was in Berlin to kill somebody. Hitler? That was too simple and too obvious, but then Cullen knew that quite often the obvious answer was the right one.

He turned to Schroeder's file. His theory of Russian involvement fell apart. If the Russians were involved, they wouldn't have gone near Schroeder. Schroeder had supported the Townsendites, the Union Party, had close contacts with the Committee to Defend America First. Given the right geography, and historical context, Schroeder could now be jack booting up the Champs Elysées. Stannard and Schroeder, an alliance as unlikely as that between Germany and Russia. What the hell was Schroeder doing? Before dispatching Stannard to Germany on Double Eagle, he'd met with Meyer Lansky, extracted the names of five potential assassins from the files of the Secret Service. It had to be an assassination, Cullen thought. Having failed to get the right man through Secret Service records, he was using a soldier.

"Your people check any of this information on Schroeder, Mr. Hoover?"

"Yeah. We have copies of all those Secret Service files anyway. It's my boys who check up on the screwballs. When we learned that Schroeder was interested in these five people, I had them checked again. Horace Bush works as a clerk in a bookstore in Grand Rapids, Michigan. My agent reports that he is really quite a mild-mannered man, and writes nasty sounding letters to everybody, Republican, Democrat, Senator, Congressman, Mayor. He simply dislikes politicians. We've rated him as harmless.

"Patrick McNeady was located on a building site in New York. He is a heavy drinker, has not held a job down for more than three consecutive weeks. His problem is that he would like to be the first Catholic President.

"Abe Brodie is in the Rockville Mental Home and has been there for the past two years.

"James Emmanuel died three months ago.

"We were unable to find Carmel Panatour. Bush and McNeady said they'd met recently with a man, who could have been Schroeder."

"What about Panatour?"

"Lives on a run-down farm in Cayenne, Louisiana. A loner, who has in the past, taken off from time to time. He's taken off now. We're still looking for him."

Cullen said, "Schroeder has obviously been looking for a man to do a job. What did he see Lansky about?"

"We're trying to find someone who Lansky will talk to. We might have to use a body from Dewey's office."

That admission must have cost Hoover a lot, Cullen thought. Ever since Hoover had grabbed the headlines by arresting Lepke Buchalter in New York, the relationship between the FBI and the New York District Attorney's Office was strained.

"Why should Lansky talk to Dewey's boys?"

"He's keeping Dewey sweet because he wants to spring Lucky Luciano, and Dewey is the only man who can do that."

"I'd like a check made on Schroeder," Cullen said. "I'd like him tailed. I want to know what he's doing."

"You'd like the FBI to check on the Deputy Head of Counter-Intelligence in this country! I need to take on the United States Army, like I need a hole in the head. Don't you read the papers these days? Don't you know, the politicians are after me again? They're calling us the American OGPU. The *Times* calls me a punk in a squad car, and that Senator Dekes says I am a Broadway glamour boy and wants an inquiry into my affairs with women!" Hoover looked outraged.

"What Schroeder's doing might blow the whole world apart," Cullen said.

"What Schroeder does in Germany, is no concern of the FBI. As you know we are restricted to operating within the United States, and if I start inquiring into Schroeder's espionage missions, I'm going to get my face rubbed in it. I can't help you, Laurence. Not this time."

Cullen got to his feet. "I understand, Mr. Hoover."

"But there's nothing to stop you investigating this on your own."

And if he was found out, Cullen thought, he would be thrown out of America on his ear, and the British Security operation blown.

* * *

On his way back to his office, Cullen thought, the only other person who knew what Schroeder was after, was Lansky. Dewey would never co-operate with Hoover in getting to Lansky. There had to be another way.

When he got to the office, he took Bill Myers into his room. Myers was American and ran the Washington office. Before joining British Security he'd been a reporter on *The New York Times*. Now he asked Myers to get him a report on the trial and conviction of Lucky Luciano, and book him on that evening's flight to New York.

Myers worked fast. When Cullen boarded the DC 3 that evening, he carried in his briefcase a lengthy summary of Luciano's arrest and trial.

On the night of February 1, 1936, more than forty brothels in Manhattan and Brooklyn were raided by detectives working under Dewey's orders. Over a hundred prostitutes and pimps were arrested, and grilled for days. In time, some of them fingered Luciano.

When enough madams, hookers and pimps had implicated Luciano as the boss, Luciano was arrested, brought to New York and charged on ninety-one counts. Bail was set at a phenomenal $350,000.

The trial was a voyeur's delight. Hundreds of whores, madams and pimps paraded into court, and despite Luciano's protests that his business was gambling and horses, he was sentenced to serve thirty to fifty years.

All the way to New York, Cullen read the story of Luciano's trial and noted the names of everyone who had tried to help him.

Saturday, December 7, 1940.
Springfield, Va.

The horse and rider galloped across the field as if they were one, soaring over the fences with a smooth motion that was almost poetic. The horse was a bay hunter, big, over seventeen hands, powerful, his coat gleaming damply with sweat in the early morning sun. The rider was a slim grey-haired man and he crouched low in the saddle as they moved, urging the horse, ever faster, ever higher.

Until he'd been given the responsibility of administering Springfield, Colonel Alan Berkeley had been in the Third Cavalry. All his life he'd loved riding and horses, and here he was, nearly fifty, sitting behind a desk and riding only twice a week.

The big bay was the best horse he'd ever had, strong, intelligent and absolutely fearless. Berkeley felt you could point him at the Empire State and he'd take off.

Berkeley rode every Saturday and every Thursday whatever the weather. This particular Saturday was beautiful. The sun had already turned silver and the woods were golden, a thick layer of leaves over the track. The air was fresh, with just a hint of dampness, and the wind of their passage cleansed his face. He pointed the bay at the high fence that separated the spare acres of Springfield from Johnson Meadow. The bay thundered up to it, lifted its head slightly, checked its stride, gathered itself and jumped. Berkeley felt the animal's shoulders heave, felt himself lifted, up, up, weightless—

There was a sharp crack and Alan Berkeley's head exploded in a shower of bone and blood. He spun sideways and fell head downwards as the horse landed in a shower of earth. Suddenly relieved of weight, the horse galloped off across the meadow, dragging Berkeley along by the stirrups, bouncing what was left off his head against the springy turf.

23

Sunday, December 8, 1940. Berlin.

By next Sunday, van Osten thought, Germany
would have a new government. But he had a premoni-
tion about next Sunday. By then he was certain he
would be dead.

The thought had nagged at him all morning, irri-
tating as an uncontrollable flicker of the eyelid. He'd
thought that when he'd become a soldier, he'd come
to terms with death. But now that death was so un-
conscionably close, he realized that one never came to
terms with dying. He wanted to live. But training and
tradition forbade the cancelation of the operation. All
his life he'd been taught to be a patriot. His eyelid
flickered. Patriots had to die.

Stannard barged cheerily into his office. "Good
morning, good morning, good morning."

They'd returned to Berlin the previous evening,
to check the equipment delivered, against the list of
equipment ordered.

"You look depressed, Paul. What's the matter?"

Van Osten smiled wryly. "I've been thinking
about next Sunday, and frightening myself stupid."

You were always frightened before, Stannard
thought, frightened, or excited, or reckless. If you

were any good, you felt nothing after the mission started. After the mission started, you were always too absorbed in what had to be done. "I've got the butterflies too," Stannard grinned encouragingly. "It'll get worse before it gets better."

"Was it like that in Spain?"

"Yes, except then you didn't know what was going to happen next."

"What made you volunteer for Spain?"

"I was a Communist," Stannard said.

"If that's true, you should be trying to kill me, not Hitler. How did you get into the American Army?"

"I was too slow in the head and not fast enough on my feet."

"But they took you?"

"Dead right, they did. The fact is, even though I say so myself, I just happen to be very good at what I'm doing. Besides, I am no longer a Communist. I resigned from the Party years ago. You volunteered for Spain too?"

Van Osten grinned ruefully. "I wanted to see what war was like."

They went downstairs and began checking the equipment. For two hours they worked meticulously, opening the boxes and counting the grenades, turning the sleds over and checking the runners, counting the ammunition belts, freeing firing mechanisms from manufacturers' protective grease.

"Any news about the Lenglen girl?" Stannard asked, busily checking that a knife moved freely in and out of its sheath.

Van Osten shook his head.

"And the Gestapo have been quiet."

"I told you that's how it would be. I think this Lenglen girl told the Gestapo about you. But they dare not interfere with you, as long as you are under Abwehr protection. We only have to stall them for seven days more."

"I wonder," Stannard said. "What will happen after all this is over, Paul?"

"How do you mean?"

"I'm putting my neck into a noose. If it gets pulled tight, I'd like to die knowing it was for something worthwhile, and not easing the way for a second Hitler."

"There will never be another Hitler," van Osten said. "If we succeed, Germany will be preserved. Germany, not Nazi Germany. Hitler's fall will be followed by an Army takeover."

"The Werhmachet by any other name, still smells of cordite."

"The SS will be purged—"

"I suppose Göring said something like that in 1934."

"I worry about that," van Osten said. "I worry whether this experience will change me into someone like Göring or Himmler. I worry whether I can cope with power, should I achieve it. I am concerned that the Germany which succeeds this one, will be different."

"If you worry about those things, you're alright."

"I want the new Germany to be a democratic Germany, a republican Germany. When we are sure that Germany is strong both inside and out, then the Army will give way to a true people's government. I would like to see a Germany that combined the best of the Weimar Republic with the strength of the Third Reich."

Stannard grinned across at him. "For everyone's sake, I hope it works."

Van Osten made a drinking gesture. *"Prosit,"* he said.

Sunday, December 8, 1940.
Arlettesburg, Va.

Arlettesburg was the kind of town you either lived in or passed through. Most people passed through. If you were traveling south west, you drove down the Main Street side of the railway cutting, past the druggist, the hamburger stand, the saddle maker, the church, the Jackson Hotel, and the boardwalked Ellman's Grocery with its advertisements for Union Smoking Leaf and Crimson Couch Tobacco. If you were traveling north east, you drove along Elm Street, on the further side of the cutting, past the town hall, the school, the hardware store, the bar, the auto repair shop, and the Gayety Cinema.

Schroeder and Viereck and Panatour were not passing through. They were in the Jackson Hotel, the tallest building in Arlettesburg, three storeys and standing on the edge of the railway cutting. From the Jackson Hotel you could look down to the neat, white station, with its rows of flower beds and wicket fencing. At each end of the station was a covered overhead bridge which joined Arlettesburg together, as well as the up and down line station platforms.

Arlettesburg had a population of five hundred or so. This population doubled twice a year for the carnival. It was a staid, matronly sort of place, where nothing much happened. Yet on December 15 it would become famous.

On December 15, unlike thousands of other Americans, the President of the United States would stop at Arlettesburg on his way to Washington. The *Tuscaloosa* on which the President was taking his fishing holiday, was due back in Pensacola on the evening of the 14th. On the 15th afternoon, the President would break journey at Arlettesburg so that he could stay with friends who lived on a large estate some thirty miles from Arlettesburg. It was a private visit and it was the President's wish that it be quiet and discreet. The only people who had advance notice of the President's intentions were the railway and the security services.

"The first thing to remember," Schroeder was saying, "is that we get two cracks at him. If things aren't right when he arrives, then we have a second chance when he leaves." They were in a room on the topmost floor of the Jackson Hotel. From its window they had a perfect view of both the station platform and the station yard beyond.

"The time the President is most vulnerable is when he is being transferred from one conveyance to another, from train to wheelchair, from wheelchair to car. The transfer has to be made with some dignity. They cannot throw the President of the United States around like a sack of potatoes. They've got to do it slowly and easily. The average time for each transfer is two minutes. You can loose a lot of bullets in two minutes."

Schroeder pointed out of the window. "The train will stop around there. The President will disembark in his wheelchair, running down special ramps. He will be wheeled across the platform, the chair carried down the steps to the yard. Remember, he is here on a private visit. There will be no crowds, no bands, no speeches. He is not being met by the Presidential car. In the yard he will be transferred to a Lincoln belonging to his friends. His friends are going to be there huddling round him as he is loaded, making everything a little slower. Panatour will have all the time in the world."

"What about his bodyguards?" Viereck asked.

"They will surround him. That is what they are trained to do. But they will not expect nor can they protect the President against an attack from the sky." Schroeder smiled at the German. "Do you approve the time and place? 14:30 hours on Sunday the 15th December, Arlettesburg, Virginia."

"Yes," Viereck said. He looked across at Panatour. "Provided I am here with him."

"Don't want you," Panatour muttered. "Don't like you."

"George has to be here with you," Schroeder said. "He has to look after the radio equipment."

Panatour frowned at him.

"So that I can talk to you from the railway bridge."

"All right," Panatour said, "if I can talk to you on the radio as well."

Monday, December 9, 1940.
Washington, D.C.

Twenty minutes after the American Airlines DC3 had landed at Washington Airport, Cullen was in a cab, speeding across Highway Bridge to Hoover's office at the Department of Justice.

Cullen had had an exhausting weekend. He'd spent most of Saturday with Sir Cossop Guthrie, the very Prussian-looking baronet who headed the Security Division of British Security Co-ordination. The main task of Guthrie's Security Division was to prevent sabotage of British installations and shipments of war materials. It was an arduous task. At that time the British had nearly $4,000 million invested in armament production factories and stocks of arms, to say nothing of the twenty million tons or so of British shipping which used American harbors. Apart from this, there was the problem of the six million Germans and four million Italians living in the United States, a large number of whom were engaged in the production, distribution, loading and transport of British war materials. America, being neutral at the time, was under no special obligation to protect British property.

Nevertheless, Roosevelt had arranged for the Security Division to work with the FBI, the local Police and Customs and Port Officials to overcome this massive threat to British arms supplies.

The Division's biggest security problem was New York Harbor. Not only could anyone on the Staten Island Ferry see which British ships were in harbor, but they could freely observe what cargoes were being loaded. In addition, there was a higher than usual proportion of immigrants in the dock labor force, which meant a higher than normal proportion of Germans and Italians, to say nothing of Nationalist Indians, anti-British Irish, and Communists who were now pro-German. Memories of the massively successful German sabotage effort in World War I were extremely vivid at BSC.

Cullen's answer to minimizing the problem of New York Harbor was based on the observed fact that immigrants not only stuck together, but observed ethnic loyalties, traditions and social structures. This was especially true of the Italians. If the Italians could be directed to support the Government's war aims, then, not only would they refrain from acts of sabotage, but they would prevent others from doing so. There was only one organization that could direct and enforce Italian immigrant support for America's war policy. The Mafia. And only one man who could direct the Mafia, the *capo di capo re.*

There were however, two problems. Sir Cossop Guthrie was opposed in principle to working with gangsters. "It makes us no different from those Fascist thugs, over there, old boy," he maintained, and it was only after extensive consultations with his superiors at BSC and at Whitehall, and the quietly expressed support of American Naval Intelligence, that he reluctantly agreed. The other problem was of course that the *capo di capo re* was serving a sentence of thirty to fifty years in a maximum security prison at Dannemora.

Cullen's main concern, however, was not the security of New York Harbor, nor the release of Luciano. All Cullen wanted to do was to trade the idea of such a release for the information Schroeder had given Lansky. He'd seen Luciano's lawyer that morning.

"As I understand it," Cullen said, "before you can apply for executive clemency, one of three conditions must have been satisfied. One, you must have obtained new evidence. In Luciano's case, this is unlikely. Dewey had it sewn up too tight, and if you had the evidence, you'd be beating down the doors of a courtroom now, to have your client released. Two, the prisoner must be suffering from a terminal illness. At Luciano's age, this is unlikely. So we are left with three, the prisoner must have rendered service to the State. The customary and only form of service a prisoner can render is relaying information about someone else. Luciano cannot and will not do that."

"You didn't come here to tell me what was impossible," the lawyer said. "Tell me what you think Luciano can do."

Cullen told him, finishing with, "We will not only give your client this opportunity, but together with Naval Intelligence, we are prepared to go on record as doing so. Two more years and your client will have the basis upon which to apply for executive clemency."

The lawyer said, "Lucky's in Dannemora. People who know refer to it as Siberia. How can he do anything from there?"

"Arrangements can be made," Cullen said, "for his transfer to a less restrictive place."

"It's an interesting idea," the lawyer admitted. "But I'll have to think about it and talk to various people."

"You do that," Cullen said, "but there is something I want, shall we say as evidence of your good faith."

"What?"

Cullen told him.

The lawyer agreed. He would have to talk to Lansky, anyway.

At three thirty that afternoon, the lawyer had telephoned Cullen and told him who Schroeder was going to kill.

Even though it was after eight o'clock when Cullen got to Pennsylvania Avenue, Hoover was still there. "Hitler," he said, "I can't seriously oppose that. In fact, I think it is a very good idea."

"It may not be in accord with the agreed joint foreign policy of our two countries," Cullen said.

"I'm not a politician," Hoover said. "Presumably Schroeder has his orders. I do not have the right to interfere, nor do I want to."

*   *   *

Back in his own office, Cullen reviewed the facts. Hitler was going to be assassinated. The assassination was a joint operation run by the Abwehr and American Intelligence. The Germans were co-operating in getting rid of Hitler and there could be only one reason for that. The Germans wanted peace. Perhaps the Americans too. But what about the British? What did they want? It was an answer, Cullen decided, that would have to come from London.

He took a large swig of black coffee, belched, and looked at his watch. It was three thirty in the morning in London. Cullen decided that the problem could wait till the English working day began and booked a priority call to Stewart Mackenzie, the Head of M16.

Cullen was dozing at his desk when the call came through. It was ten o'clock in the morning in London, and Mackenzie was at a meeting with the Prime Minister. Because it was a priority call Cullen was transferred to Downing Street.

"Yes, Cullen, what is your problem?"

Cullen told him. "The question is, sir, do we want peace?"

There was a rumble of background noise, the clunking sound of a receiver being passed round. Then the voice, rich, deep, golden, as familiar as the chimes of Big Ben. "Mr. Cullen, you wish to know my government's attitude towards a negotiated peace. Our answer is this. On the brink of defeat we rejected a subservient peace. Now, on the brink of victory we demand unconditional surrender. There will be no negotiated peace with Nazi Germany."

"I understand, sir," Cullen said, and waited while the receiver was replaced.

He sat for a while in silence, then sent an urgent radio message to Zürich for immediate transmission to Berlin. Double Eagle was to be terminated. David Stannard was to be killed.

Tuesday, December 10, 1940.
Laurel, Maryland.

Schroeder sat on the back stoop of the farmhouse listening to Panatour sob. They'd drunk a bottle and a third of Jack Daniels and Panatour had turned maudlin. Hopefully he would cry himself to sleep.

The shooting of Alan Berkeley had unhinged Panatour. Somehow the leveling of a rifle, the sight of Berkeley's skull bursting on a crisp, autumn morning, had faulted the flimsy mechanism which held him together.

Schroeder remembered that at first, Panatour had been elated. That all the way back to the farm he had babbled continuously and incoherently about Huey Long, about his father, his wife, the farm, chickens, corn liquor, and the Sho-Nuff Bar. But afterwards he had not been able to bring himself to touch the rifle. Any rifle. Not even the Garrand MI which Schroeder had procured, fitted with a telescope of 2.2 magnification.

Now Panatour was crying to return to his farm near Cayenne.

"Carl Weiss," Schroeder said. "He had no call to kill Huey. He put a bullet into him because he was paid."

There was a long silence as Panatour pondered that, followed by a loud slurping as he pulled at the Jack Daniels. "He had no call to do that," Panatour said, the sobs dying out of his voice. "Huey was a good man."

"If Huey didn't die, we would have lived off the fat of the land. Big houses, big cars. We would have had respect."

"And not on a farm with chickens and pigs," Panatour said with slowly warming enthusiasm. "We could have had a place in Baton Rouge, with help, and fine things. We could've given parties."

"Sure, sure," Schroeder murmured. "Huey liked you. Used to say to me you were his strong man. His right arm. When people would hassle Huey here in Washington, or the newspapers would badmouth him, he would say, if Carmel were here, they wouldn't do that. Not if Carmel was here."

"I did lotsa things for Huey," Panatour said excitedly. "I was his strong man."

"Yeah, Huey told me about Willie Carter. Willie Carter was a no good sonofabitch."

"A no good sonofabitch. We beat him up real good. We held him, me and Red."

"Huey said you'd done more than that."

"We broke his fingers," Panatour cried, "one by one. Snap, snap, like that. We busted his jaw. And we kicked him with our boots. They went into his belly with an oomph, oomph, and the blood came out of his nose like froth."

"Huey told me you killed him," Schroeder said. "Huey was proud of you. He's proud of you now, for what you did on Thursday."

"You think Huey knows?"

"Of course he knows. His soul knows. He knows that we have taken revenge. That man on the horse. He was the person who taught Carl Weiss to shoot. He was the man who gave Weiss the gun."

"I'm glad I shot him," Panatour said.

"And we will kill the man who paid for the bullet? With his mother's money. We will kill Franklin D. Roosevelt."

Panatour didn't say anything. After a while he stood up and went into the house, taking the Garrand with him.

24

Laurence Cullen slumped in the rear seat of the Studebaker and looked at his watch. Two o'clock in the morning and where the hell was Schroeder?

He was parked almost directly opposite Schroeder's house in College Drive. It was a large colonial looking house, too large for the Schroeders. Schroeder had bought it soon after his son's death. Only he and his wife, Evelyn, lived there. They had no other children.

For the third night in succession, Schroeder had not returned to his colonial house or to his wife Evelyn.

It was only when he'd decided to tail Schroeder that Cullen realized how much he lacked in men and equipment. To tail Schroeder properly Cullen needed at least four cars and drivers. All he had was one tired Studebaker and three men, all of whom had been working round the clock since Sunday.

If he hoped to find why Schroeder wanted Hitler killed, why he was using two assassins to do it, he had to find out where Schroeder was spending his nights. So he had waited two nights outside Schroeder's

261

house, watching the lights go on and off in the rooms as Mrs. Schroeder moved about the place. She was an economical housewife, turning off lights as she left the rooms, but where was Schroeder?

Cullen raised his head and spoke to Bill Meyers slouching across the front seat. "Any joy?"

"Not a dickie bird."

"Is he screwing someone else?"

"Not in this town," Myers said. "Not in Washington. Gossip travels fast."

Cullen sighed. They'd had the same conversation at least fourteen times before. "Where the hell is he?" he demanded.

It was uncomfortable in the car and cold. He stared at the roof lining and wondered what to do.

He could try trailing Schroeder again tomorrow. It would be tricky to keep station without being spotted in rush hour traffic. Trickier still not to lose him. If he couldn't make contact tonight, he would have to risk that.

Suddenly Cullen had an idea. He sat up and tapped Myers on the shoulder. "Find me a telephone box," he said.

They found a pay phone three streets away. While Myers waited, Cullen got out and dialed Schroeder's number. The phone rang a long time before a woman's voice answered, with the number.

"Is Max there?" Cullen asked.

"No, who is this?"

"Do you know where he is?"

"Who is this?"

"A friend of yours, Evelyn," Cullen said. "Someone who'd like to be an even closer friend. I'd like to come round and do to you what Max is doing to a young lady right now. You're a lovely woman, Evelyn. I've watched you through those pink blinds in your bathroom. You have a lovely figure, full and fleshy, just the way I like it. We can have great times, Evelyn, wonderful times. I'm coming round now."

"No, no! Don't! Who are you?"

"Max doesn't care for you. If he did he wouldn't go with the kind of girl he does. But I do. I've admired you a long time. I'm coming now." Cullen slammed the phone down, cutting out Mrs. Schroeder's protests.

He climbed back into the car and said, "Keep cruising. We might have the law around here in a few minutes."

But Mrs. Schroeder obviously had a reluctance to call the law. Police cars with screaming sirens converging on 32 College Drive would be a subject of comment and unkind gossip for weeks. Forty-five minutes later there was no sign of any police cars.

Cullen had Myers stop by the telephone box, called Mrs. Schroeder again, made even more intimate suggestions.

He saw lights go on all over the house, Mrs. Schroeder's shadow race across the living room. Forty minutes later there was the sound of a car and Schroeder's dusty, square-shouldered Packard skidded to a stop in the gravel drive outside number 32. Schroeder raced in, came out ten minutes later carrying a bag, followed by Mrs. Schroeder. They climbed into the car and roared away. Cullen noticed they turned off the lights before they left.

"Okay Bill," Cullen said. "He's all yours. For God's sake don't lose him."

Schroeder drove the Packard fast along Michigan Avenue and Monroe Street, wheeling right into South Dakota Avenue, then left into Bladensburg Road. He drove fast all the way to Bladensburg, not lifting off as he roared through the town, heading towards Green Belt Park. There wasn't much traffic and Myers had to drive for a while on parking lights to avoid alerting Schroeder to the fact that he was being tailed. Past Green Belt, Schroeder speeded up, touching 70 at times until he reached Laurel. He was obviously in a tremendous hurry, not caring whether he was being followed or spotted by a police patrol. Shortly before Laurel he turned off sharply, followed a narrow secondary road and turned off again. Myers who had stopped without lights in the middle of the secondary road gave him two minutes and then drove slowly up to the point where Schroeder had turned off.

It was a narrow track barred by a gate and two armed guards. They could see Schroeder's lights wavering against the sky at the far end of the track. As they drove past, Cullen noticed that the gates and the armed men protected the entrance to a farm. It was called Crusader Farm and belonged to Charles Rieber.

It was still early morning in London, Cullen thought, as Myers turned the car around and headed back to Washington. As they drove, Cullen composed an urgent message for the head of M16. If the head of M16 could bring his influence to bear upon the Admiralty, Cullen could deal with Charles Rieber. And if he cracked Rieber, Schroeder's involvement in Double Eagle would be blown wide open.

He thought.

Thursday, December 12, 1940. Hildesheim.

The second week of training and the group was fitter, more experienced, more versatile, functioning as a coordinated unit. They'd lost their muscle soreness and were taking pride in their new found physical fitness. They'd worked with gliders, practiced mock attacks. Yesterday they had over-run a building held by ten tough paratroopers. Stannard was well pleased with their progress.

This afternoon they had half an hour to kill while they were waiting for a squad of paratroopers to set up an ambush. The Stebsfeldwebel suggested they practice jumping. Idleness was bad, and jumping was good for the leg muscles. The ditches were eight feet across and fifteen feet deep. They were to go at it in double strides, individually first, then together.

They were going for the last jump when it happened. They were racing along together, packs swinging, booted feet pounding the earth. As usual Stannard was slightly ahead of the others, his attention fixed on the yawning black hole in front of him. The take off point was ridged with scuff marks. Automatically he looked for a place where the earth wasn't broken, which would support his thrust, where his boot wouldn't catch.

Three, two, one. He drew breath, came down heavily on his right foot, kicked it into the earth, building up recoil. His leg muscles flexed, bunched, released, his legs straightening as he launched himself. He felt his heel lift. Then his straightening right leg was scooped away and he was flying lopsidedly through the air.

His breath caught. He glimpsed mud and leaves and debris, branches, bottles and stakes, old tires and rusting metal. He tried to pull his flailing arms to his sides, tried to curve his body so he could break his fall with an arm, fall rolling. But he had been traveling too fast and leaning too far forward.

The back of his neck crashed into the far side of the ditch. He felt a horrible jarring run right through his body, his breath smash out through clenched teeth. Then he was hurtling head downwards to the debris below, trying to wrench his body round, hands clawing into the dirt. A boot clanged into his helmet, and everything went.

Thursday, December 12, 1940.
Washington, D.C.

Cullen sat in the small but luxuriously furnished offices of Crusader Gulf. Perhaps in order to make their customers feel more secure, the office had been decorated to give an impression of age, with paneled walls and an artificially low ceiling, indifferent oil paintings and antique looking furniture with extremely modern joins. A soft-spoken secretary informed Cullen that Mr. Rieber would not keep him long and offered him a choice of tea, coffee, Coca Cola or lemonade.

Cullen chose coffee. Americans made tea so badly, perhaps as an indication of continuing support for those long ago tea saboteurs in Boston.

He'd nearly finished his coffee when the soft-spoken young lady ushered him into Rieber's office, offered him a seat and more coffee.

Cullen declined.

From behind his large and impressive desk, Rieber said, "Mr. Laurence Cullen, Representative of His Majesty's Foreign Service. What have you come to do for us? Repay the twenty-one billion dollars you borrowed in 1918?"

"Not quite Mr. Rieber," Cullen said. "Not quite. The ss *Nordik*, ss *Viking*, ss *Thor*. Do these names mean anything to you?"

"They sound like ships," Rieber said cautiously.

"How very astute of you. Now let's try something else. Thirty-three thousand tons of oil. What does that sound like, Mr. Rieber?"

"A hell of a lot of oil," Rieber said.

"My words, precisely. A hell of a lot of oil. I've come to inform you, unofficially of course, that the thirty-three thousand tons of oil aboard those three ships has been or will shortly be seized by the Royal Navy."

"Why tell me about it?"

"Because the oil is yours," Cullen said. "Don't interrupt me. I know what you're going to say. That through an assignment here and a lease there, the oil doesn't belong to you but to some dummy company in Caracas or Panama or Mexico City. If that is genuinely the case, I'm wasting my time. If that is genuinely the case, I shall bid you a very good morning and leave." Cullen stood up.

"Wait a moment," Rieber cried. "Sit down. Hold your horses. Wait." He watched Cullen as he sat down, selected a cigar and lit it. "Suppose I admit the oil is mine. What then?"

"I just wanted you to know you'd lost it."

"You've got no right to seize it. It is being shipped on neutral ships to a neutral country."

"Balls!" Cullen growled. "That oil is being shipped to Sweden for trans-shipment to Germany. You know that and I know that. You know that taking into account Sweden's oil reserves, thirty-three thousand tons is more than Sweden needs for this year *and* next year."

Rieber shook his head. "You still have to prove it, feller."

"I don't have to prove anything. I just tell the Royal Navy to seize something and they do it. Just like that. And it stays seized."

"I'll sue."

"Go ahead. By the time the courts reach a decision, the war will be over. And you won't get any sympathy from the courts for supplying belligerents. So you won't be able to claim for loss of excess profits. All you can claim for is the price the Swedes would have paid you."

Rieber realized that wouldn't work. The Swedish consignee was a dummy company, and could never afford the cost of the oil, let alone the profit he would have made.

"I shall make a protest to the State Department."

Cullen smiled. "You know as well as I do, all they're concerned about is whether to hang you or shoot you."

"This is piracy," Rieber cried.

Cullen's smile broadened. "It is," he agreed. "And now if I may, I will have that second cup of coffee. Just one sugar and no arsenic, thank you."

Cullen took his time sipping coffee and watching Rieber squirm. He watched the man considering other possibilities, alternatives, counter measures. Then he came back with the dealer's eternal cry. "Alright, what's the pay off? How much do you want?"

"Not how much," Cullen said. "What."

Rieber said, "Alright. I'll play your game. What do you want?"

"Max Schroeder," Cullen said. "I want you to deliver Max Schroeder. I want to know what he's doing on your farm."

Rieber went pale. For a moment Cullen thought he would faint. Then he took a deep breath and said, "What Max Schroeder does at Crusader Farm is nothing to do with me."

"No one else would believe you," Cullen said. "Not even your friends."

"I tell you Max Schroeder and that lunatic have nothing to do with me. I don't know what they are doing. I don't care what they are doing. They're nothing to do with me."

Lunatic, Cullen thought, Carmel Panatour. "What are they doing?" Cullen repeated.

"I've told you, I don't know. All Max does is come over every evening and they sit drinking my liquor and yarning about Huey Long. In the day time the looney practices with a rifle Max gave him. I think he's shot up over five hundred bucks worth of ammunition so far."

"What do they say about Huey Long?" Cullen asked.

"Schroeder doesn't say much. He just talks to the looney about the crazy things Huey used to do."

"And the looney?"

"He's going to get revenge for Huey's death."

"But Long was shot by Carl Weiss. Weiss was gunned down by Long's bodyguard. So where's the revenge?"

"It's not the bullet," Rieber said, "but the man behind the bullet they're after."

"And who was behind the bullet?"

Rieber shook his head. "You know, people say things. Some say it was Alf Landon, others say it was Roosevelt."

Cullen didn't say anything. But the moment he left Rieber's office he began running. He ran all the way to Hoover's office on Pennsylvania Avenue.

Thursday, December 12, 1940.
Aboard U.S.S. Tuscaloosa.

Until the battleship came it had been a pleasant cruise. They hadn't caught much fish, but the President had lazed around, talked about this and that, read, fiddled with his stamp collection, been fêted at Martinique, unwound, or as he put it, recharged his batteries.

Two days previously the battleship had swept alongside the *Tuscaloosa*, towering grey and imperious above it, white clad sailors swarming across its decks, the Union Jack fluttering proudly under the warm Caribbean sun. With much panache and presentation of arms a letter from Winston Churchill had been delivered to the President.

The President had read and re-read that letter.

He'd become inattentive and withdrawn. For two days he'd sat in his deck chair and brooded. And to-night, he had asked Harry Hopkins to his state room for cocktails. It was a sign that the President wanted to sound out his ideas.

"The English are running out of money," the President said, as he mixed Martinis. "So far they have spent over four thousand eight hundred million dollars on this war. They have about two thousand millions left, a lot of it in unmarketable investments. They need more guns, more ships, more airplanes, and much, much more."

Which meant that in three months, England would be out of the war. By law, America could only supply England with armaments on a cash and carry basis. Harry Hopkins did not believe the American people would want a closer involvement than that. He watched the President's hands as he poured out and shook the Martinis. They were fine hands, moved with a delicate precision. "We will not get involved," Hopkins said. It was as much a question as a suggestion. Hopkins had mixed feelings about Britain's impending defeat. Like most Americans he had admired them for their tremendous, and lonely battle against the Nazis. But there were still many things to be done inside America. In America, the richest nation in the world, people still had not enough to eat, people still lived in slums, people still looked for work. There were millions of unfortunates, American unfortunates, who needed help first.

"We are involved, Harry," the President said softly, handing him a Martini. "We have been given much. We owe much. We cannot, and will not deserve to be the greatest nation on this earth if we abandon our moral responsibilities."

Hopkins had heard that before. America, the bastion of democracy, had a duty to fight fascist dictatorships. America had a duty to preserve the freedom and dignity of less fortunate people in the world. "The American people do not want war," he said softly.

"I realize that," the President replied. "They voted for me, not for war. But whether we want it or not there will be war. Both in Europe and in Asia a showdown is inevitable."

The President had thought it out carefully. If Britain were conquered, the Germans would have the British Fleet. Whether they had that fleet or not, in two years, they could build themselves such a fleet. They could and would control the Atlantic.

With the American fleet divided, with outmoded and insufficient aircraft, a defense of the Atlantic sea board was impossible. The Germans could cross the Atlantic in stages, taking Iceland, Greenland, Newfoundland and so on. Or they could attack from the south, from the French port of Dakar moving into Brazil where they had much support. The distance from Dakar to Brazil was much shorter than that from Brazil to the Hampton Roads and there was nothing the American Navy could do about it.

"Besides," the President went on, "we have a great opportunity to strike a blow for world freedom. We are not going to help England so that she can continue to ride rough-shod over her colonies. There will be no British Empire after this war. We have a glorious opportunity to help the development of millions of people in Asia and Africa. A heaven-sent opportunity."

The President was rambling, but it was something Hopkins had experienced before. It was a subconscious process, a kind of mental clarification.

"And so we must help England now. It would be wrong to strip them to the bone while they fight alone, so that we can fight in our own good time."

"You still have to find a way," Hopkins said. "And you have to sell it to Congress and the people."

Roosevelt flashed a mischievous grin. "Cordell

Hull and Morgenthau are working on something like
that now. What do you think if we gave England a
massive loan?"

"Impossible," Hopkins replied. "They still owe us
for the last war."

Roosevelt's grin widened. "I thought you'd say
that. The people won't stand for that. Wouldn't stand
for a gift either." He drummed his fingers on the table.
"What do you think of lending them the arms they
need? It isn't a gift, is it? And not exactly a loan? After
all, if my neighbour's house is on fire and he needs to
borrow my hose . . ."

Thursday, December 12, 1940.
Washington, D.C.

"Schroeder and Panatour," Cullen panted,
"they're going to kill the President."

"You're disturbed, Laurence," Hoover said. "Your
tie is near your navel, and you're sweating and panting. Collect yourself."

"I have confirmation." Cullen fought to regain his
breath. "Rieber . . . told me . . . Carmel Panatour
. . . the ex-Huey Long frightener . . . he is on Rieber's farm near Laurel." He told Hoover about following Schroeder the previous night, of his conversation
with Rieber, and how Panatour spent all his time at
target practice.

"I don't buy it," Hoover said. "I can't believe an
officer in the United States Army would want to kill
his Commander in Chief. It doesn't make sense."

"It's the only thing that does," Cullen said. "It's
the only theory that fits the facts. We know Schroeder
personally checked the files of five potential Presidential assassins. We know he sent Stannard to Berlin to
kill Hitler. If he picked Panatour for the same job,
why does he hide him on a farm in Maryland? Why
are the Germans cooperating with Schroeder? Assum-

ing they want to get rid of Hitler, why do they involve an American in the attempt? Surely the Army that conquered Europe must have one man as good as Stannard."

Hoover pursed his lips thoughtfully. "What are you saying, Laurence?"

"I'm saying, that Schroeder has made a deal with the Abwehr. The life of Franklin Roosevelt for the life of Adolf Hitler. A double assassination. An exchange . . . of eagles."

"But why?" Hoover asked.

"Schroeder probably thinks that Germany without Hitler will seek peace. That America without Roosevelt, will not want war."

"Boy that's sensational! Sensational!"

"It's true."

Hoover stared thoughtfully at his desk. Then he picked up the phone and ordered a detachment of FBI men to get over to Crusader Farm and bring in Schroeder and Panatour. "I hope you're right," he said putting the phone down. "I hope you're right or I'm going to get my ass busted."

While they waited, they went through Schroeder's file. The death of his son, the breakdown of his wife, the appointment of General Clark Winters as Head of G2 (C), Schroeder's refusal to co-operate with Roosevelt and British Intelligence, all these parts of his existence took on a new and sinister meaning. There was also something new on the file. A photograph of Schroeder taking a photograph.

"We often take pictures of people who come to view the President," Hoover explained. "It forms good file material. That picture was taken on the 6th November, when Roosevelt returned to Washington after the Presidential elections."

But Cullen was thinking of something else. He was still thinking about it when the agents reported that Crusader Farm was deserted and Schroeder and Panatour were not to be found.

Hoover said, "What do we do now? I can't put out a full-scale alert for someone like Schroeder without more than just a theory that fits the facts."

"Union Station," Cullen said.

"What?"

"Union Station," Cullen repeated. "That's where they're going to do it."

"What do you mean?"

"The President is on holiday. He returns to Washington by train on the 16th. The train comes in to Union Station. Viereck's letter refers to a delivery being made at Union Station. You have a picture of Schroeder at Union Station. That's where they're going to do it."

"In that case," Hoover said quietly, "they can't be far from Washington."

"They must be found and apprehended," Cullen said.

"Not on just one more theory," Hoover replied. "Schroeder is too big to be picked up on that. He must be found and kept under surveillance. He must be caught in the act."

"What do you plan to do?"

"Two things. First we check all the hotels in Washington. Then we wrap up Union Station so tight that even an ant couldn't get through."

*　　*　　*

After the meeting with Cullen, Rieber had panicked. He had telephoned Schroeder and asked him to get Panatour off the farm. Send him back to Louisiana, drop him in a weighted sack to the bottom of the Potomac, push him in front of a streetcar, but get him out. Rieber wasn't involved anymore. This little episode had already cost him twenty-five thousand dollars and thirty-three thousand tons of oil.

Schroeder had been prepared for just such an

eventuality. The previous three days two men in a battered red Studebaker had been trying to tail him. Last afternoon, he had reserved the Presidential Suite at the Tamworth—Westchester in the name of George C. Viereck, using one of the business cards he'd had printed as evidence of identity, and paying for it in advance, in cash.

Schroeder understood Rieber's concern, but would not abandon his plan. Schroeder had always believed that men made events, that individuals had a religious obligation to fulfil their destinies. His destiny was Double Eagle. Double Eagle was his place in history.

Which was why, though tired and irritable from lack of sleep, he would stay with Panatour in the Presidential Suite of the Tamworth—Westchester, even though he knew he should spend this night with Evelyn, that he had always been with Evelyn on the anniversary of their boy's death.

In three days, he thought, the man who killed Bobby would himself be dead.

Panatour was humming to himself in the next room. Schroeder realized now that Panatour was crazy. Grew crazier every day. After Berkeley's killing he had taken to roaming the farm at night, threatening the guards, risking being shot as an intruder. Schroeder had had to stay with him, even though Evelyn never liked him being away at night. Panatour was dependent upon him, needed more and more of his time, more and more careful nursing to keep him sane.

But it was only till the 15th.

Friday, December 13, 1940. Washington, D.C.

At 3:35 that morning, a young FBI agent, sorting through the piles of registration cards discovered that Panatour was staying at the Tamworth—Westchester,

in the company of a man called George C. Viereck.
He immediately informed Hoover who ordered a
squad of FBI men into the hotel, covering all en-
trances and exits, moving into rooms on the same
floor and into the lobby. From now on, Hoover told
Cullen, Panatour wouldn't be able to go to the bathroom without the FBI's knowing it.

By the evening of the 13th, the plans for the protection of the President were complete. Union Station
was going to be covered with plainclothes policemen,
FBI agents, Secret Service men. It was going to be
sewn up so tight that anyone who sneezed out of turn
would be arrested. There would be men on the platforms, on the stairways, on the elevators, in the waiting rooms, on the gantrys, on the overhead bridges.
There would be men in the plaza outside and along the
roof. There would be men on roof tops and in hotel windows overlooking the route.

Ten minutes before the President arrived, Panatour would be apprehended. Schroeder too. And on
the morning of the 16th there would be a blimp hovering over the route with six armed FBI agents and a
two-way radio system.

It was, as Hoover pointed out, the security operation of the century. Friday the 13th was proving to be
his lucky day.

25

Friday, December 13, 1940.. Berlin.

It hadn't been an accident. Stannard hadn't stumbled, hadn't made a mistake. He had been deliberately tripped. Someone in the group had wanted to
remove him from Double Eagle. It would be easy if
he could remember who had been nearest to him at
the time. But he couldn't. All he remembered was the
ditch, the momentary sickening fear as he flailed
through the air, the debris, the jarring fall, the boot
smashing against his skull. Which meant that someone
in the group was a traitor.

Van Osten said that was impossible. The fall was
an accident. He knew the whole group. No one
wanted to injure Stannard. All the group wanted to do
was complete its assignment in Lech.

David stopped the Citroen outside the Budapesterstrasse apartment. The fall had shaken him, bruised
him severely, but he was still operational. He'd returned to Berlin to collect his belongings and help van
Osten supervise the loading of the trucks which were
taking the equipment to Hildesheim.

He switched off the engine and rubbed his eyes.
Strange, there were no guards outside the building.
But then why should there be guards? He'd been at

Hildesheim all week and was only returning to the apartment for an hour. He got out of the car and stretched stiffly before walking through the deserted lobby and up the single flight of stairs to the apartment.

The apartment smelt musty and damp. Stannard washed, changed, began to pack. He'd nearly done when there was a rapid knocking on the door, a woman's voice, urgent and low pitched. "David, David Stannard, David."

Stannard picked up the Walther and walked to the door. Standing to one side, he flung the door open.

Susan Lenglen stood pale and disheveled. Looking quickly over her shoulder, she entered the room and shut the door behind her.

"Hey, look what the cat brought in," Stannard said. "What's the trouble, kid? Looking for what your Gestapo friends missed out on the last time?"

She looked at him, brown eyes wide with fear. "You've got to get out of Germany, David. You've got to get out now." Her hands shook as she lit a cigarette. She sucked smoke deep into her lungs.

Stannard walked back to his suitcase, laid the Walther beside it, and resumed his packing. "Why?" he asked.

"Because they're going to kill you."

"Your Gestapo friends have already tried that twice, and failed. What makes you think they'll succeed this time?"

"Gestapo friends! What the hell do you mean, Gestapo friends? The orders to kill you have come from London."

"What's London got to do with this?"

"M15, 6, I don't know their bloody initials and numbers. But London wants Double Eagle stopped. London wants you stopped."

"What do you know about Double Eagle?"

"Only that you're going to kill Hitler, but that isn't all there is to it. Look David, Zürich was a set up. I admit that. I lied about having been in love with you. I lied about my ex-husband. His name was David too. I met him a year and a half after Berlin. I married him because I loved him. He was killed in a Spitfire over the English Channel, covering the retreat from Dunkirk. I came back to Switzerland to work for British Intelligence, because I had to do something to prevent more people like David being killed."

"And now it's true confession time, by courtesy of NBC Blue."

"Oh, don't be ridiculous. We were friends once, David. Not Zürich. Berlin, the year of the Olympics. I couldn't let them kill you, without giving you a chance. David, please, walk out of Double Eagle now."

"What's the British interest in Double Eagle?"

She pulled nervously at her cigarette. "I don't know the whole story. It's to do with that man Schroeder, who sent you here."

"What's the matter? Don't you people want peace?"

"What kind of peace do you think you'll achieve? Do you think Europe under Göring or Himmler will be so very different from Germany under Hitler?"

"It'll be different," Stannard said. "You'll see."

"You won't. One way or the other, you won't be alive to see it."

"What do you mean, one way or the other?"

"Schroeder's canceled you," Susan said. "Whether you succeed in this mission or not, you will be killed. Do you know that your records at Springfield have been erased? There's no trace of you there. You have been forgotten."

"I don't believe you."

"Believe what you like. There are two men downstairs who have been sent to kill you. If they don't get you, Schroeder will. David, walk out of Double Eagle now. Killing Hitler isn't going to change anything. It isn't going to bring peace. Walk out now, and we'll get you out of Germany in four hours."

"Sure," Stannard said. He fastened the strap on his case and picked up the Walther. He pointed it at Susan. "Turn around and place your hands behind you, fingers locked together. We're going downstairs in a moment, and as you're so keen to save my life, you go first."

Susan stood with her back to him, shoulders hunched. "Where will you cross the border afterwards?" she asked in a low voice.

"Lauterach," Stannard replied, before he could stop himself.

"I'll be waiting," she said and walked to the door.

Stannard walked up behind her, reached forward and opened the door. Pressing the gun into her back, he looked over her shoulder to both sides of the landing. Not a soul. "Forward march," he said.

They went out onto the landing, looked down. The two men lounging at the entrance to the apartments looked up. Stannard's fist tightened on the butt of the Walther. The men looked familiar. One was burly, about 190 pounds in a dark suit and snap brimmed felt hat. The other was smaller, dark suited too, his hat pulled low over his forehead. Stannard remembered the pale gleam of a face in a doorway on his first night in Berlin.

The smaller man said, "Stannard?"

They had guns in their hands, small .32 automatics. The bigger man was beckoning with his gun. Stannard edged Susan sideways along the landing towards the stairs.

One of the men cried, "Lenglen, keep away!"

Stannard reached sideways for the stairs, missed, stumbled. For a moment he was clear of Susan.

One of the men shouted, "Lenglen, run!"

David felt himself falling, felt Susan's hand reach behind, steady him.

"Lenglen!" Both men shouted at once.

But Stannard had already raised the Walther behind Susan's figure, fired between her shoulder and the banister, a carefully calculated shot that hit the burly man high in the shoulder. Immediately Stannard was racing past the girl. The second man was leveling his gun at him. Hardly pausing in mid stride David hurled his case at him.

The man raised his arms to take the shock, was knocked backwards, his hat lifting off his head as he fell. Stannard raced across the lobby, kicked the gun out of the man's reach.

"David!" he heard Susan cry, as he kicked the man in the face, kicked him again in the throat, broke his nose with the flat of his heel.

Susan was running across the lobby towards him. "Oh Jesus, what have you done?"

"He'll live," Stannard snapped. "Let's move, girl."

He rushed out on to the Budapesterstrasse, raced up to the Citroen. Stopped. Cursed. The Citroen rested on its wheel rims. All four tires had been slashed. Cautiously he looked up and down the darkened street. It was empty. Not a person, not a vehicle to be seen. A slim figure flitted between doorways.

"Stannard."

Stannard fired towards the voice. Stood by the Citroen waiting.

"Stannard." A voice from behind him now, to his left. Stannard looked around. They were nowhere and everywhere. He was trapped.

Suddenly the street was filled with light, the sound of racing engines, and squealing tires. Two cars raced up the Budapesterstrasse with blazing headlights, hand held spots scouring the doorways. Stannard hurled Susan down behind the Citroen, flung himself on top of her. The spot picked out a man in a black windcheater and tapered black trousers. He was stuffing something into his pocket, starting to run. There was a clatter of submachine gun fire. The man staggered, took two dancing steps, threw up his arms and fell on his face. From behind them a pistol shot. Then the harsh clatter of another submachine gun. Silence.

One of the cars drew up beside the Citroen. Slowly Stannard stood up, arms upraised. A raincoated figure came towards them, pistol gleaming darkly in his hand.

"Your papers."

Stannard handed over his identity card, and the letter from Göring.

The Gestapo officer looked at it, handed it back. "Well Hauptmann Schmidt, what is happening here?"

"Shooting," Stannard said. "I think they are spies. British spies."

"Interesting. Were they shooting at you?"

"I don't believe so. Fraulein Lenglen and I were walking to my car when this started."

"You live here?"

Stannard pointed to the flat. "Yes."

"Please come with us."

"I am sorry. I am just about to keep an important appointment."

"Who with?"

"With a senior member of the Abwehr. It is on the instructions of Reichsmarshall Göring. It cannot be delayed."

"Yes," the Gestapo officer said. "I have seen your letter."

"In that case, I would be grateful if you could possibly arrange to drop us at the Tirpitzufer. You see the tires of my car are *kaput*."

"I am sorry, Hauptmann Schmidt, I cannot take you to the Tirpitzufer. I must instead ask you to accompany me to my office. From there you can telephone and cancel your appointment."

"Don't be ridiculous, man. That appointment cannot be canceled. I am acting under the orders of Reichsmarshall Göring himself."

"You said that before. I am arresting you, Hauptmann Schmidt on the orders of General Heydrich himself. I suggest you come with me and we'll let the Generals fight it out among themselves."

*   *   *

Over at Abwehr headquarters Paul van Osten, Wilhelm Tropp, and Lothar Brauer were finalizing plans for the *coup d'état*. As soon as Hitler's death was confirmed, Brauer would receive a radio message saying, "The Eagles Have Been Fed." Brauer would immediately relay the same message to Tropp, who would notify Göring's special police group. Then all three battalions of his FJR 1 would leave for Berlin.

They re-checked the objectives and troop dispositions they had discussed at Carinhall. Göring himself would be at the Luftwaffe base in Hamburg, ostensibly on a routine inspection. The news of the coup would be telephoned to him and Göring would fly to Berlin immediately. As soon as he arrived he would broadcast a message of peace to the German people. He would confirm the sad news of Hitler's death and announce that he had taken over as caretaker until such time as a successor was appointed.

It is important to give the appearance of legality and control, to make the people and the waverers believe that there was a government and that it had power. If that were done, it would all be over very quickly. The Luftwaffe would come out in support of Göring, and so would the generals who believed in him. Goebbels, always a practical man, would undoubtedly rally round as would the Army commanders who had hitherto remained neutral.

After this had been achieved, they would cut off all communications with the outside world. Göring would then issue instructions to his loyal commanders to have the SS disarmed. By Sunday night, Germany would have a new government.

*   *   *

Despite the fact that the arrests had been ordered by Heydrich, Susan and Stannard were not taken to the SD headquarters in the Wilhelmstrasse. Instead they were taken to a local Gestapo office in the Tiergarten where each of them was searched, registered and Stannard's gun taken away. Afterwards armed guards escorted them to an interrogation room in the basement.

Apart from a desk, telephones, straight backed chairs, two powerful table lamps and a Grundig tape recorder the room was bare. The walls were painted in a dark grey washable paint and there was a brown spatter across one wall. From the shadow of the desk lamp, Stannard could not tell whether it was blood or rust.

The arresting officer asked them to sit down four feet apart from each other, and opposite him. He said his name was Brandt and provided they co-operated, all this would be over in a very short time.

"I must protest at this harassment," Susan said. "I am a Swiss citizen. I have nothing to do with this . . . this war. I wish to telephone my Consulate."

"All in good time," Brandt said. "The Swiss are neutral, Madam Lenglen. You too should be neutral. You should not consort with spies."

"What do you mean by that?" Susan snapped.

Stannard said, "The men who were shooting in the street were nothing to do with us."

Brandt smiled and looked at Stannard. "You say they are British spies and I do not ask how you know that, but I believe you. You say they were nothing to do with you, and I don't believe that. What would British spies want with a Hauptmann Karl Schmidt?"

"I told you they were nothing to do with us," Stannard said.

"Lie number one," Brandt said. "Who are you?"

"My name is Karl Schmidt. I hold the rank of Hauptmann and I am attached to the Abwehr. I am on an urgent and highly confidential mission for Reichsmarshall Göring. This so-called interrogation of yours is endangering that mission." Stannard raised his voice. "Endangering the Reich."

"Lie number two," Brandt said and got to his feet. He took out his Walther and walked round the desk towards Susan, keeping Stannard covered with the gun all the time. Then, very deliberately, totally emotionlessly, he slapped Susan twice across the face.

Her head rocked with the blow. She gasped, her hair flying across her face. Stannard gripped the bottom of his chair, forced himself not to move. Take away Brandt's gun and he could break him into little pieces. But Brandt was too far away and Stannard was helpless. Worse than helpless, impotent.

"I saw an American film two weeks ago," Brandt said conversationally, "which had been banned by the good Doctor Goebbels. It depicted us as mindless thugs. Some of us are a little more sophisticated than that you know, and we don't come apart when we're shouted at. I graduated in psychology at Heidelberg and after that I studied for two years in Vienna. I do not like brutality or torture. But I find it effective when properly applied and in the right circumstances. It is not the effect of pain on the body that makes someone talk. It is the effect pain has on the mind." Brandt went back to his desk and sat down.

"What is your real name?" he asked Stannard.

"Karl Schmidt."

Brandt shrugged. "Why bother to lie. Your name is David Stannard. You're a lieutenant in the United

States Army. You entered Germany two weeks ago."

"My name is Schmidt."

"Now what are you doing in Berlin? What is your role in Double Eagle?"

Stannard looked at his watch. He should have been with van Osten twenty minutes ago. He wondered what van Osten would do when he didn't show. Would he come looking for him. Stannard thought not. They were on a tight schedule. The truck had to be loaded and be at Hildesheim by eleven. It was ten minutes to eight. The operation would get under way at midnight. Over four hours. At Springfield they hadn't trained him to resist torture. Stannard wondered if he could hold out till Double Eagle got under way.

"I know nothing about Double Eagle," he said. "I am with the Abwehr—"

Brandt silenced him with a gesture. "You are an American in Berlin with forged papers. Technically you are a spy. Technically you can be executed any time I say so. And believe me, Lieutenant Stannard, I will say so, unless you can justify your miserable existence by cooperating with me. What were you doing at Hildesheim?"

"Special training for a commando group."

"How many others were there?"

"Five."

"Their names."

Stannard hesitated, decided it couldn't make any difference now, decided Brandt probably knew already. "Van Osten, Kirkdorf, Guertner, Lessing, Lipski."

Brandt smiled. "You learn fast. What is your connection with this lady?"

"We're friends. I met her when I was working in Zürich."

"How long were you in Zürich?"

"Since August."

"And before that?"

"Attached to General von Rundstet's Army Group A in France."

Swiftly Brandt took Stannard through his career as an army officer, as a military cadet, as a student, as a boy in Bremen, rapping out the questions, giving him no time to think. Stannard felt he had done well, given the answers he had been told to give.

"There's one thing the Abwehr forgot," Brandt said as he changed the reels on the tape recorder. "There is no record of your birth in Bremen and the passport you hold is a forgery made from a blank issued to the Abwehr. You do not exist, Hauptmann Karl Schmidt, and so your death will go unnoticed."

He paused, lit a cigarette and questioned Susan very casually. Who was she, what was she doing in Germany, would she marry Schmidt, what did she think of the war, of Berlin, would she live in Germany afterwards.

Susan's replies were cryptic to the point of terseness.

Brandt said, "You are a very smart young lady. Someone's obviously taught you to answer questions." Then he pressed a buzzer which summoned a guard and having instructed the guard not to let Stannard and Susan talk to each other, went out.

Stannard looked at his watch. An hour had passed. One merciful hour. In three hours, Double Eagle would be under way.

Some ten minutes later, Brandt came back, carrying a pair of steel handcuffs from which a horizontal lever protruded. He covered them with his automatic while the guard fastened Susan's wrists behind her.

"Alright Stannard, tell me what you are doing in Berlin, tell me all about Double Eagle."

"My name is Karl Schmidt," Stannard said. "I am with the Abwehr and I am on a—"

Brandt nodded to the guard and he twisted the lever tightening the cuffs into Susan's flesh.

"You were saying," Brandt said.

"On a mission for Reichsmarshall Göring."

The guard twisted the lever. The cuffs bit into the flesh. Stannard could see puffy red weals already rising round the bands of steel. Susan kept her head down, biting her lips against the pain.

"Let me tell you what will happen," Brandt said. "Those cuffs can exert enough pressure to cut flesh and crush bone. At the moment however, only your lady friend's circulation is being interfered with. If that is kept on long enough, she will lose the use of her hands."

The guard twisted the lever again. Susan screamed.

"You fucking bastard," Stannard shouted.

* * *

As soon as he'd finished his meeting with Tropp and Brauer, van Osten booked a telephone call to his father-in-law's estate in East Prussia. He was told that a transmission line had been sabotaged, that there would be an indefinite delay. Van Osten left the call in and began to write.

By tomorrow night he would be a hero, a traitor, or dead. It was important to him that the children should understand what he had done and why. Important to him too, that Paula should know.

Paul and Paula, the captain and the countess, young, beautiful, charming, sophisticated. Their friends said they were an ideal match, that their marriage must have been made in heaven. Even as he wrote, van Osten wondered what had gone wrong. His continual absences? His commitment to I/Luft? The wars in Spain and Poland. No, a good marriage should have survived that. He realized now they'd grown out of beauty and charm and wit. The girl he'd married had become a different woman and they'd grown away from each other.

He wished it were different, remembering those sultry afternoons with Paula in the Black Forest, reading the love poetry of Heine. Whatever happened tomorrow, he would never experience that again, never feel the same way about anyone again. He still loved Paula, even though they had grown apart, even though he had immersed himself in his work and Paula had turned to the children, spent more time away from Berlin, and finally accepted with relief his suggestion that because of the air raids she should live permanently with her parents.

If not for the war it might have been different. He would have been a peace time soldier, able to come home at five o'clock in the evening. He would not have been in America and Spain and Poland. There was no end to what this damned war had done.

Before he sealed the envelope, van Osten inserted two photographs of himself, for the children. Whatever happened, he wanted them to remember him, a reflection of man's hope for immortality, he thought as he licked the envelope and sealed it.

Stannard was nearly an hour late. That was unusual. But van Osten was running out of time. He went downstairs to begin loading the equipment.

*   *   *

Blood oozed from under the thin steel bands, welled over puffy flesh, trickled slowly down Susan's nerveless fingers to the floor. She sat slumped in the chair, her body lathered in sweat, her head sunk on her chest, her hair pasted wetly to her skull. All the while she sighed hoarsely, saliva trickling from her open mouth in her fight against the continuous pain.

Stannard looked at his watch. Two hours to go. He couldn't stand it, *couldn't stand it!* It would have been different if they had tortured him, different if he was restrained. But he was free to move, free to jump up and smash Brandt's bony face. And that was the hell of it. The awareness of his own freedom and his own helplessness. Susan's hoarse cries were like bloody fingers clawing at his brain. Talk and she would be free, talk and they would both go free.

But Stannard knew it couldn't be so. He would never be free. No sooner he talked than he would be shot as a spy. Susan would die too. All that was left was Double Eagle. Double Eagle must succeed.

Two hours more. Stannard had no illusions as to what would have happened to Susan by then. Two hours. Two whole bloody hours.

There was a rapid clatter of footsteps, an imperious pounding on the door. Brandt went across and opened it, the guard covering him with the 98 K carbine.

Paul van Osten stood in the open doorway, swaddled in a field grey overcoat underneath which jackboots gleamed. The German eagle flew proudly above the peak of his cap and his collar patches glittered with the silver stars of a lieutenant colonel and the Jager oak leaves of his infantry regiment. "What the devil is going on here?" van Osten shouted. Then to the guard, "You! Weren't you taught to salute an officer in uniform?"

The guard hastily threw his arm up and cried, "Heil Hitler!" and resumed his defensive posture.

Brandt asked, "Who the hell are you?"

"Lieutenant Colonel Paul van Osten, Deputy Director of the Abwehr, Controller of Amt X West. What's your name and rank?"

"Inspector Wolff Brandt."

Van Osten stalked into the room, and loosed the handcuffs from Susan's wrists. "Torture is specifically forbidden by the Geneva Convention," he said mildly. "I suppose you know that, Inspector Brandt?"

"We shall shortly rewrite the Geneva Convention,"

Brandt announced. He was back on his side of the desk, his Walther loosely covering both van Osten and Stannard.

"What is Hauptmann Schmidt doing here? He is on an extremely urgent mission which is being personally controlled by Reichsmarshall Göring."

Brandt said, "He is here on the direct orders of General Heydrich."

"And where is Heydrich?"

"He is in Prague. But we expect him back within the hour."

"We do not have an hour," van Osten snapped. "So I suggest you release these people into my custody."

"I have my orders," Brandt said. "Schmidt can only be released on the authority of General Heydrich."

"Very well," van Osten said. He walked round the desk and picked up a telephone. "I will inform the Reichsmarshall of the General's interference. I trust you have a means of direct intercession with the Almighty, Inspector Brandt. The Reichsmarshall is not known for tolerance to those who have thwarted him. And I doubt very much whether Heydrich will find it worth his while to protect you."

"That is a cross I will have to bear," Brandt replied.

Van Osten picked up the phone, demanded an immediate connection to Göring at Carinhall. As he spoke, his eyes caught Stannard's, and he thrust his head back slightly, indicating the guard.

Stannard looked out of the corner of his eye. The guard was standing motionless, his carbine pointing at the door in deference to van Osten's rank.

"Nothing works in this damned country," van Osten snapped, slamming down the phone. "It's a wonder our trains run on time. Two hours to make a connection 80 kilometers away. It's quicker to drive." He looked at Brandt. "You are refusing to release these people into my custody?"

"That is correct."

Van Osten indicated the paper on the desk. "I need a written record of your refusal. Please write." He moved aside as Brandt approached the desk.

Brandt transferred the Walther to his left hand, rested it on the desk, placed his hand over it. Taking a pen in his right hand, he began to write. Van Osten moved closer to him, peering over his shoulder as if checking what was being written. Then without any warning he raised his right hand and chopped the edge of his palm firmly against the back of Brandt's neck.

Brandt's face smashed into the desk, and he rolled round on his shoulder, choking, palm closing over the Walther. Stannard leapt to his feet, whirled his chair round him and flung it at the guard. It caught the guard as he was turning, smashing the carbine out of his hands. Stannard went after the chair, elbows slamming into the guard's body, kneeing him in the crotch, throwing him to the floor. The guard opened his mouth to scream and Stannard hit him across the throat with a savage chop that ruptured cartilage, snapped the little bone on the side of the throat, and forced a gurgling stream of blood up through the man's mouth and nostrils.

Stannard turned and picked up the carbine. Van Osten had Brandt spreadeagled on the desk. Brandt still held the Walther, was twisting his wrist round to aim it at van Osten's body. Stannard ran forward swinging the carbine from the barrel. There was a sharp crack as Brandt fired. Van Osten reeled back, clutching his shoulder. Brandt was struggling into a sitting position, moving the Walther round for a better shot at van Osten, when the butt of the carbine smashed against the side of his head. Brandt fell sideways off the desk. Stannard jumped onto the desk, jumped off it onto Brandt's body. Using the butt of the carbine as a club he smashed it hard against Brandt's skull with a noise like an axe biting into wood.

*   *   *

"Let's get out of here," van Osten said. "My car is outside. Cover her wrists."

They went out of the room and locked the door behind them. Then van Osten shepherding them, marched out of the station to where his BMW was parked.

"Where do we go?" Stannard asked.

"Hildesheim," van Osten said tiredly. "We're late already."

26

Friday, December 13, 1940. Hildesheim.

"There are only two alternatives," van Osten said.
"We abort the operation and leave Germany, or we go
ahead with four men."

Susan, Stannard and van Osten were in Lothar
Brauer's office, van Osten seated behind Brauer's
desk, still pale with shock, the glass of brandy before
him barely touched. Susan had applied a field dressing to van Osten's shoulder on the way to Hildesheim,
but still he had lost a lot of blood. The doctors at Hildesheim had dressed the wound, dressed Susan's
wounds too, given them both pain killing injections,
promised van Osten sedatives that would last the
night. But there was no way he could take part in
Double Eagle. He could barely move his left hand
and tomorrow it would be worse.

"One of those four is a traitor," Stannard said.

Not von Kirkdorf or Guertner, van Osten thought,
Lessing or Lipski. Not that it mattered now. The operation would have to be abandoned. He was finished
in Germany. He'd had to identify himself to get to see
Brandt, and with two Gestapo men dead, neither
Göring nor Canaris could protect him. The safest
thing to do was to use the Junkers JU 52 warming up

on the tarmac outside to get Susan, Stannard and himself to Switzerland.

Stannard said, "I'll take your place."

With the throbbing in his head and the beat of the engines outside, van Osten thought he'd misheard Stannard. "You can't," he said automatically. "An American—"

"It is your only chance," Stannard interrupted. "Without it you're dead. The Gestapo will hang you from meat hooks."

"I promised Schroeder—"

"You promised Schroeder nothing. I'm in this war, Paul, I've been in it since I was picked for Springfield."

"You cannot take the risk. Look, there's a plane being made ready for Susan. Get in it and go. This is nothing to do with you."

"I want to do it," Stannard said. "It's people like us or people like Brandt, and we're going to win." Stannard paused and grinned. "Also, I owe you something."

Van Osten lit a caporal, coughed through the smoke. "If you go, I go. You take the glider and I'll meet you on the Warth road. Afterwards we can cross the border together. But I'll need your radio codes."

"I can't give you that."

Van Osten looked quickly at Susan. "The man outside has to have the codes. There is no point to the mission if the message isn't sent. If there is going to be war with America it is better that Hitler lives."

Stannard got up and walked round the room. If they were going, they should take off in twenty minutes. If he gave van Osten the codes, there was no knowing what he would do with them. Then he thought, van Osten would not send the message if Hitler still lived. He was too honorable for that. "Okay," he said. "I'll give them to you."

Van Osten clambered to his feet. "I'd better go

and brief the others. I'll see you in the hut in five minutes." He paused and looked at Susan. "I'll come back here. Your plane leaves twenty minutes after David's."

After van Osten left, Stannard and Susan looked at each other in silence. Four minutes. He went up to her and took her in his arms. "Will you be waiting at Lauterach?"

"Why?"

"You'd be nice to come home to."

She started to say something and stopped, biting her lip. Then she placed her bandaged wrists behind his head and drew him down to her. "I'll be waiting," she said, before she kissed him.

Saturday, December 14, 1940. Arlberg.

Dawn was rimming the mountain peaks when the glider cut loose with a barely perceptible jerk. Von Kirkdorf steadied the controls, waved a gloved hand at the departing Ju 52 and said, "Goodbye mother."

Stannard seated behind him, beside the rifle racks bristling with MP 38 machine pistols, turned and looked back down the fuselage. The remainder of the group were seated in a single line behind him. Guertner toying with his knife, Lipski staring thoughtfully out of the window, and Lessing dozing with his head at an awkward angle.

The only opportunity they'd all had to sleep had been in the Junker on the flight to Munich. They'd reached Munich shortly after two that morning, spent the next two hours loading the equipment on to sleds, then loading the sleds on to the glider.

The glider was a ten seater DFS 230 with high set wooden wings and a box shaped fuselage made of tubular steel and covered with canvas. For this journey the four rearward facing seats had been removed, the space filled with the two light sleds holding the skis, boots, snow shoes, and rations. Behind them were the three heavier sleds bearing the light machine gun, the mortar and the flame thrower, everything lashed to the frame to prevent the load shifting during flight.

Sleep on the run from Munich had been impossible. The seats were upright, hard and cramped. Each of them was carrying a grenade bag with six egg grenades, and helmets, six-inch double-edged knives and Walther P 38 pistols were festooned about their bodies. Despite the zeltbahns, their white parkas and over-trousers, their boots and quilted underclothes, it was bitterly cold inside the glider. The tubular frame was damp with condensation.

The glider bounced on a current of air. Von Kirkdorf banked slightly, peering through the misty perspex. He was wearing his glider pilot's badge on the outside of his parka, Stannard noticed, a soaring eagle on a wreath of oak leaves and a swastika, made of silver. They were descending slowly with soft, rushing noise, a creaking of canvas and wood. As they came below the pink tipped peaks, the light began to go, turning dense and grey, pressing around them like an amorphous curtain. The flame tipped mountains stretched for miles and through the greyness there was snow, the dark, ominous outlines of rocks and trees. A cold, inhospitable, brooding terrain. And it looked as if it was snowing.

The air buffeted them again as they descended, making the whole craft shudder. For a moment Stannard thought von Kirkdorf had lost control, had a brief vision of the glider hurtling into packed snow, splintering like matchwood. Von Kirkdorf steepened the angle of descent, brought them well below the peak, over a valley. The glider bounced unhappily on waves of air. Ahead of them another mountain soared, a harsh wall of snow reaching far into the greyness above.

"Are we there yet?" Guertner asked.

"We soon will be, young man," von Kirkdorf replied. Then to Stannard, "Does this look familiar to
you? I left my Baedeker at home."

Stannard crawled over von Kirkdorf's equipment
to the back of his seat, peered over his shoulder. To
the left, the valley ran straight down over crevasses
that seemed to extend to the foot of the range. To the
right, the valley curved between the mountains, rising
steeply, blocked in by more mountains. At the end of
the valley and halfway up the range was the flat ta-
bleland that they had picked. Von Kirkdorf was already banking the glider sharply and Stannard had to
hold on to the back of his seat for balance. "That's it,"
Stannard said, and thought, my God we're too low.

They were hemmed in by mountains as they flew
along the valley, mountains that reached up like solid
walls and were no longer tinted with pink. Ahead of
them there were patches of falling snow that looked
like smoke. Their speed seemed to increase and the
wind tore at the glider with great, ripping noises.

Von Kirkdorf sang tunelessly, "We're coming to
get you Adolf old boy, we're coming to get you now,"
and then whistled two bars from 'Alte Kameraden'.
"You remember that from the last war, David?"

"Hell, no. I'm worried I might never get a chance
to fight in this one."

Below them were trees and small blotches on the
snow that were houses. As they flew through the valley, the wooden wings seemed to brush the rugged
mountainside. They descended further, seeming to
travel faster now that they had something to judge
speed by. The glider bucked and bounced and von
Kirkdorf said, "Right men. We're going in."

The glider seemed to accelerate, suddenly threw
itself at the mountains. They were so low that Stannard could no longer see the peaks, only snow and
rock and greyness. The edge of the plateau loomed in

front of them. Above them. They were going to plough into its side.

The plateau reached forward to envelop them, blocking out the light, looming through the perspex in front of the curved nose, snow and trees, deep gulleys and solid rock. David braced himself as the glider wavered before the hillside; then they were over the lip of the plateau, hovering. There was a moment of total, absolute silence when everything seemed to stand still. Then there was a harsh scraping as the runners hit the snow followed by a vicious bounce, a soft grating noise as they rushed across the snow, a faint clattering as the glider bucked across the unevenness, snaked and swayed, slowed and finally stopped.

A rush of cold air greeted them as von Kirkdorf threw off the perspex cover.

Stannard was already on his feet and jumping over the side to land calf deep in snow.

They disembarked quickly, landing with a soft sibilance. The sleds were unfastened and eased out of the glider. Then while von Kirkdorf brewed tea, the others walked around the glider and covered it with white tarpaulin, fastening the coverings through the snow with long pegs.

It was working out well, Stannard thought. Forty minutes to unload, brew up and conceal the glider. He took out his compass, worked out the direction they should be going in, looked at the mountains, worked out a path through the snow. Fifty minutes after touch down they were on their way struggling up the steep hills, each man wearing snow shoes and drawing a sled.

27

The news of Stannard's arrest reached Heydrich in Prague where he was resolving urgent problems created by the asinine and weak-minded administration of Reichs-protector Konstantin von Neurath. He'd left immediately, reached Berlin six hours later, discovered the bodies of Brandt and the SS guard.

Incredible! There had been shots and fighting and no one had noticed. A sheepish station officer muttered something about the sounds of violence being usual in an interrogation room. Imbecile!

The Director of Berlin Police was away and he had to deal with Tropp. Surprisingly Tropp was on duty at that ungodly hour of the morning, a matter which Heydrich would investigate later. Meanwhile he wanted every available policeman out scouring Berlin for Paul van Osten, Susan Lenglen and an American with forged papers in the name of Hauptmann Karl Schmidt.

Unlike Tropp, the commander of the SS divisions in Lech was sound asleep. He had to be woken, dressed and driven half a mile in heavy snow to speak with Heydrich. A commando group was landing in the mountains above Lech. No it wasn't an exercise. They were to be intercepted. Two divisions of Waffen SS would intercept them all right, but it might also scare them off. Far better to use a crack patrol group. Hey-

300

drich himself would be in Lech later that day. The commander promised to get seven of his best men up the mountain as soon as it was light.

Heydrich looked at his watch. Too early yet to see the Führer. He called his wife, Lena, informed her a car would collect her within the hour. For the next few days it was better that his family remained away from Berlin.

It was then that he heard the raised voices and the massed tramping of feet in the corridor outside. Heydrich took the Luger out of his belt. Van Osten hadn't waited for the Führer's death to move on Berlin. The coup was already on.

His door was flung open and Reichsmarshall Göring stood there, wearing the pale blue uniform of the Commander of the Luftwaffe, his breast resplendent with medals. Behind him his bodyguard mingled uneasily with Heydrich's SS.

"Heil Hitler!" Göring saluted and walked into the room.

Heydrich leapt to his feet. "Heil Hitler!"

Göring lowered his bulk on to a chair opposite Heydrich. His face was flushed and he was sweating. His small eyes were red and irritable. "I am the bearer of bad news," Göring announced. "There are rumors that the Führer will be assassinated at Lech tomorrow."

"The source of your information, Reichsmarshall?"

"Rumors, paid informers. A report is being made ready for you tomorrow."

So Göring had come to warn him in advance of the report. Heydrich wondered if that were true or whether Tropp had tipped off Göring. Heydrich took his time selecting a cigarette and lighting it. He could deny all knowledge of the plot. On the other hand revelation of what he knew might—

"My understanding is that the SD already know of this plot but have made no move to arrest the conspirators. I have been trying to reach Himmler all night."

That put Heydrich on the defensive. He would have to explain what the SD were doing or suffer the interference of Himmler. There was no way that Heydrich wanted Himmler involved. When the plot failed, he was the only one who would be entitled to the Führer's gratitude.

"The plot has been known to us for some time," he admitted. "The conspirators will be apprehended."

"So you know who they are?"

"Already the Berlin police, the Gestapo and two divisions of Waffen SS are searching for them."

"I congratulate you, General. The Reich will remember your efforts."

"I am pleased to be of service."

"There is something else," Göring said. "I was once in charge of the police myself, so I know how difficult it is to cover all eventualities. If anything should go wrong, I want you to know that I shall not hold you responsible. I also want you to know that I would look upon you and the SD as vital elements in the continuation of all the Führer's policies."

"I am gratified," Heydrich said. As usual the Reichsmarshall was hedging his bets.

In the hour that followed he worried about how to persuade the Führer to avoid Lech. Whatever he said, the Führer would not alter his plans and he was the only man in the Reich with a stronger will than Heydrich.

Which was a problem . . .

*   *   *

They moved easily to the end of the plateau, through lightly falling snow, Stannard leading, towing the sled with the sixty-pound mortar. Behind him were Lessing and Lipski, side by side pulling the light sleds. Behind them von Kirkdorf with the flamethrower, and Guertner in the rear towing the light machine gun.

After about a mile and a half the plateau narrowed, edged its way steeply up the mountain and across a break in the range. After that Stannard knew it dipped shallowly and widened across a narrow plain that finished abruptly in deep crevasse at the end of the range. Narrow, ice-covered spurs bridged the crevasse at three points and beyond that was a narrow trail winding between the mountains. Halfway along the trail they would have to leave it, climb a long and gentle slope to the top of a mountain. From there it was downhill all the way, across the narrow plateau where van Osten had planned to drop his parachutists, falling sharply to the treeline. Stannard had decided they would make for the trees, then swing sharply across to get to the ridge above the chalet. The whole journey would take them about six hours, if there were no accidents, and it didn't snow any harder.

Stannard led them up the incline, pausing while Lessing and Lipski lined up behind each other, feeling the tug of the mortar as their passage steepened. They had made good time so far, moving with an early morning freshness and a sense of freedom after the confinement of the glider. No one spoke and the only sound was the slurp of their snowshoes, the hiss of the runners, and the occasional clink of metal striking rock.

Stannard had decided on a five-minute rest period every hour. By the second rest period, they'd climbed nearly two hundred meters, were able to look into the valley below. Standing, momentarily relieved of the weight of the sled and the mortar, Stannard looked. And saw the glider.

Two pieces of tarpaulin had been wrenched off and through the Zeiss binoculars, Stannard could see them flapping in the wind. A mistake, an accident or had someone deliberately left something unfastened? Stannard looked round the group. No one else seemed to have noticed, no one else was even looking back at the way they had come.

He'd have to leave it, Stannard decided. Even if he transferred to skis and went back, it would still take him over an hour to return, two hours to catch up with the group, and no one to tow the mortar. The glider was halfway along the plateau, not visible from below. It was only someone from above or a low flying aircraft that could spot and identify it. It was a chance he had to take. One more thing to worry about. He signaled to the group to take up their loads, and moved off angrily up the hill.

They moved quickly for another hour. Then it began to snow heavily. First the sky went grey and the light luminous, then they were surrounded by a swirling white mass that dampened the exposed part of their faces, settled on their goggles and their clothes, became a thick impenetrable curtain ten feet ahead, blotting out the valley behind them.

The snow could last for hours. If they stayed where they were they would never get to the chalet on time. On the other hand if they went on, the group would be using up reserves of strength and endurance, run the risk of getting lost. It was a question of percentages. If they stayed, the attack would have to be abandoned. If they went on, there was only a chance they would get lost.

"I can't see," Lessing said from behind him.

"Get closer to me," Stannard said and went on.

Lessing? Was it Lessing who was the Gestapo plant? The man had been surly and uncommunicative throughout their time at Hildesheim, was known to have an association with the Gestapo. If it were Lessing, he was expendable, Stannard thought. After they'd scaled the mountain.

They went up and up through soggy clinging

snow. Each splay-legged step was an effort, an achievement. Breath smoked from their panting mouths, their muscles felt taut and elongated as if stretched on a rack. The climb was slow and arduous and sometimes Stannard felt they weren't making any progress at all.

Lessing fell twice, Lipski once, and keeping track of the white shrouded figures behind him was a constant strain. Stannard estimated that they must be close to the ridge between the mountains but could not tell where the snow ended and the mountain began.

It was a hard, stamina-sapping slog, one heavy foot after the other. Think of one step at a time, Stannard told himself, one movement. Forget about the drag of the sled, forget about how far to go afterwards, forget about tiredness and the dryness in the mouth, the prickle of sweat underneath the quilted underwear. Think only of the next step, just the next step. There can't be much more to go.

It took them three hours to get to the top of the ridge and it was still snowing. At least there was one advantage in the snowstorm. The Waffen SS would not be out on exercises, and they would be totally unobserved.

Stannard called a half hour break for lunch, went to the edge of the ridge. The plain was a swirling mass of snow. From the photographs and the memory of his overflight it seemed that the route fell gently to the plain. If the weather was better they could have skied down and across it, making up time, but with two relatively inexperienced skiers in Lessing and Lipski, it was too much of a risk to take.

After lunch they set off, with new problems. They were moving so slowly that the sleds were catching up with them, spinning under-braking, throwing everyone off balance. As the slope grew steeper, the sleds became impossible to control, and Stannard had to call a stop.

Muscles stiffened in the enforced inactivity, and snow found new routes between neck and collar, and glove and wrist. The cold seeped through to the marrow, numbing nerve ends and chilling the blood, inducing a lethargy that was like death.

Forty-five minutes later the storm slowed, the dancing flakes grew fewer. Stannard who had been moving constantly rose and walked to the end of the ridge. And stopped. And stared.

Halfway across the plain, barring it, were two tents built from zeltbahns, colored a muddy green and brown. It wasn't a group that was stranded. No group would have gone out in that snowstorm. It was a patrol waiting for intruders. If someone had known Stannard's route that was the spot to pick. There was no other way to cross the plain.

If not for the sleds, if not for the inexperience of Lipski and Lessing, Stannard would have picked the trail that ran steeply down the farther side of the mountain they had just climbed. The trail fell in a series of sharp, z-like curves, dropping about three hundred meters in a little over a kilometer. To ski down it required plenty of courage and experience. To trail sleds was almost impossible.

Stannard instructed the group to change to skis. Immediately after the sharp descent, they could move east along a shallow, inclined plain, which grew less steep the further they went and ultimately joined up with van Osten's dropping point. They'd pick up time, certainly, if he could get the group down intact, and if they were not spotted by the SS patrol that had been waiting for them. If they were spotted their situation would be indefensible. Sheltered by the steepness above them, the SS could pick them off with ease as they crossed the plain.

Stannard asked Lipski and Lessing to stay close

to him asked Guertner to back them up, told everybody it would be easy, that they would take it slow.
When they were ready he moved off, skis biting into
the snow as he fought to make the first turn slowly.

The sled twisted against the towing rod, tried to
find the straightest way down, threatened to throw
him off balance. Stannard speeded up slightly,
brought the sled round in a tight curve, heard a cry
and the crashing of a body plunging through wet
snow.

He turned broadside and looked up. Lessing was
down, his sled on its side, Guertner and Lipski standing over him. Guertner waved that everything was
okay, but from where he was Stannard could not look
across the plain, to see if the SS had reacted to the
cry, or noticed the figures crowding round Lessing,
and the flurries of snow.

It took all of five minutes before Lessing was
erect, his sled righted, five precious minutes when if
the SS had noticed, they could start moving towards
them. They set off again, Stannard in the lead, edging
his skis, fighting his weight, fighting the sled all the
way. His legs ached, his spine ached with the continual pull and the continual twisting. At the speed they
were traveling, he didn't think they'd saved much
time, and he was concerned that the SS had been
warned.

Halfway down, the surface became uneven, the
sleds bumping and shuddering with wills of their
own. Lipski fell, Von Kirkdorf fell, each fall accompanied by the noise of crashing sleds, each fall adding
interminably to the time already lost. It was a slow, ag-
onizing progress. At one stage the track was almost
perpendicular, and Stannard had to risk sending the
sleds down unaccompanied, spent half an hour afterwards finding and re-organizing them. Their progress
was no longer silent.

Three quarters of the way down, the trail broad-

ened and eased. Stannard relaxed, ceased fighting the
slope, allowed his weight to carry him forward, looked
round once to confirm that Lessing and Lipski were
enjoying it too.

Ahead the trail narrowed slightly, curved between hummocks. After that, Stannard reckoned
would be the plain, an easy schuss across to the mountain overlooking the chalet. He glanced at his watch.
Forty minutes behind schedule. That wasn't too bad.
He stretched his body, enjoying a feeling almost of
liberation.

The curve was coming nearer. He looked round.
He'd pulled out twenty yards on the others. He
shifted his weight for the turn. He was thinking it
would be nice to rest once they'd crossed over, nice to
unwind for a few minutes before the important part of
the operation. His skis were biting smoothly into the
snow with a sharp hissing sound, turning him gently
and ever so smoothly.

He came round the corner, tightening the turn,
and braked instinctively. Lined across the track were
seven men in the black parkas and overtrousers of the
Waffen SS. Their skis were neatly racked against the
side of the hill, and their machine pistols were held
casually at waist level.

Stannard braked, kept on braking, spumes of
snow showering out from under his skis. Then instinctively he straightened, accelerated, started to turn the
opposite way and whipped himself round again in a
full, skidding circle. The sled wrenched at his arms.
He thrust himself forward to hold on to it. He
glimpsed the machine pistols being raised, glimpsed
snow and scrub and rock as he made the turn. Then
he released the sled and its load.

There was a harsh chorus of cries, as men, rooted
in the snow tried to move. A solid thwacking sound as
the sled broadsiding between the hummocks, scythed

through the men, its basic solid weight multiplied by the speed of its passage.

Stannard completed his turn, nearly off balance, reached behind him for the MP 38. Lessing came round, tried to slow, slewed across Lipski's path, brought him crashing down.

Stannard turned to cover the SS men. Four of them were down, the other three, lying unhurt on the two sides of the hill, readying their guns. Stannard knew he was exposed, that he couldn't take all three of them. He fired at the nearest man, watched bullets sizzle through the snow and draw blood. Then there was the sharp crackle of automatic fire behind him. Von Kirkdorf was straddling the entrance to the curve, his machine pistol blazing, spewing bullets amongst the falling and the fallen. Stannard glimpsed him standing there and the next moment, Guertner traveling very fast cannoned into him.

One SS man left. Stannard saw him move and threw himself sideways. The spatter of bullets hummed through the air as Stannard tried to get his gun aimed again. Then he saw Lessing move, try to stand up.

"Down," he shouted, but it was too late.

The SS man was firing in a high, circular pattern. Stannard heard the bullets go into Lessing with fast, light trip-hammer thuds. He moved his own gun round, firing quickly before the man could lower his aim, saw the bullets dance along the snow as he raised his sights, saw the chain of perforations across the dark front of the man's chest, perforations that swiftly turned to red.

28

They crossed over without further incident, reached van Osten's drop-off point shortly after four. The light was going fast, a deep coldness filling the air. For the first time since they left the glider, Stannard was able to take off his equipment and rest for more than five minutes.

They'd stripped Lessing's body of all identification, left him with the unburied corpses of the SS men. Stannard had towed Lessing's sled across the inclined plain to the dropping point. Now as he sat leaning his back against a sled, he wondered if Lessing was the traitor, thought it fitting that his own kind had killed him.

Stannard wasn't sure if the noise of the shooting had carried down to Lech. Sound played funny tricks in the mountains. Anyway, no one in Lech could know the result of the shooting, until their men failed to return. And no search party could reach Stannard's group before they left for the chalet. For the first time since that morning, Stannard felt safe, felt sure the operation was going to succeed.

"Hey!" It was von Kirkdorf lying flat by the raised lip of the plateau. Stannard went over, threw himself down beside him.

"Do you see what I see?"

Stannard looked through his binoculars. The road leading down to Lech was lined with SS troops. His heart sank. As long as the SS remained there, there was little point in moving, and no way to attack the chalet. Stannard swung the glasses round to the chalet. The machine gun nests were there all right, their teams in place, and the perimeter fence was being patrolled by eight guards. There were lights on in the chalet, and flags fluttering from its roof.

Suddenly there was a movement, a figure skiing fast across the lower slopes, making for the chalet, knees swiveling rhythmically, blonde hair streaking in the wind.

"That's our Eva, all right," von Kirkdorf said.

"She certainly can ski," Stannard said.

Eva Braun pulled up outside the perimeter fence in a flurry of snow. The guards saluted, raised the barrier in front of the machine guns, allowed her to ski slowly round them to the steps that led down to the chalet. Stannard watched her take the skis off, move quickly down the steps, out of his line of vision.

"Hey, David, Charlie Chaplin's coming."

Stannard didn't need the glasses to see that. A black Mercedes was climbing up the road to the chalet, followed at a distance of twenty yards, by a second black Mercedes. Immediately behind that was a large, pale grey Mercedes convertible. It's top was raised and it had a normal registration plate—WH 32290. No flags fluttered from its bonnet, though there were little silver rods on each of the front wings, to assist the driver gauge the width of the car. Greedily Stannard focused the glasses and looked into the car. Hitler was there alright, leaning back in the rear seat, his face partially obscured by his hand, acknowledging the guard of honor. Stannard kept the glasses on him. Hitler did not leap or dance or behave in the way he had been shown on the newsreels at Spring-

field. He looked perfectly normal. The only surprise
was that his skin was not the color and texture of a
newsreel.

The cars drew up inside the perimeter fence,
drawing past the machine gun teams standing to attention outside their emplacements. This would be the
perfect moment, Stannard thought, with everyone's
eyes on Hitler, the gates open, and the machine guns
unmanned.

The chauffeur walked round and opened the rear
door. Hitler climbed out, a man of medium height
with a rather pasty complexion. He was wearing a
simple field grey uniform, with only the Iron Cross
and a red and black swastika armband. The famous
cowlick was covered by a cap with gold piping. Hitler
turned and faced the guard round the permieter. Stannard peered closely at his face. It was a long face,
grown slightly flabby, moustache obscuring the shape
of the upper lip. But it was the eyes that held Stannard, pale eyes burning with a strange intensity, a
strange death wish. Hitler saluted the guards and
Stannard started. Through the glasses, Hitler seemed
only a few feet away saluting him.

Stannard lowered the glasses. Hitler was walking
away, a group of black uniformed SS men closing
round him as he went down the steps into the chalet.
Stannard felt strangely excited. It was partly seeing
the man he had come so far to kill. Partly also the
magnetism of Hitler's appearance, the haunted, burning look in those eyes. Stannard remembered the Gestapo, the horrors of Poland and the Low Countries,
remembered what had happened, what would happen
to Germany, and felt no remorse.

After Hitler went into the chalet, the SS guard of
honor trooped down the road, back to Lech. The machine gun team resumed their positions and the
guards their steady patrol round the perimeter fence.

He was only concerned with the two machine guns pointing up the mountain, Stannard told von Kirkdorf. They couldn't see beyond the chalet, but it was logical to assume that there were similar emplacements there. Those guns didn't matter. They would only add to the danger of their retreat.

The only way of getting close enough to the chalet to insure that the bombs did their damage was to get through one of the barriers, take out one of the machine gun nests. As Stannard spoke, they saw a column of black clad figures struggle down the hillside from the farmhouse above the chalet. The reserve guard taking over from the men on duty. Stannard counted them. Eight men, two for each side of the square. They need only concern themselves with the topmost two men, but they would have to insure that reinforcements could not be brought from the farmhouse.

For a while, Stannard and von Kirkdorf discussed alternative methods of attacking the chalet, and however long they spoke it all came back to the same problem. They were one man short. There was nothing they could do about it, Stannard said, so each person should try to do the work of more than one. The final plan was this.

They would jettison the snow shoes, rations, paraffin stove and everything else they did not need. As soon as that had been done, they would ski down to the ridge, Stannard trailing the flame thrower and one sled of bombs. Guertner would bring the mortar, von Kirkdorf the machine gun and Lipski the second sled of bombs. Once they had set up the mortar and the machine gun, Stannard and von Kirkdorf would take out the guards in the farmhouse with grenades. Hopefully, meanwhile Guertner and Lipski would have been able to spike one of the guns. Stannard would then ski through the gap, followed by Guertner, both

trailing the bombs. They would set them and get
away. The explosion was the sign for the entire group
to make it as best as they could to the point where
van Osten would meet them.

It wasn't much of a plan, von Kirkdorf said, but it
was the best they could do under the circumstances.
Fifteen minutes later, they had jettisoned their un-
wanted equipment and were ready to move.

The sun had nearly set, the light gone a translucent grey. Stannard ran through the method of setting
the fuses and when everyone said they were ready,
they dragged the sleds to the edge of the plateau and
waited.

Stannard paused for a moment, before grasping
the sleds by their T-shaped handles, looked down the
mountain. Then with a quick flexing of the knees he
pointed his skis downwards, felt them start to slide,
adjusted his weight and began to move quickly down
the mountainside.

The sleds bounced behind him, threatening to
pull him off balance. He had to cut his speed, move
down in slow, wide curves, hoping his white clothing
was indistinguishable against the white background.
He tried to concentrate on moving smoothly, fighting
the camber, knowing he was clearing a path for the
others to follow, knowing if he fell the noise of the
clattering sleds and the sight of a flurry of snow
might alert the guards below.

He was on the steepest part of the incline preparing to turn when he heard a sibilant rushing noise,
turned his head, saw the sled with the mortar rushing
at him. Quickly he straightened up, accelerated down
the incline, feeling the sleds he held tearing his arms
out of their sockets. The runaway sled was almost up
to him now and Stannard turned quickly uphill allowing it to clatter past and roll over the edge of the incline.

He stopped, panting, sweating. Guertner pulled up beside him in a flurry of snow. "Christ! I'm sorry, Karl. I lost it."

Stannard looked at him, hoping that the sound of the mortar crashing down the hillside had not warned the guards.

"I'm sorry, I was going too fast."

Stannard shrugged. The best skiers often went too fast. He knew. "Take one of my sleds," he said, "and let's blow hell out of them with the machine gun."

After the initial steepness, the slope flattened out gently. Stannard was able to increase his speed. He kept on going down and down, not daring to look behind, hoping that the others would keep upright and get down in one piece.

He left the higher slopes with their virgin snow, came down the path that had been skied on, the ski tracks already turning icy. His skis crunched and crackled as he carved his turns, the weight of the sled bruising his arms. His body was bathed in sweat and his breath rushed from an open mouth in a stream of smoke. His legs were stiffening, his sense of rhythm becoming fragile. Perhaps that was what had happened to Guertner. Stannard chose a path that took him over the tree line, then swooping down through a gulley, curving hard to the left high above the chalet, through a clump of trees and then crouching low, behind the ridge. He allowed the skis to run to the end of the ridge, stopped and removed them. Then he straightened up and von Kirkdorf was beside him, sweating, face red with exertion.

"That was good," von Kirkdorf said.

Stannard turned and looked for the others. For a moment he couldn't spot them; then he saw a faint movement of grey upon grey, heard the tiniest scrape of runner upon ice. Guertner emerged, a shimmering shadow amongst the trees, shepherding Lipski, moustache trailing snow and ice.

It was nearly dark and Stannard signaled them to throw themselves down behind the ridge. In half an hour the attack would begin.

Without the mortar, taking out the machine gun nest quickly was impossible. Stannard offered another plan. They'd erected machine gun nests because they were expecting an attack by a group. They wouldn't expect one man, especially if he came from the same direction as the farmhouse. At the appointed time, Stannard and von Kirkdorf would ski out from the far end of the ridge. Von Kirkdorf would conceal himself near the farmhouse, and when he saw Stannard attack the machine gun nest, he would lob his grenade into the farmhouse. The moment Stannard was within the perimeter, Guertner would come after him, trailing the two sleds with bombs. Lipski would give them covering fire with the machine gun.

"I like this even less than the last plan," von Kirkdorf said. "How are you going to take that machine gun nest?"

"You'll see," Stannard said.

Twenty minutes later Stannard had finished buckling on the Flamenwerfer, and Guertner had poised the sleds on the edge of the ridge, ready to move at a moment's notice. Von Kirkdorf said, "Well Adolf, here we come. I bet this is going to be better than Christmas." And they set off from the far end of the ridge, skiing down slowly and smoothly. Von Kirkdorf stopped off by the farmhouse, stayed crouched in its shadow. Stannard went on in the darkness heading towards the circle of light from the silent chalet. It was the moment they saw him, that would be tricky. They would demand passwords, or they would shoot. All Stannard could hope for was that he would be close enough to shoot first.

He was approaching the rim of reflected light, approaching the moment when he must be seen, when he heard the faint clatter followed by a shout. He slowed in horror. Trundling down the end of the ridge, heading directly for the perimeter fence was a sled full of bombs. The fuses were unlit, and chasing desperately behind the runaway sled, was Lipski. Stannard wanted to shout to him to stop, to take cover, realized it was too late, realized too the diversion could be put to better use. The sled accelerated rapidly down the incline, Lipski gaining fast, but not going to make it. The perimeter guard stood and stared, then realizing what the sled contained opened fire. Lipski was struck high in the chest, was lifted up, seemed to pirouette, his arms folding gracefully over his head, before he crashed down into the snow.

Stannard moved, skiing rapidly into the circle of light. Too late the machine gun crew saw him, too late they saw what he was about to do. Before they could swivel the machine gun round he was on them, pumping the flame-thrower, throwing out great sheets of flame that rushed across the snow with a crackling, explosive sound, wrapping itself round the nest. There were screams and the crackle of exploding ammunition, a deafening concussion of grenades behind him, and then he was through a blazing barricade that flew apart in a shower of sparks, past the nest with its smell of burning flesh and inside the perimeter.

The perimeter guards were turning round, taking aim. From somewhere behind them came the crackle of automatic fire. Silhouetted against the flame of the machine gun nest they were standing targets. Stannard hurled himself to the ground. Where the hell was Guertner. The men on the further machine gun nest were trying to get their gun round, then realizing they couldn't, searched for small arms. Stannard lobbed a couple of grenades in their direction, buried his head in the snow as they detonated. He hadn't got them, but it kept them quiet. He threw a third grenade which landed right in the nest. He pressed his face to the snow and thought, 'Where the hell is Guertner?' There were two machine gun nests below the house, six more guards struggling up the hill. There was no way he could get away from the chalet now. At the most he had two minutes to live.

He decided to use those two minutes. He crawled to where the slope leveled off beside the second story of the chalet. The upper story was in darkness, the lights were on below. Perhaps he thought, if Hitler crosses a window, perhaps a grenade.

Downstairs nothing moved.

He heard the swishing of snow behind him, turned, saw von Kirkdorf skid to a stop with the second sled of bombs. "David!"

The fuses were set. All they had to do was launch it over the edge into the top storey of the chalet.

Which they did.

There were twenty seconds of awesome silence, punctuated only by the confused shouting of the guards down below, twenty seconds for Stannard and von Kirkdorf to dive behind the parked cars. Then the chalet mushroomed in a great gout of flame, showering wood and stone against the night sky, lit now by bright orange flames.

"We've done it," von Kirkdorf shouted. "We've done it! Hitler is dead!"

"Let's get the hell out of here."

They skied quickly down the slope round to the back of the house. The interior was blazing beautifully. Stannard stopped and glanced through a window. And froze.

He was looking into the living room, a large and spacious room with what had once been magnificent French windows. Stannard could see clearly into the room. It was empty and the furniture covered with dust sheets.

He turned and looked down the slope. Car tracks, empty machine gun nests, open barriers. Hitler had gone. He'd been spirited away from the back of the house, long before the attack started. It was a set up, a confounded, fiendish set up.

29

Someone moved beyond the perimeter fence. A shot rang out. Von Kirkdorf choked. Stannard turned, saw von Kirkdorf looking at him strangely, saw the gaping hole in his throat, saw him fall.

Stannard threw himself down beside him, grabbed the machine pistol from his loosening fingers. "Ewald," he said, but von Kirkdorf was past hearing.

Stannard remained crouched against the snow, hoping his white smock would not be picked out by the flame of the chalet. He waited five minutes and then moved, sitting on his skis, moving slowly towards the upraised barrier. There were flashlights, the sound of men coming up the mountain far down below and to the right. Outside the circle of flame he raised himself upright and began to ski quickly through the darkness towards the secondary road that led to Warth, and as he skied his eyes began to stream, because of the cold, because of his failure and because of what had happened to men like Ewald von Kirkdorf.

*   *   *

Stannard saw the cautious flashing of a single torch, made his way to the edge of the field and the dark outline of a car. He kicked off his skis and clumped up to the car.

"Ewald?"

"No. Ewald's dead."

A long silence while Paul van Osten assimilated that. "Let's go," he said.

Stannard made to climb inside the car, saw a figure seated in the back. "What the fuck happened to you?"

"I'm sorry," Guertner said. "I'm sorry. That mad idiot Lipski let the sled go. I couldn't stop him skiing after it. Then the machine gun jammed and I thought it was all over for you, so I left."

Stannard started to say something, then realized it was pointless. The mistakes had been made, the lives lost. Sounding off at Guertner would not bring back von Kirkdorf. He climbed into the car and asked van Osten, "Do you want me to drive?"

"No," van Osten said. "You've done enough. I'll manage." He started the car and they set off, moving quickly and smoothly, without undue ostentation.

From the rear, Guertner said, "I'm sorry I panicked."

Stannard slumped in his seat and stared wearily into the darkness beyond the headlamps.

Twenty kilometers further on, he told van Osten, "I'm not going to send that radio message, Paul. It didn't work."

"What do you mean it didn't work?"

"We were set up. They knew we were coming from above the chalet. They knew we couldn't see what went on below the chalet. Hitler was spirited away before our attack ever began."

"How do you know that?" van Osten asked.

Stannard told him. Then he asked, "Who was it? You? Göring? Heydrich? Who betrayed us?"

"I did," Guertner said from behind them. "Don't move, either of you. I have my gun out. Keep driving,

Paul. Stop when you get to Au. That message will be sent."

"You!" van Osten exclaimed in disgust.

"Not me alone," Guertner said. "Us. Heydrich. The SD. You were rumbled a long time ago, Paul, right from the time you took those aerial photographs of Lech. We tried to persuade Hitler not to come to Lech today, but Hitler doesn't believe he can be assassinated. So Heydrich made the arrangements for him to get away unobserved, then warned him again, when he was in the chalet. The SD knows everything about Double Eagle, Paul."

Van Osten asked, "How did he know about the message?"

Guertner laughed. "Simple. Viereck has been turned. He gave us the counterpart of Double Eagle. The assassination of Roosevelt."

Stannard turned and looked at Guertner, looked from Guertner to van Osten. "Is that true?"

Van Osten sighed. "Yes. Schroeder agreed to it. Without Hitler and without Roosevelt, we thought we could have peace."

"And you mean, when Schroeder receives that message, Roosevelt will be killed?"

"That's why the message has to be sent," Guertner said.

They reached Au, climbed up to the village in silence. Once they had got past it, Guertner placed his gun against the back of Stannard's head. "Stop the car, Paul."

Van Osten did so.

"I know you have the codes. The arrangement was that the man outside has the codes. Give me the codes or I blow off your friend's head."

"Don't," Stannard cried, feeling the barrel of the gun boring into his skull. "Don't. We're both dead men anyway."

"I could kill you both now and take the codes," Guertner said. "What is it to be?"

"Give him the codes, Paul," Stannard said. Both of them being shot now gave Roosevelt no chance. If they survived a little longer . . .

Van Osten passed Guertner the codes. The barrel of the gun pressed harder against Stannard's head. "Get the radio, Paul," Guertner said, "and don't try to be a hero."

Van Osten got out, took the radio from the boot, passed it into the car beside Guertner. There was a faint hum as Guertner switched it on. Then one-handed he transmitted the message, while Stannard hoped that someone would deduce from the slowness of the transmission that it was a fake.

Van Osten climbed behind the wheel and asked, "What next?"

"Turn round," Guertner said. "There's a police station in Au. You will drive there and surrender yourselves."

The ordeal of the radio message over, Guertner sat back in his seat. Van Osten started the car, moved forward. Stannard leaned against the door, his hand on the lock. As van Osten swung the car round in an arc, Stannard leaned forward, pressed his weight against the door, and as it opened, rolled onto the road, rolling over and over till he was nearly in the ditch, his hands groping for the Walther.

The car stopped with a flare of brake lights. Guertner's face appeared in the rear window, then moved, disappearing. His arm appeared over the rear door, gun extended, his head a dark blur above it. Stannard lying helpless on the road, tried to press his body into it. He'd got the holster open, but hadn't got the gun. For a moment he stared into the barrel fascinated, seeing Guertner's finger whiten on the trigger. Suddenly the gun jerked, fired, was withdrawn. Stan-

nard saw confused shapes inside the car, took out the
Walther, got to his feet, ran stumblingly to the car. As
he approached there was a shot. Then the rear door
swung open. Guertner jumped out turning round,
looking for Stannard. He saw Stannard and raised his
gun though it was too late. Stannard was already
standing with feet splayed apart, left hand locked
round his right wrist, the Walther fixed firmly on
Guertner. Slowly, deliberately, Stannard fired once,
twice, three times, the shots pumping into Guertner's
body, the flashes blinding him, his deafened ears
hardly hearing the clatter of Guertner's gun hitting
the roadway.

He went over to the car. Van Osten was slumped
across the front seat, an ugly bullet wound in his
chest. Stannard opened the door, crawled in beside
him. "Guertner's dead, Paul."

Van Osten took a deep, gurgling breath. "I'm
sorry it didn't work . . . For you . . . For all of us
. . . Long live Germany . . . our Germany . . . my
children."

Stannard watched the eyes glaze, the mouth sag
open. He was too tired, too shocked to care. There
had been so many deaths. All he wanted to do was get
across the border to Switzerland. He wouldn't leave
Paul's body behind. At least he'd deprive the Nazis of
that satisfaction.

He put Paul's body on the floor between the
seats, stacked von Kirkdorf's MP38 on the seat beside
him. Then he turned the car round and drove quickly
to the border.

It took him an hour to reach the border. The road
narrowed, but Stannard didn't slow down. He kept his
foot hard on the accelerator, broadsided the car round
the last corner.

A crowd of men stood behind a wooden barrier,
and two guards turned threateningly towards the
speeding car. Stannard picked up the machine pistol

with his left hand and smashed the windscreen and pressed the trigger. The gun kicked against his chest, spraying bullets wildly in all directions. The car bucked and fought his right hand as he straightened it up and charged the barrier.

Men scattered, the barrier clouted the windscreen frame, twisted, broke. The car swayed crazily, sliding from side to side, a tire burst and it went into a long revolving skid. Stannard glimpsed the Swiss customs barrier, then the German, fired a burst from the machine pistol, then the car hit the central reservation, bounced over it and accompanied by a crackle of machine gun fire, rushed lopsidedly past the upraised barrier on the further side into Switzerland.

Stannard kept on driving, ignoring the sparks flying from the metal rim, ignoring the shouts of the Swiss customs men, driving solemnly in the middle of the road, blocking the car the customs sent after him. He was too tired, too sick at heart to care. He had survived and nothing could happen to him now.

A mile further on, Susan was waiting.

30

It was 11:31 when Bill Myers received the radio message from the FBI agent. By 11:30 he'd phoned it to Laurence Cullen. Schroeder and Panatour were lost.

They'd left the Tamworth—Westchester at ten o'clock that morning in Schroeder's Packard. Panatour had been carrying two large cases. They'd been tailed along the Mount Vernon Memorial Highway to Alexandria, and Fredericksburg. Near Richmond, Schroeder had spotted the tail and taken off, pushing the Packard to well over a hundred. By the time the agent had got on to the highway patrol frequency, Schroeder had taken to the sideroads, and was lost.

"What a ballsup," Cullen said, then thought it couldn't be important. Tomorrow was important. Today was Sunday, a day of rest. He thanked Myers for calling and said he would see him tomorrow, bright and early and sharp as a lark.

* * *

Schroeder had spotted the trailing Chevvy just before Alexandria; grey and shiny, it had been in his mirror through the light, Sunday, mid-town Washington traffic and all the way thereafter. For two days, Schroeder had known the FBI were on to him. The Tamworth—Westchester had been filled with clear-eyed, clean-shaven men, in neat white shirts and dark business suits who looked as if they never sweated. One of them had even followed him down the street yesterday, when he'd gone to a pay phone to call Viereck.

Apart from the inconvenience, the surveillance did not worry Schroeder. He was too big to be touched and his cover story was ready. He was making an evaluation of a certain personality type with a view to its usefulness in clandestine operations, and he had enough documents and orders from Clark Winters to support it. The fact that no one had interrogated him was however, a relief to Schroeder. They were waiting to catch him in the act. He had other ideas about that.

Had they used a two-car tail that morning, alternate cars, or even the difficult following from ahead technique, Schroeder might not have spotted them. But one, shiny, grey car with four burly men and on a quiet Sunday! J. Edgar Hoover was slipping! As he drove, Schroeder's eyes raked his mirror. Nothing behind. Nothing in front, either. He'd blown them. Never in his life had he been so glad of the excess horsepower American automobile manufacturers built into their engines.

Panatour sat beside him, freshly shaven, neatly suited. A bit more weight, and he could have passed as an FBI agent. "Nice morning," Panatour said. "I wish I was home." His pupils were dilated, his whole manner passive.

"You will be home, soon," Schroeder said. "Very soon."

Because of the FBI tail, Schroeder had been forced to make a detour. Though he drove fast, it was difficult to make up time on the narrow roads and by the time he saw the board of the Stardust Motel, he was running fifteen minutes late. He drove rapidly past the glowing red neon Vacancy sign and pulled up beside cabin number 12.

Viereck came out, hurried across to the car. "You're late," he said, as if that was news. Viereck too had dressed carefully that morning, looked more like an impoverished European aristocrat than ever.

Schroeder said, "Trouble with the car." He walked round to the trunk and took out the cases. "Everything's set up," he said. "You go to the Jackson Hotel. The room is booked in your name. You park the car behind the hotel. The moment the shooting is over, you walk out the back door. Leave the guns, radio, everything and walk out, understand?" Schroeder looked at Panatour, approaching them. "And take him with you."

Viereck hesitated momentarily. Schroeder knew that Viereck had no intention of taking Panatour anywhere, afterwards. "Alright. What's in this case?"

"The radio I told you about," Schroeder replied. "I'll be on the bridge over the station. If there's anything wrong, any change, you'll hear this thing buzz. When it does, lift up the receiver and you'll hear me loud and clear."

"What happens if I want to call you?"

"You can't," Schroeder said.

Panatour said, "Max, I want to talk on the radio."

"Sure," Schroeder said. "Sure. Afterwards."

"Now."

"No. We haven't got the time. Look, you go with George, here. He'll take care of you and tell you what to do."

Panatour frowned. "I want to stay with you."

"I have some things to do, and if you come with me, you will be late for the shooting. Now go with

George. He'll show you what to do, and you must do exactly what he tells you."

"I don't want to shoot no one today, Max."

"Fine. You don't shoot anybody. Huey'll know. He'll walk in your dreams again. He'll know you chickened out."

Panatour shook his head. "I won't chicken out."

"Then you go to the hotel and do exactly what George tells you. Tomorrow, we will go back to Cayenne. Everyone will be out on the streets to see you. Everyone will know you revenged Huey. Oh, we'll have such a great time in Cayenne. We'll be big men."

"We'll be like kings," Panatour said. "We'll have a big house with lots of servants and we'll be able to go to New Orleans and people will step off the sidewalk when they see us coming because they'll know we're the guys who revenged Huey Long."

"Right," Schroeder said. "Right. But you must go now. Otherwise you'll be late for the shooting."

As Panatour walked towards the car, Schroeder slipped Viereck a packet of tablets. "Tranquilizers," he said. "Give him two, if he gets noisy. Anything else, talk to him about going back to Cayenne."

"I'll deal with him," Viereck said confidently. "Goodbye."

After Viereck and Panatour had left, Schroeder went over to the motel office. He told them his car had broken down, inquired if he could rent one. Thirty minutes later, a shiny Pontiac coupé was delivered to the motel office and soon afterwards, Schroeder set off, driving slowly to Arlettesburg.

*　　*　　*

Ten minutes after Myers called, Cullen thought, if it was a day of rest why was Schroeder charging round the countryside with Panatour. Schroeder's wife was of a nervous disposition. He'd already worried her

enough by staying away all those nights. Staying
away Sundays was a bit much, and Schroeder
wouldn't have done it unless it was essential. Essential
for what? Why take Panatour to the country, the day
before he was due to shoot the President of the
United States?

Target practice? Possible, but it would have been
just as convenient to take him to a rifle club. Returning him to Louisiana? Driving him there was too
much trouble. No, Schroeder had taken Panatour out
of Washington for a purpose.

Cullen worried enough about that purpose to call
Hoover at his mother's home in Washington. Hoover
listened carefully to Cullen's theory, said he'd call
back in five minutes.

Three minutes later Hoover called. "Collect you
as soon as I get there," he shouted into the phone. "Be
ready."

Ten minutes later they were on their way, with
flashing lights and screaming sirens.

"If this blows up in my face," Hoover said, "I'll
really end up being a punk in a squad car."

Sunday, December 15, 1940.
Arlettesburg, Va.

The Secret Service man guarding the bridge that
joined High Street to Main Street said, "I can't let you
through, bud. The bridge is closed to the public."

"I'm not public," Schroeder said. "Name's Schroeder, Director of Counter Intelligence, G2. Here's my
ID. I'm here on official business."

The Secret Service man looked at Schroeder's
identification, looked from the photograph to Schroeder, and said, "I guess that'll be alright," moved aside,
waved Schroeder through on to the bridge.

There were only a few people on the bridge, a
few influential sightseers and two hard-eyed Secret

Service men, whose gaze flitted intermittently from the railway track to the small crowd that had gathered on both sides of the cutting. The time was 2:22. In eight minutes the presidential train would arrive. In nine minutes the President would be dead. In nine minutes, Double Eagle would be completed. Schroeder settled down to wait.

He'd received Stannard's message shortly after three o'clock that morning, guessed the Germans were playing it close to their chests, because there was nothing about the murder of Hitler in the newspapers or on the radio. The only thing that worried Schroeder now was whether the FBI knew about Viereck, and whether they had followed him here.

2:25. Damn Cullen and the FBI. At the investigation afterwards, the evidence of his movements might be relevant. If only he hadn't so much to do, so much to worry about. His whole scheme depended on no one being able to tie him in with Panatour.

2:27. He wished it were over. He asked for nothing but that. He would resign his commission, live quietly by the sea, satisfied inside himself that he had done something for his country, and for peace.

The signal along the line moved to the stop position. Schroeder thought he heard the sound of a klaxon. Yes, quite distinctly a klaxon. But there was another sound, a similar sound, blending with the klaxon's wail. A siren. It was louder now. Definitely a siren, drowning out the sound of the approaching train. Heads were turning along Main Street, towards the constant, wailing scream.

2:29. The train was pulling into the station. The few people expecting it craned their heads down the line. Schroeder saw the revolving blue light race along the cutting behind the heads of the crowd, heard the siren wail and die. Two men climbed out of a dusty squad car. Hoover and Cullen. They were running up the street now, running up to the bridge.

The train had stopped, but no one was alighting. The driver had missed the point for the President's coach, began to move the train slowly backwards, to where the ramps could meet the platform without a gap.

Cullen had seen Schroeder, was pointing at him. Schroeder raised his eyes to the topmost window of the Jackson Hotel. Panatour was there leaning out slightly, the rifle up near his face. Beside him the angular shadow of Viereck.

Cullen and Hoover were racing up to him, thrusting aside the Secret Service man at the head of the bridge. Panatour could be seen clearly now. Viereck, too, carrying a rifle fitted with an immense sniperscope. Below Schroeder, the train had stopped. Doors were opening, people moving about the platform. But the door of the Presidential coach remained shut.

Come on, come on, get it open and done with. Schroeder's thumb curled tensely over the transmit button of the radio in his pocket. Ah, the doors were opening now. The ramps being wheeled out, protruding like silver bones.

"SCHROEDER!" Hoover's voice from five feet away.

Schroeder turned, looked into the faces of Hoover and Cullen, looked back to the Presidential coach with its gleaming, empty ramps, looked up at the window of the Jackson Hotel. His thumb moved.

There was a dull, muffled explosion. The third floor window of the Jackson Hotel seemed to bulge outwards, a reflected flash of flame. Panatour's body wheeled out of the shattered window and fell flailing to the street.

Schroeder looked steadily at Hoover and Cullen. "A bomb," he said. "Someone's trying to murder the President."

The doors of the Presidential coach slammed shut. The Secret Service detail took up their positions with drawn guns. And from the direction of the Jackson Hotel came shrill, high-pitched screams.

* * *

Naturally the Secret Service were uptight. They clustered around the train, reinforced now by policemen, who had been originally summoned to clear the area. Schroeder had his identity checked five times and had to submit to a body search before he could get into the Pullman to see the President.

Roosevelt sat in his wheelchair behind a writing desk. Like all politicians the threat of assassination was something that he had learned to live with and had chosen to ignore, until it nearly happened. He was shaken by the attack, shaken by the fact that someone hated him enough to want to kill him. He was thinking back to that day in Miami, eight years ago, when he had been a Presidential candidate, remembering Mayor Anton Cermak, bleeding away his life in his arms. Then, he had been cool, thought and seen and acted with clarity. But this time, it had been different. It had all happened too quickly. This time, someone had been shooting at him.

He threw his head back aggressively at Schroeder. "Well, Colonel, I understand you know something about this?"

"Not something, Mr. President," Schroeder said. "Everything. G2 (C) has known of this attempt from the beginning."

"G2 (C)? Not the FBI?"

"We couldn't take any chances, Mr. President."

"Well, you sure came goddam close."

"You were never in any danger. The whole operation was under our total control."

Roosevelt looked at him in disbelief.

"Two months ago, through certain high officers in the Abwehr, we discovered the existence of a German plot to assassinate you. At the time, we could

have passed the information to the FBI, and had the
plotters apprehended. But we didn't. The FBI would
only have arrested the gunmen and our valuable
sources would have been exposed, which meant that
not only would we have lost the future use of their
services, but would not have known about any further
attempts on your life. So we cooperated."

"You what?"

"We co-operated. We pretended to help the Germans so that we could learn every detail of the operation. We helped them. Provided them with the venue,
found them a disturbed farmer from Louisiana to do
the shooting." Schroeder grinned. "Then we planted a
radio-controlled bomb in their hotel room, so that
their failure would look like an accident. We did not
want the Germans to think that American policies
could be changed through assassinations."

"They won't," Roosevelt said. He looked at
Schroeder keenly over the half-framed glasses. "I suppose I must thank you, Colonel."

Schroeder shrugged. "I was only doing my job,"
he said. "G2 (C) was only doing what was expected
of it Mr. President. It was fortunate that our sources
of information are better than anything the British
have. In fact our sources are so good, that we could
dispose of Hitler."

"I forbid that," the President said. "This is still a
neutral country. No American and no American military agency must be involved in anything like that."

"Until the war comes," Schroeder smiled.

The President hesitated. "That's a different ball
game," he said. "But any decisions about that will be
made by me and me alone. I want that clearly understood." He fitted a cigarette into a long holder. When
he had lit it, he said, "I thank you again, Colonel, and
please convey my thanks to your staff. Now, I must
consider the political consequences."

                    *   *   *

At the inquiry afterwards it was revealed that the two men had booked the room two days previously, had checked in an hour before the Presidential train was due to arrive. Their luggage had consisted of two suitcases and a small attaché case which had contained an explosive device. It was this that had providentially misfired and saved the life of the President.

Both bodies were identified with some difficulty. One was an expatriate German businessman called Viereck, the other an unbalanced Louisiana farmer called Carmel Panatour. It was quite obviously a German-inspired plot to eliminate Roosevelt.

After a private discussion with Colonel Max Schroeder, the President had announced that the assassination attempt was a matter for the utmost discretion. America was unable to yield to the demands of an outraged public for reprisals or war.

On the way back to Washington that night, Cullen said, "Schroeder came out of that smelling of roses. What the hell did he have to tell the President?"

"Whatever it was, it worked."

"He's untouchable now," Cullen said. "And he's next in line to head G2."

"His time will come," Hoover said. "It always does."

If you live long enough, Cullen thought staring out of the car window. It was a bloody screwed up world.

Wednesday, December 18, 1940.
Washington, D.C.

David Stannard stared fixedly out of the window at the rain spotting the pane. He and Susan had been rushed from Zürich by the British and he'd spent most of the night and all that morning with Laurence Cullen. From behind him, Susan said, "It's over, David. Finished."

Stannard pressed his face against the cold glass. For him it wasn't over yet. His warning sent from Zürich had been too late, but Cullen and Hoover had the situation under control, or so they said. Viereck, Panatour, van Osten, von Kirkdorf, Lessing, Lipski, Guertner, Berkeley were all dead.

There was only Schroeder. And, without proof, Schroeder could not be touched. Max Schroeder. The man who had eliminated Stannard, made him a cypher in his game of world peace. Treated him as expendable. No one cared about that.

"I'm going," Stannard said.

Susan said, "Don't be silly. He'll kill you. He has to."

"Or I will kill him."

"Cullen's manipulating you," she warned.

He walked out of the room without saying a word. He left the hotel and walked over to the office in the Munitions Building where Schroeder worked. He smiled a charming smile, had them take him up to the ninth floor, said he knew the way and knocked on Schroeder's door.

"I'm alive," he said. "I've come back. What are you going to do about it?"

Schroeder looked at him tiredly. "It's difficult to explain. Difficult to understand. What I tried to do. They are building terrible weapons. We have to stop them before millions will be killed. I had to do something. I am sorry you were the one."

"You calculated lives," Stannard said. "You thought three for one, two for one, what does it matter? But it does matter, if you're the one that's chosen. I'm very popular now. The FBI love me. The Secret Service love me. Even British Intelligence love me. What are you going to do about it?"

Schroeder said, "I did it for a good reason."

"It was my life," Stannard said. "Now that I'm

back they have all the evidence they need. And I'm going to talk."

Schroeder said, "I can't face that."

David took out the Walther he had brought back from Germany and put it on Schroeder's desk. "Do it," he said. "Now I'm writing you off."

After David Stannard left, Schroeder stared a long time at the gun. He had done what he had done for the best reasons. But there was too much blood on his hands. Perhaps Stannard had been right. It would never have worked. Slowly he reached out and picked up the gun and placed the barrel in his mouth. Then ever so gently he pressed his finger on the trigger.

*   *   *

By a strange irony, just as Colonel Max Schroeder was preparing to commit suicide, the man whom he had risked so much to kill was taking the first step that would lead to his own suicide in a bunker in Berlin five years later.

On the 18th December 1940, Hitler issued Directive No. 21, Case Barbarossa. The directive embodied everything Paul van Osten realized and tried to prevent.

Its opening paragraph read:

"The German Armed Forces must be prepared, even before the conclusion of the war against England, *to crush Soviet Russia in a rapid campaign.*"

As Paul van Osten had realized then, and Hitler realized many thousands of lives later, there was to be no blitzkreig on the way to Moscow.

Epilogue

Reynhard Heydrich was assassinated in Prague on May 29, 1942.

Franklin D. Roosevelt died at Warm Springs, Georgia, of a cerebral hemorrhage on April 12, 1945.

Adolf Hitler shot himself in his bunker in Berlin on April 30, 1945.

Hermann Göring committed suicide in Nuremberg Prison on October 15, 1946.

Charles Gladstone Rieber worked with the OSS throughout the duration of the war. On January 11, 1946 he received from President Truman a commendation for unspecified but obviously heroic services. On August 10, 1953 he suffered a massive heart attack in the much reduced offices of Crusader Gulf, and died the next day.

J. Edgar Hoover remained Director of the FBI until his death in 1972, by which time American boys had ceased to sport tin G-man badges, and the American public chose to take a more censorious view of his activities in support of law and order.

Laurence Cullen served with the British Security Office till the end of World War II, and since then worked for M15. No details of his activities are available, except the fact that he retired in 1970 at the age of sixty-five. He now lives in Cornwall with his eldest daughter.

David Stannard fought with the 3rd Marine Division at Tunis, Sicily, Cassino, Anzio, Colmar and Munich. He won a Bronze Star, a Purple Heart and a Silver Star with oak leaf cluster.

He married Susan Lenglen in February 1941. They had two sons, Paul and Gary. Paul was killed in Vietnam in 1969.

After the war Stannard served with various Allied Commissions in Germany. In April 1952, he returned to his father's law practice in Manhattan, and is now a senior partner at Hope, Myers, Stannard & Leibovitch. Though over sixty years of age he still skis regularly and visits Europe twice a year. He has, however, never returned to Lech.

ABOUT THE AUTHOR

OWEN SELA lives in London and divides his time between writing and his accounting practice. Like the spy
hero in many of his books, he collects cars. He is the
author of *The Bearer Plot, The Kiriov Tapes, The Portu-
guese Fragment* and *The Bengali Inheritance.*

DON'T MISS
THESE CURRENT
Bantam Bestsellers

☐	11001	**DR. ATKINS DIET REVOLUTION**	$2.25
☐	11161	**CHANGING** Liv Ullmann	$2.25
☐	10970	**HOW TO SPEAK SOUTHERN** Mitchell & Rawls	$1.25
☐	10077	**TRINITY** Leon Uris	$2.75
☐	12250	**ALL CREATURES GREAT AND SMALL** James Herriot	$2.50
☐	12256	**ALL THINGS BRIGHT AND BEAUTIFUL** James Herriot	$2.50
☐	11770	**ONCE IS NOT ENOUGH** Jacqueline Susann	$2.25
☐	11699	**THE LAST CHANCE DIET** Dr. Robert Linn	$2.25
☐	10150	**FUTURE SHOCK** Alvin Toffler	$2.25
☐	12196	**PASSAGES** Gail Sheehy	$2.75
☐	11255	**THE GUINNESS BOOK OF WORLD RECORDS 16th Ed.** McWhirters	$2.25
☐	12220	**LIFE AFTER LIFE** Raymond Moody, Jr.	$2.25
☐	11917	**LINDA GOODMAN'S SUN SIGNS**	$2.25
☐	10310	**ZEN AND THE ART OF MOTORCYCLE MAINTENANCE** Pirsiz	$2.50
☐	2600	**RAGTIME** E. L. Doctorow	$2.25
☐	10888	**RAISE THE TITANIC!** Clive Cussler	$2.25
☐	2491	**ASPEN** Burt Hirschfeld	$1.95
☐	2222	**HELTER SKELTER** Vincent Bugliosi	$1.95

Buy them at your local bookstore or use this handy coupon for ordering:

RELAX!
SIT DOWN
and Catch Up On Your Reading!

☐	10077	**TRINITY** by Leon Uris	$2.75
☐	2300	**THE MONEYCHANGERS** by Arthur Hailey	$1.95
☐	11266	**THE MEDITERRANEAN CAPER** by Clive Cussler	$1.95
☐	2500	**THE EAGLE HAS LANDED** by Jack Higgins	$1.95
☐	2600	**RAGTIME** by E. L. Doctorow	$2.25
☐	10360	**CONFLICT OF INTEREST** by Les Whitten	$1.95
☐	10888	**RAISE THE TITANIC!** by Clive Cussler	$2.25
☐	11966	**THE ODESSA FILE** by Frederick Forsyth	$2.25
☐	11770	**ONCE IS NOT ENOUGH** by Jacqueline Susann	$2.25
☐	11708	**JAWS 2** by Hank Searls	$2.25
☐	8844	**TINKER, TAILOR, SOLDIER, SPY** by John Le Carre	$1.95
☐	11929	**THE DOGS OF WAR** by Frederick Forsyth	$2.25
☐	10090	**THE R DOCUMENT** by Irving Wallace	$2.25
☐	10526	**INDIA ALLEN** by Elizabeth B. Coker	$1.95
☐	10357	**THE HARRAD EXPERIMENT** by Robert Rimmer	$1.95
☐	10422	**THE DEEP** by Peter Benchley	$2.25
☐	10500	**DOLORES** by Jacqueline Susann	$1.95
☐	11601	**THE LOVE MACHINE** by Jacqueline Susann	$2.25
☐	10600	**BURR** by Gore Vidal	$2.25
☐	10857	**THE DAY OF THE JACKAL** by Frederick Forsyth	$1.95
☐	11952	**DRAGONARD** by Rupert Gilchrist	$1.95
☐	2491	**ASPEN** by Burt Hirschfeld	$1.95
☐	11330	**THE BEGGARS ARE COMING** by Mary Loos	$1.95

We Deliver!
And So Do These Bestsellers.

Bantam Book Catalog

Here's your up-to-the-minute listing of every book currently available from Bantam.

This easy-to-use catalog is divided into categories and contains over 1400 titles by your favorite authors.

So don't delay—take advantage of this special opportunity to increase your reading pleasure.

Just send us your name and address and 25¢ (to help defray postage and handling costs).

BANTAM BOOKS, INC.
Dept. FC, 414 East Golf Road, Des Plaines, Ill. 60016

Mr./Mrs./Miss_____
(please print)

Address_____

City_____State_____Zip_____

Do you know someone who enjoys books? Just give us their names and addresses and we'll send them a catalog too!

Mr./Mrs./Miss_____

Address_____

City_____State_____Zip_____

Mr./Mrs./Miss_____

Address_____

City_____State_____Zip_____

FC—8/77